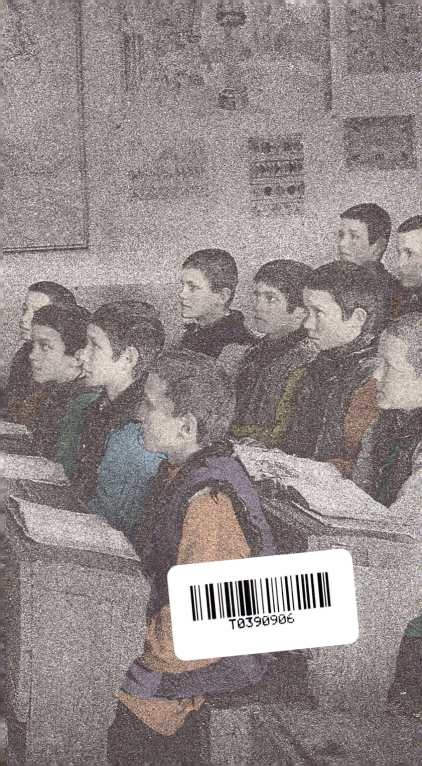

EARTH
GODS

Ukrainian Research Institute
Harvard University

Harvard Library of Ukrainian Literature 10

HURI Editorial Board

Michael S. Flier
Oleh Kotsyuba, *Director of Publications*
Serhii Plokhy, *Chairman*

Cambridge, Massachusetts

Taras Prokhasko

EARTH GODS

Writings from before the War

Introduced by
Mark Andryczyk

Translated by
Ali Kinsella,
Mark Andryczyk, and
Uilleam Blacker

50 years ॐ 1973–2023

Distributed by Harvard University Press
for the Ukrainian Research Institute
Harvard University

The Harvard Ukrainian Research Institute was established in 1973 as an integral part of Harvard University. It supports research associates and visiting scholars who are engaged in projects concerned with all aspects of Ukrainian studies. The Institute also works in close cooperation with the Committee on Ukrainian Studies, which supervises and coordinates the teaching of Ukrainian history, language, and literature at Harvard University.

Published in 2025 by the Ukrainian Research Institute at Harvard University, https://huri.harvard.edu

Copyright © 2025 by the President and Fellows of Harvard College
Translation copyright © 2025 by Ali Kinsella, Mark Andryczyk, and Uilleam Blacker

All translations in the present edition have been edited by Oleh Kotsyuba and Michelle R. Viise.

All rights reserved

Anna's Other Days published in 2025 as part of this volume under license from Kalvariia, LLC.

Printed in India on acid-free paper

ISBN 9780674291164 (hardcover), 9780674291171 (paperback), 9780674291188 (epub), 9780674291195 (PDF)

Library of Congress Control Number: 2023950148
LC record available at https://lccn.loc.gov/2023950148

Cover art by Enrique Durand-Methol, www.durandmethol.com

Cover layout developed by Mykola Leonovych, finalized by Lesyk Panasiuk, www.gladunpanasiuk.com

Book design by Mykhailo Fedyshak, bluecollider@gmail.com

Publication of this book has been made possible by the generous support of publications in Ukrainian studies at Harvard University by the following benefactors or funds endowed in their name:

>Ostap and Ursula Balaban
>Jaroslaw and Olha Duzey
>Vladimir Jurkowsky
>Myroslav and Irene Koltunik
>Damian Korduba Family
>Peter and Emily Kulyk
>Irena Lubchak
>Dr. Evhen Omelsky
>Eugene and Nila Steckiw
>Dr. Omeljan and Iryna Wolynec
>Wasyl and Natalia Yerega

♛ COLUMBIA | HARRIMAN INSTITUTE
Russian, Eurasian, and East European Studies

The publication of this book was made possible, in part, by a grant from the Harriman Institute, Columbia University.

You can support our work of publishing academic books and translations of Ukrainian literature and documents by making a tax-deductible donation in any amount, or by including HURI in your estate planning.

To find out more, please visit
https://huri.harvard.edu/give.

CONTENTS

Inside Story: An Introduction to *Earth Gods*
Mark Andryczyk   XI

Anna's Other Days
Translated by Ali Kinsella   1

   Essai de Deconstruction   **3**

   Around the Lake   **27**

   Necropolis   **61**

   A Feeling of Presence / Toward a Sense of Essence   **93**

FM Galicia
Translated by Mark Andryczyk   153

   The Year 2000   **155**

   The Year 2001   **213**

The UnSimple
Translated by Uilleam Blacker   249

   Sixty-Eight Accidental First Sentences   **253**

   Chronologically   **259**

Letters to and from Beda   262

Genetically   269

The First Old Photograph—
   The Only Undated One   275

Physiologically   281

Walk, Stand, Sit, Lie   290

Situation In Color   298

The Second Old Photograph—
   Ardzheliudzha, 1892   310

The Temptations of Saint Anthony   314

Excessive Days   347

The Third Old Photograph—
   Maybe for *Larousse*   359

Wars of the Imagination—Briefly   378

The UnSimple   387

To Say or to Stop   393

Thirty Years of the Family S.   401

Unprose   405

Have a Most Beautiful Bai (For Example)   419

If According to the Map (Legend)   465

Seven   466

Image Credits   473

Previous Publications   475

EARTH GODS

INSIDE STORY

AN INTRODUCTION TO *EARTH GODS*

Mark Andryczyk

A plant would probably write
so slowly and precisely.

— YURI ANDRUKHOVYCH

Taras Prokhasko is one of the leading voices to have emerged in Ukrainian literature since the country achieved its independence in 1991. Over the years, he has cultivated a style of writing that, in addition to slowness and precision, is marked by a delicate tone and a fable-like quality. Prokhasko's stories focus on the art and power of storytelling. To that end, Prokhasko offers texts that experiment, in myriad ways, with narration and form. *Earth Gods: Writings from before the War* collects the author's first three publications and presents them in English translation in one volume: *Anna's Other Days* (Inshi dni Anny, 1998), *FM Galicia* (FM Halychyna, 2001) and *The UnSimple* (NeprOsti, 2002). In these early works, Prokhasko probes various ways of telling a tale while providing readers with captivating prose that invites and challenges them to question and consider the act of storytelling.

*　*　*

Taras Prokhasko was born in 1968 in Ivano-Frankivsk, Ukraine. Where and when the writer spent his youth were both significant factors in his development as a writer. Prokhasko was born in the western part of Soviet Ukraine, in a region known as Galicia or, in Ukrainian, *Halychyna*. His native city was founded as Stanislaviv in 1662 and, over the years, it was part of the Polish-Lithuanian Commonwealth, the Austro-Hungarian Empire, the Western Ukrainian National Republic, the Ukrainian National Republic, and Poland. Stanislaviv, renamed Stanislav in 1932, came under Soviet rule in 1944 and, in 1962, was once again renamed, this time as Ivano-Frankivsk. Prokhasko comes from a family of Ukrainian intellectuals and community leaders and, although he grew up in Soviet Ukraine, he possessed an unwavering connection to pre-Soviet Ukrainian identity and maintained a general suspicion and rejection of Soviet authority. He began writing in the final years of the USSR and took part in civil gatherings protesting Soviet misdeeds, most notably the 1990 Revolution on Granite. As a student, Prokhasko studied biology at Lviv University, specializing in botany. As a budding writer, he performed a kaleidoscope of jobs, among others, he worked as an editor, radio operator, forester, bartender, and gardener.

Cultural life in Ivano-Frankivsk in the early years of Ukrainian independence received a significant boost with the emergence of the artistic community known as the Stanislav Phenomenon (*Stanislavskyi fenomen*).[1] A loosely-bound group of writers and artists, it included such individuals as Prokhasko, Yaroslav Dovhan, Halyna Petrosaniak, and Volodymyr Ieshkiliev. It's key figures were the writer Yuri Andrukhovych and the writer/visual artist/musician Yuri Izdryk. The latter edited the journal *Chetver* (Thursday), which became one of the most important forums for Ukraine's new post-Soviet literature. It was in *Chetver* that Prokhasko published his first writings.

Since the turn of the century, Prokhasko has consistently produced books that have been greatly anticipated by readers. Always the mainstay of courses in Ukrainian literature, they have received numerous awards. His publications include: *Inshi dni Anny* (Anna's other days, 1998), *FM Halychyna* (FM Galicia, 2001), *NeprOsti* (The UnSimple, 2002), *Leksykon taiemnykh znan´* (Lexicon of secret knowledge, 2005), *Z ts´oho mozhna bulo b zrobyty kil´ka opovidan´* (Could have made a few stories from this, 2005), *Port Frankivs´k* (Frankivsk harbor,

---

1   In his entry on the Stanislav Phenomenon in the 1998 *Short Ukrainian Encyclopedia of Current Literature*, Volodymyr Ieshkiliev points out that "the historical background for the Stanislav Phenomenon became the fall of the USSR and the condition of cultural 'openness,' which allowed for a change in aesthetic standards and artistic coordinates." See *Mala ukraïns´ka entsykolopediia aktual´noï literatury*, Volodymyr Ieshkiliev and Iurii Andrukhovych, eds. (Ivano-Frankivsk: Lileia-NV, 1998), 103.

2006), *Ukraïna* (Ukraine, coauthored with Serhiy Zhadan, 2006), *Galizien-Bukowina-Express* (coauthored with Jurko Prokhasko and Magdalena Blashchuk, 2007), *Botakie* (Because that's how it is, 2010), *Odnoï i toï samoï* (One and the same, 2013), *Oznaky zrilosty* (Signs of maturity, 2014), and *Tak, ale* (Yes, but, 2019). In 2020, *Sotvorinnia svitu: Sim dniv iz Tarasom Prokhas´kom* (The creation of the world: seven days with Taras Prokhasko) was published by journalist Tetiana Teren based on a series of conversations she had with Prokhasko over seven days. For years, Prokhasko has regularly written columns in the journals *Halyts´kyi Korespondent* and *Zbruch*.

In 2003–4, Prokhasko published a number of illuminating interviews he conducted with leading Ukrainian intellectuals—Oksana Zabuzhko, Yuri Andrukhovych, Archbishop-Metropolitan Borys Gudziak, Yuri Izdryk, Oleh Lysheha, Yaroslav Hrytsak, and Vasyl Herasymiuk—in his *Inshyi format* (A different format) series. Prokhasko also co-authored, with Marjana Prokhasko, four popular and award-winning children's books: *Khto zrobyt´ snih* (Who will make the snow, 2013), *Kudy znyklo more* (Where did the sea go, 2014), *Iak zrozumity kozu* (How to understand a goat, 2015), and *Zhyttia i snih* (Life and snow, 2017).

Prokhasko's works have been translated into Polish, German, English, and Russian. His writing in English translation has appeared in *Two Lands, New Visions: Stories from Canada and Ukraine* (1998), in the journal *Ukrainian*

Literature (2007, 2011, and 2018), and in *The White Chalk of Days: The Contemporary Ukrainian Literature Series Anthology* (2017). A translator himself, Prokhasko has translated into Ukrainian writings by Stanisław Vincenz, Venedykt Ploshchansky Andrzej Stasiuk, Kamil Barański, Leon Streit, and Czesław Chowaniec.

Prokhasko is the recipient of the 2020 Shevchenko National Prize for Literature and the 2019 BBC Book of the Year Prize in the category of essays (both for *Tak, ale*); the 2013 Yurii Shevelov Prize (for *Odnoï i toï samoï*); the 2013 BBC Children's Book of the Year Prize, the 2013 LitAktsent Children's Book Prize, and the 2013 Book of the Year Prize (all for *Khto zrobyt´ snih*, together with Marjana Prokhasko); the 2007 Joseph Conrad Award, presented by Kyiv's Polish Institute; *Korrespondent* magazine's 2006 Best Ukrainian Book of Fiction Award (for *Z tsioho mozhna zrobyty kil´ka opovidan´*); and the 1997 Smoloskyp Prize.

* * *

Anna's Other Days is a collection of four short stories united by their exploration of being. All four stories—"Essai de Deconstruction," "Around the Lake," "Necropolis," and "A Feeling of Presence / Toward a Sense of Essence"— purposely and explicitly experiment with narration, engrossing the reader with the manner in which they were written. Prokhasko tinkers with convention in order to erode the boundaries between action and contemplation, randomness and correlation, reality and the subconscious. Perhaps propelled by his training as a botanist, the author methodically anatomizes his protagonists and traces their existence through their memories of past experiences.

"Essai de Deconstruction" is divided into three dissimilar chapters. In the first, the plot unfolds in a rather traditional manner, as we are introduced to several individuals who are living in a boarding house, trying to stay out of reach of an oppressive regime. The reader is provided with detailed descriptions of living conditions but with limited background information on the story's protagonists. Importantly, we are introduced here to Irzhi, a translator, and to the concept of utilizing prose as a means of marking life. In the second chapter, Prokhasko abandons the narrative of the first one and presents entries from the narrator's diary, sharing scenes of his relationship with the story's other main characters, including discussions with Irzhi about new ways of writing prose. The final, third chapter provides a two-paragraph summary of the author's reflections on experience, death, and perpetuity. "Essai de Deconstruction" posits the idea that an individual's tracks immortalize them when this person's acquired knowledge is passed on to the next generation.

In "Around the Lake," a man named Severyn is suffering from a brain tumor and is awaiting an operation to remove it. As Roksoliana Sviato points out, in the story, the tumor can be seen as not just a malady or a defect, but an asset, because it affects Severyn's vision in a way that allows him to focus on objects he otherwise would not have been able to see.[2] And the brain, with its contours, parallels the topography of nature as two meditations (journeys) are made into (or along the surface of) the mind. The relief map that outlines the brain's surface marks the distinctions and classifications created by the mind as it grasps life's unfolding.

"Necropolis" also experiments with narration and focuses on the boundaries between author and protagonist. The reader is introduced to the writer Markus Mlynarskyi and is presented with a mix of Mlynarskyi's thoughts about his novel-to-be *Necropolis* and the actions of the novel itself. Later, at the end of the first chapter, the reader learns that what they have read up to this point makes up a letter read by Mlynarskyi's biographer Dr. Vynnyk. Mlynarskyi's *Necropolis* is a story about several individuals purchasing plots in a future cemetery. When they visit their plots, they bring their personal stories with them and share them with the other plot owners. Later, Mlynarskyi inserts himself into the novel which, together with Dr. Vynnyk's role as a narrator,

---

2   See "Roksoliana Sviato pro Tarasa Prokhas´ka" in *Literaturna defiliada: Suchasna Ukraïns´ka krytyka pro suchasnu ukraïns´ku literaturu* (Kyiv: Biblioteka "LitAktsentu," 2012), 390.

provides several viewpoints from which to explore the relationships between author, protagonist, and story.

In "A Feeling of Presence / Toward a Sense of Essence," the chief protagonist Pamva—a middle-aged filmmaker, masseur, and nurse—examines the essence of presence. Along the way, he acknowledges the importance of light in dreams and realizes that the ways he remembers his late grandfather determine how his own identity is formed. Pamva traverses a daily life adorned with pianos, cognac, coffee, cigarettes, beans, chess players, books, and relationships with both established and budding scholars, as he comes to recognize art's role in creating a sense of presence.

In the four stories that make up *Anna's Other Days*, Prokhasko takes great pains to disorient his readers and constantly makes them pay attention to the manner in which he is telling his story. The author's fragmented narrative is designed to help the reader better grasp the author's notions of being. Prokhasko's stories encourage us to ponder our existence in the world and to consider how becoming an element of narration, or part of a story, records one's being.

* * *

With *FM Galicia*, Prokhasko adopted a very different form in which to present his writings. Ironically, this form resulted from what the author considered to be "NOTLITERATURE"—a collaboration between the writer and Ivano-Frankivsk radio station Radio-Vezha (Radio-Tower) for which he did a daily reading, over the airwaves, of a one- or two-page text he had written. This program resulted in 46 short texts that were published as *FM Galicia* in 2001 by Lileia-NV. These texts offer personal reflections on topics including, among other things, Prokhasko's family, his days in the Soviet army, botany, cultural and religious figures, cities, and mountains. And, most often, they focus on seemingly mundane objects and activities. Prokhasko's delicate tone and languid pace recall the poetry of fellow writer from the Ivano-Frankivsk region Oleh Lysheha. Like Lysheha, Prokhasko leads his readers to notice oft-overlooked surroundings and find guidelines there that may help untangle life's mysteries.[3] Prokhasko also maintains this steady tenor when touching on his nation's history. His subdued manner allows him to calmly intertwine into his brief stories Ukrainian historical figures, such as Andrei Sheptytskyi who was muted and marginalized in Soviet times, and his own family members, also repressed by Soviet authorities.

---

3   To read the poetry of Oleh Lysheha (1949–2014) in English translation see Oleh Lysheha, *The Selected Poems of Oleh Lysheha*, trans. author and James Brasfield (Cambridge, MA: Harvard Ukrainian Research Institute, 1999) and Oleh Lysheha, *Dream Bridge: Selected Poems*, trans. Virlana Tklacz and Wanda Phipps (Sandpoint, ID: Lost Horse Press, 2022).

A key characteristic of Prokhasko's writing in *FM Galicia* (and in many of his other publications) is the repeated mention of the same objects. This brings a certain ritualistic aspect to his storytelling. Repetition, combined with the sharing of the personal, create a sense of intimacy between Prokhasko and his reader; it is as if the author reveals a very dear, concealed truth. At the same time, the stories that Prokhasko tells often feature a quirky detail or two, lightening the mood in what are mostly profound contemplations on existence and memory. Objects that are passed along to the author by his dear ones contain stories within them and, when the author introduces them into an *FM Galicia* episode, the past lives of those that crossed paths with him become part of his own, personal history. In *FM Galicia*, Prokhasko mastered the short form that he is known for and is revered by his readers today.

* * *

Prokhasko's constant search for new forms of expression reached another level with the short novel *The UnSimple*. The novel tells the story of an insulated community living in the fictional Carpathian mountain resort town of Yalivets in the first half of the twentieth century. The main protagonists in the novel are the photographer and filmmaker Frants, the WWI veteran Sebastian, and several related individuals with the name Anna, one of them a soldier and one an architect.

There are also the Unsimple, a group of highlander sorcerers that maintains a mysterious sway over this community.

As is the case in Prokhasko's earlier publications, narrative experiments abound in this literary work. Again, Prokhasko eschews a linear unfolding of the plot and continually disorients the reader. We learn background information about characters unexpectedly, randomly, and facts appear seemingly out of nowhere. Several times in the novel, a defining statement is made without being substantiated or expanded, then is abandoned only to be revisited and illuminated later in the novel. Major plot developments are presented in parentheses. Prokhasko also plays with chronology in the novel, creating a looping reel of the events in its protagonists' lives. Altogether, the author presents his story as a puzzle in pieces for the reader to assemble.

In *The UnSimple*, we are told several times that there are things that are more important than fate. In Yalivets, it is storytelling that is paramount. Its inhabitants communicate their own local, personal stories, passing along information in many forms: they share photos, letters, and dreams. All of these are a means of telling a story, and the ability to tell a story is deemed a powerful talent. Intonation, gestures, voice, and syntax are all the tools of the craft. But one needs to gather stories in order to be able to share them. Thus, family chronicles and inheritance are often the main topics of this storytelling; a person's power to imagine the cities and places of their family history create a personal saga.

Place is also something that is revered in the novel, for, according to Prokhasko, "a place is needed in order for something to occur."[4] In Yalivets, homes contain wisdom because memory rests within them. The buildings and the objects in them have stories of their own, as in the stories of *FM Galicia*. In the novel, Yalivets is a Babylon-like place that is well known—all of Central Europe comes there to drink its soothing gin. In *The UnSimple*, idyllic Carpathia is the place where myriad languages are spoken and understood by all—everyone is allowed to speak one's own language. It is a place with its own peculiar, artistic version of democracy—a place where a special screenwriting institute produces a play written by the people to guide their government's actions. In *The UnSimple*, Prokhasko offers a post-Soviet approach to the Carpathian region, presenting it as a place that is stylish and modern yet full of traditional mystery and ritual. His novel contributes to the myth of the Ukrainian part of the region of Galicia, a key development in Ukrainian literature in the years after the country achieved independence in 1991. The European wars of the twentieth century spill across the pages of

---

4   Taras Prokhasko, interview by Pavlo Krupa, *San Rideau* no. 2 (2004): 45.

The UnSimple. Historical facts are scattered throughout the novel, including the existence of Carpatho-Ukraine. Various peoples, from Russians to Rastafarians, intersect in wartime western Ukraine. Ukrainian historical and cultural figures, from the academic and statesman Mykhailo Hrushevskyi to the bohemian writer Osyp Shpytko, are name-dropped in the novel. In *The UnSimple*, it is anticipated that Carpatho-Ukraine will survive and that it will be from this region and from Central Europe that Ukrainian freedom will eventually emanate.

These themes, prominent throughout the novel, are interwoven in layers that resist a linear, chronological narrative. As scholar Tamara Hundorova points out when discussing *The UnSimple*, "Stories comprise a cultural reservoir; they can be combined into chains, coiled, and spun as though in a centrifuge. Stories create myth and reveal the tree of life."[5] Indeed, the author dips into the many small stories, rearranging them to tell new stories. Prokhasko's focus on storytelling also brings with it a celebration of language and symbols. At one point in the novel, an object is built purely so that words can be invented to describe it; at another point, an extensive list of the symbols used to decorate Ukrainian Easter eggs (*pysanky*) is recreated. When we are offered depictions of

---

5   Tamara Hundorova, *The Post-Chornobyl Library: Ukrainian Postmodernism of the 1990s*, trans. Sergiy Yakovenko (Boston, MA: Academic Studies Press, 2019), 162.

events, they are often unexpected and jarring. Sometimes we are charmed—and sometimes disturbed—when we learn details about the protagonists' lives. Particularly disquieting are the incestuous relations with the various Annas that are presented in the novel, which serve to accentuate the insular nature of the Yalivets community and to insinuate that all of the town's developments, though experienced by different generations of its inhabitants, are related and part of a multi-layered whole. For, as Maria G. Rewakowicz writes, "In the world of *The UnSimple*, the magic of life erases all taboos, transcends the linearity of time."[6] The mystic world of Yalivets presented by Prokhasko in his novel is associated with a certain historical time (roughly 1913 to 1951) and, occasionally, with real individuals and geographical places (as indicated above). However, it is portrayed in a manner that is heavily idealized, in contrast to the brutal nature of Soviet reality in these lands.

In the novel, birth—not death—marks the end of a story. The Unsimple continually gather stories; lives begin and end according to the stories that they tell. In his novel, Prokhasko turns things inside out and upside down to reveal how we are formed by the stories told about us, and how we, in turn, form those around us

---

6   Maria G. Rewakowicz, *Ukraine's Quest for Identity: Embracing Cultural Hybridity in Literary Imagination, 1991–2011* (Lanham, MD: Lexington Books, 2018), 84.

by the way we tell their stories. In this way, Prokhasko draws our attention to the power of storytelling.

* * *

The three books featured in this volume map different routes that Taras Prokhasko has traveled to explore how stories are told. From the postmodern deconstruction of his early stories in *Anna's Other Days*, to the brief, personal reflections of *FM Galicia*, to the interconnectedness of the mysterious, cloistered community of Yalivets in the short novel *The UnSimple*, the author has striven to push the boundaries of his nation's literature by finding new forms of composing prose. In his tales, Prokhasko invites the reader to contemplate how the story is being told to them. His stories, like the tales of his people, are full of colorful, eccentric characters who, whether they are participating in highly dramatic historical events or simply going about their daily routines, provide us with ruminations on what being is. It is my hope that this volume of Taras Prokhasko's selected prose in English translation will allow these tales to reach a wider audience and make known to them the wonderful talents of Ukraine's master storyteller.

Anna's Other Days

Translated by Ali Kinsella

ESSAI DE DECONSTRUCTION
(An Attempt at Deconstruction)

I

The analysis of time-consciousness is the age-old crux of descriptive psychology and theory of knowledge. The first thinker to be deeply sensitive to the immense difficulties to be found here was Augustine who labored almost to despair over this problem. Chapters 14–22 of Book XI of the *Confessions* must even today be thoroughly studied by everyone concerned with the problem of time.[1]

Fall is the refinement of concepts. In October, I can have more interesting thoughts about time, about Augustine, about summer. The fact that, back in spring,

1   Edmund Husserl, *The Phenomenology of Internal Time-Consciousness*, ed. Martin Heidegger, trans. James S. Churchill (Bloomington, IN: Indiana University Press, 1964), 21.

I stopped publishing articles and giving public lectures, that I ceased work on my dissertation and broke off all communication with European correspondents wasn't caused by any surveillance or prohibitions on the part of the regime (the regime, on the contrary, was interested in my productivity—I was the only one who could conduct research on the flora in this part of the mountains, which was closed off to the whole world; all the European botanical societies had to make do with my herbaria, and my silence led to misunderstandings, putting the brakes on a few continental projects), nor due to any form of disobedience or resistance. I hadn't at all lost interest in botany (I had just then started putting together a fundamentally new reference book based on nonbinary logic) or in life. I simply couldn't cope with all the minutiae established by the regime regarding the layout, cataloging, and publication of texts. I was lost. I was completely at a loss. I preferred not to write. This didn't, however, apply to my summer diary. For me, everything that happens throughout the year happens during the summer. It is by the events of summer that I distinguish the years. Each summer, I take some notes, often in the strangest ways. Maybe this is somehow connected to the herbarium—plants come about in summer, specimens are gathered and wait around all fall, until they are sorted and studied during the winter. The herbarium is a post-summer story. The collected plants are wrapped in adventures, people, places, conversations, and moods.

Summer diaries are a separate culture: travels, expeditions, hunting seasons, hikes, new places and ways of living, photography, rivers and shifts in the aesthetics of being, and later vacations, re-vacations, boyish valor, wars of the imagination, juices, fruits, and mirages. Summer is truth because it is openness.

But fall is the refinement of concepts. All summer, I read only Saint Augustine. I read only a little at a time but every morning. If Anna was around, I read out loud. We would set out the three-tiered Viennese coffeepot, held together with wire, on the uneven chair near the bed in the evening, having already ground the coffee in the coffee grinder whose drawer had the cracked bottom. We'd carefully pick up every last ground, since that summer there was nowhere near enough coffee to go around and Ms. Viki gave everyone who lived in the boarding house an equal amount, which was supposed to last three months. The beans came in tins of different sizes with different pictures and words (and also different former smells). None of the containers was actually made for coffee. I got a flat box that used to hold Grand Café cigarillos from Holland (for some reason, objects are remembered best). We all brewed our own coffee, knowing that our boxes wouldn't be refilled. Anna would come from the citadel—she didn't live in the boarding house—and I had only enough coffee for us to drink in the morning. I would get up first and pour the boiling water into the ready and waiting coffeepot.

That was when we would lie together, waiting for the coffee to percolate and return to the bottom chamber of the pot. We drank the coffee at the table, which we'd pulled up to the unusually deep windowsill; there were always cigarettes and a volume of Augustine lying on the sill. We had enough for four small cups of coffee, four cigarettes (two each), and one and a half pages of confessions (for me, each fragment of Augustine is now connected to the subtlest topography of our mornings: Anna's flannel nightgown, all of Anna's micromovements that combined to form the endless topology of her plastics. It's easier for me to hold onto this nostalgia—remembering everything, I will never forget what we said, what was spoken—it can be read word for word in Saint Augustine). I still can't break myself of those coffeepots. Even after I got to Prague, every morning, I ordered a full pot on the square near the old town hall (likewise, a few years ago, when Anna and I stopped living together, I would order a now unnecessary second coffee, always without sugar, at first unconsciously but later in hopes that she'd turn up, since it's hard to change one's routines). Ever since that summer, I have been "concerned with the problem of time." I know that the past lives on in habits and that, today, an hour from summer will last as long as there's coffee in the pot (if only I could smoke those cigarettes that Ms. Viki had). In early evening, I go to the wine bar on Vodičkova Street and drain a jug of *burčák* young wine in a couple hours. It's dark in the basement. There's only a table lamp glowing in a corner on the floor with its shade flipped upside down. I read my summer diary. I realize that, despite the compactness and totality of that summer in the boarding house—it was the time of Irzhi—the diary is nothing but records of conversations with him. The lighting doesn't change; as I read, I speak the words aloud in my mind and the burčák further dissolves the clot of intonations on the paper, their durations becoming almost identical. I always carry in my pocket at least one of Irzhi's drawings and this typed fragment: "Edmund Husserl. *The Phenomenology of Internal Time-Consciousness*. 'Introduction.' The analysis of time-consciousness is an age-old crux of descriptive psychology and theory of knowledge. The first thinker to be deeply sensitive to the immense difficulties to be found here was Augustine, who labored almost to despair over this problem. Chapters 14–22 of Book XI of the *Confessions* must even today be thoroughly studied by everyone concerned with the problem of time." Irzhi only managed to translate the first paragraph. It is thanks to the absence of Husserl that I came to know Augustine. Even now, I'm not going to write anything until I've written a book about Irzhi. And this diary, dictated by Irzhi, will finally be it. Nor will I compile a reference book because I won't be able to find an illustrator like Anna, the wife of my Anna. After Anna showed me her botanical sketches, I've refused everyone else. It's better for there to be no reference book.

Instead, there will be Irzhi. He will be more than a hero; he will be discourse, he will be style, writing. Irzhi as a way of writing. I couldn't wait for the Husserl, but Irzhi and I created our own phenomenology. We shifted our ontology from being to living, and put prose above all, right alongside God's plan.

Irzhi lived by prose. Prose was his essence, and he regarded prose as a sign of life. Just what his prose was I saw at the beginning of summer when we went to the city for a night. We crossed through yards, passed by garages, trees, chin-up bars, and trash cans; mixed with sand, the pollen from the poplars still lay around the tumid roots of the biggest trees. All of this, he said, these yards, garages, trees, chin-up bars, trash cans, this pollen from the poplars on the roots of the biggest trees, the lighting, the state of the atmosphere, temperature, even the latitude, all of this is Handke's prose. I thought then that we really were living in someone else's prose, with someone else's prose, for and by someone else's prose. But only until we could come up with our own (let's set loose the totipotency, name the unnamed, choose the unchosen, make possible the impossible). You can study your whole life without coming to any conclusions. He really liked Anna. For her, he spared not even his most precious things. Irzhi, his room, everything captured in the frame, reminded me of the Chesterfields ads. "Study without coming to any conclusions"—he said this to Anna when we were sitting in the overly large restaurant near the lake smoking Chesterfields and talking about their ads, their aesthetics of life. We thought up a general slogan for this series of photographs. He knew Anna better than I. He told me what I would learn from her, even though I had just introduced them in the middle of summer.

Every time the regime announced a state of emergency, they detained me, arrested me, and took me to a special camp outside the city. There was never a trial or sentencing. They fed us pretty well at the camp; there was a lake and a library, and they brought in beer. They just didn't ever let us go outside the boundaries. The people interned there weren't dangerous, just disagreeable to the regime. My grandpa was an officer in the army that existed before the current regime, and I myself took part in performances put on by a forbidden ecological organization. This was my sentence.

That year, summer was so unusually hot that the warmth hung around until the end of October. The water in the rivers didn't even cool off overnight; every night the walls further heated the air in the city; one's vision went yellow-green from the intensity of the rays; and almost all the insects squeezed in a few extra, overlapping generations. Allergies to the genuine haze of unrepentant pollen were the order of the day because the plants hadn't even the minimum humidity necessary for pollination, and the unrealized grains of pollen tumbled and died off in whole clumps. I really didn't want to go to the camp. What saved me was that I stopped going in to the department—it had become uninteresting. Therefore, they couldn't find me on the first day of the state of emergency. It was announced in the morning and, by lunchtime, I had already gotten pretty far on the train headed to the mountains. The train was strangely empty, save for a few old country folk who were hastily returning over the pass with their fruit, since all the markets had been closed. I bought a whole backpackful of apricots from them for next to nothing. The train was hot, so I spent the whole day and all night sitting in the vestibule near the open door. Meditating, I watched the flight of passing landscapes, objects, buildings, and then, staring continually at the movement of everything beyond the train, I most likely hallucinated. I hadn't even been smoking. Then my friend the entomologist came into the vestibule from one of the other cars. He and I met after we had spent the night on different sides of the same rock a few meters from one another, completely unaware. In the morning we saw each other and realized that we had the same method for overcoming depression: without preparing, leaving everything unfinished, bringing nothing along, to come out to these rocks, make our way to the top, and spend the night there, no matter the time of year, sitting, standing, sometimes lying down, but always holding on and always sleeping. Later, I offered him my laboratory to hide from a mobilization campaign.

The entomologist told me about Ms. Viki's boarding house. I knew the station well, back from when I studied the flora of the railroad tracks, the various immigrations, emigrations, migrations. I used to ride from station to station on the ladders of the freight cars. There was a citadel on the hill there, a real curiosity of a fortification from the beginning of the century. It was even armed with cannons, and a funicular rose up the hill from the station. Not once was the citadel needed; somehow all fronts of the war passed it by. In the end, the garrison was moved out and a few of the bastions were converted into a luxury hotel. I really liked it there. I had a room in a machine-gun bunker a little ways outside the citadel, like a separate building. One time, Anna waited there for me for several days when I had set out into the mountains on foot away from the tracks, on the trail of some expansive population, leaving Anna, who had gone with me for the entire hunting season, behind. Another time, we were there in winter right after Christmas. It was terribly cold, and we went sledding. The sled spent the night inside; the walls took forever to thaw out. Anna ate snow and we warmed ourselves upstairs, heating our clothes near the stove before we got dressed. Everyone talked only about the frost; Anna didn't allow herself to smoke. For some reason, the mirror was hung high, so Anna, who was developing a series of scenes for a new photo album, was forced to stand on a chair. I watched her strange poses, the thick wool socks on her feet, stoking the stove with seasoned beechwood until the tiles glowed. We had a lot of grapefruit with us, and we made ashtrays for our bed out of their peeled skins. Our lips were windburnt and raw, our hands frozen, and we had to tilt the glass of alcohol past our lips since the ethanol burned them. I rubbed lotion into Anna's hands. Although we had made a blanket tent on the bed to heat up a little bit of air for ourselves, the scent of the hand cream always overpowered my and Anna's smells. At some point, we bought some frozen plums. Frozen, they tasted almost exactly the same as fresh. When they thawed, though, they were completely different. We also thought we were being reborn each time we warmed up after that penetrating cold, which made every cell in our entire bodies painfully palpable. The road on the side of the mountains opposite the station, which was lined with pitch-black (especially against the backdrop of snow), twisted plum trees, led from the citadel to a narrow, room-like hideaway, closed in on all sides by rocks. Yet it was big enough for a lake, a rather large one. There were several picturesque huts standing on the shore. One housed a pub, and across from every hut was a long, wooden pier with boats tied to it. A little farther along the shore, far apart from one another, two-story villas appeared from among a thicket of mountain pine; these were the remnants of the prewar sanatorium. It would appear that Ms. Viki's boarding house was the last of its kind.

I still didn't know where I was going to live, but the entomologist said that everyone at Ms. Viki's was a runaway like me and recommended the place. My grandpa's last name is still well known and popular today. Ms. Viki took me in despite the fact that the boarding house was overcrowded. I got a room in the attic, which mostly served to dry all sorts of grasses. That same day, I found the Grand Café box near my mug in the common dining room. Besides mine, there were five other mugs. Ms. Viki herself always ate separately.

It was a little tight with groceries. Ms. Viki had thought up all sorts of dishes to make for us with whatever she could get. For breakfast, she would make us each a large mug of hot cocoa (strangely some luxury items actually made it to the village store in great numbers). She'd serve it with heaps of perfect French toast. For lunch, she only ever cooked soup: a soup civilization, the sacrament of soup, very complicated soups. A few hours later, we'd sit down to herbal tea with cake, baked from austerity recipes—from practically nothing at all. To compensate, our rather late dinner comprised innumerable vegetable dishes—beans, squash, onions, tomatoes, pulses, potatoes, mushrooms, peas, cabbage—boiled, stewed, stuffed, fried, sautéed, deep fried, baked. There were sauces for everything and a great big dish of boiled rice. Dinner ended with proper tea and a tasting of fresh preserves. Besides that, we took a spoonful of honey on an empty stomach each morning. Honey was a cult object for Ms. Viki. We could pick currants, gooseberries, apples, and cherries ourselves in the garden.

There was a large round table and a sideboard with dishes in the dining room. All the dishes were Secession. It was good that, in addition to everything else, the table service also included ashtrays, also of Secession porcelain. We could smoke during tea. Stairs from various floors and alcoves with separate rooms all converged in the dining room. The whole of the topography of the villa resembled the Prague Castle as it looks from Smíchov, when the most diverse of fragments are combined in one structure. The villa had an irregular shape due to its hodgepodge of annexes and offshoots. On every side it ended in verandas, galleries, porches, balconies, or stairs. The stairs leading to some of the rooms went straight through windows. The whole building was terribly overgrown with grape, moss, ivy, and vines I couldn't identify, all cultivated by the lady of the house. Because of this, it sometimes looked bigger and sometimes smaller than it actually was.

II

June 10.   Irzhi. For me, he was the most important person in the boardinghouse. Everything manifests in parallel—through his judgments and conclusions. A translator hiding from mobilization. A translator of

Roth, Heidegger, Rilke, Trakl. He almost never left his room. He would walk around the lake. The aesthetics of being. Everyday hermeneutics.

June 14. Irzhi on Ms. Viki. Her garden thinks; it can move from place to place. The Alps imitate the Himalayas. Wild strawberries until the snow comes, but only a few berries a day. Stale, old fur coats can serve as furniture. Moths fly out of the credenza because Heidegger lives there.

June 15. At Irzhi's. Rasta and Stronzitska came over from their rooms. Rasta is a Rastafarian guru. He's being threatened with arrest again. He tends to the marijuana in Ms. Viki's greenhouse. Ms. Viki accidentally ended up with some high-grade marijuana through a correspondence seed exchange, probably from someone in Holland. We smoked with him and Stronzitska. Rastaman vibration. Irzhi caught a wave. Stronzitska is an essayist from Vienna (she could have been a spy in the service of the Hapsburg house, Irzhi says). She smokes incessantly. And only Drum shag, but one paper isn't enough for her cigarettes, so she sticks two or three together in advance. Stronzitska has Raynaud's syndrome. She brought her own blanket. Now she has all the blankets in the whole house because her hands and feet are always freezing. She was interested in me as a famous botanist, as a former friend of a world-famous model—Anna. She recorded an interview with me for her radio program. I wasn't afraid to tell her about everything I'd seen in forbidden zones—provocative radio is her format. Things often happen only after Stronzitska tells about them. I refused to talk about Anna. She is afraid of moths. An invitation to a conference of opposition journalists from our country, Stronzitska is organizing the conference, it will take place in the boardinghouse where we live.

June 16. We went even farther into the mountains with Rasta and hired ourselves out to pick apples for a couple days. Discussions on drug-induced and sober ways of achieving visions. Attempts to analyze and systematize the visual laws (high optics) of vision. Rasta is the former European champion of cannabis reframing—two competitors go somewhere together, smoking weed the whole time, conjuring up each other's fears, phobias, provoking obsessive ideas, manias, ulterior motives, and unjustified conclusions. Whoever leads their competitor to a level of reframing from which they can never return wins.

June 20. Life in the boarding house is straight out of the nineteenth century—that's what it feels like. Our daily existence with our shared breakfasts and evening teas, the culture of preserves, the old paintings, everyone talking all at once, everyone having private conversations. Guests coming for a day or two. The absence of a storyline—there is no plot. Everything sort of stretches out in time, which ceases to be events any bigger than drinking tea or an abundance of moths at night. There is no determinism, but the logic—just one of the many possible—of the register, of the description, of the inventory of "traits." Reading Antonych with Irzhi: every day the verse with that day's date.

June 22. Took the night train to the city with Irzhi. We wanted to sleep, we smoked in the vestibule. It was on trains like this that *Being and Time* was thought up. We had to use a razor to defend ourselves from the patrol. We wounded them and jumped off the train to immediately hop on another, headed back to the mountains.

June 25. With Irzhi. We decided to listen to Ms. Stronzitska's tape—a recording of conversations with everyone who lives at Ms. Viki's. On the tape recorder our voices sound almost the same. We listen to the conversation with Ms. Hiba (it was for her sake that Ms. Stronzitska came to the boardinghouse for the summer): a film and theater director of situations—modeling scenarios, creating events directly in someone else's life, at times in reverse, at times not, at times commissioned, and at times unexpected, her involvement in a multitude of strangers' lives to the point where she has none of her own, is very dangerous for the regime. A consummate psychologist. Irzhi says, she's bored at the boarding house without drama and intrigue, she rides her bike to the citadel to play bridge with the bishops, she's looking for a plot among us that could unfold, climax, and resolve with a performance.

June 27. The invariability of phenology. Stagnant days, like the summer of '92, '94. A nighttime trek with Irzhi to the blackberry patch. A few odd lighters in our pockets. My plant philosophy is the denial of self-expression, tropisms, and contemplation. To stay, to endure. Tracelessness, coexistence, the constant feeling of existing, non-rhetoric, extra-erotica, the unattainability of the idea, and much more.

June 30. With Irzhi at the citadel. Anna is there. She is at once both happy and sad. My inability to choose. Her inability to endure. Anna lives with another Anna, a graphic artist and photographer. And Anna is her model and lover. Irzhi's lecture by the lake: conclusions for the sake of harmony with the world, the hermeneutics of holes and niches; wanderings through niches and aesthetics; free flight from being into being; entanglement as the guarantor of nonpredestination, freedom as unnecessity, freedom freely freeing itself.

July 1. Anna at the boarding house. We become lovers again with ease and nostalgia, realizing that our bodies belong to each other. Shades of various unshared experience. Anna suggests positioning her body to pose together for the other Anna. We think up compositions. We drink mineral water at night at Irzhi's.

July 2. Anna and I drink with the colonel at the pub. He has admired Anna and only now acknowledges me. In the colonel's room. Maps published under the regime—he corrects them. He's a geographer, a former minister of lands for the government, unseated by the regime, he ran illegal border crossings. A photograph with my grandfather whom he once saved from enemy fire. After some rum, he hangs by his fingers from the edge of the balcony. Deplorable memories of the First World War: during the war, he helped chart mountain routes, decipher enemy symbols, and make additional false marks (there were six coding systems).

July 3. The marijuana plant Rasta gave me is in the white porcelain vase.

July 7. Anna and I swim in the lake in the morning, daytime, evening, and night. We row the boat and the citadel floats across the lake, we swim behind the boat. We do sit-ups and strengthen our backs—the longest muscles of our backs are wet. Later, I wash her hair, but I can barely hold it all in my hands. We each smoke one of Rasta's cigarettes and experiment with that kind of eroticism. We fall asleep in unexpected places a few times.

July 9. We spend the night at Irzhi's. The floor is made up with blankets, life on the floor, bitter Japanese tea. We burn walnut shells specially collected for this in winter. Irzhi says, the more you really love people, the happier you can be.

July 10. With Irzhi. My bygone history with Anna. Growing closer over a very long time, very gradually, very completely. We became true lovers only when there was nowhere left to expand. Subtleness is holiness. She was my existence and essence, my singular motif of the riskiest, boldest, frankest, sincerest, and most grateful advances. Dances of the imagination. Standing at the edges, breaching prohibitions. The intensification of existence is a philosophical technique. Someone who has never said anything empty or extraneous, and gradually I said everything I wanted to. The conversation could be written as a continuous text without separations between the speakers. A day can only be held if it's not torn into night. Cyclamen. Rum, persimmons, large cafes. The long fear of touching each other and not getting used to it. A very thin arm whose hairs are standing on end from cold. Winter turns into spring, the sun aquariumizes the room, there's wet snow in the garden, the evening un-winterly illuminated by indirect lights. Yet, at some point, it had to turn bad. One time I returned from an expedition and immediately went to my study. She embraced me and the photographer took a picture. We contrasted too much yet complemented each other remarkably. The photo appeared on a few covers, by then Anna was already quite popular. A few things are important to me: we achieved the impossible, we learned very much from each other, we evoked unusual joy in everyone. And now we are we again, even if just for one summer.

July 13.   Into the mountains with the other Anna for a few days. We look at plants. I show her the fine aesthetics of botany. We think up a series of designs based on this. She photographs me. Sketches for my reference book. The designs let loose more and more creatures from other forms of reality. The unexpectedly quick appearance of a shared past. Destruction as a real state of the world, as a sign of vivacity. The phenomenology of a rock covered in a few layers of lichen is the phenomenology of the lichen, not of the rock. The bunches of lichens are the phenomena. Superficial, planar, topological, rhizoidal phenomenology.

July 18.   At Irzhi's, looking at photographs that Anna took, that Anna and I staged and posed for. The color of umber. Asymmetries and symmetries. The faces of medieval monks. Around the lake. Life on a single rock. The sky along your arm. Trees variously infected with mistletoe, existence among mistletoe. The silhouettes of the uninvited on invited surfaces. Irzhi says, you come up with photographs based on how you lived. But, in the end, the photos are totally different. And then you use your own photos as scripts. You are finding your own prose, freeing yourself from citation.

July 20. I'm afraid that Anna will get pregnant by Anna when she turns away from me. Anna, my lover, and Anna, Anna's lover. In this way, Anna and I are getting dangerously close. We caress each other through Anna. The traces of our touches coincide. Anna is happy and laughs both with Anna and with me.

July 22. With Irzhi. Coming up with stories. Attempts at destruction and reconstruction. Derrida. It's impossible to evaluate stories without taking up residence in them. Attempts at deconstruction. Irzhi says, I'd write a story about our summer in the boarding house. I say to really let your imagination loose. The joy of thinking up a world. I wouldn't know any motifs, I wouldn't know any reasons, I wouldn't know why. I'd see it for what it is. I'd see what shows itself. There would be no evolution, only an agglomeration of phenomena, properties, occurrences, facts. Inconsistent logic. I'd even be able to think up more than I knew. I wouldn't want to achieve anything other than to imagine what could be possible. Irzhi says writing by throwing stones into water, circles of varying intensity ripple out from each one, they enter one another. Don't worry that your story won't have much in common with your own experience; don't try to drag that into the story. I say prose on the level of auxiliary verbs, prepositional phrases. Irzhi says, a complex structure—this story is like the first chapter in a great post-summer novel of intrigue, a refined and worthy debut, yet only the first chapter exists. I say, but none of this should make the story heavy. Write lightly, with joy, so that it likewise is read with joy.

July 25. A whole other world. Anna and I take the radio operator's place and stay for a few days in the armored personnel carrier that guards the citadel during the state of emergency. Life in the contained space, life within iron, life at the radio station. We heard that they were in fact leading the military into our mountain province and introducing martial law. They were threatening everyone with arrest.

July 28. Ms. Viki planned a holiday for all of us on the first of August. I invited Anna and Anna. With Irzhi. We'll see what happens in the middle of the story. How it ends. If something happens during a night of revelry. Anna's hoping for an orgy that would let her pay attention not only to me. The colonel's dreaming about getting drunk and dancing with Anna. He doesn't even know if he'll be able to drive us across the border if they bring the military in and we find the courage to steal the APC near the citadel for our escape. Ms. Hiba probably knows everything: how the situation will eventually play out, who will have which roles. It's looking likely that Anna and I could become the object of the game. Rasta is going to try this year's marijuana, he's going to try to smoke up as many people as possible. Ms. Stronzitska, Anna, Irzhi, Anna, and I might agree to smoke. It's curious what inhibitions of Anna's the grass might evaporate. Rasta is also going to attempt a group reframing session. What's more, participants in Ms. Stronzitska's secret conference are going to start arriving on the night trains. The military might come, too.

July 29.   It turns out that Irzhi is competing in this year's October finale for the European reframing championship. And Rasta's training him. "Irzhi isn't a real Rastaman," Rasta says, "but Irzhi's potential is greater than anyone in the entire history of the championship." Irzhi has reframed moths—there were more than usual this summer. They would fly in through the window toward the lamp, until it became difficult to walk across the room without running into at least a few moths. They even landed on our hands. In the gleam of the table lamp their eyes were bright and translucent red. Irzhi would raise the moth on his hand until it was even with his gaze and stare into its eyes. Their eyes, it turned out, were large and compound. The moths couldn't hold Irzhi's stare and looked away. "Another requirement for writing"—one's gaze can never be narrower than one's peripheral vision (but this doesn't take literature into account at all).

III

Dying is the collateral of any experience. It is impossible for there to be too much experience, extraneous experience, erroneous experience. And there can be no direction other than toward experience, toward dying. The maximum coincides with death. Maximal experience is needed in order to die in your own way. So that in your death you can become an entire death forest, a whole wasteland of additional experience for someone else. Later the text becomes life that, after it appears, can only die, getting squeezed out by experience.

You never know which period you live in, or in whose, or what field you're entering. This becomes clear when the period ends, when the force of the next death ushers us into new territories of the experience of dying.

AROUND THE LAKE

The structure of the building, like that of most plants, was only needed to maintain the properties that far and away exceeded the possibilities of the structure itself. The building's properties had their own properties. The most important thing was that they really did need to be maintained. The properties dried up, went out, hid, and concealed themselves on all floors, in the attic, in the cellar, on the stairs, windowsills, balconies, roofs, and garrets. Along the gutters and following the wooden floorboards. Effort was needed to bring one or another to life; effort was needed to even keep track of them or hold their topography, periodicity, and cyclicality in one's mind.

The rooms imposed manners. Mugwort grew around the home and rubbed the walls, erasing the walls, abrading the walls. Grapevines reduced the balconies, their bunches crushing themselves when they fell from on high to the stone patio, painting it purple.

The building was tied together by a sequence of internal windows; with an auspicious sunrise or sunset and the wise placement of mirrors, you could look through the whole thing as though through amber. The hills started behind the building. The path alongside it led to the vineyard shot through with blackberries. Beyond that were the mountains. But they weren't visible from the windows or the bridge. The wind always blew from there. Blankets had to be stuffed between the windows and old overcoats under the doors to the balconies. In the mornings, the finest snow would collect in their pockets and pleats and under collars—the snow the wind was made up of and which penetrated even the cracks in the glass. To prevent the building from going completely cold, it was necessary to light the stoves while it was still dark, starting with the coldest, emptiest rooms.

To get to the bridge, you had to go up steps that started not far from the door, steps into the hills. Then take the bridge and turn toward the building, passing it at the level of the second-floor windows, and keep going. A ravine with train tracks at the bottom separated the house from the edge of the city; the bridge connected the edge of the city to the building, hills, vineyards, and shortcut to the mountains. The tracks led to the quarry. At one time, it had been possible to slip between the metal trestles and jump from the bridge straight into the sand on the platform when the train was leaving: the trains reached the station faster than the trams snaked through the whole city. Now that they'd stopped excavating sand, there was already a lake there; the tracks hadn't been used since summer. But various railroad lanterns, mostly blue, on very short posts, still glowed every evening along the tracks. Their light fell onto the stalks swaying in the breeze—the remains of the last generation of non-native plants sown here by the trains, the accidental ephemera from a single season, deprived of the ability to reproduce, wasted by the prospects on this embankment. Their exaggerated shadows moved along the banks of the ravine, and it seemed as though the stalks and barren capsules themselves had stopped the trains.

Strangely, the road to the building passed landmarks in the same order as symbols listed in the legend on the topographic map of the city: single-story homes with gardens, railroad tracks, ravines, individual buildings, vineyards, individual trees... One of the individual trees was an araucaria. This araucaria grew in a basket in the middle of Severyn's room in a house in the hills (individual buildings, vineyards) for a few dozen years and was never counted by the topographers.

Snow fell, but it only stayed in the coldest places—on the crotches of trees, on the bridge, on the poppy heads. The snow turned the territory into a room. In this snow, hands didn't even get cold right away. The footprints on the bridge went all the way down to the wet boards; the ashes didn't rest, couldn't rest on the uneven surface of the snow, there was so much excess moisture in the snow that it burst into the structure of the ashes, washing them away and pulling them, now dissolved, in gray streaks into the pores of the snow. Snow makes winter imperceptible, it passes without allowing itself to be remembered, recalled, recreated in the imagination. This is a sign of the seasons. It's why they're not boring. But the experience of previous winters only hints at what needs to be confirmed once again.

The inside of Markus's thick overcoat still held air captured in Severyn's apartment. The coat carried air from place to place, Khrystyian could smell it when Markus undid his top buttons to take two cigarettes from his pocket. The Mlynarskyi brothers always stopped on the bridge to smoke one cigarette each when they were coming back from Severyn's. Khrystyian's lips recognized the proffered cigarette as a Gauloise. A passing tractor trailer going towards the mountains lit Markus up in yellow light; Severyn could have seen shadows on the patches of snow if he'd been standing behind them; the wind disrupted the integrity of the circulation, stealing a portion of smoke from their mouths; the light in Severyn's window went out right when the tractor disappeared over the hill, almost like his window was one of its headlights. It got dark. The araucaria in Severyn's window lost its color and appeared as finely detailed black branches. It was clear that in the room it was brighter than here; perhaps the moon was shining over the hills.

The Mlynarskyis were visiting Severyn before his operation. They left him a tomogram of his brain that clearly showed the tumor. To Severyn, the tomogram looked like a tangled relief map, and the tumor looked like the smudge of a lake. It could also have been not a map but an aerial photograph: from up high, you could see that the lake was bulging out—the broad strip along the bank was very shallow, barely under water, but the one closest to the water was already swallowed by the lake. Khrystyian showed in detail how he'd get to the tumor, where the cuts would be. Markus had to convince Severyn once and for all of the urgency of the next day's operation. Even though he himself would not have agreed to be deprived of access to another world as Severyn's disease made possible—from time to time the neoplasm pressed on his oculomotor nerve and his eye could not perform the seamless, minute movement-transitions, movement-touches to all points of the visible at any given moment (it is precisely this property that is the ability to see the seen), his eye would freeze immobile for a long time, fixating on the elementary ultrastructures of vision and everything except for the ultrastructure would turn into a blurry spot until his eye crawled to another microstructure. Severyn could spend whole hours or days like this—however long the attack lasted—not seeing anything except for the tiniest components—actually, no larger than one-off points of view. It was like using a binocular microscope to examine flower structures or cross sections in plant morphology—it's not so much that the ultrastructures get larger, but that they become self-sufficient, they stand out from the homogeneity, take up the entire field of vision, become distinct from what's analogous by being determined and defined. In addition to this, there was an effect of interrupted genesis—the majority of the subsequent frames was skipped. "Bird," Khrystyian said when the image of the araucaria against the curtain took on a red background, moved a bit to the side, stopped, returned to its place, and then wouldn't stop vibrating thanks to the switching on and off of the now indistinct yellow light from the depths of the room; Markus thought how good it was to have enough shared experience that this rhetoric was sufficient. Bird had entered Severyn's room and set a match to an old letter to light the stove. She was going to twist herself into a pretzel and snuggle against the stove, recently cooled by the mountain air, until it got warm enough, regardless of the fact that, at first, it would be too cold but, by the end, it would be too hot to touch. In the middle of the night, Bird will light it again. In moments of insomnia, she is capable, like a plant, of not moving and not getting bored, she can just be as long as necessary. Perhaps she just needs to soak up some warmth in order to last a while longer. Bird is still young and very pretty, she's like the sandy bank of a lake in a pine forest. But she is completely deaf and, therefore, couldn't learn the local language. She settled into the garret of the house

Severyn lived in, and all summer she gathered various berries and spoke the words of a language with many vowels. Severyn named her Bird. At first, Bird went to Severyn to gather the remnants of the plants that weren't needed for the herbaria, but, when he fell ill and more and more found himself helpless, losing his orientation, falling into another space and time, Bird took care of him. When everything was fine, she only tended the stove, and, in the summer, she looked after the grapes on the balcony.

Sometimes Bird uttered a long sentence to Severyn. Then he would remember it and repeat it to Markus—it turned out that Bird spoke Estonian, but it was unclear how she ended up here in the mountains—and Markus could translate a little of it with his antique Estonian-German dictionary and then translate that directly from German. "By the way, she said that everything that passes is not the past as long as the memory of skin and folds feels the past touches; and also that life is never too short, no matter its length. It is complete, there's only not enough time to learn how to feel that" (they couldn't do a more precise translation).

Khrystyian tossed his unfinished cigarette, but it caught on some part of the bridge. The ember sent a bunch of sparks flying that went out faster than they should have, each one hit by a different snowflake. Khrystyian Mlynarskyi couldn't let his hands get cold before the operation and he needed to get some sleep.

Severyn couldn't sleep. He sat on the floor somewhere between the araucaria and the stove. Impressions moved across his closed eyelids. Bird wanted to be near him. She knew this would help him and that she herself would experience stronger feelings. She knew that directed, conscious thinking about Severyn would stir up unexpected otherworldly visions and the sense of her having lived his experience.

A person's inner world is that which is now on the inner side of their eyelids. This is what most makes people like plants. Because the most important thing is the quantity and kind of light that lands on their exteriors. Self-awareness depends on lighting. Therefore, Bird sat down in such a way as to receive the same light as Severyn...

...

...

yellow spots with wavy edges moved away from the middle under pressure from the smooth violet cracks that grew, jutted out, and changed the direction of the current, sometimes the violet stream got paler, and it was apparent that it was flowing along a riverbed made by a very sharp and sedimentary rock, laid out by some broken and twisted geometric ornament;

a wind picked up and the yellow spots drifted to the middle, the wind blew evenly from four sides, the spots lost their color, became gray, punctured by lively white holes, his body couldn't maintain horizontal balance, his head was constantly tipping the scales, and then newer and newer influxes of fluid flowed with such force that the walls of his capillaries ached from the excessive strain, Severyn turned onto his back and ended up underneath the spots, the wind, sinking down all the way to the support;

    the earth really is that which you can envelope with your body, all the nearby surfaces can bend, sway, dip, even your earth snagged on wobbly planes will descend, turn, and spin—yet still you won't lose it, it won't abandon you, rather it will hold on and squeeze into your body; then can you let it go, and your body, having released the earth to its place, will slide wandering into the depths, there's no need to turn outstretched palms to the earth, for even the backs of hands can perfectly sense the slightest details and lightest touches;

    the compact, unreachable ground, a few dozen tiny stones that are more or less connected to the ground, the very long, thin brown grass pressed to the earth and made white by a former snow, there are epithelial scales on it, dead but strung together in the places where the spikes once were;

    Severyn engirdled everything within reach with his palms, pressed his face to what his hands enclosed, and lived there for a few seconds, going from end to end along a path left by an ant;

    the path led him to the foot of an enormous slope, the plane of which took up his entire field of vision;

it was apparent that this whole slope was located in the sub-alpine zone—no trees, no bushes, only stiff, short grass dotted with ruined islands of blueberry bushes, also short yet very old; he looked around and saw that he was standing on a rocky outcrop of the slope, that the slope continued still far below and this was only its spur;

the surface of the slope was bounded by streams that started somewhere up above, he traipsed upstream along them, crossing from stream to stream wherever there was less water—the streams were cluttered with clumps of ripped-up grass, streams along slabs and stairs, streams warmed in the sun, stream-roads that didn't quench thirst but engendered the desire to drink of them, kneeling at the water and lowering your entire face into them, then the water immediately becomes saltier from the washed-off sweat and there's no need to draw it in with your lips because it flows in between them on its own, flooding all the channels of the relief of your lips;

the earth is deprived of sky because, on this slope, everything that doesn't lie directly on the earth is in the sky, the sky grates against the surface, right before the top Severyn felt a mass of a different air crawl over from behind the mountain and roll along the plane, wrapping itself in the scraps of a scent found on this side with such force that he couldn't contain everything he had inside, his insides blew away, the wind dried out the least moisture inside his body, and it was impossible to feel or even think about anything other than this;

due to the unevenness of the surface and the enormous internal pressure from the lava, individual pieces broke off immediately forming into spheres of various magnitude. At first, they were sticky and picked up everything that ended up on the slope—water, stones, lichens, the wings of dead insects carried there by the wind, Severyn's words, and multicolored spots, later not losing but gaining speed and volume, they solidified from their periphery to center like the vacuoles of an unbelievably sweet berry, like lumps of cherry glue, ultimately, like amber;

the amber skipped down and gathered in quite a large pile, it was constantly rebuilding itself, for as each clump fell, it dislodged dozens of others that had just settled in; the words in the middle of the amber had no time to arrange themselves into permanent sequences: they created illegal combinations that suddenly made possible things that simply hadn't been possible to think due to rhetorical obstacles;

Severyn began identifying a little something he knew from experience: how large summer flowers cut and placed in water cool off a room, how you drive away ravens by running to the walnut they've tossed on the rocks in a place where there aren't any walnut trees at all, how car headlights at night illuminate the fall trees along the road and the eyes of cats sitting in those trees, how to scurry up and down the grapevines leading to the high balcony, discerning the living branches from the dead, cut-off ones that are still somehow holding onto the walls, how you can't get rid of the experience of the delicacy of someone else on your fingertips even if you pinch them together with all your might, how the steam from a mug moistens the skin of your upper lip and brings back the smell of random beds you fall asleep in dressed, how you drink a cognac in one swallow, holding it too long against your mucous membrane, the roof of your mouth going numb from the excess alcohol, the vessels swelling and bulging into the cavity of your mouth, your tongue—surprised by the change in relief—strokes your palate again and again, despite Severyn's mad opposition;

to stop these irreversible changes to his environment, Severyn started catching the globs of cherry glue and shoving them in his mouth, they rolled through him not quite dried out, his fingers stuck together, his lips, he moved like he was hunting moths, the crushed gluey lumps stretched into thin threads whose sagging stretched them further and further; soon, a mesh of transparent fibers joined his lip to his tongue, all of his fingers together, and each one to his lips; the glue stuck to everything Severyn touched and the network multiplied, creating a spider web, thick paints, a tricky antenna, a system of resin veins on a cross section of a pine, a tangle of chimerical knots or a map of railroad junctions around a large European city, the focused shadow of a fine beetle wing, or the labyrinths of dactyloscopy;

the glue turned out to be some kind of organic saliva, probably a supersaturated solution of hormonal compounds; thousands of multicolored grains of pollen and spores of the most refined shapes, broken stamens, the seeds of crushed berries, and fragments of mashed dried fruits landed on the net in a single, dense layer, squeezing past one another, and occupying the minutest free sections;

the multicolored mixture of branches swayed, bent and sagged, scrunched and stretched, rejoined with itself in new places;

the walls of the seed swelled, absorbing the least bit of moisture, sent out roots and rhizoids, surface cells began dividing, layering upon the distorted contours of their burst walls, the green cones, the threads couldn't bear the load, they sagged still more and broke, the ends were either forcefully drawn back to where they were attached or swung freely, bouncing like a bob in a clock, they curled up into spirals and balls, their seedlings jutting out;

Severyn didn't know these plants, which meant he hadn't been there before; floristry had been not his refuge from his disease, but above all a coordinate system just as the town halls, opera theaters, Vincentians, Dominicans, Cistercians, Carmelites, and Redemptorists serve as landmarks in cities;

he himself was a sort of man of floristic registers and simultaneously the most oft-repeated entry in the register;

his disease took him to a parallel world of vegetal ultrastructures, bent him to gaze at the level of plants, he understood leaves, shoots, and flowers to be the landscape, and the infinite variability of the analogy of vegetal ultrastructures—often one plant differs more from another than from a non-plant—allowed him to navigate macrolandscapes when his disease struck and his field of vision was reduced to discrete structures;

by a few fixed morphological structures, Severyn identified a floral combination that was an inimitable sign of the place, not only did he remain a leading authority, but he became invaluable for anyone who needed to be shown some plant, he started working with botanists, pharmacists, biologists, herbalists, gardeners, photographers, florists;

the territory of his brain was a substance where plants existed in a way not intrinsic to them—gathered together, named, defined; Severyn belonged to them in that they were simply the boundaries of consciousness, the landscape of his consciousness; landscape is a particular form of experience, Severyn didn't know where he was or what to do next, the threads had frozen, building him into a static carapace, the ends that had twisted into spirals now straightened out, hardened, and flew off in different directions like arrows wrapped in colorful yarn, the seedlings budded, and the petals of various high mountain flowers burst forth from them, oversaturated with bright pigments and covered in pollen—Severyn ended up in the center of a floral sphere as though he had gotten lost in a Christmas tree or an enlarged model of a cell;

he knew that these flowers could be trusted unconditionally—bulbous, hairy, ones with bent stems, asymmetrical flowers, different colors and short-lived blooms, but ants were already running up and down the needles; they ate the grains of pollen and shined violet, yellow, orange, and burgundy, they crawled onto Severyn, leaving an acid trail behind themselves like they were digesting a Secession tattoo in the form of long, smoothly curved stems, and furthermore the construction warmed up from the inside from the excessive exchange, synthesis, and decay until green vapors became visible, it smelled like potent, roasted substances, and drops of the juices settled in the lungs;

Severyn looked upon himself from the outside, he positioned his point of view a little higher on the slope—from here, he looked like a bird stretched out by a couple of strings, or like a tall and, therefore, bent in a few places patch of grass preserved in a plant press, he moved his gaze farther away up the slope to the very top of the water in the stream, so it was like the viewer was going uphill backwards, ever staring at Severyn;

either the flowers were in the way of seeing everything or it was all too far away, but, when he turned around, he was standing on the very spur of the slope, Severyn ran a few dozen meters along the slabs covered in dry bunches of Icelandic moss, neither growing nor shrinking, crouching so as not to be blown over, and he ran into a cloud that started practically on the earth, he lay down on a rock and looked at the gap between the edge of the cloud and the earth—the change in scale did not violate the proportions: the bottom of the cloud was the sky, the relief of the slab was an implausible forest of lichenous growths and rainwater gathered in crevices and cracks, it was a perfect, even instinctual, yet inaccessible landscape, the gap never ended, it was very quiet, only somewhere in the depths of his inner ear did Severyn hear a rhythm that coincided alternatingly with the friction of his pleura or with the force of squinting his eyelids, and, from the intensity of his staring, only the shade of the cloud's gray changed from brilliant white to a muddy citrus barely illuminated from its depths, if he lay on his belly the clouds pressed directly on his back and their surface could provide the same support as the earth, his gaze dissolved in the absolute uncertainty of the clouds, he could turn his head such that it seemed he was lying on the boundless uneven bottom of a snow pile, his earring quickly cooled and chilled the tendons in his neck;

only three colors were left on earth—green, brown, and black—but the chaos of their combinations and diffusions created a hallucinatory polygon going through all the stages of cellular division that his eye's optical memory could still reproduce a few seconds after it had already looked at something else—the clouds, his palm, the inside of his eyelids;

the sky and earth were joined by dry and empty stalks of sorrel, no telling where they began or where they ended because they could equally belong to both margins, even the direction the translucent drops of condensed water—which, like lenses, enlarged the dead facets of the stalks—crawled, meant nothing, they could pull themselves up or drip down with equal force;

Severyn sat up on his elbows and bent his face toward a puddle of distilled water in a stone depression with a complex shoreline (bays, cliffs, shoals, fjords, bends, peninsulas), the mosses and lichens reflected in it looked like enormous trees, the briars of a fantastic orchard, and, in spite of its size, the lake divided everything from everything else, only lakes can separate the fragments of their own shores like this;

from the hard rocks and the dry lichen, apt to crumble to a powder, his elbows were rubbed raw like from a sheet being used for a folk cure, Severyn examined the landscape with the lake and realized that he knew it well, at least its typology, some surprises could perhaps be compared to the way the shadows of the peripatetic clouds distort the topography of mountain ridges, or to how two puddles merge after heavy rains during the day and, at night, you step in water where it never was before (puddles don't change from rain to rain thanks to the immutability of their bases): all these variational series had no effect on recognition, just like cuts don't alter the lines on our palms;

the landscape with the lake not only made space in itself for the elements of Severyn's experience but, as it turns out, was itself the chief motif of all his memories of experience and all his dreams about pre-experience;

it's impossible to remember one and the same thing twice, with the exception of a few landscapes that follow you, upon which your basic experience is built, all wars of the imagination are played out, where definitive conclusions are drawn, where nostalgia for the unchosen hides, and you live as the person you truly are, all experience leads to the recognition of these landscapes, and the landscapes become experience itself;

the experience of a landscape is the external, outward-facing part of the genome that can be added to, experience is a way of looking for mutations, a way of risking exposure to mutations, to the diversity of the world that is contained in a single life, it is those few landscapes worth daring for, they dictate our way of thinking, and our way of thinking is our fate;

the water in the hole reached a few patches of Icelandic moss and totally soaked them, making the moss dirty-green and gelatinous, individual contours dissolved, spirals of a russet infusion eddied from it into the water, gradually settling and dissolving in the further layers of the water, Severyn knew no other being that had more to teach him, and he touched the whirlpool most affected by the moss's antibiotics;

after a few swallows, he was seized by such bitterness that, for a second, all his vessels constricted, when his blood could finally push through, his hands were trembling, and the contours of his vision had blurred, the bitterness penetrated to the farthest alcove of his body—to lick his shoulder now, thigh, or fingers, would all be very bitter, the bitterness was like the color black—the absence and sum of all possible flavors;

the bitterness made possible the absence of all layers of his own body—scrunched and squashed at the same time—up until the extreme points in all directions, in this way, the experience of bitterness is analogous to the experience of cold, pain, or disease;

Severyn really wanted a smoke—the flavor of smoking depends on the state of the soft palate, just then a cigarette would have been sweet, smoking is a game, an element of rage that must exist in the biographies of pain, cold, and disease, which don't allow for any games;

these are separate biographies, for they can't be fit into a general life story, perhaps only as a riddle, and there are totally different rules of existence (you can't have fun with exceptional women, certain plants, or lakes, but you can with herbaria);

he got up and his feet instantly got wet, forcing the water from the clump of moss—the water here had nowhere else to get absorbed.

Severyn opened his eyes. The stove was lit, Bird was sitting next to him, as usual, in some pose that was impossible to imitate. A few dry branches fell off the araucaria—when taking out the trash, he always thought his life was unusual because it is unusual to simply have araucaria branches in the trash. He looked at the clock; exactly ten minutes had passed and there were still ten left. Bird was apparently very far away. With her eyes closed, her face took on striking medieval features. The cigarettes were on Severyn's tomogram near his foot. His mouth tasted bitter like he'd eaten the skins of young walnuts, or a grapefruit, or a tea of Icelandic moss; it would be nice to smoke, but he had to hurry to get to the right spot.

As soon as he saw the tomogram, the map of his brain, and realized which lake he'd been at, he wanted to return to his tumor for those ten minutes again in order to examine it, perhaps restore even just a bit of what disappeared under the water or crumbled from erosion; for this, it was necessary to use the map to reconstruct the landscape of the surroundings from the line of water to the farthest offshoots of his brain, to stroll around the lake. It takes effort to remember yourself.

Severyn's feet were freezing. He looked at Bird's eyelids—impressions of the flames glowed on them, and shadows of the tree's compound branches intersected...

...

...

the white trunks of beeches, a reeking liquid on the wet chestnuts, the smooth, slippery bark of the waterlogged walnut, the forest of eternal fall, the archeological samples of deciduous trees, the leaves of the final layer snow-bleached and dried until they're metallic, anemones, hepatica muscaria, caltha, pulsatilla, violets, blue ravines, yellow shadows, the unwinding of ferns, plants have the most to teach you (indirect experience);

the initial green of summer, determination makes no sense, evaporating juices, a sign of misunderstanding—allergies, arms cut by grass, the smell of parks when first mown, other smells shoving their way through the broken window of the mountain train, green grass stains on your shirt, distinguishing sights by their smells, leaves ground in a mortar, teas from the herbarium (floral teas);

teas that taste like different places, from herbarium samples gathered in different corners, the places identifiable by the flavor, by the smell of the tea, there are no two places with identical components, plants are bearers of concepts (animals, of images);

indirect experience, experience that awakens various vortexes, experience as a risk to take a chance at the danger of mutations, indirect experience can be squeezed from anything, even from extraneous, excess experience, indirect experience justifies a waste of time, the experience of the absence of experience, when you're not thinking about anything, you can think about how you're not thinking about anything (the consciousness of consciousness);

mucous membranes can be trusted, eyelids can be trusted, whatever happens on them is much more important than what goes on behind them, white contours of the movement on the water's surface demarcating an orange field even though the lake is far away, through the warmth of the alpine meadow come sharp and indivisible skeins of cold air formed at the distance between the trees of the pre-alpine forest, the air from there, where there's a lot of water, gathers into a dense mass in one place (even though the lake is very far away);

floral teas collected in different places, each one somewhere he'd been, even if just to find the plants needed to fill the absences in the archives, each one of those places had something else, flora includes thoughts, fragments of experience, the memory of skin and postulates of mucous membranes, which is why places change slowly and the photos of your mountains unerringly define the decades, even without taking technological advancements in photography into consideration, and they mark an old age related neither to the loss of strength nor level of experience but only to the openness and the displacement of coordinate covalent bonds, the concept of eternity is frightening, in its place there is only day and there is duration, and the essence of anything that so endures is no longer the essence of the thing enduring, but the essence of enduring, often, co-enduring, like with the araucaria, incidentally, it's obvious that it's also suffering, based on the experience of the araucaria, it is easy to deduce that the green is just foaming, it's only starting to get better, not losing any new branches, annual rings, channels of bark and stems that hold the fruits, the need for analogies to the crown are reflected in the roots, yet the analogies are overly primitive, even though they proved correct in the case of the walnut, it's worth listening to asymmetry (the short period when irises are in bloom);

the short period when irises are in bloom falls on the last days in the city before summer, which will take place in the mountains, every day looking in the city, in the small gardens near the strange pseudo-palaces on the side streets, where there are too many of these buildings, looking for the hues and configurations of irises, at night following a map of daytime discoveries and bringing individual flowers for the vial that—in a month or perhaps even sooner, two to three weeks—will blend into the monotone, barely altered order such that the first won't look anything like the last, Bird will take the wilted flowers and arrange their petals into an impression of her dream, and the dreams will show what is really possible (making possible the impossible);

even though it is very far to the lake, even though the road is different every time, every time there is a different biography before arriving at the lake, every time you yourself and your memories are different, you sense the lake through the tilt of the earth—now it won't stop until it reaches the deepest place, it is going to lean like that and you roll through your experience, through objects, landscapes, reflections, shadows that can't be covered with sand, through weeds and seaweeds, across cities that were only just thought up and attempts to construct a life story, barely managing to put one foot in front of the other, jumping from one clump of blueberries and moss to another, and—turning around when you're already in the air—bypassing nests of valuable mottled eggs that belong to sleeping birds who scattered uneaten berries about their nest, despite your incredible speed, you examine the minutest ultrastructures (because it's only they that can give you even a modicum of orientation in the chase, turning your head back for a long time, you end up in corridors that you're flying down, flying to the openings that let in some light from the outside and always seem tighter, for a long time you disappear in the citadels, lost in the very soundings and writings of what's in the citadel or the city's botanical garden, in the botanical garden's citadel [in the citadel's botanical garden]);

conscious of the consciousness of the reference book, of the text, of the signs—that which leads thinking that was converted to a reference book, the floristic logic of the range, of the introduction, of expansion, of extinction, of the interaction of everything with everything else, of the register of names, and plants is only substance for properties including verbal ones, a parallel linguistics, non-Latin, horsetail, squills, juniper, crocus, alchemy, sowbread, lady's slipper, snake's head, monkshood, viper's grass, hawkweed (mistletoe);

making possible the impossible, remembering a few geneses, remembering a genesis that doesn't exist, the genesis of time, changing fate along with those whom you lead into the mountains looking for medicines, drugs, paints, fibers of wind, underground springs, mineral waters, analgesics and hallucinogens, seeds, rhizomes, roads and observatories, looking for the lake, lakes and errors on the maps, places where thought happens, living landscapes transfer to the imagination as the basis for the brain's landscape, and the creation of an imaginary landscape leads to unknown places that you recognize and know everything about, verbal associations turn out to be a sequence of concrete space, real objects become symbols of properties located on the landscape of the brain, and they grow like plants from the herbaria, photographs record the plants in places where they no longer exist, habits develop unrelated to things, the habits become sense and meaning in a life deprived of sense and meaning, letters are written as an escape from discourse, as anticipated responses to their own letters, and dialogs lag behind the destinations of lived experience, you're afraid of the ordinary logic of common sense, you stifle your memory in order to not remember the ultrastructures because there are so many of them that you can think up unlived biographies knowing it all, stringing your unordinary pursuits on the excess experience of ultrastructures (the need for reduction);

reducing the events of your own life, your own experience to the fundamental, to a few definitive fragments, to just what you're sure really happened, to what you can recall immediately, to what you can't make up or imagine because it has some detail that you can't invent without knowing, without feeling, and it's not even possible to calculate precisely which tropism gives a sense of liveliness to the whole system, reducing it to a few scenes whose ultrastructures are instantly forgotten, to a woman who's all other women in different ways, to water without which you will unconsciously get sick, to the wind with its invented smell that you can't find anywhere, to the pain after which you live without any of the fear that will later turn out to be the culmination of your story, to the cold that gripped your body, giving your soul the chance to endure without support, to go through the orchard, the flower box on the balcony, the way out to the ridge, swimming in summer, frozen night coffee, the smell of a large number of books, a few touches that changed your worldview, picking apples in fall, holding onto the rock with your whole body, examining the structure of a cell in a microscope, building words, inventing a secret vocabulary of properties and signs, the walls and the ceiling shift and turn in the glow of the hospital nightlight, and some pure substance goes straight into your vein and the shadows become burdens (and the feeling that you're alive is stronger the greater the reduction in the inventory of simultaneous feelings);

animals flashed, disappearing among the plants and rocks, behind the walls, and under the roofs, every escape reminds him of a person, but people refused to be identified by their burned insect wings, lizard run, startled bats, hacked-up worms, swallows' nests, nimble shadows of predatory birds, mole hills, phantasmagoric fungi on the bodies of large beasts, the numbness of moths, heavy and sprinkled with powder. Only traces remained: imprints of the most precious traits in the sand, in the snow, sticky shadows, oft-distorted voices that awaken more than snapshots, snapshots that the imagination cannot change, reflections in fluctuant water, glows, the warmth of touches on objects, a smell unchanged for innumerable years, remembering everything said, which is initially very memorable and later is forgotten together and all at once, hair catches on unshaven cheeks, cracked lips miss each other, palms sweat and dry like boards on a wall facing the river, prickly fingertips scrape skin where joints meet, lick dusty eyes, being is co-being like lichens (like the mistletoe in the citadel's botanical garden); the agglomeration of the mistletoe in the trees creates another tree without phenology, an evergreen construction of tumors on the bare drawings of trees is another orchard, the rudimentary landscapes, abandoned places, flora's revenge, overgrown train tracks that skirt the city, the bastions filled with endless rains, the uneven city with steps instead of streets, and the streets are a continuation of rooms, burrow-buildings, nest-buildings, gaps, gutters, everything united by a single balcony, the forbidden city, a border it's not wise to cross, plants carried onto roofs, Secession train stations, multistory rock gardens, bridges that are held up by the wind, having time to think of something else that will appear through the fog, bas-reliefs between the first and second floors, at the windows and doors, this country belongs to those who know which plants grow where in the city, who've described them, defined them, gathered herbaria, that which is thought up is positioned so it can't be missed when wandering around town just like the citadel, the large summer square, the ramparts, or cemetery, or a bookstore (many, many days await this city);

everything starts with fonts, depression is also a conflict with discourse, context, text, fonts stretch this out, unwind, the best can't be read at all but are just graffiti on the walls, everything suddenly goes green like a page overly illuminated by the sun, at first the vision gets cloudy and then it's paralyzed, again the attacks of disease, again the ultrastructures, a parallel world, but with the lack of plant landmarks you get lost like you're looking through a sweater, pawing at the finest lines of a face through hair like the topography of wet ceilings, the classification of venation and an outline of leaf edges, the riverbank where it's only stones, and each stone must be distinguished (and remembering the stones, you can call to mind the bank);

inventing experience, biographies, chronicles, and geographies of life you don't know what was real because you know too much about what everything's made of and the principles of composition to be sure if you froze the same way like before when you were really cold, to not pour vodka from mouth to mouth, to not touch the very long and wet muscles of the back, to not turn over in the snow, to not add a little milk to your coffee, to not cure yourself with mulled wine inhalations, to not speak other languages (without touching the lake);

one had to jump down, the hole led to the small, sandy alcove between the two cliffs on the sandy bank, the sand was so wet, washed so many times;

Severyn couldn't shift his gaze and saw only what was happening step by step—the relief of the sand which looked like a mountain chain and massifs, uplifted earth, smooth stones with deep pores, empty snail shells, bleached branches and snippets of roots, the unbelievable tangle of dead seaweed, wet seeds, the colorful spots of the smallest lichens that had already started taking over the bare bank;

he was walking in the water already, the water reached halfway up his body, it was imperceptible, that's how warm it was, like air, and the landscape of the bottom was no different from that of the bank, farther on the kelp got very long and wide, Severyn could no longer see the bottom, he couldn't make out that down there, probably, the unchanging territory continued, even though it seemed like the contours of some kind of constructions were coming through the weeds in places, he took a breath and dove, almost immediately releasing everything from his lungs to get as far as possible;

he's not going to swim up, he'll rip out his disease in these depths where the ultrastructures can no longer be, where the form of water is indivisible, the water was so transparent that farther from the surface the sun got no darker, it was like opening your eyes and seeing shadows without cause, shadows of clouds, of the spaces between clouds, and of the movement of streams on a few planes, the shifting of squares, the layering, the perforated background, the translucent layers, the nimble connections, concentrated circles of light, various solutions, polyhedra of dust, the misalignment of the edges of leaves, petals, outgrowths, cellar membranes, permeation, complementariness, spiral twists, variability, the chaos of flickering forms that simply spreads from the center to the edges, is carried to the middle, gathers at the borders, runs from top to bottom, gets tossed up, divides unevenly, the impressive difference in speeds, the indestructibility of trajectories;

his lungs emptied such that the water would have flooded in if he had held his lips together even a little less tightly, Severyn felt very alive, he understood with his whole body that he existed—as joyfully, gravely, and wisely as possible—he stopped moving and he was immediately carried up, there was less and less water above him, a yellow spot swam to meet him, Severyn passed it too fast and struggled to turn face down; it was Bird forcing her way to the bottom, she was intact, his gaze didn't break her into the ultrastructures of the secret topography;

the other side of the surface, then in two halves—already above, yet still under the water, just above the field of the lake, the water is lower yet, the boundaries of the banks are firm;

from up high, everything around the lake was visible—on the shore itself, divided by lines of stones laid out perpendicular to the edges of the water, lines of sown plants, of ditches, cracks, walls, or simply drawn in the sand, the most diverse landscapes (mountains, fragments of cities, forests, barrens, botanical gardens, canals)—stretched out in narrow strips far from the lake like rays with no concern for each other—came together; something different was happening on every segment of the shore, these neighbors were sometimes unbelievable, forbidden, unlikely, but lakes inherently unite everything with everything else, while distancing everything from everything else;

Severyn saw himself on every patch, he led different people through the mountains, their interests becoming his new trade, their needs, his needs, their goal, his goal; distinctly periodizing his life, he'd slept on snow, in others' beds, in burrows, he'd mowed hay, photographed plants, counted animals, waited for women in foothill towns, carried trash he gathered out of the mountains, mulled wine, lined his shoes with moss, prepared cross-sections and microscope slides, flown a hang glider to inaccessible rocks, thought up and put together alpine and rock gardens, frozen and thawed out without remembering where he'd drunk, killing his memory, had fallen into cold rivers, swum across lakes, caught snakes with his bare hands, and lain ill after snakebites, collected herbaria, dried roots, leaves, invented teas that defined their places, climbed grapevines up to balconies, climbed cliffs with no equipment, not cared about self-expression or self-realization, switched from train to train, looked for mineral springs, temples, plants, hallucinogenic mushrooms, led crazy researchers who didn't understand dosage out of the mountains to the city, fainted from headaches, spent months dying and recovering in hospitals, examined ultrastructures, suddenly sat up after not being able to get out of bed, knocked out by unexpected onslaught of ultrastructures, had lost his way for long periods of time and wandered blindly, he'd studied plants and their locales, lived in a parallel world of ultrastructures without getting lost, and, despite his blindness, gathered berries in homeopathic doses, been saturated with smoke, the smells of grasses, of streams, of bark, of large, hairy dogs, fallen into an abyss when an attack of ultrastructures had transformed the rocks into enlarged landscapes that he couldn't keep his hands on, he'd fed birds and beasts, told women about the ultrastructures, about totally different amazing worlds nearby, done with them what he had learned from plants, been left alone when they couldn't handle life alongside disease, he'd grown cyclamen and stolen irises, bought maps of the mountains from used bookstores, hidden in citadels, smoked innumerable cigarettes, each one somehow different, each time he was different, in a different place, knowing something different and in love with different people, meditating on water, fire, stones, clouds, remembering something else, he'd gathered walnuts, injected analgesics into his veins, smoked near the stove, mostly kept quiet, walked the Mlynarskyis to the bridge, was the best at identifying plants, knew the mountains best;

 Severyn felt his speed was very great, he could no longer make out faces, then arms, then figures; roofs, spires, bridges, footbridges, mansards, verandas, galleries, porches, balconies, chimneys, trees, vineyards, cliffs, log cabins, river islands, bastions and forts of the citadel, orchards, gardens, blackberry brambles, steps, chapels, cliffs, barrens, and trash heaps, train tracks all ran toward the lake, on all sides this ended in mountains, endless passes from mountains to mountains, this beauty gave a calm; from higher up the totality of all landscapes looked like cytological microphotography, like a topographic map, like the tomogram of a brain; all this agglomeration was understood as a form that contained a lake, a spot that unites duration...

...

...

...Severyn opened his eyes and looked at the clock; twenty minutes had gone by, Bird was still meditating. He grabbed the cigarettes, extinguished the fire in the stove, lit the tomogram with his lighter and tossed it in the smoldering stove. He gave the araucaria a little milk that was supposed to be for coffee, drank his cold coffee, and threw on a very big and heavy overcoat sewn from blankets, took a cigarette out of the tin, and put it in his side pocket alone.

He wanted to call to Bird, but he decided that he shouldn't interrupt her. But he didn't put her sweaters away, rather tossed them on the floor around her. He was in a hurry to make the night train to the mountains. Bird would soon see where to go if she wanted.

Severyn decided to light his Gauloise only when he reached the bridge. The taste of the coffee would last until then.

NECROPOLIS

A Gift for Olenka

I

Markus Mlynarskyi wrote, "It could turn out that the meaning of all your existences, of all being is recombination. The creation of some sort of text by way of protracted genetic recombinations, steps. Recombinations, which—through endless attempts, innumerous uncertain moves—have to lead to a concrete structure that someone thought up. Perhaps this is how the Appearance (Manifestation) of God is supposed to happen. Or it could perhaps be that the most essential recombination is rhetorical. Perhaps, in the end, there will be the word, too. And we'll pick it up, we'll make our way to it, reciting texts and tossing out the texts that aren't it. Just like with plastics. We change space, we alter space by moving through space. It's unknown which movement, which action will turn out to be the decisive one, which selection of simultaneous worldly movements will create the space that will stop everything, so the stasis of eternity can last in that shared positioning."

Here's where Markus should have stopped himself, but he kept going, violating his own calculations: "The problem lies only in the fact that, in order to comprehend the totality of recombinations, to connect, to unite simultaneous discrete tropisms into a single (really, the only) system, a solid system where the cause of anything isn't only something else or their combination, but a non-encompassing state and the juxtaposition of all other elements, not only a discrete moment in time, but also their stratification, their layering from the beginning of time itself..."

Before this, Mlynarskyi hadn't written anything other than a philosophical treatise that came to no conclusion. To be precise, the treatise had turned into a chronicle—abstract ontological observations were refined from a meditation on completely concrete everyday events, so that Markus alone could have used the chronicle to recreate what had been observed.

To be sure, in addition to the treatise, he also had a diary that he kept on his desk near the window that looked out onto a closed-off courtyard. There he only made entries about what he'd seen throughout the day through that window (irrespective of the almost total lack of activity in the yard and the absolute absence of what the locals call "living nature," despite Markus's strict taboo against writing in the diary any reflections or associations that would have somehow led out of the space limited by the solid wall of buildings around the yard, Markus saw so much every day that his work with the diary took up a portion of the time that he'd have liked to have spent sleeping; some of the entries therefore had a touch of insomnia; during one nighttime carousal in the kitchen, Mlynarskyi decided to make his daily entry in the presence of his friends and told them what kind of diary it was, even reading them a few fragments—not the ones he loved most and not the ones he thought most interesting—rather he just closed his eyes and opened the notebook randomly a few times; his friends were taken not so much with his entries, as with the very idea of recording the variability of invariance, modeling a variety of interesting variations for a long time; later they seamlessly moved on to other topics, but when they got together a few days later without Mlynarskyi, they were completely serious when they agreed to employ different discrete methods to provoke at least some kind of events in Markus's yard; the game didn't last long, but it was precisely at this time that chimerical realities began appearing in the diary, each one of which could have been developed into a story, so Markus decided to string them together with some imagination and write a novel).

Mlynarskyi's novel was supposed to be called *Necropolis* (city of the dead). Let's say a group of individuals that didn't know each other buy plots in a yet nonexistent cemetery at auction. These people long ago lost interest in normal city life. They lost their friends, acquaintances, were left without families, all their real ties to the City erased, they were alone, destitute, unneeded, barely alive. They didn't want to and could not live like the masses, and the masses militantly disliked their primitive lifestyle, and, when they broke, the masses simply stopped noticing them. This is exactly why they all hazarded this step: to at least take care of the wordly forms of an otherworldly life. Having taken this step, however, they are afraid both of what they've done and of themselves. Perhaps it is this fear, mixed with the secret desire to strengthen it further (somehow or another, real, living experience, acute existence) and mixed with the attempt to break free from fear's grasp at least here, that forces each of them to go to the Cemetery once, and then again and again, hiding from accidental witnesses, and later from each other as well, gradually getting used to their own plots, to their own land, gradually bringing more and more of what tied them to life. They secretly know this is chimerical, yet still worthwhile communication: avoiding and gravitating toward each other, observing and hiding, studying the timetables, schedules, routes, manners, directions, habits, and preferences, ultimately demonstrating, knowing that they are being scrutinized from maybe a few points of view, pretending like they don't know, but in such a way that they understand they know more than is even possible, approaching ever more complex intersections of this widely known game. Eventually, it happens that somewhere, sometime two people don't pass each other by but open up to each other. What is happiness to them is unbearable to everyone who witnesses them. They open up and open others up, the most timid. They begin arranging their places and, in time, it looks more and more like a barn raising, and the semantics of the cemetery are eventually erased; they bring their habits here, start to move in, tend to their own niches for the first time, adapting only their own tastes. Yet more ways of communication appear, but they are all destructured as individuals, each one bears the burden of habits that, until recently, were an imitation of sense, they are deprived of experience that goes beyond the bounds of their own experience of emptiness (the experience of their own emptiness), they have fallen behind the development of terminology and nomenclature, to them it is important to think in words and concepts, their feelings significantly exceed the possibilities to express those feelings—someone gets the idea to form a chamber orchestra—they pass out instruments in the order they should sit in the orchestra, and they sit according to how their plots are laid out—swapping plots (there emerged some steadfast couples, fellowships, for whom the matter of direct proximity was of principal importance), swapping instruments causes no harm, for initially no one can play anything—now their main task is to hold uninterrupted rehearsals of funeral marches—they are so emptied and so thirsty for something better that they rather quickly master their instruments at the level of the dilettante (taking into account even the swaps they made)—for a while, marches satisfy them, but soon that is not enough—among them there is one talentless composer who, in fact, conducts the orchestra, trains the musicians—he is assigned to write something suitable—for the composer this was his first real event, his first opportunity to become a real composer, he tries long and hard to compose, but the world of the cemetery is ephemeral, the composer is good and refined, but his talent is illusive—still he brings a score—it is Mozart, a symphony the composer copied by hand in the library, but only the parts in their orchestra—everyone really likes the music and learns their parts without much effort, but the combined performance is atrocious, they all lack lightness, looseness, the ability to listen to intonations. They all lack freedom.

Mlynarskyi decided that the novel would not have a specific time frame or even overly marked features of a temporal nature. Even the genesis of the events would have to be blurred in time. There wouldn't be any ordinary features that belonged to a particular decade. Nor any stylistic signs in the writing that would hint at a decade more convincingly than an actual mention of the year. No clear or detailed psychological traits beyond the characters' actions. And the logic of the novel's development would be the logic of the intransigence of further progress on the grounds of what had previously happened—what came would be determined by what had been only such that what had been would increasingly limit the possible options, simply fill in the free moves. This irrational logic was the logic of available opportunities. He would love this weakness of his characters. He would cut off the story lines so as to return to them after a certain amount of time, but with this time unaccounted for; there would be sudden breaks in the lines, uncertainties and lacunae that wouldn't be followed in which anything could have happened. He would know little about his characters and would have to fill what he didn't know with stuff he made up. They would have to speak to themselves. He would release a few microscopic viruses into the text that, having used up the unanticipated possibilities of his text, would snatch them from the text and multiply, spreading out in them into the unknown beyond the text.

Mlynarskyi even thought up a rather elegant ending for his novel. He would introduce himself into the text, turn himself into an owner of one of the cemetery plots, one of the musicians in the orchestra. He would still be himself with all his attempts to tell the story; the novel itself would then become the author's telling of how he wrote a novel about the events in which he was an equal participant. And, at the very end, he would be exposed as a self-observer, in fact, the true Mlynarskyi.

This, of course, was a positive-sense virus. And a very interesting one that could shift perspective in different ways, perspective from the novel, perspective on the novel, perspective in the novel.

Then, somewhere in Mlynarskyi's endless treatise, the first inklings of recombination appeared. That day when (according to the diary entry) the rain started with the chestnuts and the chrysanthemums thrown to the ground began wilting from their lower petals, Markus had already written, "The main sign of all combinations is their limitlessness. Classification registers of the components of a certain combination, just like with the selection of the combination itself, is conditional. Combinations are open systems, into which any adjacent elements can be introduced, up to unlimitedness. Everything can be reduced to a single combination."

Mlynarskyi was not in the least concerned by the disorder of his sentences. He gladly offered the half-accidental, half-considered locutions the opportunity to draw into the text unexpected and unanticipated motifs, associations, detritus of nearby constructions. Thus, the sentences reminded Markus of the ripples on water from a stone tossed in. Only, in Mlynarskyi's imagination, the film of the vision was projected in reverse—the rings converged from the periphery to the center, getting closer and tighter until, from underneath the water, a stone burst forth, taking an entire sphere back with it, coming out at a smooth trajectory, losing its aureole of moisture, drying up before one's eyes. Here Markus broke off his vision in order to allow for a multiplicity of final states of the trajectory.

Moreover, Markus Mlynarskyi was shocked by the course of the self-willed recombinations that the novel he'd thought up was meanwhile teeming with. Once, and then again and again, Mlynarskyi noted strange changes in the concept, and later he had to admit that all his versions turned out to be fatal (they weren't capable of even being refined); instead, a single line came to dominate, one that was not an expression of the involuntary, but the result of uncontrolled recombinations of individual fragments, phrases, sketches, comments, and traits... Markus agreed to go through all the steps of its logic.

It was based on a single dogma: the residents of Necropolis could not be buried in their plots; Necropolis was not to become a cemetery. So they all had to be cleared from the city and killed. This was nearly impossible since they did not leave the city, some of them rarely even since childhood. The balloon remained. (This is a very important turn. Approaching this turn time and time again, yet returning to its start, Mlynarskyi became convinced of what ultimately led him to the final *Necropolis*. The final *Necropolis*, to be sure, came much later, but, for now, Markus realized what fate, accident, relativity, and everything related to this meant.

From the treatise: "The essence of both fate and accident is one and the same: the accumulation of consecutive recombinations generated by the recombination process itself. And this is irreproducibility...")

The hot air balloon proved to be precisely this irreproducibility. They were flying for the second time. The first time, their irrational orchestra flew so that there, in a patch of the uncertain unfirm firmament, in a state lighter than air, they could play their Mozart, ridded of their earthly fears, complexes, habits, manias, neuroses, and doubts. Existential music. Naturally, they succeeded, naturally only once, only there. Clearly, they returned oh-so excited. This was ecstasy, euphoria, eruption, tremors, trances, dissolution, and condensation. Obviously, they had no use for the all-city panic, for the disquietude of the government, the work of experts, the introduction of a curfew, the state of emergency, patrols at the Market, sentries on the roofs of private and government buildings, checkpoints at the ways out of the city, the bans on mass assemblies. They knew nothing of the greatest sensation in the city—a few of the most modern cannons had been brought to the city.

The second and final flight made even more sense. The music that occurred during the flight could not be reproduced on earth. That's why the second flight was the despair of hopes, a new dimension, the last chance, revenge and contempt. It was a physiological addiction.

It was completely natural (and, in this, there is nothing symbolic) that they flew without an anchor, without ballast (the sandbags were tossed overboard when they were still even with the lowest trees), loaded down with musical instruments, and the only sign of at least some foresight was the uncorked flask of *vyshnivka* cherry brandy. It was also justifiable that the commander of the farthest cannon outpost gave the order to open fire on the inscrutable, chimerical flying apparatus hanging above the city's western border (having previously flown over the city at a height at which nothing is inaccessible to special optics) and from which came sounds similar to the work at the shuttered radio station. A special committee acknowledged the total destruction of the apparatus—which made expert examination absolutely impossible—as the only mistake.

Mlynarskyi was almost convinced that those on the balloon hadn't managed to notice either the cannonade or the hit itself. Except for, perhaps, the Composer, but he was a good composer and could sense how their orchestra lacked a percussion section, which everyone had turned down as a sign of low intelligence.

They put the hot air balloon together randomly, fitting parts together from the largest crate in the attic of the two-story building where the only woman who was a Necropolis owner lived. A few times in putting the balloon together, lacking as they did the slightest practical thinking or technical understanding, they created something so utterly unsuitable that it was at first taken for a machine for conducting some very specialized and very secret work. But, when the hot air balloon finally emerged (which was exactly what had lain dismantled in the trunk), no one needed say a word to concoct their incontestable, joint plan.

The house at one time belonged to a well-known traveler and cataloger of flora. Every year, he wandered alone along the riskiest routes, leaving his small daughter unsupervised. He returned with the first snow, loaded down with dried objects, always bringing home some lizards, birds, and beasts, having lost or abandoned part of his expensive impedimenta due to its onerousness. He would sit in his office all winter processing the materials from his expedition. His daughter would bring him breakfasts and dinners, shake out his ashtray, water the flowers in the solarium, and feed all the living things. She was allowed to examine anything in the office, laboratory, library, and attic where he kept his collection and equipment for his next expedition, which her father mostly bought during his lunchtime excursions to the restaurant. She subsequently delved further into the subject of her father's research, helping to compile registers, editing what he had typed on his typewriter. In the final years, she knew everything, even the details of his planned routes. Nothing else interested her. She was sure that her father had not become a collaborator. He simply did not give up his wanderings or academic work with the arrival of the new regime. She was aware of how abnormal her feeling of guilt was for that spring trip to the coast when her father submitted a report on his latest expedition to the publishing house, was arrested, released, and buried, not having been saved by the best hospital. Since then, she had lived alone. No one bothered the house, the editors sent some money, and no one visited her until the orchestra's second rehearsal, which she offered to hold at her home. From then on, they never looked for another place to hold rehearsals; often one of the orchestra members would stay until late, someone might spend the night; they came alone, in pairs, sometimes all of them would come one after another and later take leave in the most random order.

She didn't live in poverty; she lived among totally impractical luxury. But those accumulated things—books, clothes, devices, instruments, plants, weapons, equipment—created an exotic environment that existed as a separate world and in which it was possible to exist autonomously from the world without suffering from a lack of impressions, phenomena, inventories and names, secrets and adventures. There wasn't even enough time to thoroughly catalog that world. But, on the contrary, there was more than enough space—the walls, stairs, corridors, doors and internal windows, furniture and paintings split the space of the building into an infinity of sub-, para-, super-, trans-, interspaces that had not lost their ability to intersect each other, they oozed from one another, were unclosed, had no solid borders, and morphed from the slightest shift of objects.

The animals would not submit to any training. They simply loved her and required neither cages nor tethers. She identified them by the creak of the floor—the length, weight, and speed of each beast's steps extracted a unique melody from the parquet, complicated by the fact that each individual board creaked according to a formula inherent only to it, often not coinciding with the direction of the movement of the body along the floor, being more reminiscent of problems laid out on a chessboard. She recognized each of them by the hypertrophied semblance of the shadow that passed across the office ceiling, transformed by the game of insufficient light into a sphere, seeping through the matte glass into the hallway. She lost the most significant part of her consciousness when she was congested and her sense of smell ceased to function. She experienced all the sweaters found in wardrobes as one-night stands—accidental and quickly fleeting contacts. Sometimes she smoked a pipe to mask the smell of the rooms' memories with the spirit of one of her father's tobacco mixes.

When Mlynarskyi caught her on the terrace, a cool rain was falling. She sat in an icy armchair, wrapped up in her winter cloak, squeezing a mug of grog between her knees, and not flicking the ashes from her *pakhitoska*, that thin, corn-husk cigarette in her hand hanging over her abandoned book (although the pakhitoska wasn't touching the book, a bronze sign of its heat appeared on the page). He felt he had never been closer to anyone than this woman. He had never yet given anyone so much of his knowledge, his secret knowledge, his most scrutinized and most defining habits. He had never before been so generous. And he had not experienced such gratitude. She immediately recognized the inevitability of his habits in his attempt at the maximum alignment of the desired order of the world with the natural, the chaotically natural.

Gradually, Mlynarskyi gave her all of his external experience, until he even ran out of knowledge. She demanded new experiences, experiencing what she hadn't lived through. Most often, she hardly noticed what Markus gave her, the burden of Markus's experience, taking it as constant and shared. This woman on the terrace had herself become a fragment.

Mlynarskyi got scared. He was not afraid of devastation, was not afraid of self-abnegation, self-destruction. He was not scared by the fact that she made anything else impossible, nor by the fact that everything he did at a certain point was her whim—foreseeing associations caused by cognition—the day before, Markus consciously engaged in events to be able to give her the experience of them. Markus achieved a certain experience, legitimizing the previously named—the possibility of naming forced him to make possible the happenings. And the whims were increasingly liberated from the dominant of rationalism, goodness, beauty, and intellect, approaching the recognition of the value of being *per se*.

And Markus knew that her incomprehensible ability to become the final reason for causation would lead (even if in the course of randomness) to the essence. But then neither Necropolis nor the balloon would be random.

Markus was not even afraid of responsibility. He was simply afraid for her. Everything changes from a change in something else—Markus would save (or lose?), would save her by not being with her. So Mlynarskyi stopped writing his novel.

There was a thaw. The leaves that had lain on the ground since fall were liberated from the snow to fall again, lifted by a warm wind. The warm wind melted the snow beginning to fall from clouds that had gathered over the course of a few days. The snow fell to earth as a cold rain, covering itself in leaves, much more slowly.

In his treatise Mlynarskyi wrote, "Being is, inherently, co-being. The concurrent existence of everything with everything and the coexistence of everything."

In reality, though, at that time Mlynarskyi was only interested in problems connected to the further fate of *Necropolis*. He understood that his sketch of the novel was already a text, was already something of the everything, it already coexisted, it was reality. For Mlynarskyi, the idea of the novel was already commensurate and capable of being the start of independent chains, strung on presence in the contemporaneous being of all possibilities of all future moments and the possibility of precisely these moments coming.

Necropolis was a reality in a world where there was generally nothing unreal, only different forms of reality. Mlynarskyi had to finish revealing the form of *Necropolis*'s reality and include it in the series of mutually transitive forms. Here, a situation arose similar to the status of Mlynarskyi's treatise. The treatise was the transference of Markus's everyday existential experience into the experience of philosophy, the experience of consciousness. The new form or structure of *Necropolis* needed to be a model of imaginary experience—the experience of the imagination—according to Mlynarskyi's philosophical outlines. As usual, an unexpected recombination appeared: in this case, *Necropolis* was a reflection of a reflection, a system of mirrors that could be extended on and on (Mlynarskyi was sure they weren't Venetian mirrors, rather something much older, made of silver and tarnished, that noticeably distorted the image when tossing it back and forth. Even the first mirror offered a clear impression only if it was kept at a certain focal length).

It was then that Mlynarskyi felt ecstatic calm (the feeling of calm threw Markus into a fit, he shook, froze, and barely spoke, imagining the essence of his calm) from a single non-concrete thought. Calm enveloped Mlynarskyi to such an extent that he did not need to crystallize his thoughts; he felt the calm of harmony between the world and his own understanding of the world (he knew that everything hinged on this, that he lived only to produce explanations of the world that would harmonize with the world; he knew how rarely these explanations came along, how all-encompassing they appeared in the moment, how short-lasting their effect; what an illusion of non-futility, of sense they created, the pleasure of fulfilling an obligation they offered, the relief, how they justified the entire preceding period and what hope they gave to the next period), but the understanding of the mechanisms of this calm being layered on the uninterrupted repetition of that thought led to a fit. It is somehow possible to catch this thought by comparing the notes in the treatise and the diary. Without a doubt, they are about one and the same thing. "For all its diversity, uniqueness, and endless variations, experience can ultimately be reduced to a few things, a few feelings, states: the measure and circumstances of their appearance are insignificant alongside the fact that it, the experience, simply was; in this way, they are compared to experience and do not occur as greater or lesser, just different." (Then Mlynarskyi goes on and arrives at cognition as the one thing to which absolutely everything can be reduced, a single and final structure that does not even set apart humans from all living things. Further yet, we run into a thought that, it would seem, contradicts the first, but is in fact its repetition if you turn the imaginary cube of thinking to a different side: "The measure of only one phenomenon [fear, hunger, risk] can be the starting point of experience.")

And in the diary: "The snow was deep. There were more and more tracks on it. Later, the snow melted and froze a couple times, deforming the impressions of the thaw and capturing the deformations of the freeze. Every morning, the relief was weird and different, the bizarre self-contained topography changed, possessing only three degrees of freedom—the primary snow with the original impressions, the melting, and the freezing. Knowing this (and the number of repetitions) it is probably possible with some effort to return through the thickets of recombinations to the ur-principle, the authentic traces, and further to the impeccable inviolability of the surface of the snow."

It was precisely this recombination of Mlynarskyi's observations on recombinations in the snow that proved decisive for the course of recombinations with *Necropolis*. Meanwhile, Markus created variations of the constructions of *Necropolis*: in one of them, *Necropolis* was a succinct, lyrical story that retold a city's history (the reality of this story is somewhat special, stories like this are integral, inviolable, and self-sufficient regardless of whether they are more or less full of details, here only consistency is important) that the author had heard while visiting some city, the text of the story was read by a screenwriter and the screenplay he wrote added some spectacle to *Necropolis*; the screenwriter shifted the accents, introduced dialogs, and emphasized individual portraits, a few scenes that were so obvious they weren't even mentioned in the story were developed in great detail, down to the second; the script was read by a director, who offered ample comments, additions, clarifications, notes (really, it was this text—almost the director's journal—that was submitted), moving even further away from the spirit of the story, the director mailed it to his cinematographer who filtered everything that was written through his imaginary camera, reality changed with respect to the lens's ability to see, the cinematographer's internal monologue ran through the text; the final fragment in the chain of texts was a transcript of recommendations for the film from the whole group with additions and inventions, clarifications and stratifications-limitations from the gaffers, effects artist, sound engineer, designer, make-up artist, costume designer, and this text was a repetition, that is, it had the beauty of a deserted construction, but the ruins of the story were so diseased and blasphemous, the chimera of the project so ugly and unrealizable that the director, not wanting to lose the nice plot, himself took up writing a new screenplay, liberating it from all its divergent branches. Of course the text of this script turned out to be the absolutely unchanged text of the story (which the director had not even seen or heard about), succinct and lyrical, and the director decided to make an animated movie. Another of Mlynarskyi's versions was the bane of a printing press because the text of *Necropolis* was supposed to be set on the sixth line of a musical staff that already featured the notes to a Mozart march and an avant-garde jazz piece; yet another was a split text—the first chapter offered portraits of the characters, the second gave thorough descriptions of the minutest details, the third only had all the dialogs, the fourth contained appropriate reflections, internal states, and the monologues, the fifth was like an encyclopedia made up of excerpts from eclectically compiled geographic, historical, technical, physiological, ethnographic, and linguistic knowledge, and only in the sixth was the bare skeleton of the plot revealed, the sequence of events; in one of the ideas, *Necropolis* was written on divided pages, starting from a first shared phrase, every sentence on each half differed from the analogous one on the other by only one word. And there were many, many other versions of *Necropolis*.

Later it got hot, summer baked the city, and Mlynarskyi became depressed (thinking up the versions lasted a few months and dragged Markus into an unchanging state of the constant lightness of being), he went to the countryside, drank linden tea, ate wild strawberries, swam in the river, and, starting at the very beginning, read his treatise every evening, not more than a few pages a day, reproducing the images of his own life with every entry.

At the end of summer, Mlynarskyi reached the March entry on the deformation of snow. And it was apparent that he had been sufficiently prepared by the treatise and his summer impressions of impressionlessness, because he was able to experience anew that thought, that state, to revive all the alchemy (Merab Mamardashvili calls this "falling into a thought," compared to "falling into being"). What's more, its continuation turned out to be obvious: knowing the end of that *Necropolis* (and Mlynarskyi considered the discovery of the hot air balloon and the decision to fly to be the real end), knowing those people and their city, and having gone through all the recombinations of their actions (that relate and—this is most important—don't relate to the plot line), he could restore all states, the state of each one at the moment when they went to the auction where the plots of the future cemetery were being sold. That's the only way to find out what creates Necropolis. Who creates Necropolis.

All of September, Mlynarskyi worked twenty hours a day compiling a cumbersome register-description of the schema of recombinations. He selected action, verb as his ur-structure. The research looked like an inventory of the most numerous variations of actions that branched from a few definitive ones to ever more refined and exquisite ones, and to increasingly detailed ones; from one verb to entire phrases with subordinate clauses that characterized the most specific actions (for example, the chapter "Smoking" was cut by a few dozen planes into a few hundred subchapters such as smoking a pipe, smoking skinny cigarettes, smoking tobacco rolled in newspaper—this was only one plane cutting through it—while other planes offered smoking in the mountains, smoking indoors, smoking alone, smoking cigarette after cigarette. This was how it was split up until more complicated concepts such as "in bed in the early morning smoking her cigarettes with that barely perceptible elegant flavor of the smoky smell of the ashtray on your breast ashes sometimes fall on the covers turning into a gray stain from overly aggressive rubbing lasts longer than usual only holding the cigarette keeps you from sleeping however what's being said is actually ramblings consciousness agrees with the dimension set by the direction of the coordinate axes of the cigarettes' position").

The most complicated was the description of the planes that emerged with the mutual penetration of irregular figure-subchapters. This was already a topology, a geometry of uninterrupted planes. From every most favorable point, not breaking off for even a moment, it was possible to cross from one point of the register to another, to another elementary chapter, and later either to a more generalized subchapter of that group or to a specific one from a totally different group. And thus, traveling along the curved horizontals and verticals, one could get all the way to the ur-word "cognize," ultimately all the way to the hot air balloon. By October, Mlynarskyi had finished his colossal map of being (thanks to the help of a friend who was a hacker). All that remained, while limiting himself to the real possibilities available to the characters of *Necropolis*, was for him to follow the phantasmagorical, crooked path from the balloon to the auction. But there was nothing strange in the fact that Markus had lost interest in his project: first of all, he had very little left compared to what he'd already done, and, second of all, the maneuvers of Necropolis had lost all value against the background of the universal and totipotential code. Mlynarskyi believed *Necropolis* was an interesting and fruitful period in his philosophical oeuvre, his life, and the sum of his experiences and impressions. Ultimately, he was grateful to the people of Necropolis.

In December, sometime before Christmas, a theater festival was held in the city. It was a holiday and Markus spent all his days talking with friends and acquaintances who came in from out of town, having sex with the actors, watching all the performances, writing articles for various newspapers and journals, feasting, and organizing receptions. He spent his nights in the most diverse assemblies and delivered a brilliant lecture on the philosophy of theater at a seminar. Meanwhile, at his home, he accommodated actors from the theater of plastic dance and their choreographer—the ingenious Spanish Arab X.—with whom Markus had been friends for many years. X. was a hermit, he turned up only at the theater and only on the days his group performed. The rest of the time, he sat in Mlynarskyi's apartment, taking the opportunity to be alone among Markus's papers. He knew Markus was intentionally staying away, encouraging him to calmly study all that Markus had written recently.

Among the papers, X. found the map of being. It impressed him so much that it made reading anything else impossible; it stuck with him for quite a while. For the first time in his life, X. wrote down some notes from a text. A year later, X.'s theater brought its own program to the city. Among other plastic compositions, the premiere of *Necropolis* was shown, a plastic construction based on the motifs of the idea of M. Mlynarskyi, who was confused and gladly accepted an invitation to the premiere, promising to even speak from the stage a bit after the dance.

The only evidence of these events is a mention in the newspaper a few paragraphs long: the atmosphere of the premiere was more magical than throughout the previous year's entire festival, and, for two hours, a genuine artistic bacchanalia went on in the foyer, on the stairs, in the hallways. Among the guests, there were many who had never before been successfully lured to the city. Mlynarskyi did not speak because, after the performance, which ended in triumph, he was nowhere to be found.

In the morning, a friend of Mlynarskyi's went to X. and told him that, in the middle of the first act, Mlynarskyi was overcome by an unbearable headache, he fainted, freaked out, and asked her to leave the theater with him. His fever lasted all night, she made him compresses, later he fell asleep for a bit, and, in the morning, Markus was gone. On January 2, X.'s theater left, and Markus returned on January 7; on January 20 X. arrived, forbade recording the plastics of *Necropolis* in any way, photographic or otherwise; on March 1, Mlynarskyi himself went to X., they were seen on all-day odysseys of coffee shops, wine cellars, bars, pubs, taverns, and saloons.

Mlynarskyi's relationship with X. didn't suffer. *Necropolis* was performed for the last time in November. Throughout this whole time, Mlynarskyi avoided all inquiries or conversations about *Necropolis* almost to the point of rudeness.

Everything was gradually forgotten.

Thus ends a letter that Doctor Vynnyk, author of the most-read biography of Markus Mlynarskyi, received right as he was preparing the updated second edition of this bestseller. To be fair, there was also a poetic postscript. Initially, the author noted that one of Markus's closest friends had told him the whole story a few years back; later he explained that he was trying to recall as much as possible of what he'd heard, but he preferred to toss out some of what he'd forgotten rather than think or remember too hard (in this, Vynnyk felt some of Mlynarskyi's spirit). But, in his final addendum, he swore he knew absolutely nothing more, could not add anything or report in greater detail and, therefore, would remain anonymous. Vynnyk, who labored unduly thoroughly over Mlynarskyi's biography, was hearing about *Necropolis* for the first time. He was curious to learn more about that friend of Markus's who knew something of it, but the second edition of *The Endless Variability of the Invariable* was printed without any mention of the mystery of *Necropolis*.

II

All was found. All was found. Although it was just one person, there was a person who knew about *Necropolis*. Who had even been involved in it. At a compulsory hospital for alcoholics in Mlynarskyi's hometown, Vynnyk found a totally destroyed seventy-year-old cellist who had played in the city theater's orchestra in his youth. He remembered well almost all the themes of the various ballets, operettas, and vaudevilles. He remembered that he played in *Necropolis* when some traveling theater arrived; the scores were theirs, but he couldn't remember the music at all. Vynnyk sat with the old man until midnight in an unnaturally clean examination room. He rolled him cigarette after cigarette, listening to his phantasmagorical stories about the life of a theater musician. He even mulled a decent glühwein from contraband wine in the autoclave, risking getting kicked out of the hospital. The cellist got lost on a tangent. He no longer had the strength to draw out the story of *Necropolis* (it seemed to him from the very beginning offensively unwise to speak only about a single episode); Vynnyk had waited long enough.

There were six men and one woman who danced. Although they didn't so much dance as perform different acts. Mainly the woman did something with one of them. The others were either on stage doing their own thing or exited altogether. Sometimes the woman with two, three, four, or five men. She also looked nice alone; a few times they were all together. The stage was divided by various contours into a great number of spaces. There were windows on the stage; there were hanging punctuation marks of fabric, cords, and a synthetic film. Lamps of different strengths were used, affixed in different places. The lights were both special and ordinary bulbs, table lamps and projectors, as well as flashlights turned on and left anywhere at random. Besides that, the grip manipulated a complex system of lights directed at the stage. Different levels. Scaffolding, swings, cubes, benches, candles, and candelabra. Water flowed. From faucets, from balloons with holes, from tilted dishes. The water either spread out or collected in vessels. Animals wandered freely about the stage—dogs, cats, here and there garter snakes wriggled, hedgehogs hid. A few beasts slept soundly, a few were tied up and trying to break free. Birds sat, from somewhere butterflies flew away, very many butterflies, wasps, moths. The insects flew through the bands of light, bands of smoke.

The smoke came from cigarettes left in ashtrays, papers burned, grasses were thrown. There were myriad plants. Ivy spilled, there were vases, vats, vials of flowers. It smelled like a mixture of broken bottles of perfume, spices, and freshly brewed coffee.

An entire army of shadow workers carried furniture, rigs, plants, books on and off. They rearranged the objects on a few tables. They rearranged the pieces on a few chessboards, poured drinks from bottles into goblets, mixed them. They either poured them out or drank them up. They shifted paintings and moved sculptures. Someone sat down at the piano—and lived there, not touching the floor. The grip changed the slides projected onto all the planes. The workers herded the dogs, looked in the telescopes, microscopes (one girl constantly changed the slides on specimen table), and binoculars, ground leaves and grass, pounded roots in a mortar.

The ones who danced were always showing up in different costumes. It was so chaotic that, after a certain time, no one involved could extract themselves from it anymore, and did not what they would have liked, but what was dictated by the strict order of chaos. Besides, from time to time, they would declaim phrases, poems, and extracts of prose from different places in the theater.

The music for the ballet (the cellist stubbornly called it a ballet) forced them to throw their instruments after each performance, notwithstanding the psychological load of playing their part, and run from the orchestra pit. The music was crazy, pathological, and compelling. It did not let up until the moment it tossed you aside. It is not known precisely why one musician or another went crazy from it—or was it all because of their pasts?—but they started with the whole orchestra and played till the end, losing some combination of instruments along the way and not paying attention to their absence. The cellist held out each time, but now he slept. Dr. Vynnyk went to the hotel and also slept, but he remembered what to think about when he woke up—about the fact that he had to retell what he'd heard in the hospital and record it on tape, that—by overlaying the register of plastics onto Mlynarskyi's outlines described in the letter—he could write *Necropolis*.

Another strange thing: lying down to sleep, you always forget overnight what you were thinking about, but, in the morning, nothing is necessary to freely continue on that line of thought. And nothing is forgotten because of night.

Nothing was found in Vynnyk's archive except for an approximation of *Necropolis*. When they had started razing the building and the orchard was half hewn, having taken the last bundles of empty frames, the doctor's friends turned their attention to the fact that the headlights were creating a dull shimmering along a thin, illusory, tangled, broken line in the tree closest to the balcony. It was a cassette tape hurled into the crown, here and there resolutely enmeshed in the branches, in places extremely taut, but basically free, so windblown that the tape curved beyond the imaginary contour of the crown and changed the configuration of the outline.

When it was pulled out, the tape tore in a few places. In one place it was so tightly tangled that they had to break the branch.

The tape was damaged—it was not meant to become involved in the circulation of the tree's sap. A few pieces had totally lost their color, others were coated in dust, covered in Irish moss, some places had been eaten by moths (they probably got disoriented and flew to the tree through the open windows), the film was streaked with stripes of the formic acid of ants and the slime of slugs, some fragments were absorbed by a hardened glue like amber, bark beetles had chewed through it more than once.

Listening to the tape made a break in time. Beyond the ultrasounds of bats and mosquitoes, beyond the overflows in the capillaries, the application of radio interference (all of this can perhaps be explained by the influence of a constant magnetic field from the proximity of powerful antennas) right behind the orchard, excerpts of free verse spoken aloud by Vynnyk emerged. The synchronous interlinear translation constructed an indubitable *Necropolis*. It turns out that the voice was copied only by the genotexts of our being, for repeated listening only let the wasteland of effacement, openness, purity, and waiting endure.

A FEELING
OF PRESENCE /
TOWARD A SENSE
OF ESSENCE

|

The fact that there was a long, compact fence on the right was important not only because it meant there was nothing else on the right, and not because it would have been impossible to turn anywhere if she had raised her head, but, above all, because it affected the lighting. It would have been good to remember it, although obviously there was no way to isolate the effects of the fence.

She drank from the standpipe on the street. Piles of leaves had gathered around the pipe and she had to step on them. This made it even harder to drink, for she had to bend over more. Chestnuts too big to fall through the holes rolled around the grate beneath the standpipe. Glued to the grate with water, the leaves formed something like an oilcloth and the sound of the stream against it was somehow off. Then it made a gap in the leaves in one spot and so only caught on their crumbly, wetted edges. She bent over and turned her face to the sky. The center of the very powerful jet was empty. The water was like a wrapper. She needed to only just touch her lips to the stream. The stream was somewhat distorted and flew farther than it should have; drops fell onto a pile of leaves without a trace, not even wetting the surface. A trickle flowed from the corner of her mouth to her ear and beyond onto her clavicle. Occasionally, the ends of her hair got wet and looked like paintbrushes someone had licked. He realized he was very thirsty. The girl was becoming more diaphanous from the layers of fog added with every step.

Further on the stream passed by the island. But only on one side; on the other, the riverbed—cluttered with enormous stones upon which previous water levels were distinctly marked, with the bleached jumbles of branches, with logs, with miniature sand dunes brought in and held by algae—was totally dry. And almost immediately everything began moving as though someone were spinning you on a lace tied above your shoes. The river turned to the right so sharply that it began flowing parallel to itself, just in reverse.

It wasn't until he drew the map that he finally understood the whole topography: tracing the line from left to right with his pencil, stopping as closely as possible to the previous segment to go back from right to left; the angle had to be minimal. Only later would he be able to draw the same on the outside, so the width of the river would be apparent. Everything went upside down when the current hit that corner and turned toward the canyon (for before that the left bank was low and continued all the way to the forest). The canyon was very deep and wide—we simply don't have any rivers like that. The water was turbid from the whirlpool at the bend.

In all those times, he had counted and recorded a few hundred names for everything that had been and had happened on both shores and in the waters. These fragments were always unchanged, but the speed of the current made it impossible to examine everything. There were hanging bridges, paths, gazebos, trash cans, huts, gardens and flower beds, pits, beehives, a road, the piers of collapsed bridges and the twisted detritus of railroad tracks, flocks of birds, animals drinking water, anthills, autumnal nests, boats on taut chains. Many people lived there. This time, he noticed rather large entrances to burrows that ran along the entire right bank and came out somewhere on the other side before the bend. Light and the distant forests on the low shore could be seen through these caves. It turned out that this shore was utterly thin, the burrows made holes in its thickness, not much deeper than a stone wall.

Perhaps it made no sense, but it seemed to Pamva that the fragment with the river was always last. Likely some other dreams ended with it. For a few years, he dreamed of this river from time to time. Most impressive was the fact that, after that bend, it became very quiet despite the life teeming in the canyon; not even the noise of the water could be heard. He had to wait some time after waking up for sounds to finally retake the space.

Right now there were no sounds. He didn't have the strength to stand any more. He had to do something that would make a sound. He took matches from his pants pocket and shook the box. The boards of the walls just barely squeaked, shrinking from the ever increasing cold. Pamva lay dressed. Under the woolen blanket it was very warm, but the room was so cold he could feel it in his lungs. In that cold, the scent of apples seemed to get stronger, overlapping with the cold, with the dampness. The apples were heaped in an enormous pile on the other bed. The room was too small to dissolve the spirit of so many Reinette Symyrenkos. Outside the window it was dark, but not as dark as when he lay down. Pamva had a premonition that he had slept too long and missed the evening train to the city. He could not get up, could not crawl out from that warmth. The wool was like a vagina. An onset of childish sensations—not getting up, squeezing his eyes tightly, not going anywhere, not leaving. For some reason, it was only in the fall that he superstitiously didn't want to return to the city. To stay for the whole winter, which was, ultimately, still a long way off. To stay here, primitive and motionless.

It was Saturday. The train to the city left late in the evening. Pamva didn't know what time it was. He had lain down when it was already totally dark. Maybe an hour had passed, or maybe it was truly night, and the train had left. The next one wasn't until the morning, and it would be almost just as dark. Fall does not distinguish between periods of the night. Pamva found a pack of Gitanes in the pocket of his flannel shirt, took out two cigarettes, and fumblingly smoked there in bed, promising himself to get up after he had smoked them one by one. The whole time he was careful not to stick his arm out from under the blanket lest he invite the cold into the covers.

There hadn't been Gitanes in their city for a long time. It was for the Gitanes that Pamva had gone to the train station in the morning long before the train was scheduled. Someone told him that his favorite cigarettes had turned up in one of the nighttime shops near the station. He still almost missed his train looking for them. He went to the mountains. To the place where his grandpa used to live. When he was a child, Pamva was almost never there. But now he tried to go as often as possible. There was an empty house, an orchard, and a well. Today, he had to pick the apples. You can't wait until the frost comes, but it's good to let them hang on the trees as long as you can. Apples cannot hit each other or the ground. Each one must be picked separately. You have to sort them—his grandpa had grafted a few varieties onto the trees, a different one on each branch. Pamva picked apples all day, stuffed them in all his pockets sitting on the tree so that he wouldn't have to get down each time, later he piled them on the bed. If he closed his eyes, it was all apples.

It was wet after the overnight rain. Fortunately, only on the grass, for the apples dried in the wind and he didn't have to wipe each one off. In the morning, Pamva had removed his shoes; they were so full of holes on the bottom that his feet would have gotten soaked immediately. He didn't want to have to walk around in wet shoes, so he spent the whole day barefoot. His feet froze, but at least he didn't destroy any branches. He dressed in strange old things to protect himself from the damp and wind, and partially for the sake of the many pockets. He wrapped himself up in some scarves. Clumsiness and helplessness attained holiness. His hands could not feel anything at all except for the difference in the roughness of the skins of different varieties. A cigarette stuck to his wet lips, his fingers, not ready for work, slid all the way down to the ember, burning holes on the inner sides of his pointer and middle finger. He didn't even feel the burn.

Pamva had long ago ceased trying to remember how space changes from emptiness, nakedness, and the erasure of boundaries, how the best correlation between coldness and the brightness of sunlight is established, how leaves all lose their own smells and begin to smell the same, how the special plastics of resisting constraint appears. It seemed to him that, with this, he was depriving the world of its final properties, that it was not necessary to take something away by remembering.

Instead, picking apples, finding all the walnuts, raking leaves, pouring out the water from the barrel under the trees, turning over the barrel, leaving some of the late berries for the birds, stuffing moss into the chinks in the walls—this took on some sort of strange importance; he stubbornly wouldn't leave until everything was done. It was also important to be admitted into certainty, finality. And to be frozen, clumsy, speechless, and patient.

A few times, flocks of birds flew by lower than he was.

On a shelf, he found a bottle with a drop of cognac and did not drink it for a few hours.

He wasn't thinking about anything; only noticing that, when you can't reach an apple, you can always stretch a bit farther. One time, he imagined how the day would have sounded on a piano, if all of them—Pamva, the trees, the apples, the birds, the moles, the walnuts, the grass, the light, the cold—could hold on to the soundboard and keyboard. Or if they could at least behave at the piano like he had walked, climbed, stretched, fallen, rolled, bent, squatted, hopped, stooped, and exhaled today. When it was getting dark, Pamva brewed all the coffee that was left right in the can. And, warming his hands, got into bed. And now he was reaching the end of his second cigarette timekeeper.

He lay with the extinguished filter in his hand for a while. At first, he listened for which train was passing near the house and what direction it was headed in (a heavy freight train coming from the city), then he ate an apple he found he was lying on, it fell out of his pocket and he slept with it, the apple was warm, finally he thought—how could he combine into a single maxim such paradoxical things: it's nice to lie, the nice wool, it's nice to smoke while lying, it's nice to eat a warm apple, it's nice not to want to get up, it's nice to get up when you don't want to, it's nice to return to bed, it's nice not to return to bed when you're leaving, it's nice to go to the station in the night, it's nice to wait for the train, it's nice to miss the train, it's nice to go, it's nice to stay, it's nice to not sleep, it's nice to feel niceness, it's nice to know you feel that niceness itself is nice, there is nothing else, but niceness cannot be the sense, there are, after all, things more essential than niceness, and these things, incidentally, are still nice—and nothing else can be given up as easily something nice, yet even this, in turn, feels nice...

Pamva didn't turn on the light. He covered the apples with the blanket he had just been sleeping under, threw off all his rags, grabbed a large sack of walnuts and apples. He finished the water that was in the bucket.

He put on a tight, knitted cap, stuck a cigarette behind his ear, and went outside.

Walking past the walnut tree, he saw that the tree was completely naked. Walnut trees are not ungainly without their leaves; they look rather more like a Hnizdovsky drawing. A secret mechanism was revealed—a single thick branch knocked on the roof, swaying in the wind. The leaves had all fallen at once. Right when he was in the house. Pamva imagined that tomorrow, if it was dry, the patchy plane of the fallen leaves would shine in the sun like a pockmarked sheet of tin, and would gradually become homogenous, continuous. The few leaves at the top of the tree would resemble an illustration from a children's book about fall. Now Pamva could only see what was against the backdrop of the sky—the edge of the roof and all the walnut's branches.

It became clear after a few dozen steps that the sack was too heavy. Now he still had to go to the cemetery. Sometime over those days, the thirtieth anniversary of his grandpa's death had passed. Pamva wasn't sure if it was today or tomorrow. Not because he didn't remember the date, but because he wasn't sure what day it was. The cemetery was between the house and the station. Pamva left the sack at a spot along the rails and ran into the deep ravine. In the morning, he thought he'd seen crocuses and was surprised by the abnormality of their repeat blooming. Once he even wanted to take a few flowers to a botanist he knew: he slipped them into a book, subsequently forgot where, and eventually he sold the book. Along with the plants. He was already over thirty when it became strangely unsettling not to know plants; it was like not understanding the language others spoke to you in. He bought up tons of albums, reference books, and studied one type of plant every day. Above all, he had learned that it was a fall crocus. Then he calmed down—just as unexpectedly and groundlessly. Sometime then he thought up something *soloristic* for the piano in which he translated onto the keys all the steps in the sequence of identifying some difficult species found in the reference book.[2] For another piece he selected a text, a register of Latin plant names ordered in a certain way.

It was totally dark, and he had to grope blindly for the fall crocuses. When Pamva climbed up onto the tracks and sparked his lighter, he saw that his bouquet was half made up of some elongated leaves that had the same contour as the flowers when they closed for the night. Under the trees in the cemetery, it was even darker. He had to use the tall crucifix with the primitively carved and multicolored wooden cross as his guide. A real spear was stuck in the red wound under the pronounced ribs—the tip was made from a repurposed can. Setting his flowers on the frozen ground, Pamva began to pray, but he grudgingly could not stop his thoughts:

---

2   *Soloristics* is a neologism the author has coined. Later on in the text, it is defined as "making sound for the sake of movement" (see p. 132) (ed.).

when he remembered his grandpa, he always existed in a certain fragment from his own life, which, for some reason, caused him to remember an episode about his grandpa. Pamva was always different but the same—for he was thinking about him; these individual moments could be sewn together, removing them from everything else, to get an independent story, a genesis, a self-sufficient plot, likely totally warranted, or to compose a separate Pamva. He decided to monitor this.

Pamva started to run. It seemed he needed to run fast. He got used to striding from railroad tie to tie, and, when they weren't in the right spot, he practically fell from his burden or hit his foot hard. He screamed as he ran. He was completely wet. The delicate skin on his long scars burned from the sweat. Right before the train station, everything lost its reality, for a few types of different projectors, lamps, and signal lights shined in his eyes. The cigarette behind his ear got wet and slipped out.

The smell of wine burst out of the station doors (if he had somehow been forced to define his life for the last month, it would have been daily red wine). Lots of men and women sat in the hall on wooden barrels. A bottle of young wine stood before them. They all held in their hands some kind of vessel with different quantities of liquid. Apparently, they had been drunk on wine for a few days now. They spoke a foreign language. These were peasants who were bringing wine from beyond the mountains to the city Pamva was from. The evening train had left long ago, and there were still a few hours until the morning one. Pamva shifted to feel if his knife had accidentally slipped from his belt around his sacrum. Ever since childhood he had felt the strange need to never be without a knife. He sat on his sack and lit up. Almost immediately a few men turned to him and gestured that they wanted to smoke. Pamva had already counted his remaining Gitanes—for waiting for the train, on the train, the walk from the station home. He wouldn't get new cigarettes until he was home. But he generously gave away half of what he had. While the men were lighting their cigarettes, holding them in hands stained with grape juice, a woman brought Pamva a jar of wine. All the women were young, pretty, strong, and looked hardy from drinking. There were wine stains on their lips, their sweaters, their fingertips, and the backs of their hands, more or less wiped off. The women were tickled to see how Pamva drank. He had just started feeling sickly chilled—his shirt wet with sweat had dried. The wine was as cold as his body. The cold accompanied him all the way to his stomach, but Pamva drank quickly, waiting for the arrival of a warmth of a totally different, metaphysical provenance. People were constantly talking, to him as well, but he didn't understand anything. They called him over. He drank more and more, began to laugh, full of the joy of the here and now. He remembered he had walnuts and he shelled a whole pile. It was very difficult to pluck the meat from the shell since his fingers were frozen and burned, and now he was tipsy. Pamva wanted to teach them a trick—he grabbed half a shelled walnut, held it in his mouth a second, and then touched that walnut to some salt sprinkled on a newspaper on one of the suitcases. The youngest woman wanted to do the same, but she didn't lick the walnut, the salt didn't stick, and she ate a plain walnut. Not like that. Pamva grabbed another half, held it in two fingers, gave it to the woman to lick, dipped it in the salt, and placed it in her mouth. The woman was obedient and now marveled at the unusual taste. Pamva gave her a sip of wine from his jar, and she laughed. Not like that. Licking a walnut and dipping it in salt, she gave it to Pamva, took a sip of wine, leaned over Pamva, and passed the wine from her mouth to his. Like that. Pamva thought that the men might react differently, but they laughed and watched with interest, marveling at the understanding, recognizing the advent of a new language.

Pamva needed a piano. And there was one; among the packages, there was a small children's piano whose construction did not even allow for strings, someone had obviously bought a souvenir for some children. With his right hand he played a few chromatic notes; with his left, the rhythm on the soundboard (also with his fingers). One foot ended up in a puddle of wine, his shoe squished in time nicely. The peasants all got to their feet, and gathered round Pamva, the men held each others' shoulders, the women clapped their hands. At first, it was quite simple, but then they started getting increasingly used to his rhythmic variations. Pamva could no longer see anything, maybe the men were dancing around him, or maybe everything was spinning in his head. He shook from ecstasy. Someone tossed an old wool blouse with tattered sleeves onto his shoulders. The onslaught of foreign smells pushed out the ordinary ones, they immediately began to tilt and turn, disappear, rush in, and change just like the world before his eyes. Near the end, Pamva frantically drummed the wrong chords.

He came to when they had already left the mountains and the foothills. The train car was cold and almost empty. The winegrowers slept on the benches, their shoes and woolen socks blocked the aisle. Someone had thought to grab his sack. The moon shone so brightly that it was clear as day in the car even though no lights were on, outside the window every reed in the ditch the train was traveling along could be made out. The shadows on the moon were intensely dark, almost artificially blackened. The youngest woman was not asleep; she approached Pamva's bench and set the piano on his knees. Pamva did not want to play, though it would have been worth it, and not just because of the girl—it would be good to recall what he played at the station, it had two felicitous themes for his piece that was due on Monday—the motifs of numbness in the orchard and drunkenness on young wine. His pants were somewhat damp—either drowned in wine or he had lain somewhere near a puddle, or it was urine, or it was that humid in the car. Maybe the piece wasn't needed at all. Not for the film, not for Francis, not for Anna, not for him. He would turn back and stay there for a long time. Pamva started looking in his pockets for the scrap of paper on which he had written everything that he had to do in the coming days. He took various objects out of his pockets and set them on the toy piano: matches, a lighter with no gas but with a flint, a lighter with gas but no flint (to light up, you had to hold them in both hands and unite the flint of one with the gas of the other), a wooden rosary, several pits from last year's plums, a few different pencils. The girl took this to be the start of some new story, the next phrase, a continuation of the game. She was partly right. Pamva cultivated a world of pockets, of things in pockets. Sometimes, he wouldn't take anything out of his pockets for months, just to later chance on an unexpected register. He always put something interesting in his pocket so that he could examine it for a while when he had the chance. From time to time, he would play diverse meditative solitaires out of the contents of his pockets. On a leather string—a few silver rings removed when picking apples, amber overflowing with its own inner world, a small bottle of eleuthero extract. The girl decided to sniff the small bottle of cologne, a few nuts, a little bit of shell, and large individual coral beads. At last, the list on a shred of the cigarette wrapper: Gitanes pick apples walnuts shell beans cover window in basement barrel grab walnuts books coffee shop (select clothes) gallery massage meet Anna green thickets for light. Such lists could be published as self-sufficient minimalist writings, like diaries or notes are published. He was fated to spend those days in the city, every point on the list was tied to a promise. Everything is always reduced to biding. You need to bide—this is the most important explanation of your whole life. You can only choose or want to choose the way of biding. To indeed write the piece for the film, or at least to make the piece itself possible. Make it possible to be fated to bide. When the whole world, everything on earth, and earth itself is a large piano with different alcoves; or life with everything that's necessary, only on the piano itself; or an odyssey from one random piano to another in order to perform a piece, though, you need a few different instruments, preferably in different places. That almost never happens. Pamva immediately stopped on the second option, remembering the two others as unused methods for something else.

He took a pencil and crossed out the items in the register that had already happened on Saturday. He started putting everything back in his pockets, took the rings off the cord and put them on his fingers, and he threaded the biggest coral bead on the string, tied a knot, and placed it around the girl's neck, slipping the bead under her sweater. The bead hung right between her breasts. The girl looked at the pack of Gitanes. Pamva took the last cigarette out and went out to the vestibule. A moment later, this youngest woman came out. She stood in front of him. Pamva was smoking very slowly and saw how extraordinarily pretty she was. The smoke was drifting toward her, he took her by the shoulders and put her in his place near the window and himself stood so that the smoke was pulled out through the crack.

She grabbed his hand with the cigarette. Pamva thought she wanted a drag. Instead she took the cigarette from between his fingers and threw it to the ground, and placed his empty hand on her chest such that he could feel the coral bead. She leaned into Pamva, holding his palm in both her hands. Pamva grew so sad that he wanted to cry. He felt that this was the last time such a young woman would touch him, and he didn't know if anyone would ever need to nestle into him again; he was certain there was no way anyone would ever approach him so spontaneously. He was overcome by terrible nostalgia; he thought about how old all the women he had loved his whole life were, they who were now in more pain and less enlightened than he, through whom he became aware of his own aging. The girl's hair parted surprisingly easily.

He kissed her on her nape and on her neck. The girl was slight and Pamva's fingers long, so, when he held his palm against her back, hooking his fingertips on the two narrow and hard bands of muscle along her spine, it seemed that his thumbs could feel the relief of his own palms through her belly.

He knew that he wanted to return with her to the mountains, he thought he knew he could. He would gladly just be there with her long enough to get completely used to being with her, used to her, to her body, so as to lose unexpectedness, for her to become ordinary, known, uninterrupted, continuous, water, wood, the bed, a shirt, the view from the window. The girl suddenly turned her back to him but did it so gracefully that Pamva's lips did not slip a millimeter from her neck, and his palms ended up on her belly; she bent forward and pressed her arms onto the glass, muscles quivered in her belly, Pamva understood that it was all just fingers, a neck, a sacrum, pressure, wine.

Everything most genuine is extraordinarily cruel.

He embraced the girl strongly right underneath her breasts, pulled her toward him, and slowly turned her around—like she had been before. She left behind two warm palm prints on the frozen glass. Pamva thrust his hand under her mussed hair onto her skin, squeezed her hair in his fist, and leaned one of the girl's cheeks against the cold window, pressing his forehead against the other. He held her like that until she started breathing calmly, then he broke off all touching and even stepped back.

Not to dwell too long on what had happened, he took a photograph out of his deepest pocket and showed it to her. It showed a woman dressed in white standing with her hands on the shoulders of a young girl on the shore of some small lake; behind them, off to the side but on the other shore, sat (on a dock that looked like a wooden crate) a man younger than the woman wearing black and strange shoes not suited to summer, his head nearly shaven. They all stared ahead calmly, almost indifferently, but somehow as though focusing on something else. The woman had soft features and long hair.

Pamva knew that the girl would look. And she did, having seen only herself and a little of Pamva's very thoughtful face in the window. The woman in the photograph gazed as though she was looking in the eyes not of the person looking at the photo, but whoever stood over their shoulder.

It's plausible the youngest girl could not determine the time the photograph was from—sometime in the mid-thirties. She glanced at Pamva just as un-here-and-now-ly and went back to the car. Pamva found the unfinished Gitane on the floor and smoked it, scraping broken ice off the window with the spent match.

He insisted that the film's composition be just like in the photo: to shoot fragments of the lakeshore with completely different scenes, but always so that something on the other side was visible, and at the very end to raise a camera above the lake in order to show that incompatible things are happening simultaneously around the lake. Well, and to attempt to achieve the detachment in the woman's, girl's, and man's looks.

When the train entered the city, Pamva went into the car to get his sack. He got off as soon as the train stopped. It was still totally dark, it was good that he had stood in the vestibule, because, in the early morning, it had grown even colder and he would have frozen outside from the shock.

Pamva reminded himself how, at twenty-five, he thought he already knew all the main structures of life, that they would begin to simply repeat—of course, slightly differently each time—but that nothing fundamentally new would happen. However, from then to now, living had only become more interesting.

Through the fog—the farther Pamva went, the thicker it got—the train station reminded him of a giant steamship that trains drove into. It seemed the sea was close. Pamva stopped often to rest. Leaves were being burned on every street. Sometimes, he had to walk through very long swaths of smoke. Here and there, the piles were just beginning to smolder; in other places, what remained were mounds of white ash that still retained the form of the leaves. Not far from home, a car with yellow fog lights was driving toward Pamva, which meant he could only ascertain its distance by the sound, for the intensity of the light was always the same. Only when it was very close did it become clear that it was a tractor trailer without a trailer. In his courtyard, Pamva was frightened by the surprise of realizing someone was watching him, sitting in a dark car (plus the windows were fogged up). Pamva had once dreamed something similar—he was driving through a well-lit town at night, the windows were opaque just like this, he stopped, opened the door, asked directions of someone who thrust his arm into the car—some small Volkswagen—and drew a map on the window. He drove on following the map, but it was cold outside and inside it was warm, the windows were still perspiring, especially along the lines of the map, which started disappearing, and it was not possible to get there any other way, he had to make it before the map disappeared completely, because, for some reason, it was also impossible to redraw it.

It was still dark, but the presence of the slightest illumination from above the rooftops could be perceived on the wall. Without turning on the lights, Pamva carried the sack down the long corridor to his room, knowing perfectly the distance to the walls, wardrobes, and bookshelves in every spot along the hallway. His whole life he had lived only in this apartment (Pamva used to imagine how strange and unnatural it must have been for people in the first hallways to get their bearings, to turn off into different branches). He poured all the walnuts out onto the floor of the room. On this side of the building, there were streetlights. Pamva found a box of cigarettes in the pocket of his winter coat on the hanger and went out onto the balcony. The grapes no longer fenced him off from the street, only the stalks were left. There was a small pitcher of coffee that he had made before he left—he really loved nearly frozen coffee, really loved being on the balcony as much as possible, and, when leaving home, he loved to prepare himself some coffee, cigarettes, a fresh book or magazine, and a laundered sweater, only to find it all at home as soon as he returned.

He sat a little too long on the balcony because he had barely slept at all these days and was afraid that he would not be able to fight the desire to lie in a warm bed, to stretch out after the sack and benches, would fall asleep and not manage to collect the books for the morning. He thought that, irrespective of the fact that the day was overbooked with various events, the day would not be as full or saturated as yesterday (though he himself did not know where yesterday was or today, for the days do not end if you don't cut them off, this is the only way to drag one day into the next), the flow of his present was linear, not diffuse; and almost no music emerged from it.

When he started living there alone, both rooms, the hallway, the kitchen, the pantry, and even the balcony were cluttered with things unchanged since his childhood. Everything had its own story, its own supplemental meaning (even supplemental meanings). The majority of things were impractical. He loved that world. He remembered all the chronicles and it often seemed to him that he himself had experienced ancient events. He did not understand how you could live in uninteresting, contemporary buildings suitable only for biding. For the longest time, he did not know the new city. He did not need to buy any clothing—the wardrobe contained more good, ancient clothes than it was possible to wear through. When he bought a book, it would subsequently turn out that the same one, but in an older edition, was already in the enormous disorderly library. Pamva lived among so many old snapshots that he couldn't get used to contemporary faces. Sometimes, he wore such expensive rings or brooches that they could not be taken as anything other than costume jewelry.

He would then spend a long time researching the genetics of each thing—what it was and how it affected his own evolution. He discovered that the whole collection was somehow also spread out within him. And all was not okay—together with the things, he had inherited a multitude of complexes, defects, diseases, fears, oddities, habits, curses and sins, mistakes and misunderstandings. One day, he discovered that he simply no longer needed to have all of that, he wanted neither to save old things nor possess them, nor know that they were nearby. He wanted an empty apartment, a life liberated from the dictate, the discourse of things. Pamva started selling them. For the longest time, he was able to live well on that, traveling the world over.

Now, in the empty room, there was only an enormous open grand piano and a strange bed that Pamva himself contrived and built. A few pieces of graphic art and leaves from the herbarium remained on the white walls. He saved the photographs the longest, but, when he found some long wooden chests with glass negatives, he burned all the photographs. The negatives stood on a narrow shelf that delicately crossed the entire length of one wall. All the clothes fit on a wall hanger with lots of hooks fitted between the double doors to the balcony. Lots of unnecessary books still remained packed into trunks in the hallway, and a large credenza with windows and numerous compartments that held all the dishes and all the provisions stood in the kitchen along with a large table.

As for the bed, technically speaking there wasn't one. There was a large box taller than Pamva but without a lid, and, instead of a bottom, mattresses, blankets, and pillows were laid out. The box, or rather pen, was constructed from boards. There were small shelves on the interior side of the pen where Pamva kept his cigarettes, ashtray, a few bottles of alcohol, the most necessary medicines, some magazines, a collection of knives (the knives, just like the pencils in the pitchers on the piano, had been collected recently, Pamva had found all of them himself), music notebooks, wallets (really they were just old jars of Dutch tobacco) with money, paper cards with handwritten registers of the negatives in the chests. In order to get into bed, he had to climb up one ladder to the top of the pen and climb down another.

It was growing light out. In the hallway, Pamva selected the books that had been ordered for today. He was glad to get rid of them—twelve volumes at once, a whole collection of Balzac. Pamva was a masseur. He had irreproachable hands for this—strong, nimble, and large. For many years, he was the best (or at least the most popular) masseur in the city. At first, he worked with a ballet troupe at the theater. He got to know the bohemians and went on their tours. When he went out walking, he always ran into women he had massaged. Later he was invited to the circus. This was perhaps the most interesting period of his life. Besides, he was still very young. When his fingers began to find other diversions—rock climbing, pottery (his hands remembered a few hundred female bodies, each with its inimitable subtleties of surface, and he molded reliefs, fragments of the microscopic geographies of bodies, then folded them into hollow tubes with strange topological formations resulting; they were only comprehensible when you took them in your hands—your skin recognized and followed the folds and bends), now the soloristics of the piano—it turned out that Pamva's hands had thought up a biography for him—he stopped having enough time for his regular work, so Pamva switched to private practice. He did two or three sessions a day, always going to the patient's home, trying to select those who needed long courses of treatment. Still, he had free access to the theater bar and got invitations to the performances when he ran into dancers. Sometimes, he went to the theater, but only for rehearsals.

 Pamva tied all of the Balzac novels he could find up into two tall stacks, put on his shoes, which had warmed up a bit near the stove, took a massive swig of cognac from the bottle, and went outside, holding it in his mouth. If not for the yellow leaves, the morning could have been taken for early spring—that's what the sky, air, and wind were like. There wasn't anyone on the streets. Pamva wanted to make it to the bus stop without swallowing and smoke a cigarette there, but the tram peeked out from over the hill and he had to run to catch it. He had to get to the professor's by nine to give her a massage before bed. She read all night and slept a little in the morning. Pamva had been going to see her once a week for many years. At first, he accepted her money, but, in time, he stopped. Now he was even bringing her books. The professor read a lot, sometimes rereading the same thing several times. What Pamva brought her was not enough; he often saw her through the glass of the bookstore—she would stand on a ladder selecting books from the upper shelves of the stacks. A few days later, she would sell back everything she had bought to that same bookstore, always losing money on the commissions. Pamva asked her to sell his books, too. The few times she tried to give him the money Pamva didn't take it, so then the professor started baking something for his visits, usually *tsvibak* fruit cake.

The street was empty, and the tram approached so fast it was rocking from side to side. It blew the leaves off the rails. The rays of sunlight were filled with dust. Pamva didn't know if he should swallow the cognac and smoke when the roof of his mouth stopped burning, or hold it in for a few stops. For now, he didn't swallow. Balzac reminded him of his childhood, summer, the hot floorboards of the porch—these were some of his first books. Now he tried to select novels for the professor such that she repeated, even belatedly, his reading history. The concordance with the seasons of the year, phenology had special significance.

He had to go to the old center. The fall, the cold, the emptiness suited well the quick pace of the tram along the narrow, empty streets with their myriad turns. There were a few people inside the tram, and it smelled like soap, eaux de toilette, and perfumes not effaced by other smells.

Pamva crossed through the small stone courtyard covered by glass three stories up and got to a Secession entryway with stained-glass windows. There was also glass up above the stairs and people kept flower boxes along the stairs. On the professor's floor, he could hear a radio playing the pope's mass from the Vatican. Pamva entered the apartment, went down the hallway to the matte glass door, and peeked in the room—the professor was sitting near the large tube receiver attending the mass. Pamva really liked that the names of cities were written on the dial. He went into the kitchen to wait for the end of the broadcast.

Before anything else, he swallowed the cognac and lit his cigarette, flicking the ashes into the porcelain ashtray, in the middle of which was a special stand that held a box of long, thick matches such that they were halfway exposed. For breakfast, he had tsvibak with coffee from the coffeepot wrapped in a shawl. He took a few small bottles with various homemade liqueurs out of the credenza, set them up in a row, and drank them in turn from a small goblet. This was their arrangement—Pamva had to eat breakfast. Then he lit another cigarette and decided to roll some very long and slender pakhitoska corn-husk cigarettes, sprinkling ground mugwort leaves on the paper.

It was good that the professor was old and withered. Lately, Pamva hadn't wanted to massage young women. There were two reasons for this: when giving the massage, he had to keep himself from being overtaken by the beauty of the body, from imbuing his movements with the slightest hint of a caress, and, when he really was with a woman, he was careful not to use massage techniques that might either ruthlessly or indifferently bring her to instantaneous orgasm or utterly soothe, anesthetize, or put her to sleep.

The room smelled annoyingly like mugwort smoke—Pamva singed her sore spots with the pakhitoskas, this belonged to the highest form of art. Before that, the whole time he was delicately massaging her with his hands, a young cat sat nearby, following his fingers and jumping on his hands from time to time. The professor got helplessly angry, but Pamva was not bothered. He liked listening to the old woman tell him about the books she'd read, not forcing Pamva to talk, from which he suffered incredibly with most of his patients. After the massage, she had to lie for a bit. During that time, Pamva always sat at the piano. A piano like that one could have perhaps interested only Pamva—it was completely out of tune, the top was covered in books, and the inside filled with jars of jelly. Moreover, there were cracks that ran the length of the entire body. A significant portion of the keys sank in and needed to be lifted manually. Behind the board, the aperture for the keys was stuffed with basil to keep the moths out. Pamva repeated on the piano all the same manipulations that he had just finished on the old woman's body. This was extraordinarily easy, for they were similar: the piano rang awfully, the basil stalks and jars muffled every sound as though the left pedal were depressed, Pamva didn't extricate the keys that stuck with the first hit, and the sounds it was possible to make with the keys were ever fewer.

Meanwhile, the professor had packed up a slice of tsvibak in a napkin and put it and a small bottle of cherry liqueur, vyshnivka, in the pocket of Pamva's winter coat. For the next time, she requested something of Márquez's (which came, in Pamva's history, at the end of March, the forest is wet, water cannot seep through the layers of endless fallen leaves, the sky is very blue, the sun comes through the smooth branches of the still bare trees, there are leaves only on a few bushes, a defunct railroad in the middle of the forest on a shriveled embankment, the rails and ties are warmed, thousands of deliriously amorous pairs of frogs, all dreadfully shrieking), but Pamva recommended instead she reread Bachmann's stories; he'd bring them.

Outside, it no longer smelled of coal smoke and sulfur from the train station—this meant the weather would clear up for good, it would not rain. It was still late morning, but the sun was shining so intensely that there was no shady side of the narrow streets. Absolutely, totally shadeless illumination. Behind closed eyelids, there was also only a flat, unmarked orange field, with no artifacts. His feet were cold, the wind hugged the earth and blew straight through all the holes in his shoes. Pamva entered a small coffee shop in the large square; you could tell it used to be an apartment, there were three rooms and in each one a tiled stove, the windows were just as they had been in the apartment—small and with double frames.

They met there every Sunday—exactly when no one else was there yet. Pamva arrived and allowed himself to light the stove that they sat next to. They drank strong coffee with a spoonful of vodka tipped into each cup.

Their cameraman was a water truck driver. He could only borrow the camera for a few days, so each film had to be thoroughly thought through in advance and shot in one take without mistakes or corrections. Soon, it would be winter, the streets would not be watered, and he would drive a truck that swept and collected snow.

The chess player was an actor and a sound engineer, but they didn't make any films with live or even spoken sound. He only recorded Pamva's music on a tape player and later layered it onto the film.

The gallerist set the light; in exceptional cases, he did necessary set design and make-up. He sold paintings in a private gallery, knew all the artists and photographers, and sometimes invited them for consultations. His state constantly depended on the paintings among which he was forced to live.

Pamva, too, was an actor, but he also did the music: the ideas, scripts, and direction they either came up with all together or by taking turns. Pamva felt he was beginning to lose them. They had been making amateur films on an 8-mm camera for many years. They never showed them anywhere other than in their closest circle. Then they met Pamva. At first, he only acted in various roles for them and thought up the music; this was the best. Later he started to feel the need to make his own films, but they didn't always understand him.

Pamva rarely worried about something as much as he had lately about Saint Francis. All these feelings of poverty, the joy of renouncing one thing and instead accepting something else, the creation of a complex codex and ritual that still made life simple if you believed in them, the physiology of bare feet, clothes with holes, unfussy food, irresponsible wanderings, and the self-certainty of prayer. The mechanics of an accessible ecstasy. It seemed to Pamva that this was that level of the absurd where it became as natural as rain, snow, and the whole world. The absurd as traces of unattainable thinking. He persuaded everyone that they needed to learn about Francis, he himself felt like Francis, and gradually made a Francis out of everyone. But then he set himself to abandoning filmmaking and scriptwriting, he would just deliver the piece and do everything that they said in those fragments and where they said it. He never thought that he could agree in advance to the cruelest of losses. Ultimately, there was no end in sight. The last thing you can lose is the ability to lose, and that would lead to an achievement that you could again lose. Pamva even supposed that really nothing would happen, not on the surface, not below—for the loss itself he had already experienced a few times in his mind.

They started to undress. Everyone had brought some clothes for the film, and they had to change and take pictures to see how it looked. It was cold. The driver, naked to the waist, brought four glasses of vodka right away, they drank them and felt nothing—the ecstasy had begun. Pamva said that Franciscanness was not when the naked man wasn't cold, but when, already freezing, you undress. Their clothes remained on the chairs. They went outside, the sun had already warmed things up a bit. They stood in front of the door: Pamva in shoes with no socks, ragged pants, and a raincoat with nothing underneath; the gallerist was barefoot, wearing only a long baggy sweater; the chess player was also barefoot, he had white canvas pants rolled up, a few shirts, all on top of each other, fingerless gloves, a scarf tied around his head. They stood like that for a bit—they smoked, said hi to their friends, stepping aside from the door for them, looked at themselves in the glass, moved weirdly, observing their shadows—they needed to get good and frozen. Finally the driver started shooting: one at a time, in twos, all together, faces, from behind, from the side, from a distance, from the other side of the square. Pamva asked him not to shoot the shadows and reflections. Finally, they ran out of film. They went to the stove, got dressed, wiped their dirty feet, drank Pamva's vyshnivka straight from the bottle. Now it was good, like before.

Taking their leave, they drank more vodka (tomorrow Pamva would bring the piece, the driver would develop the photos and get the camera, the gallerist would borrow the necessary lights from the gallery, the chess player would calculate the time for each fragment and outline the sequence of scenes; the day after tomorrow, they would go before morning in the water truck to the lake in the forest, and, in two or three hours, they would all need to return to the city). Pamva left with the chess player, he still had a little time.

The chess player made his living playing chess for money in the square, which is why he was called the chess player. He had a very showy style of play, and he always garnered the most spectators. From the very first move, he did everything he could to create as many dangerous, unsolvable positions on the board as possible. He moved his pieces almost up to his opponent's, put the majority of them on the squares where they could be struck, yet he protected them with others, usually one piece insured several squares at once, in this way, he simultaneously stockpiled a few dozen fraught moments, achieving a certain stasis, not taking anything, even when it was necessary. Finally, the possibilities of the chessboard would be exhausted. Then a continuous chain of taking turns capturing pieces would begin, without stopping until they each had only two left. And, in these situations, the chess player could play so safely and reliably that he never lost.

They were already waiting for him in the square, the spectators started getting their money out. Pamva wanted to watch a little, but it turned out that, due to his agitation, cold, and fast drinking, he was so drunk he couldn't focus. He sat on the neighboring bench, but, again, this wasn't good: he couldn't sit, couldn't rest his elbows on his knees or lean his back against the bench. He walked up slowly along the alley, lots of small, sharp red stones made their way through the holes in his shoes, and Pamva stepped off the path, kicking up bunches of leaves, sometimes forcing his way through some bushes, through entire swaths of junipers and yews, almost like in the mountains. Ravens simply stepped aside, a few held nuts in their beaks.

Pamva walked through the whole park—which seemed small, but it went uphill—he went into a hotel bar and ordered a double bitter coffee (the hotel and the bar were very expensive, so Pamva asked for a drop of cold milk to stretch his coffee) and took the cup outside. He sat on a low fence holding a cigarette in his lips, waiting for someone to get a light from—because, although he had matches, he didn't feel like looking for them, then lighting one and shielding the flame from the wind. He knew a good way to warm up—you had to hold your cup not with your hands, for then only your hands got warm, but squeeze it between your knees. He was finally able to get a light and heard, when he asked for it, that his own voice had changed, due to the challenges of articulation. He drank so slowly that the flavor of the coffee and milk changed a couple times as it cooled.

Right behind the hotel there was a small bazaar. Pamva suddenly had an unbearable desire for ham. He bought a little from a butcher. Pamva loved the stalls of the winter bazaar when there was very little of everything, but everything was strangely high-quality and mythological. It was crowded near a separate row, chimerical smoke constructions drifted out—they were selling tobacco. Pamva had fun trying the hand-rolleds with different types of tobacco, inquiring as to their provenance, feeling the note paper with his fingers. He liked the archaism of the situation: lots of men smoked very seriously, attending to their own impressions and watching for the slightest changes in others'. Maybe because the tobaccos reminded him of the flavor of Gitanes Caporal, or maybe because it was important to feel like he was one of those people, but, without thinking or considering it, Pamva bought a glass of each of the various tobaccos, pouring them all into a single bag. He suspected that he could assemble a genuine Gitane at home.

When Pamva returned, four figures remained on the chess player's board. Pamva sat on the bench to the side. It was turned to face the park. There was no one in his field of vision. The sun was warming him through his broadcloth. These last days of fall, Pamva did not want to move or exert himself, it seemed most correct to sit without moving, warming in the rays, absorbing warmth for winter. Pamva squinted his eyes and turned his face to the sun. He left a narrow slit underneath his eyelids so he could only see a squashed fragment of the sun wrapped in threads of light, tangled in a bright spider web from within. It seemed to Pamva, or so he imagined, that he was on the bottom of a viscous, supersaturated solution of fall in an incredibly tall, clear glass. The trees were outside the glass, the top of the glass ended in the sky, and at the bottom were Pamva and the sediment of leaves.

Sounds are also necessary to synchronize the flow of time with the course of the vision. It was almost as quiet at the bottom of the glass as in a canyon. Pamva could not even totally hear his own voice when he started to say something to the chess player. He had won a lot of money and wanted to treat Pamva to a beer. Pamva noticed that even what he was thinking yet not saying sounded somewhat distorted. Two dogs were sitting on the bench—small, very intelligent, they cuddled up to Pamva yet did not lie down, but sat like people, one of them had no fur on its head, only eyebrows and a bit around the eyes, its skin was dry and smooth and gathered in supple folds at its nape. The dogs came from who knows where, asked for nothing, just waited calmly until they were given what smelled so good in his pocket. Pamva fed the dogs his ham and left with the chess player. The dogs did not run after them but stayed sitting on the bench.

It seemed to Pamva that the chess player was singlemindedly accomplishing something that Pamva did not know about, and he could barely keep up with him. The sounds either lagged behind or were ahead of what they were supposed to belong to, therefore, what the sounds were supposed to belong to yet followed or preceded was either slowly drawn out or quickly compressed: still in the park, he hit his head against a branch, but there weren't any branches to be seen, and anyway he had bent over, so what could he have caught himself on and where could that package of tobaccos have gone if the chess player hadn't picked it up; or where they drank their beer and the sun had so distorted his vision through ordinary glass that, from the outside, the inside looked like a terrarium with different creatures and interior illumination (and, from the inside, as though you're sitting near a window in a basement with the sun in the west and you can only see the people who are closest but then upside down, or in a Sunday tram that's going from cemetery to cemetery past Pamva's building but with such a concentrated smell of chrysanthemums that it would be nauseating if it were any other smell than chrysanthemums).

Pamva had to meet Anna a little past nine; he was home by four and felt totally fine. He again did not go to the gallery (he had to check out the new lamps), he didn't need to make soup. However, he sat down to sort through the beans. He had before his eyes the hallucinogenically colored irregular spheres of beans that overwhelmed any background for so long that, for some time afterwards, his eyes saw only hallucinogenic beans against the background of which everything was crawling.

Obviously, sorting things with your fingers organizes your thinking in a sort of a meditative way—rosaries, spinning cylinders with text, a well-tempered clavier. When your fingers automatically do something well, then you can think about what you can't think about when thinking about what your fingers are doing. Pamva thought about Anna.

Anna wasn't coming for long. Since neither he nor she could imagine love in her city, she would either come for a short while or they would go somewhere together.

Anna was much younger than Pamva and looked younger yet. They met when she was a student at the university. She was already married and knew that she would never live with Pamva, but she could not live entirely without him. It seemed to him that her love had some sort of typological character—she loved not Pamva himself but the aesthetics of his type: his type of body, type of thinking, type of face, even his type of biography and experience, his type of aesthetics of life. And he felt incredible tenderness, which grew into constant fear for her and a premature readiness to cut down anyone who ever gave cause. For a very long time, Pamva was tormented by the uncertainty of their status, it was important to him to see her every day during the day, however, she herself gradually turned everything in the other direction, she insisted on bodily compensation, wanted his body. Everything is in the transcription of corporeal love. To express everything through the rhetoric of the body. Ultimately, this approach proved rational and psychotherapeutic, for the form of their relations took on self-sufficiency. Beyond that, she did not exist beyond Pamva. And not only because she had never had a better or more suitable man; above all she made Pamva her hero, her object, the subject of her research and contemplations. It was strange that Anna was a philosopher, stranger yet that she worked as a philosopher at the center for postmodern studies. She worked on the problems of the body and the text, the textuality of the body, and the corporeality of texts, she wrote a book on Pamva's music (soloristics: making sound for the sake of movement), and Pamva was her only access to primary experience. Maybe he was also a text in a philosophical sense, but, in Anna's life, only Pamva existed as an unwritten and unread subject for philosophizing. Sometimes, Pamva thought that he could stop caring how to live, for there were books that took upon themselves all his responsibilities.

Pamva set the beans aside when it started getting dark in the kitchen. He had just undressed. He could not remember—did he really force his way to the old, battered piano in the restaurant with the beer, pushing out the piano man, or was it a nightmare? (He even tried to drink in places where there was at least one instrument, because he sometimes reached a state wherein it was physically impossible not to play, but just as often Pamva dreamed that he was playing something of his own on a piano in an unfamiliar place, and he was touching that piano for the first time, at the same time, it was always understood that some additional feeling of presence was present.) Yet, he was sure that Anna was the only woman in his life with whom he could not philosophize.

Pamva carried the beans into the laboratory. The laboratory was in the other room (the other room was a laboratory). All the beans were kept on the floor near the window. The window could be made completely dark. Pamva took a spade and shoveled two full buckets of sand from the crate that stood in the middle of the room. In recent weeks, the "laboratory" that was recorded in his register of tasks meant picking over a few more beans, adding them to the ones that were drying, taking two buckets of sand out to the trash bin in the yard. He poured the sand into a separate pile, maybe someone could use it. The wind picked up and blew scraps of some paper into Pamva's pile, Pamva buried them with the sand from the bucket. Here and there in the pile there were miniature houses, bridges from toy train sets, juniper twigs that looked like shrunken trees. For the longest time he was building a model canyon in the crate. The laboratory existed to discover light. Pamva had once realized that his dreams wouldn't be as strong as they were if not for the light. He wanted to recreate it and make an ordinary but very high-quality filmstrip about the canyon. In the middle of the empty room, he set up a crate of sand, molded a riverbed, banks, built up all the details of the landscape, and added water. He had three cameras. One he affixed to a movable boom up above, the second set up on a tripod, and the third he held as he moved around the maquette. He tried all possible ways—through a thick layer of multicolored solutions, with a diverse combination of lamps, through different plants, painted sheets of paper, steam, glass, smoke, and muslin, too.

It resulted in very pretty slides, but there was no feeling of presence. Once, he had meditated on the different women he'd been with. They appeared in strange forms. One only as a reflection in moving water; another had a flickering line of fire rather than the contours of her figure; yet another disappeared right at the moment of the flash from the spark of the lighter without gas; and the last one existed very close but was pressed up against some fabric from one side, and he was a step away from her on the other. Despite all this, Pamva knew that they were present, and he was near essence, and that the unusual manifestations came from perception. But the photos of the canyon made with the maquette were alien. It had no canyonness, and he was not in the canyon as it had been. Pamva let the water out of the crate and began carrying the sand out. Very little still remained. It was better not to try overly hard to be present. It was better to wait until it will again happen for real. It was better to experience those things by living through them. And every living-through would appear as though nothing happened between it and the previous one. That was possible. And, in the disassembled laboratory, he could grow hyacinths and crocuses, or even Moroccan marijuana (the trash bins stood in the middle of a yard confined by very pretty, long, two-story buildings with uninterrupted balconies and gutters that went straight into the underground sewers, iron steps at different levels; every evening a different combination of windows glowed, lighting up a different territory each time; Pamva always spent at least a few minutes there).

Very little time remained until Anna's arrival. Pamva wanted to bathe. The water took a long time to warm up, not only because the gas flow was weak because everyone had started running their furnaces, but, above all, because the river was already extraordinarily cold. He took a bottle of rum into the bathroom. Rum anesthetized him before Anna's arrivals.

Pamva had not started to wash himself, just warmed up in the water when the telephone rang. He had to walk naked through the entire apartment. They said that he had to report for night duty that evening—Pamva worked as a nurse on the staff of the ambulance cardiology team. He was overheated and frozen, on top of which he got worked up and started to shake so violently that his muscles hurt from the trembling. He had to lie in the tub for a bit longer, but at the end rinsed himself with cold water.

Pamva sat at the kitchen table. All the doors of the credenza were open; from time to time, he would get up, take something out, and sit back down at the table. Pamva loved unexpected calls. First of all, because more than anything he valued overexertion; moreover, it was always interesting. Pamva even liked the rhythm of a very clear, thought-out, consistent assemblage. He drank some terribly strong coffee, ate a spoonful of honey, swallowed four aspirins, and dissolved some glucose and ascorbic acid in a glass of water, squeezed the juice of two grapefruit, supplemented a small bottle of eleuthero with some cognac and drank it all at once. Finally, he brewed some strong tea and lit up a cigarette. But he couldn't sit. He left his burning cigarette and went to get dressed. Then he grabbed the tape player, a fresh tape, the microphone, and took it into the kitchen. The cigarette had almost completely burned down; Pamva lit another one off it. He was wearing pants, shoes, and an undershirt; his suspenders hung off to the sides. He rubbed some rum into his forehead and a lotion with aloe into his hands. He got the tape player ready to record, threw his heavy winter coat onto his shoulders; meanwhile, the second cigarette was now smoldering.

This time he was forced to light a match, and he started talking. He wanted to say that sometimes everything comes apart, unravels, loses its direction but masters surfaces and planes, that there exists destruction that denies the possibility of a purity of style, ruins rhetorical constructions, and calls into question logocentrism, the acknowledgement of destruction returns the freedom to not choose, and you can, therefore, be among everything and with everyone, this is not rhetoric, but linguistics, because chaos defends against inevitability, otherwise you come to terms with the fact that everything hinges on women who experience orgasm.

Pamva spoke a little about those days. About the fact that, sometimes, you live as though you are masking one flavor with another, but that's not the one you need either, then something else, also bad, further on it's a bit better, you need to just adjust it a bit and eventually it's no good at all. Especially for Anna, he emphasized that the text of a story about the day had to depend on the day—on the rhythm, saturation, density, mood, and force of pressure. It is precisely there that he stopped liking what he had said, he spoke a bit more, but then rewound it to the beginning and erased everything he had recorded. He wanted to try again. Ultimately, you sometimes have to say what you understand. The most important thing—Pamva immediately tried formulating an imperative—was to know and to make known what you understand. When they were together, there was no suitable moment, and now there was no Anna, and it seemed unnecessary to do this without her, even if it was for her.

Pamva was pleased to anticipate what would happen. He could easily imagine how Anna would show up, how she would be moving when no one else was around, she would eat the dinner he prepared, drink something, listen to his voice, maybe go out on the balcony, climb into bed, she would wait, fall asleep, so night would pass faster. And Pamva also knew, besides this, that he'd be able to come for a minute in the middle of the night, he just didn't know how. This confidence in the nearly impossible felt especially acute. He switched to the radio and whirled through different spaces of the ether. He suddenly noticed that the frequency dial was a strong source of light. Leonard Cohen was singing in some city; Pamva made his tape player record this off the radio. The challenges were great, but the song was nearly complete. Pamva again rewound it to the beginning, listened to Cohen, and realized that he would leave him for Anna. There was very little time left. He quickly recited his favorite Brodsky poems into the microphone, struggling to pronounce the Russian words. The tape recorded how Pamva took a drag on his cigarette and how he blew out the smoke.

 He quickly took off his coat, put on a few sweaters, pulled up the suspenders and put the coat back on. He swallowed two tablets of nitroglycerin and went out to the stairs, tucking the key into their hiding place. In the long hallway, on the first floor between the stairs and the gate, the wind swept up the hard, dry leaves. They continued moving and scratching the concrete floor loudly like the claws of small beasts. The whole yard was filled with the moon. A frost had begun and it seemed that the moonlight was its cause. There were no clouds around the moon, but when Pamva walked quickly through the yard raising his face to the sky, something moved—either the moon itself or the most illuminated fragment of sky. The bigger puddles looked warm, while the smaller ones had transformed into ice all the way to the bottom. And only where a leaf lay was the water preserved.

 Pamva knew how to get to the hospital without taking the streets, by only going through yards. Intense tachycardia—the result of sleeplessness and all the stimulants—interfered with his breathing. He felt a tickle coming from his adrenal glands—full of adrenaline and all sorts of other hormones—and spreading across his back as though his blood vessels were occupied by various insects; it was difficult to bear. His body was hypertonic—every movement was made to expend as much energy as possible; it was all Pamva could do not to perform a somersault.

Some people were sitting under a gazebo in one of the yards, Pamva saw the fires of three cigarettes. People knew him in this neighborhood; moreover, he was older, so he felt no danger. He had gone quite a ways from the gazebo when he heard someone running behind him. Pamva turned around and saw a big dog charging along the alleyway straight for him. Pamva took a few steps forward, heavily stomping his feet and growling like an animal; he stuck out his arms. The dog stopped but did not retreat and still had not called off its attack. Pamva had to stare at it continuously and keep his body tense. He slowly withdrew step by step and the dog followed, just as tensely and slowly, waiting for him to turn even slightly away so it could attack. Pamva felt a greater stirring inside than from the nitroglycerin. They took approximately ten steps like that and apparently crossed some boundary, for the dog suddenly relaxed, shook itself, wagged its tail, and lost all interest in Pamva. Pamva took a few more steps backward, and then nearly fell when he turned around because his feet got tangled.

He had so obviously grown weak that he felt how difficult it was to execute each subsequent phase of a single step, stretched out in time. All of his adrenaline had rushed out and dispersed. Pamva sat down and waited out the most intense weakness. Then he moved off in the direction of the hospital, having lost the spatial sensation of the shape of his own body. His eyes were closing, he thought about smoking but he couldn't do it and didn't want to. He imagined down to the smallest tropisms what it's like to lie down and know you can't fall asleep.

Pamva briefly said hello to his team and told them where to find him, and then went to their car. He crawled inside, lay on the stretcher, tucked his face into his coat, covered himself with a blanket and fell asleep. He dreamed of a rock far out in the sea; it was clear that this was the southern European Atlantic; the whole rock, the whole mountain was totally covered in vases—smallish flower pots—with rare African plants not usually cultivated, all the plants were in bloom. Pamva flew high above the rock, somewhere around the height of two of him, but it was like he was skating, standing vertically on his feet, yet maintaining his balance—like going down from the hills on ice skates. However, he could not fly where he wanted, rather moved with some current—obviously what they call an airstream. Most captivating was the fact that Pamva was at the bottom of the stream (but not bound by anything firm), and, above him, somewhere right beneath the surface, almost motionless colored fish swam by one after another. The surface of the stream was set off against the bottom of the sky by its blackness.

They woke Pamva at the gate to a one-story villa that had only in recent years been subdivided into a few apartments. The former galleries were glassed in and served as pantries and closets. This one stood out from an entire row of other villas by the fact that there were lights on in all its windows. The gardens behind each of them went down to the river. This was the edge of the city. A few police patrols stood near the gate, they were smoking and sharing all the details of what was happening. Pamva didn't want to know anything. He grabbed the stretcher and took the path through the orchard to the porch. The smell of leaves, the thickets of the orchard, the feeling of the river, the separation from the lights of the city, the men near the entry, the spirit of overturned earth—all of this gave the impression of a village in the plains.

The door was wide open, so from the porch he could smell the somewhat sour odor of the home, and, in the bedroom, the stream of cold, acerbic air from the yard was most striking. The man lay not far from the door, he hadn't even been moved to a bed. There were a few holes in his thick, black sweater, but the blood did not pour out, rather it gathered in the structures of the sweater, it crawled across the whole front so that it didn't even look like a stain—it could have been the shade of the wool.

But the sweater was wet and cold to the touch. Pamva felt so helpless he almost cried; he was conscious of his presence there, but it was like none of it had happened. He knew these hands and this mouth well; they had often performed CPR and intravenous injections—the man got ill in certain weather, usually at the end of the night. He had just had a complicated heart operation; many times they had sat in this room until morning, not daring to leave him without supervision. Pamva did not want to know what had happened, he felt sorry and desperate—not one of the efforts invested into this life had anticipated such an end, all their pains turned out to be not futile, but ineffectual. And the worst was that making an effort meant being or becoming defenseless.

One of the patrollers and a young woman—obviously a relative, but Pamva had never seen her—also got in the car. They slowly pulled away from the unlit and sporadically pitted streets along the river. Pamva had to sit on the floor. He saw headlights through the rear window and soon the silhouette of the water truck on the bank. Pamva asked them to stop the ambulance, he jumped out onto the road after telling the doctor he'd be at their station in an hour—he wouldn't be needed for that hour anyway—and ran to the river, to the water truck. At first, he took the street, but then he went along the broad, even, stony bank. Running, he felt lots of chestnuts in his pocket—all day he had been collecting chestnuts in different places for some reason—now they were falling out on the stones. The water truck driver was pumping water from the river. In the spot where the hose entered the river, the water was clear gray, for that's where the shadow of the cistern ended and a long band illuminated by the moon began. Pamva climbed in the cab and the driver poured him some coffee from his thermos. The coffee was permeated with the taste of the cork.

They went in the direction of Pamva's building. Pamva always took a few cassette tapes when he was on duty in order to listen to music with the driver of their team while waiting for calls. Now he took one out and put it in the tape player. Cohen started singing immediately—this was the cassette he meant to leave for Anna where the key was. Pamva wanted to swap it out for another, but the driver caught his arm, and they listened to the entire cycle of the epistles to Postumus.

The light was on in Pamva's windows. Lighted from inside, the balcony looked like a fragment of a stage prepared for a performance. Pamva went home and the water truck drove on very slowly, barely moistening the piles of leaves—if it had gotten the road wet, it would have turned into ice. The apartment was quiet. The light was turned on only in the bed; Anna's things were in the kitchen, some dirty cups were still out—Anna always drank her next cup of coffee or tea from a fresh cup and lined them up on the table in front of her. Pamva stood on the ladder and looked in at the bed. Anna was sleeping. She was almost covered, but she was completely naked. Pamva barely forced himself not to undress and lie down next to her for at least a few minutes. He was sure that then he would not get up, trying through his strange half-sleep to keep track of two things: if Anna was there and if it was time to get up.

Pamva turned off the lamp, set the cassette recording on the pillow, went out onto the balcony, and lit a whole newspaper on fire. The fire unexpectedly generated a lot of light—Pamva could no longer see anything outside the illumination; he imagined how strange that spot must look from far away, when the individual buildings aren't visible, nor the balconies, nor the windows, and it becomes impossible to connect the fire with any concrete structures. The water truck pulled up directly under the balcony, Pamva lowered himself a little on the grapevine and then jumped on the tank. They got to the hospital really fast. They only had to stop once because a big pack of dogs was running down the street.

At home, Pamva had grabbed a lot of walnuts, so he could keep his team busy with something and not have to talk, play chess or cards. But they had not yet returned. In the meantime, the telephone operator took a call, Pamva took the address and went all the way to the gate, worrying that minutes were passing. He wanted to be with Anna now. But in her. Feeling the presence of only his self that is in Anna, the self that perceives her from inside, and only of that Anna who is inside, whom he feels from the inside, discarding all else. He wanted to experience the topography, not the shifting, monotonous touch, not some climax.

Anna never acknowledged this. She silently demanded an overfilling that would have bordered on overuse. She drew complex maps on her body in different colored inks, which Pamva was supposed to traverse across her skin; she stretched out on the piano, feeling the vibrations in her internal organs, especially the lower octaves; she slowly attacked Pamva who wielded the stick, and he was forced to equally slowly defend himself, thinking up some strange plastics around the stick; sometimes, they hung from monkey bars and had to manage without using their arms or other support; she took kittens to bed, rubbed valerian drops all over herself, and wasn't at all embarrassed that there were so many of them all together; once she brought an enormous armful of very fragrant flowers, set them all out everywhere, stuffed them in the pillows—that was really extraordinarily good—but it was just by chance they did not die. Pamva remembered his unwritten piece. He thought if he could squeeze in next to Anna at the piano and not restrain her but restrain his own sounds, then he would hear a truly soloristic concert (he, however, could not provoke Anna to such a thing, knowing that she would purposefully listen).

The car finally came. Ten minutes had already passed. Pamva did not even let the car come to a stop—he opened the door and jumped in while the car was still moving.

Everyone was very tired, but Pamva gave them the address with the kind of intonation that allowed for no hesitation.

II

Pamva never knew that there could be so many sounds in a nighttime apartment similar to the crying of a child.

Pamva looked out the kitchen window onto part of the cemetery and a fragment of the botanical garden (he wanted to go there on November 1 when candles were lit all over the cemetery), it started getting light out, the enormous greenhouses looked like monstrous beasts that slept standing on the lawn.

Pamva saw a plate with used syringes on the table before him, in each one there was a little blood—they had given the woman a few intravenous injections; it's a good thing she left the door open.

Pamva didn't go to the ICU where they took the woman because there was a small child sleeping in the bedroom.

Pamva noticed a small, genuine pump organ next to the child's bed, he couldn't wait for morning when he could play it, though he was terribly afraid of the moment when the child would wake up.

Pamva did not know how to behave with children, did not know how long to stay, did not know if he should call Anna over or take the child home.

Searching for a mug in the credenza, Pamva found a few ampules of ketamine, then he dumped everything out of the trash can and discovered a disposable syringe—the woman could come back completely different; it was unlikely she would stay in the ICU long.

Pamva decided to record the start of the piece, but, from time to time, he'd fall asleep for a few seconds, long enough that he dreamed a few images, a few lines drifted out, and awkward locutions settled into the text.

Pamva eventually decided not to write anything—he would play the piece on the pump organ, bring the tape recorder, and right away set down the music for the film playing just how he wanted to at that moment.

Pamva knew that the music that he wanted would only be a trace of someone's idea that Pamva was not capable of comprehending; how to be with the instrument would depend on him: would he play with one hand or tie his wrists together, or stretch out the fingers of one hand on the keyboard with the other, or get good and drunk throughout the performance, or spread flowers out on the keyboard, or hit the keys with his fist or forehead, or spin on his head, or cut his fingers and bleed, or bandage his wounded fingertips, or put on gloves, or fill the innards of the pump organ with walnuts, or fall asleep, or lie down on the floor and reach for the instrument, or close his eyes, or turn off the lights, or climb onto the pump organ and play it with his toes, and then slide off and maybe hit the pedals over and over without touching the keys, maybe hold one note, maybe sing along to some other melodies, maybe not play at all, but look for something on the receiver or do absolutely nothing at all, just be.

Pamva thought he heard someone playing the pump organ just the way he'd imagined. He darted to the room—everything was quiet, the child still slept.

Pamva guessed that he had half an hour before he woke up.

Pamva felt a sweater on the railing of the crib and took it into the kitchen because he was a little cold; it was a coarse burgundy woman's sweater with buttons—large, wooden, worn smooth from touches—it was clear that the buttons were made from a very soft wood, they were probably much older than the sweater.

Pamva had to eat something because his stomach started grumbling, he looked in the fridge—a little cheese, a bottle of milk, a bottle of mineral water, butter, a piece of boiled meat, honey in a jar, some leftover vodka, lemons—he'd give the child the cheese and milk for breakfast; he ate the meat and two large spoonfuls of honey.

Pamva wanted to mix the vodka with the mineral water and add some lemon juice, he grabbed the water but it turned out that his hand had fallen asleep and he couldn't hold the bottle and it broke (Pamva could not figure out whether it was due to his heart, though his heart felt fine, or if he had pinned his arm when he fell asleep sitting up).

Instead, Pamva brewed tea and poured ample vodka into the hot liquid in the mug.

Pamva imagined he would drink some tea and go to the bedroom, his child would be sleeping there, he'd get in bed trying not to wake his wife—very dear to him but completely unknown (Pamva could not call to mind either her face or her body, obviously it was someone whom he had really never seen), and, in the morning, he would embrace her when it was light in the room but their son still slept.

Pamva went outside so the smoke wouldn't drift into the bedroom, it was time to call Anna (yesterday, Pamva dreamed of spending the whole day with Anna at home, not going anywhere), it was light enough to see through the greenhouses and now it was not they that were the chimeras, but what could be dimly made out inside them.

Pamva understood well that his cigarette would go out any time now, he would go back inside, then Anna would come, and that this state of a few minutes would be extraordinarily unstable, but he still could not convince himself that something else would be different, that this moment would cease stretching out and continuing endlessly, that some of the slightest changes were possible in the world, in him, that the distance would become normal, that it would be far, farther, close and closer, that it would be possible to cover the distances.

Pamva went up the stairs and, for the time, forbade himself from loving the states, from recording them, remembering, systematizing, and above all trying to summon them—he needed to return to the child without getting stuck on anything.

Pamva also thought that when he wrote his piece sometime later, he would end it approximately like this: the performer has no other task than to create a feeling of presence.

FM Galicia

Translated by Mark Andryczyk

THE YEAR 2000

November 18

For a city to be considered a genuine, traditional, European city, two elements are required, which, in fact, define it as a city. A city may lack a sewer system and it will still be a city. But it cannot lack a fortification wall or a tower—two opposing things, whose clandestine duel is the very sign of the existence of a city. The wall is necessary to make the city stand out against a backdrop of fields, to distinguish it from the surrounding area, and thus render it a tangible, noteworthy point on a map; the tower is necessary in order to oppose any forced demarcation of a city. It is essential to look out from a tower beyond the walls and see the neighboring territories and distant landscapes and even more distant horizons. Because it's necessary to know from where the sun appears and to where it disappears to avert the thought that it just turns on and shuts off above one's head at certain times of the day.

For the sun has a tendency to rise and set in beautiful and important places—above the sea, the forest, the mountains, and the rivers. Looking at these places from a tower, city dwellers realize that they, too, could end up over there, that they passed through these walls voluntarily, and that they can, at least occasionally, cross its boundaries.

Ivano-Frankivsk has walls. But it has no tower. That is why each one of us needs to find his own tower from which the mountains can be seen. Because we're not just a ditch lying between two rivers: we are a place, located below the level of nearby mountains. Only if they learn how to grasp the nearness of the mountains, will residents of Ivano-Frankivsk obtain their tower, after which Ivano-Frankivsk will qualify as a city.

Through our urban worldview, the mountains can become streets, courtyards, squares. The mountains don't need us. They are self-sufficient and immaculate. We need them very much. If only as images and as points of orientation. Because, for us, the Carpathian Mountains signify a trip southward, towards warmth and life at its fullest. For us, the Carpathians are something which cannot be captured. They are the knowledge of a safe hiding place, of the most elemental respite, of the ultimate opportunity for escape, should it become necessary. The mountains are that neglected orchard on the edge of our yard. An orchard that we have not tended to for quite some time. But all the trees in that orchard are healthy and fruitful. Its existence comforts any blows. You are aware that it, if necessary, it awaits you and is ready to receive...

November 19

Anyone who has witnessed winter, spring, summer, and fall will never see anything radically new.

The seasons exist in order to never bore us—that is why we forget about them so quickly. Over a certain period of time, the traits of the previous season are erased and the upcoming year's fall will turn out to be as poignant as last year's.

But the seasons require attention. We can't just treat the highly refined changes that occur between the seasons as shifting weather patterns—it became cold, it became wet or otherwise unpleasant in some way.

We act superficially. Even our language demonstrates such inattentiveness. Arabs possess several dozen words that correspond to shades in the color of sand. Just for sand. While Eskimo-Aleut languages have a hundred different words that describe the various states of snow—color, hardness, pliancy. They don't have the word "snow." Their language has equivalents for one word, for example, "morning, shiny snow, which is difficult to walk upon because it is hard on top and deep underneath"—this is all just one word. And this constitutes being attentive to one's surroundings. And when we're trying to be poetic, we say—the leaves have yellowed, the yellow leaves. But can they be so uniform? Can they really just be yellow? And can they be the same yellow when on the tree, when falling, and when on the ground? And, when on the ground, don't they change color depending on whether they lie separately or are gathered in a pile, or whether they have been lying for a few minutes or several days and nights? And what if there has been frost or rain?

And fall is not just defined by the shades of leaves. It has countless other characteristics. The fact that they have been forgotten does not mean that they shouldn't be seen and that we shouldn't try to remember them. There is no truer method for organizing one's everyday life than wisely adhering to phenology—to the flow of changes in the seasons. If you implement this methodology, you needn't worry about your mind—it will be free of confusion. And now everything that you do will contain that special joy of making sense. Food will be better, dreams more interesting, wine more healing. You need to just sense winter, spring, summer, and fall flowing through you.

November 22

For some reason, we do not consider our territory to be a fertile land. Transcarpathia, Moldova, and, perhaps, the Kosiv region—those are the fertile lands, while all we have are potatoes, beans, some squash, and onions. But our region—the Prykarpattia (Ciscarpathia) foothills—is an apple paradise. You won't find such winter apples anywhere else, except, perhaps, somewhere in northern France, but they're hard to find in the winter anyway because the whole harvest is used to make calvados. And we have the most prized Rennet apples, and winter apples can last—if treated with love and care—until summer, without losing their taste or smell, even though they leave a trace of their fragrance in spaces where they have been stored.

In wintertime, mountain orchardists make their way to the stations in snowy hordes, bringing apples to the Ivano-Frankivsk market by train. If one of their sacks should tear along the way, those yellow-red apple billiard balls might use that which they had absorbed from the sun to warm the whole dreary Chervona Ruta train-car, or maybe they'll singe the hopeless frigidity of the snows with their cooled skin.

Sometimes that is exactly what takes place. And then the apples need to be gathered. But once, it so happened, that not one single winter apple that had been spilled along the railroad tracks had been touched by anyone. They just lay there like that and then melted through snow's thickness and eventually seeped into the ground, maybe without even having deteriorated; no one can say for sure because, when the snow thawed, no traces remained. And no one picked up those apples because they spilled from a sack belonging to Mr. Boiko. Mr. Boiko was carrying a sack of red winter apples to the train station. It was still dark and freezing cold. His winter hat was tied tightly, his head bent from the weight sitting on his neck. That is why he didn't hear the train approaching from the rear, and the apples spilled out along the train tracks.

The reason people didn't gather them was not because, in wintertime, there were no flowers to lay at this spot, but because the apples served to remind them how difficult it was to escape one's fate. Because Mr. Boiko had been hit by trains in the past, having gotten his wagon stuck while crossing the tracks. Never had this happened to anyone else. He had always survived, unscathed, while his wagons had been smashed into splinters. For him, trains probably had been like lightning bolts.

I don't know why, but I find this story to be very optimistic. But it also reminds me that you never really know who will end up eating the harvest you have gathered.

November 23

Once the snows came, it became more difficult to determine what this fall had been like. It wasn't until today, upon arriving in the mountains, that I realized that it had been, it seems, a very dry one. Because where there had always been a lot of water, there now was little.

The bucket needed to be lowered to the full length of the chain. And, even then, it barely reached the surface of the water. Whether it was from the wood shavings that had crumbled off the windlass or because of something else inside, the water smelled of wood. It's as if it had been aged for a long time in a vessel made of wood prone to humidity. This is sort of the way that cognac, calvados, and rum are made. The aftertaste of the wood didn't bother me. I wanted to drink as much water as I could from this very well.

If ninety percent of my body is made up of water, then, obviously, the whole state of such a system is dependent on the type of water it is. Even the brain consists mostly of water. This means that thoughts should adjust according to the type and quality of the water.

If that is so, then water needs to be adjusted. It is necessary to squeeze out the dirty water with the clean, as is usually done with a reservoir. There is, however, a complication—if you pour dirty water into clean water, then all of the water becomes dirty, and when you add clean water to dirty water, it nonetheless remains dirty.

(This is one of the life's truths, formulated by my son). But, regardless of this complication, it's worth trying to adjust it, at least partially.

You just have to find a well that is most suitable to you, because drinking the same water as everyone else is dangerous—imagine if everyone were to become identical, the way two buckets of water are. I found my well. Not to get too poetic, but after I drank that water, I truly started to feel different, and this lasted for a long time. Because, if I flood all of my internal pipes with it, then it seems to start becoming me, and I it. And this will keep me going for a while. And then, later, I'll set off once again, from home to the mountains, to my well. Meanwhile, the snow will melt and the water will rise. It will no longer smell like wood. And, by that time, I'll notice whether there have been any changes in me between today and that day.

November 24

When you live in the mountains, firewood becomes an important part of your life, like bread, milk, a bed, a shirt, a warm jacket. Firewood becomes an extension of you—it's as if it's a part of your body. You see condensed warmth in that timber, without which your body ceases to be yours. Upon it, in fact, your existence is dependent. And a pile of logs can be regarded as a peculiar anatomical structure that is part of your organism. That's why you can't even think of treating it as something that is foreign or supernatural; you just want to make sure there's lots of it.

Up against the walls, arranged stacks such as these transform houses into true fortresses. In such a lair, one can survive any attack. And they will come. The frost will press up against the walls so hard that the wooden framework inside will crack and, at least a couple of times, the snow will blow up against the door so that you'll have to climb out through the window, crawl over the snow heaps up to the door and shovel the snow. The wind will transform the windows into vibrating membranes and the chimney and the attic into territories settled by various unfamiliar creatures.

And then your choice is simple—don't burn it and become one with the wind, the frost and the snow, or burn it and transform the wood into warmth for your body.

That's after you've lived in the mountains for a while. Winter's progression, its calendar, its marked-off days—all of these are traced by the gradual shrinking of that pile of wood.

But when you only come to the mountains occasionally, firewood is not treated as daily bread but as some kind of delicacy, as gourmet food, like a cordial. My firewood, in fact, is most similar to aged cognac. Because, in addition to last year's spruce logs, I also have a stash of beech logs that has been stored for over twenty years. They are pure white, almost transparent, and sonorous. And they provide a warmth that is simultaneously intense and delicate, and, most importantly—long lasting. They've learned not to hurry. It seems to get warmer when you're just holding such a log in your hand.

In Austria, they use such aged beech to make crucial components for violins. From one of my logs, they could make about twenty. I am aware of how many violins I have burned over all these years. I am aware how much money I could have made, had I just taken one suitcase full of logs to Vienna. But I also know that I'll continue to burn them little by little, offering them to my friends and children, as one offers conversation or wine. And I'll spill the ashes onto the plot where garlic spends the winter, awaiting its time. Let it warm up as well.

November 25

After the snow has fallen and it looks like it will lie there for a while, I start to feel better about my household chores. I know that my arms and shoulders will get a break because I will be provided with transportation. Snow, in itself, is a form of transportation. It can move anything: people, barrels, sacks, logs. Actually, it only becomes capable of transporting when combined with an inclined surface. But where I do my household chores, all the surfaces are somewhat inclined. Besides the snow and the hills, I also have a sled. And that is what provides me with hope that my arms and my shoulders will be relieved.

I don't know how other people are able to do it, but I never leave my sled just lying there on the road. It lives in my house, in the best spot. That's how they used to treat livestock, letting them in the house for the winter. The sled greatly affects both the look and the mood of the house. It's especially pleasant to wake up in the middle of the night and see the sled's skeleton in my room, lit up by reddened oven tiles (for there is no other source of outer light). At first, you can't figure out where you are, at what road rest stop it is that you have paused your journey. Then you realize that, indeed, it is your sled that is resting for the night in your house. And it becomes very pleasant to fall asleep knowing that tomorrow there will be the day, there will be snow, and there will be the sled. You need the sled to take care of some very important things. Take the borrowed shredder across the river, and, while riding back, walk along the railroad tracks to find a large rock with which to press down the shredded cabbage. You have to ride into the forest and, shaking off the clouds of snow from the spruces, chop off some twigs—some thick spruce branches. They'll be needed to cover those roots left in the soil. Although these twigs aren't heavy, carrying a whole armful of them is very cumbersome. But, on the sled, it's very easy. You, of course, have to tie them on with a rope. The twigs look unbelievably beautiful against the snow. I would like to send this carriage down from the mountaintop so that it would ride for a long time. May this mobile green blot intersect the snow slope's gigantic screen. Instead, I sit on it by myself and begin to steer with my boot. And I ride down to the house. I fly into a haystack which, unlike the sled, I have left outdoors for the winter.

November 26

I've understood for a while now that every person needs to be in possession of a very detailed knowledge of two or three landscapes. That provides enough concrete landscapes to enable one to think. Because a person cannot think without having placed certain pictures onto the landscape that has been fixated forever in one's mind. Moreover, these varieties of terrain suffice for the combination of dreams. Dreams always take place based on a very dear, fundamental, landscape that has been fixed, along with language, in the earliest days of childhood. The alchemy of dreams comes from the endless other fragments, witnessed at various times in various places, heaped onto the background of your fundamental territory.

    I very often dream of my hill in the mountains, the house, everything surrounding it, the nearby forest, apexes, and abysses. Actually, my place grows, it becomes filled with all kinds of strange details, additions, new trees grow; the rooms get bigger, as do the number of entrances, exits, and corridors—new paths of combination become possible. Of course, all this becomes inhabited by a large number of people who, broken off into groups of interest, do their own thing. Most often, I walk from group to group.

Another typical motif—I'm home alone or with someone who is very close to me. It's nighttime, it's cold and quiet. And we know that surrounding us—in the ravines, behind the trees, perhaps already by the walls—are some sort of armed enemies. We keep the lights off, listening in. We grab makeshift weapons lying nearby—knives, scythes, ropes, pitchforks. Sometimes there's one old-fashioned musket for the two of us. In such dreams, we're almost always able to leave the house and its surroundings through one of the exits that don't exist in reality and, moving past mute figures, make it through the orchard in the direction of the forest. One time, in order to do this, it became necessary to shoot the pneumatic rifle through the glass straight into the eye of the attacker who had attempted to look into the dark window by pressing his face against the glass. But today, for example, I had a real nightmare. I walked out at night to have a smoke, stood by the wall. Suddenly, a car came out of the darkness and flew between me and the nearest tree. And this kept repeating. And then everything became clear—I noticed that, while I had been gone, a transnational highway had been laid out through my orchard. Right through the orchard. Once a secluded house by the forest, it now found itself right by the road. This was worse than hundreds of attackers with rifles. This was the nightmare in which my world came to an end. Waking up, I said a prayer, asking not to live to see such changes. To die before our world changes in such a way.

November 29

Whenever I begin to think that my life is starting to resemble a tangled ball of thin rubber bands—many fragments with many ends, all jumbled together—I then begin to think about people who have experienced more difficult times. And most people have. A calm, unemotional comparison always exposes how cheerful my biography is when measured up to anyone else's. Dad once told me an old Hutsul tale about a man who was tired of living and who, in his prayers, would ask the Lord to offer him an easier fate. God, of course, heard the pleading of the downtrodden man and led him to a giant hall in which crosses were stacked—every cross a particular fate of an actual person. Then he allowed the man to choose which one he wanted for himself. The man searched for a while and then chose the smallest and lightest one.

"But that one is your cross, it is your fate," said the Lord. And that's the way it really is.

We are too involved with love—actually, pity—for ourselves to understand that we need nothing else but thankfulness to the Creator for every day of existence. I respect the thankful. They are joyful and good. Those who are thankful to the Creator understand that it is precisely that which is needed by others whom he has created. My aunt said that what a person needs most of all is gratefulness. In time, I proved to myself that she was correct. For, in essence, everything is dependent on gratefulness. That is why I understand people who accept gifts with enthusiasm. That enthusiasm is made up of gratefulness, not self-assurance. That is why I also understand people who give, never accepting thanks in return. They know that the latter know to whom they are thankful. And if not, then thank God that, when someone needed something, you were in a position to give.

As for difficult times—they disappear when you fathom that the day is a gift. Because, just by possessing that day, you have received something. And you believe that your day is better than other possible similar days. You just need to understand that, if you are hungry today, then it is because you were full yesterday and will be full tomorrow. And it's the same with coldness, pain, despair, fear, and other real things, which let you know that you are alive. The greatest wisdom, then, is the simple, daily prayer, given to us without any expectation of gratitude: Lord! Thy will be done, not mine.

November 30

After Grandpa's funeral, I noticed that various people would approach me and, among other things, cautiously begin asking me about some kind of grass that is used for smoking. It reminded me of plots in films about secret drug addicts. I, of course, was convinced that Grandpa had nothing to do with grass that is smoked and I tried to convince all those who had approached me of this. Old village men would walk away doubting my honesty.

I remember the way Grandpa smoked. He had a plain but high-quality pipe and a nice little bag for tobacco. He loved to take a break from work, lean up on his hoe, shovel, scythe, or rake and smoke a bit in the shadow of the plum tree or on the knoll overgrown with sweet briar, depending on the weather. And it was by that plum tree that he had his worst asthma attack, the result of having spent many days on the Lysol-covered concrete floor of a solitary confinement cell.

After the attack, Grandpa stopped smoking. For several months after, he would keep dried plums in his pocket so that he could eat them to help suppress his cravings to smoke, and a bunch of kids would follow him, asking for a plum. Grandpa left behind some almost poisonous makhorka tobacco dating back to the end of the 1950s, half a pack of Herzegovina-Flor cigarettes, and a couple of packs of small filtered Soviet cigarettes unimaginatively named "Minty." But I knew nothing about any grass. By the way, those old men would keep coming up to me, sometimes once a year, sometimes more frequently, asking that, even if I continued to refuse giving them that grass, I at least show it to them. I came to understand that all this represented some kind of secret my grandpa had had.

Several years later—in the attic, of course, among homemade Christmas ornaments, I found a little metal box of Lviv ground coffee. Upon opening it, I was astounded by the extraordinary fragrance that was released. It was the smell of an orchard in summer, honey poured over magic herbs, the most delicious fruits, and the essence of the most delicate petals. And I recalled that scent, although I had believed that a distant recollection of it was really just another childhood fairytale. Grandpa would put a pinch of this herb in his tobacco and this would make the smoke very pleasant. This little box contained that grass those wise old men were searching for. As it turned out, it was a treasure more valuable than Grandpa's whole inheritance. This secret mix he had discovered was a real masterpiece. It makes poor tobacco good, and good tobacco—amazing. If Grandpa wanted to, and if he had lived in a different part of the world, he could have become the magnate, the champion and the hero of all smokers. Instead, he passed that chance along to me. Maybe someday I'll be up for it. But today, I just pull a pinch of herb from the little box, mix it with Dutch tobacco and throw myself a little party. And I think about Grandpa. And, to this day, I don't know what grass is contained therein.

December 1

Every now and then, I enjoy reading the Lives of the Saints. There are very few books existing that contain so many amazing stories. They are a waterfall of people's fates. Besides providing instruction, they also offer a great number of fantastic narratives. I'm convinced that, in all the literatures and among all the peoples of the world, there is no such collection of stories.

But even these lives and these stories can be systematized by looking into how it is that the saints became saints. In turns out that, in addition to the most important requirement—absolute faith—several other acts were also required. Chief among them was an honorable death. Martyrdom was important, but an honorable death was your guarantee that you would become a saint. The saints died in horrible ways. All the descriptions of brutality found in today's literature cannot compare with those terrible manners of dying that were assigned to the saints. The phantasmagorical imagination displayed by the authors of those deaths refute any declarations made by pessimists who contend that, in today's world, humankind has declined. Because then, at the start of the millennium, the fantasies and the industriousness of the executioners knew no bounds. But the variety of deaths is only an insignificant feature of belles lettres. What is important is the conduct of those who were destined to die. None of them wavered, bowed down, or encountered doubt. They accepted their hours or minutes of death almost joyfully. Besides, there are things that our simple minds cannot fathom—parents witnessing the torture of their children and vice versa. But no one allowed themselves the opportunity to flee the situation or to be cowardly. The path of a righteous and virtuous life. Few were able to stay true to it. And those that were can be divided into two categories—ascetics and those who relentlessly helped others. Other possible paths—acts for the good of the church committed above and beyond the call of duty, or producing miracles and wonders. And the saints I like best are those who came up with something that you keep thinking about to this day.

Especially important for one's reflection and reasoning is the life of Saint Simeon Stylites. A person who, out of a thousand possible ways to live, chose the strangest—20 years of prayer on top of a tall pillar, on which no stray move was possible. Day after day, for twenty years, for every minute, only in this spot. Completely ignoring that which we call life's opportunities. Just two leaves of cabbage a day for twenty years. And that's it for the food. For the rest of the time—conversations with God. No outside impressions; no journeys, meetings, or entertainment. And, most importantly: no complaints, an inhuman patience. A pragmatist might consider such a life to be useless, an escape. But, actually, Simeon is among those who provide life with at least a little bit of sense.

Whenever I start to get bored and impatient, I always think about Simeon Stylites. How did he deal with it?

December 2

Today, I was subjected to a series of strange coincidences that could be considered magical. Because now and then when we think about someone, even subconsciously, we conjure up their image over and over throughout the day.

In the morning, I went to shave, or perhaps just wash my face. Looking in the mirror, I said to myself: "Bohumil! Hrabal!"[1] And, before evening, I entered a winery. And there, the spirit of Hrabal crossed paths with me once again (surely, if he were to appear just like that it would be in the company of wine). In the winery, a visiting Czech gentleman told me about Hrabal's death. The story was very emotional. And it was extra appealing because it wasn't true. But the Czechs, the countrymen of

---

1 Bohumil Hrabal (1914–1997) was a prominent Czech writer. He died when he fell out of a fifth-floor hospital window (tr.).

the Great Bohumil Hrabal, believe in it. The Czech gentleman said the following: while Hrabal was lying in the hospital unable to use his legs, he became engrossed with some birds that were stirring just outside the window. Mr. Bohumil crawled up to the windowsill and crumbled some bread from his hospital tray for the birds. And he increasingly leaned out the window, listening in to the birds' conversation, up until the moment that he lost his balance and fell out the window, dropping to his death.

In reality, it is a proven fact that the elderly Hrabal neglected his medicine, illness, and frailty. Maybe he wanted to take on the role of that wooden angel he had described, the one that splintered into pieces in the courtyard of a Prague church. Or maybe he had been called by one of those who had often appeared to him, and to his grandfather, and to his father after a few jugs of Moravian wine—Christ, Friedrich the Great, Lao Tse.

Hrabal is probably the greatest poet in contemporary Czech culture among those who wrote down stories they had overheard. Scraps of the conversations of ordinary citizens of Prague were ground into the well-puddled-stream of Bohumil's fantasy and became masterpieces. The whole world knew of him, while Hrabal continued to work, either at a factory that was wreaking havoc on his brain or at a paper recycling facility to which various Prague weirdos would bring used paper. His kingdom was the enchanting Czech language, with wine, ghosts, and the tales of the half-insane and their oversaturated lives. "Bohumil! Hrabal!"—he would address his reflection with the scolding voice of his mother. The reflection was silent. And Bohumil wrote down stories. He died the same summer that those other wrinkled elders like him did—Jacques-Yves Cousteau, Bulat Okudzhava,[2] Mother Theresa.

And today, in this insinuating manner, he came to me the way that earlier, the immortal elders had come to him.

And what's really strange—almost all people whom I admire had some kind of connection with this deceased man.

December 4

The arrival of the concept of what in Ukraine they now call by the English word "second-hand"—the market for used clothes—can be considered to be one of the most important events in recent years. It greatly affected our daily lives. Let's recall Soviet times, when clothing was rather expensive and most fellow citizens wore sad, identical suits, coats, jackets, and hats. Because of this, our

---

2   Bulat Okudzhava (1924–1997) was a poet and musician of Georgian and Armenian heritage. He is considered to be one of the pioneers of the "author song" musical genre popular during the Soviet era (tr.).

people were recognizable throughout the world in the way that Indians or Africans are when they wear their national costumes. Second-hand provided two or three major possibilities—to have lots of affordable clothes, to have everyone dressed differently, and, most importantly, to find something that fit you well.

But there is a great danger hidden within it. As we know, clothing, more than anything else, accumulates the energy of its owner. Thus, every one of us, by donning something worn by the anonymous, takes on the remnants of something good or bad, calm or nervous, happy or tragic. It is not possible to ever deduce which it is; it is not possible to determine it in any manner. The grand circulation of the clothing spirits is like the massive spreading of various viruses that enter genetic codes, seeping into them, snatching for themselves something from the previous master, and then inhabiting the next person with all of this.

I thought of these things when I got dressed this morning—there was not one single thing that I myself had purchased. Everything had been given to me, everything was someone else's, everything with traces of someone else's life. A jacket given as a gift, which had been purchased at a Prague store stocked with goods hailing from various "colonies." A sweater that earlier had belonged to a famous avant-garde actress from a German youth theater. A shirt previously worn by a Kurdish freedom fighter who was also a Lviv University student. An absurd pair of pants, wide at the waist and of a stupid color, presented to me as a sign of recognition by the Maltese Order. A belt given to me by Grandpa on the day I turned seven, and on which I have noted every new place where I have been. Complimentary socks obtained by an actual German count when he flew on Lufthansa Airlines. Army boots that had taken part in the storming of the palace of the President of Georgia, Zviad Gamsakhurdia.[3] Also—an earring given to me as a present, a silver ring, a watch, a knife. A Franciscan cross brought from Assisi. I did not choose any of these things myself. They came to me from various parts and they brought with them fragments of the lives and fates of others. But my advantage over the second-hand is that I know what to expect from each of these things.

December 6

My great-grandfather was very strict with his children. He didn't beat them, but he gave them a very stern upbringing. At home, to this day we have a whip—a sixer (with six leather belts), which was called a quirt. No one ever beat me. I didn't experience it my whole childhood.

---

3   Zviad Gamsakhurdia (1939–1993) was the first democratically elected president of post-Soviet Georgia. He was overthrown in a coup d'état launched in December 1991 (tr.).

Perhaps my dad slapped me on the wrist a couple of times, and my grandfather hit me only three times. But those three times were so unusual that I remembered them for my whole life. Actually, those three spankings were as useful as three university degrees.

Grandpa was very gentle and loving towards me, but he possessed a fiery nature. His anger was short-lived but excruciating, although it never jeopardized his relationships with others.

The first time he hit me was with a scythe handle, which caused me to fly into the ditch by the railroad tracks. And this was very timely. Because a train was approaching very fast and I, still a little boy at the time, almost stepped out right in front of it as I was crossing the tracks to go to grandpa, who was returning from the harvest.

Another time, some friends as old as my grandpa visited and sat at the table, conversing and sipping some gin. I was there, too, and, when I was asked a question to which the answer was supposed to be either "yes" or "no," I started babbling on, not noticing that the old men had had enough. Then grandpa grabbed a link of kielbasa and hit me for a second time.

The third time was actually completely unclear to me at first. Grandpa and I sat in the house; it was raining and there was no work to be done. A member of our family stopped by and, talking about various things, asked where my father had been. Grandpa said that he did not know, but I knew that he knew that my dad had gone with his buddies to the mountains and that he was aware of the path that they had taken. I began telling this to the family member. But I didn't finish telling him because I received a very painful and out-of-nowhere blow in a certain tender place. My grandpa had learned how to do this at a special training camp in Holland. When our guest left, Grandpa apologized to me and told me never to say that which is unnecessary.

So, I was hit infrequently. But three hits accomplished more than daily beatings would have. Now I never cross railroad tracks when a train is coming, I never interrupt those older than me and instead hear them out, I never reply to questions the answers to which no one really wants to know, and I never tell of the paths taken by those whom I love.

December 7

Today, I was scolded: so-and-so or so-and-so, who raised you, would never have conducted themselves in such a way. In other words, what happened to all the guidance you received, your upbringing? At first, I was shocked—I truly did not want it to be this way. I would like to be the person I was brought up to be. But, after a few hours, it hit me—my God!—well, I've been raised by so many different, extraordinary people. I loved all of them, I was enamored with all of them, and I've absorbed something from, and remembered something about, each one of them. But these people themselves were so dissimilar that they often had difficulty agreeing on anything. I didn't recognize this as a child, because I didn't comprehend it. I now realize that certain individuals who raised me, each of whom had the same amount of influence on me, were all equally exceptional. That's why coming to a conclusion based on one, as criminologists say, episode, is incorrect, illogical, and impossible.

And, in addition to living relatives, two irrefutable factors that have had a direct influence on me have to be taken into account—the dictate of blood, that eccentric twisting of heredities, and, of course, myths—stories about those whom I never met in my life but without whom I cannot imagine my worldview.

Take this story about my great-grandmother, for example. When it became too dangerous for my great-grandfather to remain here, in Galicia, Sheptytskyi[4] was able to get him to America. After a period of time, my great-grandmother joined him there. She settled in a small town, and, being the wife of a priest, had

---

4   Andrei Sheptytskyi (1865–1944) was the Metropolitan Archbishop of the Ukrainian Greek Catholic Church and one of the most important and powerful figures in twentieth-century Ukraine. Treated as an enemy by the Soviet Union, he was a hero of the Ukrainian national political and cultural movement. See also note 15 on p. 321 (tr.).

to participate in the social life there. But my great-grandmother had one important need—she was a heavy smoker. And in America at that time, a woman who smoked was looked upon with disdain. Smoking in public was simply forbidden. My great-grandmother couldn't last more than half an hour without a cigarette. She truly loved her husband, but she just could not suffer such torture. She stayed in America for a bit longer and then took her child, who had been born there, and returned to her homeland. Forever. She kept smoking and later died of lung cancer. This was foreseeable but, ultimately, not obligatory. What was obligatory was not succumbing to the decrees and dictates of social mandates. And what can be said about this? How can her conduct be logically justified, and moreover, how can all this be applied to an interpretation of my behavior? And to the fact that, in one particular episode, I did not act like so-and-so or so-and-so who had raised me.

December 8

Athletes have a strange heart condition—the heart begins to ache when exertion decreases.

This reminds me of my own coexistence with many men whom I dearly love. They are the ones I usually meet up with, we waste one another's time, we do something, talk, joke around, walk somewhere, drink something.

Life goes on, passes by, fades away. It's like exertion for athletes. It's always there... But sometimes they are not around, they've gone off somewhere. And then, without that familiar exertion, the heart begins to ache. Lungs shrivel, as do all respiratory tracts. Air is lacking. You sharply begin to fathom that, without all those Yurkos, Olehs, Vlodkos, Andriis, Ivans, Romans, and Bohdans, you cannot continue along your own path. You see how, without them, you become an iceberg that has been dragged to some port, in order to be melted down and drunk up by unknown, strange people. If I ever were to wish I were a woman, then it would only be so I could be everything for those few men that are worthy of heaven on earth. Hell is other people. That was said by someone without much thought. Because other people are heaven. Other people, more specifically those people mentioned here, are that arrow in your chest, which hurts you but, if you pull it out, you die.

And, if there is anything worthy of your precious life, it is, in fact, this—seeing, hearing, sensing, touching. Let it be pointless, let it not result in anything—no houses will be built, no orchard will grow, no children will be born. Let scars on your body and your heart be all that remain. But if you grant these people part of your own fate, then you will be giving a gift to those children that already exist. They will know that Dad knew what he was doing.

Your little partisan army will not occupy any new territory, but it exists so as to not allow any occupiers onto your native land. Because it truly is yours. And neither you nor we will ever be able to fashion a true hell on this parcel. Here, even if you don't want it, only paradise is possible.

December 9

I believe that most offenses should be forgiven. I believe that society should not be divided into the guilty and the not-guilty. However... Today, I came across a manifestation of something that frightened me ten years ago. Here's what happened. It was the Ukrainian revolution. We, students from Lviv, were organizing a very risky demonstration in Kyiv. Marching toward us was a riot police brigade. This was scary, but most of us were used to it. That day, doubt had emerged within the police. So they didn't start beating us right away. Several leaders of the student corps, including me, were packed into a car and taken to the commanders of the Kyiv special forces. There were people there whose last names were the very symbols of brutality, but it's not worth listing them now because they are the ones who are in power in today's Ukraine. And it was then, at that interrogation ten years ago, that I suddenly understood: a time will come—the one for which, in fact, we are fighting now—when I will be forced to attest to these very people my allegiance to a sovereign Ukrainian state. I understood that neither my absolute belief in

Ukraine, nor my indisputable patriotic upbringing, nor that which I do now so that Ukraine may continue to exist, nor all that my family has done—nothing will protect me from that situation when I will be forced to prove to all those generals and their cronies that I am for Ukraine and for its statehood. It's absurd, but absurd things such as these are precisely those that usually come to fruition. And today, I finally experienced this as reality. I am all for forgiving, I am against revising biographies, but I desire that which, it would seem, is completely normal—that the forgiven understand that they have been forgiven and that the guilty know that they are guilty, and thus do not continue their offences. I don't want to have to prove to people responsible for all sorts of malevolence back then that I am for this country and for this state. I don't want former enemies to judge what I have done for my people. And I don't want to have to answer to boys from the special services who were members of the Komsomol[5] to its dying days and who are now responsible for the safety of my country. Even though I have lost the biggest game of my life and things have not turned out the way we had wanted them to, my former brothers-in-arms and I should not have to fear the harassment of those who change colors when it's convenient.

---

5   The Komsomol, or All-Union Leninist Young Communist League, was a Soviet youth organization that served to prepare future members of the Communist Party (tr.).

December 14

We, Ukrainians, are used to the idea that various summer preparations of jams, salads, fruit spreads, fall salting and marinating—all these tomatoes, pickles, mushrooms, which women prepare late into the night in order to make it in time for winter—are a characteristic of our way of life. That the homemakers in the opulent world don't even think about such things because they can buy absolutely everything, either fresh or similarly conserved, in the nearest store. And this is true to a certain extent. Most women in Western Europe or America would never convince themselves to work so hard in the summer and fall in order to assure themselves that their families will get through the winter and early spring without being affected by the lack of harvests. But this argument also contains a counter-argument, which challenges its absoluteness.

As it turns out—and I heard about this from actual Americans—their grandpas and grandmas, who lived through the Great Depression of the 1930s and experienced famine, one which you didn't cause but for which you can prepare, do the same thing. People that have experienced famine—not just a certain number of days of lacking food during some kind of extreme situation but an enduring non-eating, a constant thinking about food—will never cease being frugal and forethoughtful when it comes to reserves. Because reserves, like our people say, do not cause problems.

I also make juice out of apples for the winter. I justify it to myself with the thought that, otherwise, the apples will rot. But, really, I simply know that I won't be able to buy these necessary juices for my kids. And it's not about winter, it's about the impossibility of living frivolously. Actually, I'm even worse than that. I can't even slice off a piece of meat and eat it with bread for breakfast. Because, when there is meat, I realize that it is there by chance and that it won't last long. Like some kind of reptile, I prefer not to eat any bread, or anything else, with it, so that I can eat a maximum portion of meat. Let it last in my organism for a while.

And I remember one more detail. It was during the coup d'état attempt in Moscow. Once again, there was disorder and confusion—what is really happening? I was in the mountains then. And wouldn't leave my radio's side, listening to updates every hour. But the people there were not doing the same. They were standing in line for bread, so that they'd have enough of it to last for a while.

December 15

Many of us possess a secret map—it could be a real map, it could be one that's been painted by hand, it could be a certain photograph or an illustration in a book, some kind of painting in an atlas, a diagram in an encyclopedia.

It could be an old photo featuring unknown people or someone's painting. Sometimes this map could even be a picture of a certain author, a statue, or, perhaps, even a city-square. This map could exist in the form of an old sweater, a spoon, a beat-up knife, or a chipped cup. It could be dissolved in a certain type of wine or chopped up and ground with coffee of a certain quality. I won't even mention spices and perfumes, a few words written in a certain font, herbariums, numismatic, or philatelic collections. Or attics and basements, beds and dressers, melodies and pianos.

It could be carried in someone's face, sometimes in that of a stranger, or it could be chiseled onto somebody's tombstone. Thus, that secret map could be hidden in just about anything. What unites all of them, however, is that they all show you the path to your own lost paradise. It's a chart of your paradise and the means of getting there.

I also possess such a map. I grew up on a balcony. My aunt transformed this balcony into something that was incredible. It was large and covered with vines. It faced three of the cardinal directions. And my aunt was the most amazing floriculturist in the world. She was never concerned with the size of the flowerbed, because it was never about having a lot of flowers. She was only concerned with having a lot of different kinds of flowers. In a few boxes and reinforced large pots grew several hundred of the most exotic plants. Searching far and wide, she would find at least one seed of a certain very strange plant. One seed—one plant. That was the principle. Floriculturists from various corners of the world would send her letters containing seeds. The balcony on which I grew up was like a tropical coastline. All that was missing were coral reefs. I bathed in basins that had been set up in the sun in order to warm up the water. Later, this water, like in the jungles, was used to water the plants.

When my aunt died, I sketched a chart of her garden. I wrote out all the names. This is the map of my lost paradise. I warm myself with the thought that someday I will be able to reproduce that whole paradise on a different balcony.

December 16

While I was still a student in the Department of Biology, I realized that biology itself provides as much a fundamental foundation for education, for a worldview, and for comprehending philosophical formations, logical constructions, and even artistic creations and metaphors, as does, perhaps, linguistics. Simply put, biology can be the basis for everything the mind requires. But today I met up with a former classmate, whom I had not seen for many years—a fellow biologist who had changed professions and was now informing me about a whole system of observations he had made concerning the influence of various biological sciences on the psyche.

Entomologists (insect specialists) always become collectors. Moreover, they are collectors by nature—they collect everything, even experiences and emotions, which they carefully systematize. Botanists are a varied sort. Some almost become philologists, others become erudite practical workers—gardeners, horticulturists, mushroom-pickers, floriculturists—while the rest become experts of every corner of a certain region. They know exactly where everything grows.

A separate category is made up of all who work with a microscope. Herpetologists, ichthyologists, and physiologists constitute another bunch of weirdos. But completely apart from all of these are ornithologists—those who study birds. To decide to become an ornithologist is already a sign of an infirm psyche. Ornithologists can be recognized immediately and unmistakably. They are unique. Something pulls them from the earth up into heaven. They probably corral birds into God-knows what and travel somewhere with these harnesses. Ornithologists do not see the ground—only the sky, the tree tops. These are their roots. Just think about it: to count, based on their contours, flocks composed of thousands as they move; to plot paths between us and Africa; to put a ring on captured birds' legs and receive telegrams from the island of Java, should one of those birds happen to die there; to be able to differentiate between twenty shades of pink in the tiny feathers on a little belly. To recognize nests and eggs of various sizes and colors. To constantly look into binoculars, lorgnettes, and clear tubes. To know which trolley will get you to see a certain migrating flock on time. All these things do not lead to a normal psychic state.

I know this from my own experiences of coexisting with birds: thrushes would nibble on bushes of berries, and I would then gather them; crows always sat on the building outside my window; sparrows would not allow swallows into their nests on my balcony; a rook drowned in my bucket of water; a crow lived with me for a while; my kids found a frozen parrot that later flew freely around my house; a stork fell, weakened by a long flight, while I was on my post when I was in the army; pigeons that my neighbors would fry up on Saturdays; a crane that flew to my forest from bombarded Serbia; crows from which I stole nuts in the army... If plants are notions, and animals are pictures, then birds are symbols and signs. I was not surprised that my acquaintance had become a theologian. Because, in some way, birds are similar to angels.

December 17

During childhood nobody understands this. During childhood this is considered to be a father's weakness. A child cannot understand that efforts are made to extend the night, because children sometimes can't wait for tomorrow to come. Children get up early and want to stay up as long as possible. It's the same with teenagers. It seems that medical claims about the need for sleep are foolish. But later... Later, unexpectedly, the moment arrives when you begin to realize that the only thing that you will truly be lacking for the next few decades is sleep. You can still work at night and gather your strength the day after a sleepless night and continue being functional. Even if you are very tired, you can still suddenly decide not to go to sleep if you should get the chance to watch a good movie, read a book, drink with your friends, make love. However, all that enthusiasm will not last long. Because when you've lived for a good number of years but are not yet old, then a few hours of sleep are your treasure, an extra hour a luxury, and a half day of sleep an obsessive dream. Because it is only here that you can wait out a pause between attacks from a lengthy list of aggressors. You don't event really need dreams. For although it turns out that dreams are the greatest thing you can acquire during this slice of life, you can settle for just crashing for a bit. Like a wild animal surrounded by traps, you slowly make it over to your bed and disappear into your nook. Into darkness, depth, snugness, and tightness. You willingly become a hedgehog, a mole, an amphibian, a larva who doesn't know what is happening around it. You strive to return to warmth and snugness from which you have been distancing since childhood. To that place where resting in a womb is equivalent to happiness. Where you can be, where you can exist in the form of a bulb, or a root, or seeds. And then only one thing that bothers you is that, tomorrow, day will come again. That you'll be given light, water, and heat. In the morning, you will have a few minutes of more joy than you can imagine, you'll experience all states of explosion—including a moment of silence, and including the decompressing and compressing of air. Because, for a few minutes, you'll know that you're almost not sleeping but that you still may. A few minutes filled to the rim with life before you open your eyes and thank God that you have seen light once again.

December 19

All snow is first and foremost about volume. But every snowfall is full of movement, dynamics. That is why snow is measured in centimeters of thickness and in cubic meters while snowfall, sometimes, in terms of intensity. That is, every snowfall has its own chronometer—a sand clock, an hourglass, a change in the thickness of snow either on a roof, in a certain fixed place, or at a meteorological center. The time during which snow falls needs to fit into somebody else's time. And it does so very successfully.

It was a winter without snow. But the city, swarming with all sorts of minutiae, conducted itself as if it knew for sure—that there will soon be a snowfall. And it began a few hours before dusk. Within fifteen minutes, everything was white. In the air, at first, and then, later, on surfaces. Although when it is white in the air—that is, vertically—then it seems that it is very white on surfaces, too—horizontally, or somewhat slanted. After a bit of time, snow had amassed in creases, between branches in gutters, and on balconies. After even yet another period of counted time, snow had stuck itself to those lines on which it is impossible to lie, making it necessary to stick to it and hold on. Snow's next gesture—it now looks like a spiderweb. In other words, it enveloped certain invisible frameworks of geometric figures with weakly defined counters that are situated in the air. Such as trees and utility lines. A bit later, the snow was beginning to overtake the tree trunks. It started with stumps—they were the first to become unnoticeable, covered.

And then, suddenly, everything halted and became the opposite—the empty clouds, which had unloaded their whole fill of snow, scattered with relief. It began to get brighter. The sun started to give off its heat. The whole top layer of snow began melting, regardless of what surface it had accumulated on—horizontal, vertical, slanted, or glittering. At a certain moment, the snow began to turn into water. The clocks changed—the snow timer transformed into an hourglass of warm water. And then I saw the old woman. She walked very slowly. She had gone to get some bread and milk. Step by step she conquered that half-kilometer. She had left the house before the snow had begun and now, when everything was melting—she was returning. She was the most perfect chronometer, a super weather station. On her old-fashioned, prewar hat everything that had taken place in the past hour was preserved—twenty centimeters of snow, which had come down densely, but had not melted on top of this autonomous zone. The old woman, her hat, and the level of snow on it were an archaism, as is ever timer that has completed its counting off.

December 20

It was thirty years ago. I know for sure because that same photographic developer kicked in—very intense snow. When such a thick snow began to fall upon our road—one that was laid out in Austrian cobblestones and along which a ditch was dug, into which water would flow in the summer and snow would accumulate in the winter—when it would snow, along that road of ours, one man in particular would set off for our mountain. He had a long gray beard, was always dressed in the same old puffy jacket and artificial leather boots. He held an artificial leather bag in his hands that looked not like a sack but like a briefcase. He was the only wandering panhandler who would appear on our mountain. He had his own password: "Give me some guelder rose berries," the panhandler would say. He would be given bundles of guelder rose berries cut beneath the snow, when the berries are sweet, taut, and ready to squirt out juice from every inadvertent touch. Of course the guelder rose berries were some sort of extraordinary, deep metaphor. Or even a token of diplomacy. Asking only for guelder rose berries would present him not as a beggar but as an agent of some sort of unusual and unclear mission. And the diplomacy lay in the fact that, beside guelder rose berries, he was given lunch, given a shot of aged spruce liqueur, a few apples, a head of garlic, and some dried apples or plums or mushrooms in a long brown envelop in which the Warsaw newspaper *Nashe Slovo* would arrive.

But the great wisdom of this wanderer lay in the fact that he only asked for that which everyone had and that was not a necessity. Because everyone who would cut guelder rose berries from beneath the snow could get by without them when it was necessary to give them to the man from the snow.

In time, I saw that everything around our house subsisted along that principle—give to those that ask that which you can give up, and ask for, that is, know how to ask for, only that which you can actually be given. That is, what is known as ecology—the knowledge about life in one common home.

Ants would carve out paths in sugar, and no one drowned them, mice would chew-up nuts, wasps would build nests in the warm attic, hawks could pick out some chickens for themselves, hedgehogs and snakes were given plates full of milk. Some black chokeberries were saved for the birds. No one would chase bats from below the roof. Hares would run up to get some bark and cabbage scraps. In the middle of winter, hay and salt were always available for deer and elk. Mole holes were not flooded with boiling water.

We all lived together, everyone had everything that they needed, and everyone was happy. We could rely on one another. And, with our common efforts, we could support more than one wanderer, who asked only for guelder rose berries from beneath the snow but received much more.

December 21

There are freezing temperatures outside today. I am dressed rather lightly—without doubling my pants, without a sweater, and in a fall jacket. On my feet—light shoes, on my head, a beret. Without a scarf and without gloves. I am walking outside a lot, but I'm not cold. And I can't understand why I was so cold in such a temperature when I was in the army. Although I was much more suitably dressed back then. Everyone was cold, just one hour of standing in the snow and it felt like your feet were going to fall off; your hands would freeze after only a few minutes without gloves, everything felt cold. Clearly, the amount of one's inner warmth must somehow be determined by one's level of freedom, dependence, or liberty.

In the Soviet army I was truly convinced that hell is not hot at all but quite the opposite—terribly cold. We lived in armored personnel carriers during heat waves. It was almost 176°F. We would fry eggs on those APCs, our hands were constantly singed from accidental contact with the overheated metal. But all of that seemed superficial—that is, it only affects your surface, your shell. It only irritated, ruined, and tortured your skin. The cold was much deeper and more primary. Most importantly, it hollowed you out—in order to itself become the contents of your form during days-long, autonomous trips. Autonomous—meaning that it is just you, your DNA, just the tiny generator of the radio station, which cannot offer heat, only snows, freezing, and forests. Then burning hell began. Then it burned. Burned from the inside, in your bones, you felt every cell as if it were a bottle of water placed out into freezing temperature. Hopelessness would ensue from which you could try to run away but, in the end, you could not. Because there was no warmth to be found, and there was ice within you.

I jumped out of a warm armored car on whose interior walls ice was forming into the dead of night, because it seemed that the freezing temperatures inside would suffocate you while the even-colder outside temperature would not be as horrible a constraint as being closed-off. Everything that was in a bottle became ice, bread froze, even paper became frozen. I will not dare to call this cold. This was a limit, a pain, a cleanliness, an act of blessing, of rebirth. This was life. And this, in fact, was hell. Because it was endlessness, boundlessness, the construction and sounding of complete silence. This was madness. The freezing temperature disabled our heads. But that's tomorrow's story.

December 22

So then—today we have a continuation of that story about the freezing temperature. About how it turns a person into a madman.

Many times I've seen people being crushed—through coldness, beating, pain, disease, greed, fear, the death of dear ones, poverty, derision; they crushed people with shovels, buckets of bleach, violence and plotting, lying and indifference. I saw how people tried to crush others and how the latter either became crushed or didn't. But only once have I seen how a perfectly respectable person became crushed in such a manner that he no longer resembled a person. Even after a year, his speech, intonation, voice, glance, gait, and movements did not return.

Something changed in his mind. It was the freezing that crushed him. An impeccable and intelligent, witty and elegant officer from Saint Petersburg went with us into the crackling freezing of the northern forests. He was placed in one of the armored personnel carriers. He composed himself and acted surprisingly well, properly, and with dignity. Our column raced through boundless forests. The rule was that we had to get to a certain place regardless of any losses. That is, no one cared about anyone that was left behind along the way.

And it turned out that the APC with the impeccable officer broke down somewhere in the deepest thickets. Three people were left in the middle of snows and one-hundred-kilometer forests together with tons of absolutely useless metal, which, however, could not be abandoned. The hiding place turned into a trap. For over a week they sat without food, without warmth, without contact or news, without a watch or any knowledge of what was going on. The situation was such that the cold was horrific but would not let them die. Life had entered a new dimension—a minimal smoldering on the verge of being put out. We made it to our destination and worked in that kind of cold weather for a whole week. But we were working. We were freezing but we were not planning to die. We didn't have time for that.

When, after a week, we began gathering our lost colleagues and finally got to that armored personnel carrier it was difficult to look at the officer. He had become a scared wild animal, he couldn't speak, think, or move. Like something out of a Jack London story. His eyes had become frozen and lifeless. He ceased being wise, good, and active. His brain and all of his senses had become frozen. We had to lead him as if he were a blind and dumb paraplegic. After he warmed up, he didn't cease being frozen.

Something similar happens with fruits which can remain fresh for a long time when frozen but return to their original state when they thaw. They can only be used for compote and they have to be used very quickly because otherwise they will rot.

December 23

Lately, I have lost the ability to distinguish not only between years, but also between days of the week. That is why the idea of a "Sunday stroll" has become an archaism for me. And so it's not all that strange that this Sunday stroll took place on a Thursday. Actually, it was quite a perfect day for a walk—sunny, snowy, and frosty. Snow is especially conducive to strolling because it alters the space—it makes it more porcelaneous—it becomes divided, portioned, and partitioned into its various fragments. I chanced upon the most prestigious neighborhood in my city. This is an extraordinary neighborhood with magical blocks that lies to the right of a small park and to the left of the railway tracks. The fantastic world of a different city, of quiet streets—upon which you can walk outnumbering automobiles—of villas and orchards. It is the villas that are the most interesting. This corner of the world overflows with them. There are many of them and they are all different. Each of these villas acts as an illustration to a long story. Each of these stories includes an introduction, a conclusion, a peak, a culmination. They feature stability followed by collapse, one that is unnoticeable at first but then becomes steep, and later tumbles toward ruin. So, that should be the end of the story. But not in this case, because the villas are stalwart and lasting. That is why old stories are replaced with new ones. And then everything begins anew—an idea, a peak, a culmination, stability. It is also clear that a collapse is coming. Without a certain aftertaste of collapse, buildings such as these lose their taste. It is especially interesting to see these villas as the materialization of someone's concept of an ideal building. Someone came up with the idea of having his own palace. Usually, it was the reflection of certain dreams about Vienna, Prague, Krakow, or, at least, Lviv. But how their dream was supposed to look was imagined poorly by the owners. That is why builders took this task upon themselves. Their dramas are also engraved into each building, while the buildings are in fact the manifestation of everything that did not work out in the lives of these architects, builders, engineers, and decorators.

And, nonetheless, the buildings turned out well. It is our good fortune that there is a small area such as this in our city. And it is our good fortune that one can take a Sunday stroll there. Even if takes place on a Thursday.

December 24

I've long had a dream that I will dare to share for the first time today. A few years ago, I noticed people suffering from depression and realized how I could help them. I came up with the idea of a special guest house where depression could be treated. I want to gather those in need and take them to the mountains. During any of the year's seasons. Even in the cold weather, like today, which could actually be beneficial—because freezing highlights all types of psychic darkness and shadows. So, it could all look like this: I place an ad in a newspaper announcing that there is a certain guest house that is accepting people that are suffering from depression. Some service fee would need to be listed that would cover, for instance, the cost of food, drink, transportation, and my remuneration for healing the patients. The advertisement would provide an address at which one would need to show up. And then that person would need to go to that address—be it in Dora, Liubizhnia, Kvasy, Vorokhta, Mykulychyn, Zelena, Huta, or some place like that—and say that they wanted to be healed.

And I would already be there. I would meet the ailing person and would stay up with them all night, sharing a bottle or a barrel. I would talk to that person and tell them a few stories. I would be happy and the ailing one would see happiness gushing out of me. We would go out into the night to look at the stars. It would be very cold. Everything would be freezing.

We won't light a fire, we'll endure. Then we'll lie down for a few hours. The sleep will be full of dreams, because, due to the cold, we'll be waking up every half hour. The patient and I will sleep in such a way as to heat one another with our bodies and our breaths. Then morning will come. It will be splendid. The sky will be colorful, while the mountains will be like a reproduction of a black and white engraving. We will be lacking food. We'll only have enough onions and garlic. But there will be nothing to eat with them. We will stink of onions. And we'll wash it down with even stinkier drinks. Morning will seem like evening. Our hands, with skin cracked by discomfort, will pour something for one another. I'll pull some books and photos from an old closet. We'll read and flip through them. And then—overcoming the desire to sleep—we'll start doing heavy physical work not guided by any logic—we'll carry something, we'll dig, we'll gather. Later, we will be able to lie down for a bit, but not fall asleep, and discuss that which we are thinking about, and then, once again, go, sit, bathe, drink vodka, wine, coffee, milk, not eat anything but canned seafood, converse, recall, dream, carry a weight on our back, risk falling under a rock, a wave, a chopped tree, a sack, an avalanche.

I will ask the ailing ones to stay, to just stay with me longer. And their sickness will wane with time. We'll be able to make it through this, if we live a bit together.

December 27

I decided a long time ago for myself, and can advise everyone else, too, that pondering God's plan and the various acts of God is completely hopeless. Because an instrument thinking about a craftsman is absurd. It's not on that level, it is not that, which can be thought through. There is a lack in the method and in the dimension of thinking, there is a lack of imagination. And yet there is nothing more enticing than to try and contemplate God's plan, the upcoming plot twists that He has come up with.

I know that in those rare moments when human logic or desire are one with God's logic and God's desire—in those rare moments wonders and miracles occur. However, it is senseless to follow them as signs because, once again, this would only be logical according to human logic.

I don't understand the meaning of everything that is happening. And I don't ask for such understanding. But it is clear that the Lord is amenable to me and to many whom I know. He caresses us. He has surrounded us with a whole sentry of guards and angels. That's why everything works out for us. We are unconstrained and our heaviest burden comes from worrying about this supernatural lightness. Because really, we don't offer anything in return except for faith, love, and hope, while we receive everything. For some reason, we are being cared for. We are born, we give birth, and we die rather easily. Our arms and legs are supple, our breathing is free. Our eyes see farther and they see more, while our ears hear heavenly music. Our fingertips travel along the greatest of the world's paths. Our children love us and we love them. And we are also loved by the most refined women and the most dignified men. They are ready to renew our faith, love, and hope at any minute. Warm rains are poured over us, our bodies recall the scents of mountain rivers. We are nurtured like the strangest flowers in an unkempt garden. When we are hit or bitten, our wounds quickly heal and don't rot. We, like birds, find food every day, and bees and other insects don't take away from us but, instead, bring us nectar. Viruses live in us but do not harm us. And other such things.

I don't think that this is God testing us with temptation. The Lord is preparing us for something. It is His personal idea. And I know that we will be able to be reliable. It is unknown when and how we will return the favor. Even if we'll have to take part in some kind of public meeting of the Final judgment.

December 30

Sometimes, it turns out that you drink at night in the kitchen of your own home. In such cases, the guest that shows up is unexpected but very much anticipated. In such cases, all the home dwellers are sleeping. Something is brought from the nearby corner store while everything else is improvised and composed of dinner's leftovers and other strategic provisions. Usually, onions with oil and vinegar are prepared with the possible addition of tomato juice. There is drinking, talking, recalling and singing, and a listening to favorite music.

And, at some point during all this, the moment arrives when you cannot resist showing your guest something that captivates you. This could be a stamp collection arranged in special albums, coins, photographs, an assortment of knives or lighters, a collection of pencils or souvenirs. You can show postcards or perhaps a scrapbook. Some noted down fragments of a dream, a rifle. You can take him to the farthest room and play something on the piano. Sometimes, it comes down to turning on the light in the room where the children are sleeping to show how beautifully they are sleeping. You can show off your aquarium with fish or orchards filled with cacti. This displaying will surely be accompanied by such lavish stories that the guest will realize that he's missed out on something in his life. Although, really, that's just what you'd like to think. It's just that stroke of life's opportunities that fits you like a glove.

I also have such a thing. I show botanical atlases. And I talk not about plants but about atlases. Their authors would surely be surprised if they could hear all that.

Because atlases are the world's best literature. The most beautiful, the most factual, and the most perfect. They have an extraordinary magic—a parade of portraits of flawless plants, of those that either you see every day but don't know their names or those that you will never see in your lifetime and which will become an everlasting rebuke of your own helplessness. Botanical atlases, obviously, are distinguished by their style. And in that there is a certain subtle charm. The German ones—extraordinarily pedantic drawings, which tell you more about a plant than the actual living plant itself. The Czech ones—predominantly photographic. The Polish ones—popular and cherished. The Soviet ones—either very academic or geared toward kids. The catalogues of the British Kew Botanical Gardens—like a register of every one that lived anywhere in the world. And many more, too. You demonstrate these piles of books and talk about what is different in each of them. You are either understood or you are not. But, that night, all of the participants of the kitchen meeting will dream of graceful plants.

December 31

The possibility to choose, which is considered to be the highest form of human freedom, is actually every person's greatest captivity. It is fate. You are forced to choose, by nature you cannot not choose. Because, even if you don't choose, you have still made a choice not to choose. A choice is a required test that not everyone passes. And choice is a special responsibility to those who are close to you as well as to all of humanity. In fact, the path of your choice is the most valuable thing that you can do for all of humanity. Because each one of your choices, and their complexity and consistency especially, highlights this potential path. By making your own choice you point to a potential path for someone else.

These are things that are obvious and straightforward. But for inquiries regarding choice there is another aspect that no one seriously considers. That is—the question of that which has not been chosen. That which we reject affects us a lot more than that which we choose. Because the chosen immediately becomes reality and, thus, acquires a temporal dimension. And that which has time must have an end. That is, our chosen things become ours only during the time of their actuality and, later, pass or evolve into something that barely evokes that original thing that you actually chose.

On the other hand, the register of the unchosen—the gigantic list of spurned possibilities, people, relationships, words, places and acts, senses and worrying, melodies, smells and tastes, touches and feels—accumulates in that non-reality. All of this has not been realized, and thus is infinite. It is a cemetery that is always with you. That kind of baggage, in fact, leads to aging and exhaustion, although it is from it that art and literature are unpacked and from there the best music is played, and it is there that the most beautiful faces in the world glimmer. It is true, however, that it is there that all kinds of delusions, fears, and revulsions contort and shriek in the weak. In that baggage, there is always an old coat in whose pocket a lost ticket resides. It's a fringe special pass into schizophrenia, which is the most often recurring proof of the existence of the chosen and the unchosen. While in the strong, the unchosen develops that which makes mammals into humans—some kind of opaque nostalgia, a sadness that does not ruin but instead inspires a certain lack of fear and a certain unbearable lightness of being.

THE YEAR 2001

January 4

In that very moment when despair, disbelief, and the gloomiest perception of the world squeeze us into the grimmest of corridors—one that is tight, wet, hot and cold, or completely dark; when the turn ahead is not visible, while the walls get closer and tighter; when you wander through putrid water, going deeper and deeper with each step, aligning your face with its surface, where the most disgusting vestiges of someone else's party float. And when it seems that your next step will be your final one but you haven't yet lost your faith in fate, a confidence in your path, and a love for your community—one that is ready to flood you with the opposite of all this—it is then, in those short moments, that the rigid wall which impedes us transforms into a soft, tender, and illuminated opening. Through that slit, that which is wonderful in the world appears to us. It is then that angels, like noble birds, fly, and children's fears turn out to be wise fluffy animals. From your body, eyes, and ears, from every finger—a most beautiful flower emerges that is able to extinguish any stench for a minute. That is when the true beauty of life emerges. If you add up all those ecstasies of beauty which, after all, vindicate entire years, then you will accumulate a few days or hours, or maybe, even minutes. Because beauty is conferred to us in seconds. It is given in doses, like homeopathic remedies. If you can't withstand the dose then you can die from a heart attack. It is varied, this beauty. It has as many manifestations as shadows that scamper along the inner surface of an eye lash on a sunny day, or like that fragment of the greatest dream in the world that transformed into a moment of awakening and cannot be fathomed. It is something that is uncatchable, it is impossible to capture it with a photography camera, a video camera, or a dictaphone. It's just a current running along your skin, in your mucous membrane, and on the bottom of your eye socket: an astonishing woman walks before you on the street, but you only see one of her cheeks, a hawk descends from a blue fall sky, the wind blows petals off of a flowering tree, you dive into the clear bed of a mountain river, a nighttime moth looks at you with large red eyes, you ride in a car on a fall road at night and headlights illuminate trees on the roadside, you stand in the morning on a mountain amidst the sun and all that is below you is covered by an even layer of clouds, a naïve and pleasant postcard that flies out of a randomly selected book, twelve white horses in the glow of the moon race up hills, an arrow flies. After such a list, a so-called carte blanche comes into play—a white card, a free card where everyone can note down their manifestations of beauty.

January 7

Of all the holidays, Christmas best gives us the chance to sense our humanity, our kindness.[6] We, all of a sudden, end up in the illusory role of a caregiver instead of the one being cared for. The essence of God's Christmas miracle is that we, people, have the opportunity to receive God in our own form. To that end, it's the only time that an impression that God has become dependent on our laws, our nature, our understanding, and our kindness, is formed. We begin to understand that, after this, He will become different—more understandable,

---

6   Until May 2023, Christmas in Ukraine was celebrated on January 7, following the Gregorian calendar. The decision to switch to the Revised Julian calendar (for fixed holidays only—that is, all religious holidays except Easter) was announced by the Ukrainian Greek Catholic Church in February and by the Orthodox Church of Ukraine in May 2023 (following a Council of Bishops meeting) (ed.).

closer, more merciful, and more loving. That is the first mystery of Christmas.

The second one, probably, is formed by the strange cogency and perfection of the simple Christmas storyline. In that storyline, like in a genetic code, everything that concerns humanity is contained. Maybe that is why it is only from such a storyline that a phenomenon such as the nativity scene developed. Gradually, the nativity scene grew into a model of the world, into a design of the cosmos, into a cosmological encyclopedia.

The yearly repetition of the nativity scene does not weaken but, rather, strengthens its comprehension. With every year, Christmas is understood in an ever deeper and clearer manner. And that is the third mystery. Christmas can be its own season of the year. Always awaited, always dreamed about, always unexpected. The story of your Christmas occupies its own string of beads. You can view it as an independent timeline of your life, which does not depend on the stories of other seasons of the year. In the chronology of Christmas, there are no special events, just light, comfort, gentleness, and wisdom. And even when something bad takes place during Christmas, it takes on a different sense, a different feel, and a different light.

During Christmas, we are drawn to our dear ones. This is yet another phenomenon of the great story. At some point, my grandfather could not restrain himself and went to his mother on Christmas Eve. He came from a very remote and safe mountain hideaway. On Christmas, the house was completely surrounded and he was captured. He spent many years in prisons and in exile. But he had no regrets for what he had done that Christmas. And none of the following Christmas days were bitter because of that Christmas. For Christmas is a separate season of the year, a separate story, a separate biography, and even the separate character of each person, of each family.

January 13

Again and again, I am convinced that people retained much from cold-blooded organisms whose lives directly depend on changes in the temperature of their surroundings. It's understood that we, too, change depending on whether it is cold or warm. But this is not what I have in mind. The remains of cold-bloodedness are first and foremost traced on the level of brain function.

A drop in temperature alters the entire arrangement of thought, of a worldview, of the mechanism of memory, and of the possibility of imagination. When it is hot, thoughts cannot be the same as those when it is cold. I recall two of my significant army dreams and visions. Back when it was possible to fry an egg on the surface of an armored personnel carrier, I dreamed of cold mountain streams, snow on mountain ridges, blue pools, ventilators in spacious rooms with shaded windows, chilled carbonated beverages, rains, walks through a snowy forest. On the other hand, as soon as winter arrived with its deadly freezing temperatures and an inch-thick layer of large icy crystals formed on the inner walls of the armored personnel carrier, then the vision became the opposite—a warm bed, lighted stoves, sleeping together with cats, scorching sand, hot wines and soups, puffy sweaters and hats, multi-hour hot baths. And thus is the simple dependence of dreams, memory, and imagination on temperature.

Truth be told, it's a bit different nowadays. With age, I began loving winter during the winter and summer during the summer. I no longer liked overly warmed homes. That is why I am happy that my old and ramshackle apartment is heated by stoves and not radiators. There is a certain charm in all of this. When the stoves cool overnight it gets cold in the morning, even in your bed, but you have to get up into an even greater cold, throw an old coat on your back and, first and foremost, light the stoves. It is very pleasant to warm up the kitchen, the bathroom, to heat water to be used for washing in buckets and pots. You cannot leave the house until the fire has been put out in the stoves. And when you are ready to head out, then it is not warm anywhere but in the kitchen, because the rooms warm up more slowly than the stove tiles do. It's also very pleasant not to heat one of the rooms to save energy and there you'll have the coldness of a storeroom.

It is pleasant to burn nut shells, letters, greeting cards, and branches of a Christmas tree in the stove. And then to remove the ash with a little shovel and save it for the garden in the spring. It is pleasant to smoke into the stove, listen to the whirring of the wind and the blizzards in the chimney labyrinths at night. And it is also pleasant to not depend on government heating schedules—then you can freeze in the winter or warm the house during cold summer rains. And most importantly—the daily changes in warmth of the dwelling offer the opportunity to live in a natural rhythm and not be the object of a large comfortable incubator. That is why I want to live where stoves exist.

January 15

Living in my home (in addition to various people) is an extraordinary plant—an araucaria. If you look through the window from the street, you can see it. The araucaria is still shorter than me, although it's over a hundred years old. They grow very slowly, these araucaria, in their Andes. For araucaria are Andes evergreens. And they live some three thousand years. They were rather fashionable in European dwellings at the beginning of the century. The Secession style adored ornaments such as these. And truth be told, it really is beautiful. It has paw-like branches, four on each level. It usually does not contain more than three levels. The rest gradually droop, die off, and are moved out of the way. And fresh millimeters begin to grow on the top. This araucaria was given to my grandma as a gift in return for some sort of successful medical treatment back in the 1920s. At that time, it was no taller than sixteen inches, although it was older than my grandma who, actually, was not yet a grandma. Based on its life span, the araucaria was an infant. At first, the plant did not notice anything. Later, it began scrutinizing more and more everything that went on in the house, and all our experiences came to be preserved in its tree rings. Because it's been proven that plants—especially such perfect ones—while, perhaps, not fully capable of thought, do, at the very least, understand, sense, and remember everything.

Sometimes it's scary to be in its presence. Because it's not so easy to have witnessed past events and then live on for a few more thousand years, having outlived us all, everyone close to it now. For it, we probably are like some kind of half-real, half-imagined childhood memory. Perhaps, it barely notices us, if one takes the difference in our life spans into consideration. Surely, it's not able to comprehend individual episodes that take place with us as they happen—in the same way that a camera with an unbelievably long shutter speed does not capture something that has moved somewhere else.

In that way, trees that live slowly don't notice, cannot notice, the existence of seasonal butterflies.

I bathe it every now and then. And, every time I take out the trash, I see that my trash bin is unique because it contains araucaria branches.

Not long ago, I purchased another little evergreen from the Andes. Perhaps it's as old as I am. I'm convinced that at least this araucaria will survive to see better years.

January 18

Any work with words, especially with words that are spoken, resides between one side where there is skepticism and another side where there is hope that cannot be destroyed. Skepticism—because you understand how little a word and speaking mean, you realize that your babbling will not lead to anything useful. Because every person is capable of doing that which is the worst in people and then no word can stop them. But there is a hope. A belief that all words find their addressee, no sentence is worthless, every detail contributes to that construction where it is needed most. That is why you work with words. You end up in the role of a craftsperson who makes luxurious goods or a salesman in a very peculiar and expensive antique store. Your goods are needed only by the few and those who need them don't always know about the existence of your store. So you have to wait. Because it's impossible not to wait until it happens. And when you see the delight, tears, and smile of the one who found you then you can no longer do anything else. I am convinced that no person exists—even if they are bad or stupid—who has not lived up to that moment when they meet that word or sentence that is addressed specifically to them. They, even if for a short time, transform into the best and most intelligent person in the world. It is because of such metamorphoses that it is worth living among people and loving them more than yourself. And it is worth giving birth to words, sentences, and pictures, sending them at random in all directions, handing them out to those who, unbeknownst to themselves, are suffering because they a lack a needed word... Deed... Gesture... Kiss... Blow... Hug... Glance... Gift... Melody... Fruit... Road... Direction or example.

January 21

Lately, many systems have appeared through which basic conversations between people become a study of communication technologies. These theories presuppose a learning of certain universal methods of making friends, dealing with enemies and, generally looking very likable. Gestures are given particular attention. More specifically—the instantaneous compositions of movement, facial expressions, and the look in one's eyes that form a gesture. However, it is worth considering who belongs to whom—a gesture to a person or a person to a gesture. Who controls whom, who can express whom. Perhaps (Milan Kundera mused about something similar) there exists a certain world of gestures that remain unchanged for centuries and must be realized in some manner. For this purpose, gestures select bodies for themselves which could best share, preserve, and repeat them. A gesture becomes the fate of the body that it has chosen. When one body ends—the gesture moves on to another. Maybe, in fact, these viruses cum gestures actually steer the world and all of life's mechanisms.

This is all easy to believe if you recall what it is that you find to be most important in how you perceive your loved ones. Words, events, and faces can be forgotten, but a few characteristic gestures, like crossbow arrows, strike you right in the throat, and that direct hit recreates everything that is tied to their carrier. At other times, you see a gesture that is most dear to you in some stranger. And, once again, your soul is scalded by tenderness, delirium, and sadness. An understanding of one of the most important senses in the world appears.

I trust Kundera, I want to trust my own experience. And that is why I don't trust American textbooks of communication technologies. I want to know that the gestures that live within me are the most important component of my biography. One of the most verified senses of our life. You can rid yourself of many things, but the gestures that are inherent to you need to be cared for and they will watch over you. It's like it is with de Saint-Exupéry—a responsibility for those whom you have tamed. But, in this case, the responsibility is mutual.

January 24

The greatest joy a person, or any other living thing, can possess is communication. No matter what some may think, it is through communication that all things having to do with happiness come together. Without communication, everything loses its sense, and no pleasures can bring it back. That is why anything having to do with poor communication always results in drama. And complete misunderstanding—in a tragedy. There are various types of misunderstanding—on purpose or not on purpose, sudden or drawn out, fleeting or endless, radical or compromising. They're all tragic. And, first and foremost, they are based on an opposition of desires and intentions—this is the first level of misunderstanding. The second level is more complicated—when interests are common, but there are different worldviews and manners of coexistence. And even higher is the level on which everything concurs, except for an understanding of words—meanings, shades, emphases, the history of a word and its various synonyms.

These tragedies are the most unpleasant ones, and there is almost no way out of such a situation. The saddest thing is when everybody thinks that they've done everything they could to understand someone else and to make themselves as easily understood as possible. What remains, then, is nothing but sorrow, reproach, and distrust. I once knew a turtle. And I knew its owners. Both the owners and the turtle were very pleasant and loved one another; they did all they could to make sure that everyone was satisfied and happy. I remember the look that turtle had when it communicated with its owners. But one day the turtle carelessly crawled to the edge of the balcony and fell helplessly down onto the pavement. Luckily, it was found right away and taken back home. As it turned out, it was still alive—the shell had been only chipped a little bit. They treated it and it seemed like everything was back to normal. But something was not quite right—happiness had disappeared. At first, the turtle became indifferent and soon, as a result, so did the people.

Gone were communication, contact, and understanding. Remaining were sorrow, reproach, and distrust. And that is how they lived. On one occasion, I gazed into the turtle's eyes for a long time and came to understand everything. It had become different—having fallen, the turtle had damaged its brain. Permanently. Simply put, it had gone crazy. And we could not know what was going on in its head—perhaps total darkness, perhaps the brightest of searchlights, maybe it had forgotten everything or, maybe it had excruciating headaches every night. Maybe it tickled between its brain and its skull, or maybe all sounds and smells irritated it. We could not know. We could not come to an understanding. We could not advise. We could not save it because we could not fully communicate. It, by the way, will live for another 240 years. With all of the above, but without us.

January 25

"A fable, that's all," this is what they say in the mountains when they are inferring that something is not worthy of attention or is trivial. "Tell us the latest fable," they say on the street as night approaches, when a couple of friends sit by the fountain, enjoying a few beers at the end of a day of partying. It is then that true-yet-fantastic life stories are told, having been passed along by an acquaintance. And literary scholars refer to a fable as a short, allegorical work, in which usually animals, or other natural phenomena, embody various human characteristics, traits, and conditions.

For too long, people have abused that last definition of a fable. As a result, an enormous number of mistakes and superstitions have occurred that twist the truths of natural science. Animals have become erroneous symbols, strapped with the burden of human faults and digressions that are alien to them. Yet, this can be looked at from another point of view. Instead of utilizing animals cum protagonists when telling human stories, we can simply study actual situations that animals find themselves in and then recognize in those situations that which has happened, is happening, and may happen to us. So here's a short and true, non-fable story about how foxes acquire dwellings.

For foxes, to live comfortably in luxurious burrows is of paramount importance. But they are incapable of, don't want to, and don't know how to dig them. Wonderful burrows are made by badgers—deep, dry, sophisticated, multi-roomed. Toilets and bedrooms are in separate rooms; corridors branch out; there are several entrances and exits. Badgers are born to be builders, while foxes need to find badgers' burrows and take them over. It is impossible to do this by force. A badger's jaw is among the most powerful, and a strike with its paw can kill two foxes, along with their babies. But there is another way, another approach. Badgers are extremely tidy animals. They hate—they cannot stand—the smell of a toilet. Foxes take advantage of this. Upon discovering a badger's dwelling, they relieve themselves right at the entrance. The first time around, the badger gathers the feces and buries it somewhere. And then the foxes do it again. And the badgers do it again. This goes on for several consecutive days. The tired and disillusioned badgers gather their whole family, including their pregnant ones, infants, teenagers, and the helpless aged, and abandon their homestead. They cannot take it anymore. They prefer to go to a different place and build a new, ideal home—sophisticated, dry, and deep. And the foxes with pleasure settle in the trashed, vacated burrow.

January 26

Several times in my life I had to gather people for certain combative events. And it turned out that there are no guidelines for finding the solider within a soldier. Actually, there are very few soldiers. Most of the people that you love, respect, and trust are not soldiers. And that is very good, it really is better that way. But only until that moment arrives when you need to find soldiers. And then you need to find some kind of test, some type of assessment, and tryout.

Of course, sometimes you can spot them with a naked eye. But in such instances those soldiers are just too soldierly. You'd be better off without them in your unit. They would certainly mess things up. So then—what test would work for this?

After lengthy observations, calculations, and analyses, I found a clear way of determining who is who. Strangely enough, doing this does not require any physical characteristics nor any intellectual qualities. The most important thing is to see how this or that person eats.

This is a flawless indicator. I have designated four types of people, based on their manner of eating, that are more important for me than the classical categorization based on temperament. So here are the categories: a strong type and a weak type. And each of them is split in two: strong-intensive and strong-calm, weak-intensive and weak-calm. This is enough to determine what a person is all about and what you can expect from them. The best soldiers belong to one type—strong-calm. All the others could be impeccable in one situation or another but never in all instances.

And so I gathered who don't make errors, those who don't doubt. They eat in a particular manner. It's impossible to confuse them with anyone else. And this method based on eating type is more valuable than any recommendations or autobiographies. This method is greater than an x-ray or a brain tomogram. It's a definition.

I have assembled those units based on such a process of selection. And they have already fulfilled their mission. There were no hiccups. But, to this day, I still find it uncomfortable to run into those who were not selected. Because I know how they eat...

January 27

A meal, any meal, has a distinct ritualistic significance, especially a common meal. A common meal is like an inner circle, a brotherhood, an exchange of confirmations and guarantees, a sign of similarity and camaraderie; it's like being involved in a crime or taking part in a heroic deed. I have shared a meal in the most diverse, and sometimes uncertain, exotic, and wild situations. Holiday parties, family lunches and dinners, wakes, nighttime breakfasts, the distribution of dry rations and improvised drinking snacks with the guys, the feeding of one's own children and of other's children, friends and foes, feedings in the hospital and food in the train, the last of what is edible in the mountains and the final grains of various cereals, cooked together, sliced sandwiches, receptions of the highest order, feeding by random people who had put me up for the night. Delicious, improvised suppers and the finishing off of meat scraps in restaurants, mystical Christmas Eve dinners and Easter eggs. And countless other lofty and lowly manifestations of the ritual of common meals.

But a particular one stands out in my memory—an unforgettable breakfast in Kyiv. It was about an hour before the hunger strike demonstration was to begin on the Maidan—Independence Square.[7] Several tens of students entered the cafeteria on the street just above the square for what could end up being our final breakfast. We ate boiled eggs, cheese, sour cream, crepes, and omelets; we drank coffee and sweet tea. Strangely, it

---

7 In October 1990, hundreds of students occupied Lenin Square in Kyiv, in Soviet Ukraine, demanding reforms in Soviet political and military spheres. Many of the participants went on a hunger strike. In independent Ukraine, the Square was renamed Maidan Nezalezhnosti (Independence Square) and was the site of both the Orange Revolution (2004) and Revolution of Dignity (2013–14), the latter often referred to as EuroMaidan (tr.).

was eerily good—calm, placid, filling, and immediate. The October sun broke through the huge windows in a special way and filled the whole cafeteria space. Less than one hour remained before the deciding moment. And then, suddenly, the doors opened and members of the riot police began entering the hall—wearing helmets and carrying batons and shields. They entered one after another, forming a seemingly endless line.

"And in just such a primitive fashion unsuccessful revolutions come to an end," I thought to myself, "in a cafeteria, when all the participants in the rebellion are satiated and helpless."

But a minute later, it became evident that this was not the end of the revolution. Because the riot police warriors did not pay any attention to us. They, too, had come to eat breakfast—they had been brought in from various cities in the morning and, before tending to their duties, before the battle that was to take place in those above-mentioned forty minutes, the soldiers wanted to eat. They ate eggs, sour cream, kefir, cheese, and crepes, and sat at the neighboring tables. They did not realize that they had been brought to Kyiv because of those sitting next to them. We finished the meal together. We exited in two separate groups and had a smoke after the meal. We had a smoke and dumped our cigarette butts into the same trash can. And we parted. Within five minutes, we had run onto the Maidan and sat down on the granite, having begun the hunger strike, the rebellion, and they took up their positions, surrounding the Maidan with a ring of iron. All sorts of things happened in the days that followed. But, on that first day, we ate together.

January 28

In the education and upbringing of each of us who lives in this smallish land known as Western Ukraine there is one major flaw. All of us know our closest geography very poorly. We have been taught to know our way around France, Russia, Germany, America, and Asia; even if we have never been there, we can imagine cities and landscapes, we know a few customs and manners of thinking. Closing our eyes, we can erect a spatial model of various parts of the world—where something is located, what is below, above and next to it. And this is very good. But most of us cannot do the same with even seven oblasts—Ivano-Frankivsk, Lviv, Ternopil, Transcarpathia, Volhynia, Rivne, and Chernivtsi. Of course, everyone knows well the environs of one's own village, knows pretty well a few oblast centers and the road from a city to one's native village. We also know somewhat about forests on the edge of the city and certain vacation spots. Everything else is terra incognita. We seek the exotic far beyond the borders of our fatherland. While Western Ukraine is a land where, every step you take, there is something different. The natural conditions of a fractured landscape create a unique situation in which every village and every town is different. Touring the nearest areas promises more impressions than can be expected. Different people, different buildings, a different language, and even forests, water, and grasses that are different. A variety of assorted countries is contained here. And sometimes—various worlds exist right next to one another. There isn't enough life to fully absorb this land. But you never feel like a complete stranger here. Because our slice of land is cobweb and lace. Like threads, people's stories unwind in various directions simultaneously, come together, unravel, get tangled up, form knots, tear but do not disappear. In this land, it is impossible to touch one hair and not have it affect another. There is nothing here that does not at least in some manner pertain to your fiber, your coil. It is quite simple to explore this lace—grab a seat on any local train or bus and get off at the, let's say, tenth stop. The day you spend at this locale will be unforgettable. Because it will certainly turn out that this place is not accidental.

February 7

To this day, children's favorite souvenirs from Kosiv, Kolomyia, Kuty and Vyzhnytsia markets are little cheese horses. They are sold by masters of this craft for loose change and appear to be something ordinary and primitive. But they truly are among the greatest wonders of the Hutsul region.

First of all—the cheese. The cheese in these horses is nothing like other types of cheeses. It is dry, very tasty, and fibrous. One can almost completely tear apart a horse by ripping off thin strips, or whole clusters, of fiber along its body. This cheese is impeccable with wine. When you fill your mouth with dry red wine and a piece of the horse, the cheese becomes like rubber, like a viscous, elastic, nutritious substance. The taste of the cheese is the greatest concentration of the manifestations of the essence of dairy. According to the laws of ecology and energy transfer, one old little horse equals several haycocks of the most fragrant grass from the sunny Alpine meadows of Carpathian Chornohora. A few such horses could constitute several days of food for a mountain climber or, let's say, a Montgolfier—that is, a hot air balloon pilot.

But it's not just about the taste. The appearance of the little horses is such that it is impossible to stop looking at them. Their so-called primitivism contains a certain harmony and significance that takes our memory back a few millennia—when there weren't many things around but each thing was immensely important. Some kind of Trypillian aesthetic dug out of the ground and out of the deepest layers of the subconscious. Meanwhile, cheese is one of the least malleable of materials. At one time, the horses were made exclusively by shepherds in the mountain meadows. But more than a hundred years ago the little meadow sculptures lost their significance in being secret dispatches from the meadow, and now they are made exclusively by women.

When you add a bit of glogg to milk, the milk sours. From this, a cheese is made that is both runny and viscous. Slices of that cheese are placed into hot water where a figure is quickly formed—a little horse, a buck, a lamb, or braided bread. The horses can be mounted, can come with weapons, or even with barrels tossed over a saddle.

The formed sculptures then need to be dropped into a salt solution to harden the cheese. The firmness of the cheese figure depends on the concentration of salt.

The roots of these creations are even less known than the origins of our mountains. But these clumps of particularly drawn-out cheese are genuine symbols of a mountainous country. If some kind of contraband would ever need to be taken out of the Carpathians, then cheese horses would be best suited for that. Because they are extraordinary. You immediately realize that this is something arcane and yet very significant.

February 10

Some time ago, I came to realize that, if a weapon is aimed at you, it doesn't necessarily mean anything, because if it truly is aimed at you, then there is nothing you can do about it, and if it is only vaguely aimed at you, then it will not be shot. I have been aimed at many times and nothing really came of it. I needed to just stay calm, even though, in the past, I've been commanded to do some ridiculous things with a weapon pointed at me—jump out of a moving train or off a towering bridge, give up something that was very important to me, or some other impossible feat. But these are all fragments that are soon forgotten. They rarely actually fired and almost always inaccurately. Only once was I accurately shot at—I almost died instead of my buddy. But nothing came of it. They missed me. And this is what bought my buddy a bit more life. I seldom had such reliable buddies. And such ideal ones. His name was Rudko. I named him. Large, wolf-like, but yellow and with long hair. With the marvelous eyes of a tiger or bobcat—amber, deep, and wise. And those eyebrows. Completely human-like, brown eyebrows. He was all grown up, and with a massive collection of nasty experiences, when he showed up on our mountain. He immediately became attached to me. In the beginning, he would occasionally bark at me when I would pet him, because tenderness seemed somewhat strange and cunning to him. But he soon got used to it. Only I was capable of petting him the way he wanted to be petted. Even though he began living with us, Rudko never entered the house. I suspect that he was claustrophobic. He kept order in the yard—he didn't allow anyone into it but members of the family, he mercilessly harassed postal carriers, he barked at all the trains. He hated anything that represented the slightest change in the rhythm of our lives. And, besides that, for some reason, he defended me from certain family members and determined that I should not have anything to do with them. Infrequently, he could get upset and gnaw someone. Gnaw them, not bite them. Soon, the list of those who had been gnawed was identical to the list of those who lived near us. And it was then that the older adult neighbors decided that it was time to get rid of him. One of them had a rifle; the others would stake out Rudko. The dog sensed something and stopped visiting the neighboring areas.

I was running in the ravine when buckshot whistled over my head. Surprisingly, I didn't fall to the ground. I peeked out of the ravine and heard a couple more whistles by my head and saw the neighbors cum hunters, who were shooting in my direction. They were shooting because the only thing sticking out of the ravine was my head, which, with its color and shagginess, recalled some part of Rudko's body. After the sharpshooters had come to their senses, they kissed and hugged me for a long time. And, as if speaking to someone who had returned from the dead, they promised me they would no longer harass my buddy. Of course, as it is written in ancient books, in time, they easily rescinded their promise. I think that, if they had shot and killed me that day, this would have happened even sooner.

February 15

This was 800 years ago. In the days before the Great Fast, Francis of Assisi, who had already become a saint but had not yet been canonized, was in a city named Perugia. There was a large lake with a small island in its center. Francis stopped during his journey to spend the night in the modest dwelling of a man who, recognizing the saintliness of the guest, received him with extraordinary attention. During the night, a great inspiration came to the saint—to refrain, like Christ had, from eating anything throughout the whole Great Fast. The place he was to do that was on the island in the lake. In the morning, Francis asked the man to take him to the island, leave him there without any food, and not come back there for forty days—up until the sixth Thursday. Also, the man was not to tell anyone that Francis was staying there—the saint did not want his students or followers to witness his spiritual act. So they sailed out. The spring water made his feet cold when he exited the boat. The man nonetheless left the ascetic two small loaves of bread—in case the latter could not make it completely without any food after all—and sailed back, confirming that he would keep his promise to stay silent about this. Francis found a place on the uninhabited island where tree branches were thickly interwoven and stayed there, in that nature's gazebo, in order to remain untouched for over a month thinking about God.

After forty days, the man sailed back out to the island. He found Francis in that very same place. The latter was pale but looked as active and energetic as always. Having lost sense of the flow of passing days, Francis didn't even think the time of his heroic fast had concluded. He was prepared to be there even longer.

The man noticed that one of the loaves remained untouched and a bit less than half of the other one was missing. The saint explained this by stating that he could have gotten by without any bread at all but he felt that it would have been arrogant to go through this fast like Christ had—without a crumb of bread. Thus, that piece of bread was eaten so as not to measure up to what Jesus was able to do.

This was 800 years ago. But certain events occur in such a way that it seems like they took place yesterday—or even more likely—are taking place this very moment.

February 22

This story is a short one, as are all tragedies, which differ from misfortune and drama in temporal parameters. By their brevity, in fact. Tragedies are not long lasting. Their effects—those can last very long. But then it is not a tragedy. So—this story is tragic. It is so short that it has not yet even become a history, and can't even develop into a story, except in one's imagination.

Tokaj. An amazing land that has the finest wine as its blood. Tokaj. There is no entry with that name in the Ukrainian Soviet Encyclopedia. While in the third volume of the Ukrainian General Encyclopedia published in Lviv, Stanislaviv, and Kolomyia in the 1930s there is such an entry. Of course, they don't know about the tragedy yet. Because no encyclopedia can predict a tragic coincidence that will take place in 65 years. So, in that encyclopedia, Tokaj is found between Toynbee (an English philanthropist) and Tocantins (a 1,615 miles long river in eastern Brazil). A Hungarian town by the Hegyalja foothills (we will come back to that entry). Six thousand inhabitants, famous wine. Spectacular white wine... As for Hegyalja, it is a trachyte mountain range that extends from Prešov to Tokaj, 3,582 feet high. On its sides are vineyards of Tokaj wines. Those are from the Ukrainian General Encyclopedia. And now, from that same year. Velhagen und Klafing Press in Leipzig. *Das Bild der Erde*—a picture of the world—"a new atlas in 100 pages of maps." Tokaj is on the Tysa. That Tysa which a week ago became dead and poisonous, like thousands of sacks of mashed plum pits. The fish died, the plants died, as did the wells. Because cyanide leaked into the Tysa and then into the Danube.

In the small, snowy town of Bardejov which is in Slovakia near Prešov, where the Hegyalja begin, which end in Tokaj, there is a medieval little street with a building in which the Tokaj Wines winery lives. 50 varieties on tap, a ten-liter jar for 200 korunas (about four dollars), that is, forty cents for a liter of the most valuable juice of the lands of Central Europe. The men, drinking one glass after another of the fragrant wine, cried. "Listen, man," said one of them, "there, in Tokaj, on the shores of the Tysa, every other house has a stork's nest. What will they eat? Our poison? But they'll die. And the grapes, too. This is the last of the wine for several years going forward." They cried and drank and prayed to God that this misfortune would pass as quickly as possible, disappear. So that the least number of stories would grow out of it. Because, here in Central Europe, everything is so close.

February 25

The sense of what one's homeland is involves myriad concepts. The broadest being: state, society, nation, language, land, history, people, myths, culture. But, as it turns out, lately it seems that the only ones that remain dependable, ours, truly Ukrainian, and faithful, are myths and, of course, land. Crippled, damaged and littered, yet insanely beautiful. You begin to appreciate Native Americans, you begin to appreciate the Chechens who, perhaps, continue to exist only because the rock has managed to remain. There is a sense that soon our true fatherland, too, will exist only in its manifestation as land. But that land will not cease being native to you, being yours. Notwithstanding what state it belongs to, what people walk upon it, what language they speak, in which culture they bathe, and to which history they pray. And, in these Ukrainian landscapes, even lichens on a dead tree and splintered rocks will remain true to our myths, which can at least hold on to the wind, if that's all that's left to hold on to.

I felt all of this not too long ago when I spent time in the most obscure corner of the former Lemko land. The former—because no Lemkos, nor even Lemko songs, remain there today. Only a resplendent wasteland, the jagged relief of which captured the intonations of Lemko mythological cosmology forever. This is an almost uninhabited corner that is divided between southeast Poland and northeast Slovakia. The toponomy has been preserved—the place names—Magura, Bekheriv (Becherov), Konechna (Konieczno), Hladyshiv (Gładyszów), Horlytsia (Gorlice), Banytsia (Banica), Kryva, Volovets, Nyzkyi Beskyd (Beskidy Środkowe). What have remained are those that don't betray—the mountains, the valleys, and streams. What have remained are antique souvenirs—churches seemingly assembled out of matches, characteristic local houses. Those are called *khyzhi*—long and gentle, a living area for people and livestock, for cattle, together under one roof; what have remained are talisman-paths between the mountains, valleys, streams, churches, and *khyzhi*. There are very few people, we don't have areas with so few people (except for the Gorgany mountains), and it's not those people anymore—every one of those people were taken away back in 1947. A few of them, actually, did return, but they returned different than they were. At every step here, you can learn two disciplines—how unused wooden buildings are ruined and how processes of natural forest renewal take place on abandoned territories. But, regardless of all the sadness concerning these mountains of ours, which, formally, no longer belong to us, two thoughts initially emerge. Number one—this is a true homeland on that faithful level of land and myths. Number two—it's good that only the land and the myths remain, and nothing else that could destroy or offend them. And, P. S. — if our land becomes alien to us, then the last Ukrainian natives will have the sacred Lemko reservation for their retreat.

March 9

City dwellers are used to assessing the weather and various natural phenomena according only to convenience and comfort. Villagers, people tending the land, gardeners, foresters, and beekeepers think a bit more universally—they think not about themselves but about the wild animals, insects, trees, buds, sprouts, bulbs, seeds, flowers, leaves, fruits, berries, and roots that they tend to. In fact, they only tend to them in order to eat them, or to give them to those that live in cities—those who assess the weather only based on their own comfort. Such a narrowed worldview is the reason for the greatest misfortunes of humanity. But it has been like this forever, and it turns out that those few people who hear the singing of the grass simply cannot and will never be able to convince those who don't hear it to pay attention to it. The snow from the day before yesterday was considered in various ways: as an unpleasantry, a joy, a joke, happiness, a difficulty, an obstacle, senselessness, an absurdity, and as a fragment that really doesn't mean anything and—besides a few rescheduled flights—doesn't alter anything. Because, nonetheless, it's spring already, and this short-lived snowy protest will be quashed in a few days. So, the snow fell the day before yesterday and, a couple of days later—that is, today—only traces remain of it. It seems like it really did not alter anything.

But such an assertion is correct only in a system of the coordinates of human—that is, anthropocentric—logic. Because, actually, two days of snow saved an entire tribe and an entire army of God's creatures. This small courageous and beautiful nation has already suffered from human invasion. Every day, its finest men, its most beautiful, pregnant women, and its greatest thinkers were murdered with human hands and their bodies were driven to the city and displayed in squares there, only to slowly decay. Moreover, people ruined their homesteads, dug up their treasures, and exchanged them for cheap thrill money.

A day of snowfall and a few days of snow-covered ground gave this nation an opportunity to rest. In a short time, spared from a new attack by people, the forest tribes of crocuses, snowdrops and scilla managed to do a lot. Some of them inserted fertile seeds in the dirt; others died off, and, by doing so, rescued the underground perennial bulbs from destruction; while most of them simply stopped being attractive and, as a result, lost their defenselessness.

Thus, the two-day snow towards the end of March was not for naught. Maybe next spring a small tribe will be able to assemble a new large army because of it.

The UnSimple

Translated by Uilleam Blacker

For whomever does not read this essay, life will be an unsimple experience, since the Unsimple will pass him or her by with their explicit plots—even more than this, they will simply turn off the sound and the light.

YAROSLAV DOVHAN [1]

---

[1] Yaroslav Dovhan (b. 1956) is a well-known poet from Taras Prokhasko's hometown, Ivano-Frankivsk (tr.).

SIXTY-EIGHT ACCIDENTAL FIRST SENTENCES

1. In the fall of 1951, it would not at all have seemed strange to go west. At that time, even the east had begun slowly to shift in that direction. Nevertheless, in November 1951, Sebastian and Anna left Mokra and went into the east, of which there was, after all, a great deal more. To be more precise, they headed for the eastern south, or, we could say, the southeast.

2. It was not the war that had delayed the journey for so many years. The war could do little to change anything in their lives. Sebastian had decided on the bold step of breaking with his family's tradition of showing children important places from the family history when those children turned fifteen. Because, when Anna turned fifteen, Sebastian understood that everything was repeating itself, and that Anna was the only possible woman in the entire world for him. And it was

not just that he could be only with her, but also that he couldn't be without her. Meanwhile, in Yalivets, that place from the family history that he was meant to show her, the Unsimple were waiting for her. And Sebastian knew that they would easily persuade his daughter to stay with them.

After all, they had predicted that she would become an Unsimple at the moment of her birth.

3. In April 1951, Anna began to sense that her father, Sebastian, was the only possible man for her, and they began to make love.

That spring, there was no lack of wanderers travelling by hitherto unheard-of roads and carrying fantastic rumors with them. This was how Sebastian found out that the Unsimple had vanished from Yalivets. After that, nothing more was heard of them.

Sebastian and Anna spent the summer submerged in their lovemaking, oblivious to the various armies flowing back and forth around them. Nothing blocked them from going east, south, or southeast. When it got really cold, and the roads contracted into tight, well-defined lines, they finally left Mokra, aiming to be in Yalivets within a few days. The journey had been put off for three years. But Sebastian feared nothing—he had once again found a real woman. Of the same breed as always.

4. He had no idea how he would truly be able to show his daughter all the places in the mountains between Mokra and Yalivets. Instead of four days, the journey would need to last four seasons. Only in this way, and at all times—by day, by night, in the morning, and in the evening—would Anna be able to see how different this road looked in its collective totality. He looked at the map, read the names aloud, and immediately began to feel better. Even the fact that the map meant nothing to Anna could not dampen his mood.

He was, however, a little disturbed by the trees along the way, which he hadn't seen for so many years: the growth of trees is what most often makes a landscape unexpectedly unrecognizable. Their growth is also proof beyond doubt that trees that mean something to us should never be abandoned.

And as for the actual trip—no journey knows what might become of it, what its true causes or consequences may be.

5. Frants once told Sebastian that there are things in the world much more important than what is called fate. He had in mind, first and foremost, place. Where there is a place, there is a history (if a history is woven, it means there must be a corresponding place). To find a place is to give a start to history. To invent a place is to discover a plot. And plots, after all, are also more important than fate. There are places where there is nothing

left to tell, and sometimes it is enough simply to speak the names of places in the correct sequence in order to take command of the most interesting history, one that will be more captivating than any biography. Toponymy can lead one astray, but it is also perfectly possible to rely on nothing more.

6. And something like that happened to Sebastian. He found Yalivets, which Frants had invented. He became fascinated by linguistics. Toponymy captivated him, and not just because he was fascinated by its details. Pleska, Opresa, Tempa, Apeska, Pidpula, Sebastian. Shesa, Sheshul, Menchul, Bilyn, Dumen, Petros, Sebastian.

Before there were any mountains, their names were already assigned. It was the same with his women—they had not yet come into being when his blood had already begun to mix with the blood that would become theirs.

From then on, he became dedicated to keeping to this limited toponymy and curtailed genetics.

7. Frantsysk met Sebastian on a cliff beyond Yalivets. Sebastian was on his way home from Africa and was shooting birds. His sniper rifle did not allow him to feel the kill. Through the gun's sight, he saw only a kind of movie. The shot did not so much cut the film short as introduce a new scene into the script. He had already shot a fair number of small birds that were flying over Yalivets on their way, as it happens, to Africa.

Winter would soon be happening. Winter must always change something. Winter gives a purpose—this is its defining characteristic. It closes the openness of summer, and this fact itself has to find expression somehow.

Frantsysk was looking for something to make a new animated film about. And suddenly here, just before winter, a cliff above the town, in the middle of the town, a flock of birds flying over a mountain to Africa, to Asia Minor, to the fields of saffron and aloe and hibiscus between enormous dog roses, a short way from the long, slender Nile, a pile of many-colored birds, shot through the eye, laid one on top of the other so that their different colors contrast even more sharply with one another, in each right eye a reflection of their intercontinental journey, in each left a red stain, and not a feather damaged, and a light wind gently brushing and tangling the ghostly down of the weightless little bodies, and the eye of the marksman at the other end of the sight. And the marksman. A red white African.

8. Sebastian's hands were frozen. He had gotten frostbite one Saharan night. Since then, his hands could not bear gloves. Sebastian asked Frants what pianists were supposed to do in such cold.

They looked around in all directions and everywhere was beauty. Because it was fall, and fall was sliding into winter. Frants named various mountains without even indicating which was which. Then he invited Sebastian to his home. It had been a long time since he had had guests—it had been a long time since he had met any strangers on the cliffs. That may well have been the first time they drank coffee mixed with grapefruit juice. When Anna brought their coffee out onto the glazed veranda, where vine branches burned in the copper stove, Sebastian asked her to stay for a moment and show them what could be seen from the window. Anna recited: Pleska, Opresa, Tempa, Pidpula, Shesa, Seshul, Menchul, Bilyn, Dumen, Petros.

It was late fall, 1913. Frants said that there are things far more important than what is called fate. He suggested that Sebastian try living in Yalivets for a while. It was getting dark, and before bringing them a second pot—almost pure juice, only a drop of coffee—Anna went to make Sebastian's bed, since she could not yet do this in the dark.

CHRONOLOGICALLY

1. In the fall of 1913, Sebastian stayed in Yalivets. He was twenty years old. He had been born on the other side of the Carpathians, on the Borzhava river, in 1893. In 1909, he spent a whole month in Trieste with his parents, and, a year later, he went to fight in Africa. He returned home via the Black Sea and Constanţa, then the Rodna mountains, Hryniava, and Pip Ivan. He crossed Chornohora, passing by Hoverla and Petros. It was late fall, 1913.

2. Yalivets had appeared on the map twenty-five years earlier.
The place had been thought up by Frantsysk, who was usually known as Frants. Frantsysk had lived in cities for twenty years—Lviv, Stanislav, Vyzhnytsia, Mukachevo. He had learned to draw with one artist only (an artist who had once worked with Brehm and had later made

and forged prints); he had had to, had wanted to, and had been able to travel with the artist from place to place. Then he was shown a camera, and he stopped drawing. Later, however, very near Morshyn, the illustrator died. He had been accompanied by a professor of botany from Krakow—they had been on their way to Chornohora to make a study of the plants of the Hutsul country.[2] In Stanislav, the professor had come across Frants, and several days after this the latter would find a place where he felt at home—comfortable and happy. A year later, he returned to that place and began to build a town.

Within five years, Yalivets would become the most magical resort in all of Central Europe, and quite fashionable.

3. Anna, because of whom Sebastian remained in Yalivets, had originally been named Stefaniia. The real Anna was her mother, Frantsysk's wife. She had tried to conquer her fear of heights, since she was a mountaineer.

---

[2] The Hutsuls are an ethnic sub-group of Ukrainians who live mainly in the Ukrainian Carpathian mountains. Their rich folk culture has inspired numerous writers and artists from Ukraine, Poland, and beyond. Perhaps the most famous literary work on the Hutsuls is the early twentieth-century writer Mykhailo Kotsiubynskyi's novella *Shadows of Forgotten Ancestors* (1912), which was the basis for the internationally successful film of the same name by Sergei Parajanov (Sarkis Paradzhanian in Armenian, Serhii Paradzhanov in Ukrainian), which was released in 1965 (tr.).

She had come to the resort with a friend of hers, a speleologist. They were both masters in their chosen fields. The only difference was that she would only climb up, and he would only climb down—but what they both lacked most of all was space. When Anna became pregnant with Frantsysk's child, she decided to give birth there, in Yalivets. And by the time Stefaniia was born, Anna had no desire to go back to where she had come from.

She died in a duel, to which she had been challenged by her husband. Frantsysk immediately changed Stefaniia's name to Anna. He brought his daughter up alone, until the day he invited Sebastian, who was on his way home to the Borzhava from Africa, into their home. Frants realized then that, from now on, she would either submit to Sebastian or to no one at all.

LETTERS TO AND FROM BEDA

1. The only person who knew them all over several decades was old Beda. It was said that he was one of the Unsimple. He was certainly acquainted with them. When Frants taught Anna to read and write (for a long time, he had not wanted to do this because he realized that Anna would not write but rather record, and that she would not read but rather re-read, and Frants considered this useless), she began to show an interest in learning about the beginnings of Yalivets and about her mother. Old Beda was the only one who could know about such things, and Anna would write him letters with questions. The answers would arrive either very quickly or would take so long that she would begin to fear she had written the address incorrectly, that the letter had ended up somewhere where there would be nobody to write back and say that Beda could not possibly have been there, ever.

Around this time, Beda began living in an armored car, traveling from place to place, but always within a certain radius of Yalivets. Once Beda told a story.

2. After the first year of living in the armored car, he was sure that he would remember its interior down to the tiniest detail until the end of his life. Then the car ran over a mine that had been left behind by the Italians when they had been building a tunnel in the Iablunytskyi pass. Beda was almost killed. He was found by some Hutsuls. His body was badly damaged, and not in the way that one is damaged by a knife, a saber, or an axe—the wounds rather resembled cracks in the surface of the earth. They stuffed him into a barrel of honey and fed him goat's milk curdled in hot wine. A couple of gypsy violinists undertook the job of repairing the car. Nine months later, Beda climbed out of the honey. The armored car stood in the garden and the children had climbed on it to shake the fall apples from the high branches of a tree. From a winter Calville, most likely. Beda, then, thought that he had memorized the inside of his vehicle down to the last detail. He climbed up the ladder to the hatch, and, tiring quickly, realized that he could not remember exactly how he had climbed that ladder nine months previously. He closed his eyes and could not picture what was where inside the car, where everything had once been so familiar. He tried to comfort himself, telling himself that it was because he was

now in a different skin. Or that, during the repairs, the fiddlers had discarded some parts. But he could not quite put himself at ease. That is what old Beda wrote.

Anna sent him letters with questions about her family. He replied, answering the questions and always adding something about himself; although she never asked him for this, she read it with interest.

3. Some of Anna's letters went something like this.
...I'm not asking you to tell me everything...

...I also have so much to tell you about Yalivets, Frantsysk, my mother, the Unsimple. You're the only one in the whole world who knew all of them...

...I don't even know why I want to know all this, but I feel them without their voices. I feel my own body, I'm starting to think like it. I realize suddenly that I'm not self-sufficient. That I depend on all of them, because my body thinks through them...

...it's not something that makes me feel bad, this dependence, but I want to know which parts of me belong to whom: which belong to Frants, which to my mother, which to the Unsimple, which to Yalivets, and which are mine...

...hesitation is something greater than a mistake...
...tell me something else...
...tell me more...
...how did Yalivets look long ago...
...I say this: I love you so much, it is and it is...

...I know that my mother arrived when Yalivets became fashionable. There wasn't a resort like it anywhere in the world...

...my dad always spoke about our ancestors using the word "probably"...

4. Old Beda would answer (If I could remember everything they said, everything we talked about. Even without what I said. And if they had told me everything they said without me. But they also remembered little, only a few phrases. When you don't remember how you spoke, how you were spoken to, then you have nobody. You won't hear the voices. You have to hear a voice. A voice is a living thing and a voice gives life. A voice is more powerful than an image. Frants told me that there are things more important than fate. Let's say: intonation, syntax. If you want to be yourself, never give up your own intonations. He spoke with the same voice as always throughout the whole war. I can't speak with you a second time only about this. I can't tell you everything you want to hear. I can speak. And then you can hear what you want. But not vice versa. But you also won't remember everything. What has been said passes. We feel good now because we're talking so well. I like hearing myself talking to you. No one in your family ever recognized standard syntax. You know what your family phrases are—it is and it is, we should and we should, irrational coherence is absolute, I love you so very much... Hesitation is more than

a mistake, or less. But for longer. They say that your grandfather—your mom's dad, he wasn't from round here, but from somewhere near Sharish—had a little garden. He dreamed of living there in his old age. Lying on a bed made of snail shells, smoking opium, and rolling glass balls with his feet. He walled off a small scrap of land and sowed it with a single variety of high-quality grass. In the middle, he erected a really tall pole and grew ivy, beans and wild grapes along it. Alongside, he dug a pit and filled it up with snail shells. They said he had seen something similar once behind a high wall in Hradčany when he had been lost and climbed up a cherry tree to get his bearings. He would lie on that bed of shells when he smoked. He would lay his head on a great, flat rock, on which only lichen grew. He wandered in the White Tatras, collected spores, and infected or impregnated the rock with them. He made the glass balls himself; in their centers were living cyclamen. You could set the balls in motion, they would roll and come to a stop, and the cyclamen would have spun around, but slowly they would begin to twist, turning downwards toward the earth and upwards toward the sun. The garden was destroyed when your mother was still little, and your grandfather escaped with her and the other children to the mountains. Frants isn't local either. Nobody can say where he came from, where you all come from originally. He decided to settle in Yalivets because he thought that he could avoid experiences there, that there wouldn't be any stories there. He didn't want anything to happen around him that he couldn't keep up with, that he would have to force himself to remember. He was still very young. He didn't know that things just don't work like that: first, life will seethe around you no matter where you are, perhaps trivially and monotonously, but always unrelenting, never repeating, constantly changing. And second, you don't have to remember anything anyway, you don't have to force yourself to keep up. What needs to remain will come and take root by itself. A sort of botanical geography—the exhaustive joy of germination. I know that the first Anna appeared around the time Yalivets became fashionable. Patients came from all around to drink gin. The town already looked just as it does now, except without your inventions. Little hotels and guesthouses with bars were built. You could drink by yourself in your room, in pairs or in groups, three times a day, on an empty stomach and in the night, or all night, or they could wake you at a certain time during the night and serve you a measure in bed. You could fall asleep wherever you were drinking, or drink with a doctor or psychotherapist. I liked to get drunk on a swing. Anna was an excellent climber. She could feel the weight of every inch of her own surface and was able to spread it across a vertical wall. You don't need a wide perspective up there. And the most important thing is that you're always with a rope. She had thought she didn't care about anything—but, in truth, she started to be afraid. She started coming to Yalivets after a serious injury. Although she could climb well again, she was now afraid. She couldn't fully explain it, because she was barely able to speak, although she thought with every millimeter of her body. Frants then was twice the size that he is now—you can imagine what they felt. Frants never told anyone about this, but I know that they were happiest when Anna became pregnant. And there's no "maybe" about it. For some reason, it is believed that death is the end of a story. In fact, stories end when someone is born. Don't be offended, but when you were born the story of Frants and your mother ended…)

Anna liked the fact that Beda wrote on wrappers that still smelled of various fruit teas they had once contained.

GENETICALLY

1. Frantsysk considered himself a surface person. He loved surfaces. He felt confident on them. He was unsure whether there was any sense in going deeper than what is seen with the naked eye. Although he listened attentively to sounds coming from behind any sort of membrane. And he would sniff the streams that flowed out of pores. He observed every movement, but, when he looked at someone, he did not try to imagine what that person might be thinking. He was unable to analyze the essence of anything, because the over-abundance of superficial details provided more than enough answers. Many times, he noticed that he could be completely satisfied with those explanations for various phenomena that can be accessed without knowledge of the fundamental relations between things. Most often, he used the simplest figure of thought—analogy. He generally thought about what was similar to what. Or, more precisely, what

reminds one of what. Here, he mixed forms with tastes, sounds with smells, characteristics with touches, the sensations of the internal organs with heat and cold.

2. But there was one philosophical question that genuinely interested him.

Frants contemplated reduction. He observed how the immensity of human life, the infinity of infinite seconds, could be reduced to a few words of the kind that, for example, can be found written about a person in an encyclopedia (of all books, Frants recognized only the *Larousse Encyclopedic Dictionary*, and his library consisted of a dozen or so editions of *Larousse*).

One of his favorite distractions was to invent entries of just a few words or sentences in the style of *Larousse* about people he knew or had met. He even wrote down some entries about himself. Over the years, he had amassed several hundred. And although each one contained something that distinguished it from the others, the fact remained that his entire—granted, as yet unfinished—life could be set down in a few dozen well-ordered words. This excited Frants and never failed to amaze him; it gave him hope that he was living his life very well.

3. Further proof of Frantsysk's superficiality was that he knew nothing about his family roots. Even of his mother and father he knew only what he had seen

himself as a child. For some reason, they had never spoken with him about the past, and it had never crossed his mind to ask them about anything. He spent his whole childhood alone, drawing everything that he saw. His parents died while he was away, when he already had his own teacher in a different town. Eventually, Frants realized that not once, not even in the first years of his life, had he painted his mother or father. Their reduction was practically absolute.

It was most likely the fear of continuing this emptiness that drove him to tell his daughter as much as possible about himself. He even tried to explain the construction of the world in such a way that she would always remember that it had been her father who had first told her about this or that.

About her mother, however, his Anna, he also knew only about the time they had spent together—a little more than two years. But that was still enough for the girl to learn everything she needed to know about her mother.

All her life, except for the last few months, Anna had not spent a single day apart from her father. Even after she became Sebastian's wife.

4. In September 1914, she volunteered for the army and, after a few weeks training, was sent to the front in eastern Galicia. Sebastian and Frantsysk remained alone in a small building not far from the main street

in Yalivets. There was no news from the front. Then, in spring 1915, a courier arrived in the town and handed Sebastian (Frants had been beheaded the day before, and the following day his funeral was due to take place) an infant—the daughter of the heroic volunteer, Anna Yalivtsivska. Sebastian never found out exactly when the child had been born, or what pregnant Anna had done in the midst of the most terrible battles of the World War. But he knew for sure that this was his daughter. He called her Anna, or rather "second Anna" (it wasn't until after her death that he often referred to her simply as "the second").

5. The second Anna grew more and more similar to the first. Or maybe they were both similar to the very first—only old Beda could know this. As for Sebastian, he grew accustomed to comparing himself daily to Frantsysk.

He brought up his Anna by himself and would let no woman near her. In the end, eighteen-year-old Anna, of her own free will, chose a man for herself. The man was, of course, Sebastian.

6. This time, there was nothing he didn't know about the pregnancy of his woman. Indeed, only he was present at the birth of their daughter (and, at the same time, his granddaughter). And Sebastian saw how the birth became the end of the story. Because, at the very beginning of this new story, his dearest, second Anna died just moments before the third Anna came to rest in his arms.

Somewhere in the bitter depths within him, Sebastian sensed the whirl and flow of underground waters, he felt worlds being sketched out and erased, he felt the transformation of the previous twenty years into a seedling. It occurred to him that he didn't need the Unsimple to realize that something like this had already happened to him once, and that, with this newborn woman, he would live to see a similar end. He realized that this was not a question of the curious blood of the women of his family, but rather of his own unstoppable desire to be poured into it. He realized it wasn't that they had to die young, but rather that he had no right to see them more than one at a time.

7. Sebastian went out onto the veranda. The Unsimple had probably been there for some time already, but they had sat quietly on the benches, waiting until the birth was over.

For supper, Sebastian had shot almost a hundred of the thrushes that had recently been eating all the berries on the young rowan tree. He baked the birds whole, after plucking them and brushing them with saffron.

Two women—a seeress and a snake-charmer—washed Anna and wrapped her in colorful blankets.

The men, meanwhile, managed to feed the child and declared that there was no need to tell her anything—she herself was Unsimple. And they also said what Frants had said: that there are things far more important than fate. Apparently, he was thinking of heredity.

After supper, Sebastian could not get to sleep. He was trying to remember whether Anna had ever said anything about where she would like to be buried, and about how to feed the child tomorrow. Then he began to think about Pastor Mendel's experiments with peas and decided that the child was going to be happy.[3] He tried to imagine himself in fifteen years' time—in 1951—and immediately fell asleep.

---

3   Gregor Mendel was an Austrian scientist and Augustinian friar. His experiments with pea plants in the 1850s and 1860s were important contributions to the modern understanding of genetics, in particular of heredity (tr.).

THE FIRST OLD PHOTOGRAPH— THE ONLY UNDATED ONE

1. A low wall composed of flat stone slabs of irregular shape. Furthermore, the slabs also differ greatly in size—there are small, thin ones, like closed hands, and also larger ones, long enough for a person to lie down on quite comfortably. These are the thickest, but not one of them retains the same thickness along its entire length. The majority, however, are of medium size. If you were to hold one of these in front of you, with one end tucked under your chin, it would barely reach down to your waist. The wall has one strange quality: although it looks solid enough and gives the impression that it has no end (just as all marked boundaries should) the unfilled gaps between the horizontally laid slabs somehow arouse the desire to move and rearrange them, or to remove each one and make something new of it.

2. It is important that all the stones are completely clean. On the whole wall, not a single scrap of moss is to be found, not a single little tree, nor blade of grass. Even if the leaves of the beech trees happened to fall on the wall (and the wall is wide enough, and the leaves are yellowing already and occasionally fall off in the dry wind, as always happens at the end of August—all this is evident even from a black-and-white photograph), someone has carefully swept them up from the surface of the stones, which are warmed by the afternoon sun.

Between the trees, beyond the wall, there is a cubic building, also made of stone. The stone is impeccably smoothed and polished, and the whole building appears to be a windowless monolith. The relief on the façade is designed to look like four drawers, so that the cube also resembles an enormous chest of drawers. The building is made in such a way that the top drawer appears to protrude slightly. Engraved on a relatively small enameled metal plaque, in simple, thick, squat script, is the word YUNIPERUS.

3. In front of the wall, there is a fragment of road paved with river stones. The road begins at the bottom of the postcard, in the middle, and leads up toward the top left-hand corner, skirting round a tall, leaning cedar pine, before disappearing once again near the center—naturally, at the top. In the distance, the road curves

in such a way as to serve as a sort of backdrop for the rest of the photo. The wall is always on the right, and on the left is a narrow canal with bare, concrete banks. Further to the left, beyond the canal, is a sliver of a high, wooden platform, on which there are several deck chairs and some planters with slender junipers.

4. Frantsysk, in a white linen coat with large buttons, stands on the very edge of the canal, on the bank nearest the road. He has some clothes slung across one arm. The clothes are the same color as his coat, but it is possible to make out a shirt and a pair of pants. In his other hand is a pair of black shoes. From his posture, it is clear that he has just turned away from the water. And in the water is the head of a person swimming with the current along the canal.

5. The face is impossible to make out, but Sebastian knows it is he. It had been a habit of theirs: they would go for strolls through the town, Sebastian slowly swimming the canals and Frants walking along the bank.

All the streets in Yalivets were lined with canals. In this way, water from the many streams that flowed down the cliffs above the town was collected in a swimming pool at its lower edge. Sebastian could swim for hours in the mountain water, and he and Frants would converse the whole time. From the look of it, the photograph must have been taken near the end of the summer of

1914. Because there was one occasion on which a young instructor in the art of survival, whom they had invited to one of the lodging houses in September to give private courses, had accompanied them. A teacher of Esperanto and the owner of a hectograph had also made the journey to Yalivets at that time. But only the instructor had asked to come on their stroll through the town.

6. Immediately after the swim and having taken the photograph, the instructor suggested going somewhere to drink gin, but Sebastian and Frants had a fancy for some fresh, light gooseberry wine, and so took the instructor to see Beda, to the armored car, which stood between two islands of mountain pines. Beda had been collecting various berries all summer and now several ten-liter glass jugs of fermenting, different-colored fruits stood in his car being heated by the metal walls of the vehicle.

First, they tried a little of each wine, and then drank all the gooseberry. The instructor became extremely talkative and began to test Sebastian, to see if he could solve some simple survival problems. It turned out that Sebastian had a serious lack of knowledge in this field and could quite easily perish in the most innocuous of situations. Although Sebastian himself had a clear enough idea of what survival meant. In fact, his idea of it was so clear that he had, in the end, stopped caring about it. And had survived all the same.

7. In Africa, he had had plenty of brushes with death, but survival had been more important—because it was interesting, because this was Africa. Eventually he understood, by looking at the ground beneath his feet wherever he was, even when urinating in the morning, that he was on a different continent, on unknown ground. Thus, he became convinced that Africa exists. Because before then the long list of place names, the numerous variations—in architecture, in the layout of the stars, in skull structure and in customs—had all been neutralized by the unfailing uniformity of squares of ground and the grass on them.

8. It was when this grass began to burn around him that he first discovered survival. The wind, which normally brought only psychological disorders, drove the fire outward in all four directions from the place where it had landed on the parched earth. But then, having anticipated the fire (it is possible that he ran precisely to the place from which the wind was driving the fire in all four directions), Sebastian found himself caught in a rain that had been gathering itself all year and which now flowed over the hard, red earth in a multitude of parallel streams, and for which a human being is as insignificant as the tiniest sand turtle and as significant as those millions, myriads of thirsty seedlings cast off by dying stems during many months without a single drop of water.

The instructor was indignant at Sebastian's ignorance. He could not believe that someone could allow themselves to live so calmly without a clue about how to avoid everyday dangers. So Sebastian decided not to say another word about survival.

9. Thus, the only undated photo was taken on June 28, 1914. It should be written on the back of the photograph, with a hard pencil at least.

Even if the inscription were rubbed off—and anything written in pencil is bound to be rubbed off eventually, usually when there is nobody left to check what has been written—the hard, graphite tip of the pencil will have left an indentation of the inscription on the surface of the paper.

PHYSIOLOGICALLY

1. Every man needs a teacher.
Men, generally, should study.
Outstanding men distinguish themselves not only by their ability to study and learn, but also because they always know and always remember from whom, exactly, they learned what, even if it was by accident. And while, for women, remembering their teachers is a sign of benevolence, for men it is the most crucial element of what is learned.

The most distinguished men not only study their whole lives (to study is to be aware of what happens around you), but also very quickly become someone else's teacher, ensuring this awareness of what is experienced. In this very way, schooling becomes never-ending, and this, together with one's family tree, serves to ensure the maximum likelihood that, during the course of one's life, the world should not change to such a degree as to make life, for this very reason, totally undesirable.

(Later, both Frantsysk and Sebastian would see how much some women know without having teachers at all; how wise women become wiser when they learn how to study; and how, when the wisest remember those from whom they gathered their experience, making it their own without being forced, they turn into something which no man will ever be able to achieve. And for the very reason that these women have nothing other than the possibility of gaining this, no man will ever manage to learn it.)

2. The illustrator who taught Frants had studied with Brehm.[4] Brehm had studied among animals. Over the years, the illustrator told Frants stories about Brehm's teachers. For years, Frants observed animals and drew their habits. Later, this zoological knowledge would become the foundation for the education of his daughter. And, of course, he also taught Sebastian all this, when the latter made the decision to stay forever in Yalivets and began to live in Frants's home. For this reason, Sebastian's children in their turn knew these stories equally well.

3. The second Anna interested the Unsimple precisely because of her ability to understand animals, to become

---

4   Alfred Brehm was a German zoologist. His book *Brehms Tierleben*, published in several volumes in the 1860s and illustrated by Fedor Flinzer, was popular throughout Europe (tr.).

like them, and to live with this or that type of animal without arousing in them an uneasy sense of otherness. As for Sebastian, he liked it how every morning, as part of her exercises, Anna would, for a few moments, turn into a cat or a lemur. And, while sleeping with her, he would find himself sharing his bed with such delicate creatures as spiders and bark beetles.

4. Frantsysk noticed fairly early on that he had a somewhat prolonged physiology. Obviously, the physiology of every creature depends on its environment, but, nevertheless, in Frants's case this relationship was somewhat exaggerated. He was convinced that, in part, what should happen in his body in actual fact took place far beyond its shell. And vice versa: in order to occur, certain external things had to make use of his physiological mechanisms.

It struck Frants that he was in some ways similar to a fungus, interwoven into the fabric of a tree, or to spiders whose digestion takes place in the body of their prey, or to a mollusk with an external skeleton, like a fish, whose sperm, once released, swims freely through the water until it impregnates something.

He saw how there was not enough space in his head for certain thoughts, and how they dispersed themselves across fragments of the landscape. For it was enough just to look at a plot of land in order to read whichever thought had settled there. And, if he wanted to recall something in particular, he had to take an imaginary walk through familiar places, browsing through and picking out the required memories.

And, making love to Anna, he knew exactly how she looked on the inside, because he was convinced that he had passed whole along her internal road.

5. His own personal physiology stopped bothering him immediately after his teacher repeated to him what Brehm had said: that dogs have a sense of smell a million times better than a human's. This was inconceivable: no imagination could even come close to grasping such an idea. But Frants, reducing the number in his imagination to only ten times better, was fascinated by the way everything that happens on the outside is exaggeratedly repeated inside a dog's head by the drafts which rush through the corridors of their brains. (This he told to Sebastian who afterwards always tried to be careful with certain strong smells, so that the dogs would not be irritated by that from which they could not escape. Sebastian almost cried whenever he walked to his sniper's position and had to rub his boots with tobacco solution so that the dogs, having once breathed in that smell, would lose their desire and ability to follow him). (Frants developed such a respect for dogs that, on settling down in Yalivets, he acquired several very different ones. From respect, he never trained them. The dogs lived, were born, and died free. Considering the lives

the other dogs around Yalivets led, his dogs seemed to be grateful to him for this. And after all, it was they who were the real intelligentsia in Yalivets).

6. Although it is true that one of them, perhaps the most intelligent, who was named Lukač in honor of the Serb forester who had taught the Unsimple to grow trees a little more slowly, like wild vines, and during the war had planted thickets around Yalivets that proved impassable for soldiers, had to be killed by Frants himself.

7. Lukač was bitten by a rabid ermine.
He was already in a bad way and would certainly soon have entered his final death throes. As always with rabies, convulsions intensified at the sight of water, from a breath of air on the face, from light, from loud voices, from a touch to the skin, or from turning the neck.

Lukač lay in the orangery in the shade of a young bergamot tree. The flowers of the passion fruit had just come into bloom, with all their little crosses, hammers, nails, and spears, and Frants had had to cover the whole bush with a dampened cloth piano cover so that the pungent scent of passion would not irritate Lukač (before, he had loved that scent so much that, when the passion fruit was in flower, he would sleep for days underneath the tree, not leaving the orangery for even a moment).

The bergamot grew at the very end of a long alley. Frantsysk walked towards it through the whole orangery, a machete in his hand, passing the exotic plants one by one. The dog moved only its eyes in order to look at the face, the hand, the sword, and then slightly raised his head, exposing his throat. But Frants did it differently—he put his arms round Lukač and pressed the dog's head downwards, stretching out its vertebrae; the blow began at the back of the brain but did not stop there.

Despite the speed of the operation, Lukač would still have had time to smell his own blood, and Frants could hear the tissues rip distinctly as he drew the blade through them. It was as though those sounds came from his own inner ear, from inside his own neck (the way sometimes you hear your own voice when you shout under a waterfall).

8. The killing so pained Frants that sometimes he imagined that Lukač was looking at him through the eyes of the dog's children, that Lukač's movements, posture, and expressions sometimes welled up under the fur of his sons and grandsons. That Lukač was immortal.

Frants had simply not lived enough to realize that things just were not so. While Sebastian would later have plenty of opportunity to be convinced that it is possible to enter the same river more than once, living with his wife, and daughter, and granddaughter.

Sebastian saw nothing strange in the fact that Frants himself died the same way as Lukač (perhaps he did not smell the blood, but he must surely have heard the sounds of tearing tissue), although he was not killed so carefully.

9. And, in the same way, Sebastian saw no allusions when, twenty years after Frants's death, right in the middle of a bridge over the Tysa, an army dog attacked him. Sebastian just squatted down a little, so as to counter the dog's lunging weight, and stuck his sheepskin-clad elbow into the dog's flying muzzle. The muzzle closed around his left arm tighter than a pair of pincers, but with his right hand Sebastian pulled a long razor from the pocket of his coat and in one swipe cut off the dog's head, which stayed clamped onto his elbow, while the body fell onto the boards of the bridge.

10. With his elongated physiology, Frants could not feel comfortable just anywhere. He preferred most of all places where, just like an embryo in the placenta, his physiology was free to grow in the greatest of comfort.

Beda had been right when he wrote to Anna that this was a sort of botanical geography. Frants found a place that made travel unnecessary.

Before the premiere of one of his films at the Yuniperus cinema, he even told the audience who had come from all over Europe: "I live like grass, like a juniper, so as not to be anywhere else after the seed has taken root; waiting for the world, which is passed on through me; to see it not only from below, but projected right onto the heavens, that is, enlarged and distorted enough to be interesting; after all, my place will always be at the center of European history, for in these lands history in its various forms comes of its own accord to our doorsteps."

11. In Yalivets, or rather in the place where Yalivets had not yet appeared, Frants began to live most genuinely. He was even somewhat ashamed of his constant happiness.

12. On the day that he and the professor stopped between Petros and Sheshul, Frants felt that he was wandering across islands in the sky. Only a few of the highest peaks reached above the clouds. The setting sun fell only on them. The red surface of the clouds flowed about them, forming gulfs, lagoons, straits, river basins, deltas, and estuaries. Whatever was underneath was of no consequence.

On the gentle slope Frants found berries. Because of the lack of summer climate on this mountain tundra, they grew all at the same time—woodland strawberries, black bilberries, raspberries, blackberries, and red bilberries. Frants lost himself, he became absorbed in some sort of cosmic movements, he could not stop himself, he ate so many berries that he was forced to lie down, and then he felt that he was being lowered to the bottom of some wondrous bosom, he could hold it no longer and emptied himself.

A little higher up, it was still spring, and the fragrant first flowers were in bloom.

Higher still, the snow was slowly melting.

Frants ran down the slope and darted into the beeches, among which it was still fall. On his run through the seasons, he emptied himself again. The professor in the meantime set up their tent. They ate a few of the little cheese horses that the Hutsuls make and brewed a pot of tea from the leaves of all the berries. Then the night began. In the moonlight, everything seemed to be covered with snow. The Romanian mountains were like a distant strip of shoreline, and the ground unceasingly gave off a heat that smelled of vermouth.

WALK, STAND, SIT, LIE

1. If places really are the truest plots, then Yalivets's peak as a town was without doubt the time when the town architect was Anna, the daughter of Frantsysk.

For the children of animators who never leave their father's side, becoming an architect is not difficult. Especially in a town thought up by their father. After her first sketch, in 1900 (when Anna was seven), a new cinema, the Yuniperus, was built in the shape of a chest of drawers especially for screenings of Frants's animated films.

When she was still a child, Anna drew plans for a swimming pool in the shape of a grebe's nest that floated on a lake; underground tunnels with openings, like those moles make, on various streets in the town; a bar in which the exit was designed in such a way that, on leaving, one found oneself not outside, as one might expect, but in another, absolutely identical room; a four-story pinecone building; and an enormous, two-story sunflower villa.

2. Because Anna thought with her body. She could feel every movement not only in its entirety but also as sequences of contractions and relaxations of muscle fibers, of the bending of joints, of the easing and explosion of blood flow, of the intake and expulsion of streams of air. For this reason, the sentences of her thoughts were spatial constructions. She also viewed buildings by circling around their exteriors. And, also, as spaces in which the shifting of various mobile and semi-mobile constructions—of fingers, spines, skulls, knees, jaws—takes place.

3. However, Frantsysk noticed that, in the beginning, Anna's imagination could not overcome the limits of symmetry. He realized that enchantment with the wonder of natural symmetry is the child's first step towards the conscious reproduction of the beauty of the harmony of the world.

4. Anna had a fairly restricted upbringing.
When she was still called Stefaniia, and only her mother was Anna, Frants understood that the most important thing in bringing up children is to be with them as much as possible. It is possible that he took this too literally: after the death of his wife, for almost twenty years, there was not a single moment when he and Anna were apart. Always together. Either in the same room, or out together, or doing something in the garden within sight of one another. Even when bathing, Anna never

locked the bathroom door. It was important for them to always be able to hear what the other was saying. This was the sole principle of Frantsysk's pedagogy. Strangely, she was happy living like this. When she began to work seriously as an architect, she would even tremble with joy as they sat working at different tables in their big study—she annotated her sketches and made drafts, while her father drew his animations.

5. All their life together, Frantsysk spoke not so much to her as merely aloud. Everything that Anna heard their dogs heard too. Anna rarely asked questions and, at the same time, learned to constantly speak of her impressions, trying to find the most accurate combinations of words.

Often, she would interrupt Frants—tell me the same thing again, only not so briefly.

Anna could neither read nor write, but she looked over the illustrations in *Larousse* every day. Music she heard performed only by the resort band or by Hutsul musicians: *floiars, tsymbalists, husliars*, and *trembitars*.[5] She played only the Jew's harp. She could draw a circle impeccably, although she formed it from two symmetrical halves. With the same accuracy, she could draw any ellipse,

---

5   Players of traditional Hutsul folk instruments: *floiara* (a wooden flute); *tsymbaly* (a version of a hammer dulcimer); *husli* (a type of stringed instrument, similar to a zither); *trembita* (a long wooden horn played in the mountains, the Hutsul equivalent of an alphorn) (tr.).

and she could also continue a straight line indefinitely, resting from time to time for a few minutes or months. About her mother she knew everything that a young girl should know. She played with her dogs and in this way had contact with creatures of the same age as herself.

6. She lived twice as much, every day experiencing both her own life and Frantsysk's.

7. Unexpectedly even for herself, Anna began to draw beans. The movement with which this was done gave her the greatest physical pleasure. Thousands of repetitions did not reduce the pleasure. Anna began to think about this.

She saw beans everywhere—in river stones and in the moon, in curled up dogs and in the pose in which she most often fell asleep, in sheep's kidneys and lungs, hearts and halves of the brain, in lumps of *budz* cheese and in the caps of mushrooms, in the bodies of birds and in fetuses, in her breasts and in the two beloved pelvic bones that stuck out beneath her stomach, in the banks of small lakes and in the concentric lines showing the rising elevation of mountains on geographical maps. In the end, she decided that it was precisely the bean that was the most perfect form for isolating a small space from a larger one.

8. All this Anna told old Beda when she brought a whole sack of large blue beans to his armored car. They dragged the sack onto the roof of the car and poured

the whole lot into the top hatch. Anna looked inside and gasped—inside, the car was filled with beans of different sizes and colors, and the beans at the top of the heap slowly slithered downwards, like lava flowing down a volcano. Beda gathered beans from all over Yalivets to take them to the market in Kosiv.

He must have said something afterwards to the UnSimple, because they came and had little Anna appointed as the town architect.

9. When Frants chose a place, he always took care that he felt good there in all four states—walking, standing, sitting, and lying—in which a human being can be.

With Anna, things were different. She lived from the very beginning in such a place. After becoming an architect, Anna began to have different thoughts. She remembered very well what Frants had taught her, and even better what Frants himself had learned. But, for the first time, she began to think that he had not told her everything.

10. It is possible to fall—and under certain buildings they placed large air cushions onto which you could jump straight from the balconies.

It is possible to hang—they stretched long lines between two mountains and, using special handles (Anna found them among her mother's climbing gear), you could slide right down to the central square, hanging for a few moments over the roofs and lower trees.

It is possible to swing—they installed trapezes on the buildings so that you could fly across to the opposite side of the street.

And it is also possible to roll, to jump, to crawl, to burrow—and all this was also considered in the reconstruction of Yalivets. More and more patients began to come to the gin resort.[6] Sebastian was already fighting in Africa then, and the terrorist Sichynskyi escaped from the Stanislaviv prison.

11. Frants saw clearly that Anna could think up nothing new, because even while falling (or, say, during flight—if we ever manage to achieve it) a person either stands, or lies, or sits in the air.

But the innovations pleased him, and he proposed pouring water over the streets just before the winter. Yalivets, for a few months, became one big ice rink. Only by gripping the railings that ran along the streets was it possible to somehow scramble one's way to the upper part of the town. But Frants was good at walking on slippery surfaces.

12. Wandering with Frantsysk in the nearby mountains, Anna saw many different Hutsul villages. Looking closer, she understood what it meant to have one's own house. Maintaining a house gives the daily search for food sense. Having a house is like laying aside leftovers

---

6   The town's name means "juniper" in Ukrainian. Juniper berries are a crucial ingredient of any gin (tr.).

or sharing food with someone. Or, sometimes, sharing the responsibility for finding food.

If the body is the gate to the soul, then a house is the terrace onto which the soul is allowed to come out.

She saw that, for most people, a house is the foundation for biography and an express consequence of existence. And it is also where memory rests, since it is with objects that memory finds it easiest to persist.

She was enchanted by that particular Hutsul habit of building one's house on one's own far away from the houses of others. In an unspoiled place. When a house is built, it becomes wiser than all prophets and seers—it will always tell you what you should do next.

13. Another characteristic of beauty. To be accessible, beauty must be able to be formulated in words. And therefore—to be reduced. A house gives that reduced space in which it is possible to create beauty by one's own efforts.

Anna considered the basic conditions for beauty in the home to be space, light, draughts, passages between the divisions of space. For this reason, she designed several buildings in the style of the Hutsul *grazhda*.[7] Separate rooms and different parts of the house opened directly onto a square courtyard that was enclosed on all sides by those same rooms.

---

7   A *grazhda* is the name of a typical Hutsul dwelling, in which living quarters and agricultural buildings are laid out in a rectangle around a central courtyard (tr.).

14. The source of all beauty that can be controlled by human beings, of all aesthetics, are, undoubtedly, plants (and, in the end, food also; here the ideal and the material are one as nowhere else). On the other hand, few things represent such a perfect embodiment of ethics as the process of caring for plants. To say nothing of the fact that watching the changing of the seasons of the year is the simplest way to one's own private philosophy. For this reason, the Serbian forester Lukač planted flowering bushes brought from Macedonia in the courtyards of the grazhdas: barberry, camellia, heather, cornelian cherry dogwood, deadly nightshade, forsythia, hydrangea, jasmine, magnolia, rhododendron, clematis.

15. Anna ordered that the city itself be surrounded with transparent, zigzag Hutsul fencing made from long, thin wooden strips called *vorynnia*. Entry to the town was through real *rozlohy* gates, which consisted of two posts with holes that held removable horizontal poles, or *zavorotnytsi*.

There was no particular need for this, but Anna wanted to revive as many words as possible that are necessary when talking about fences—*gary, zavorynie, huzhva, byltsia, kiechka, spyzh*.[8]

8   *Rozlohy* are a specific type of gate used in traditional Hutsul villages. The other words are dialect terms for different parts of fences or gates that would be unfamiliar to most readers of the original, too: *gary*—holes in the upright posts on each side of the gates; *zavorynie*—another type of gate; *huzhva*—a steamed tree branch used for binding a fence; *byltsia*—railings or barriers; *kiechka*—a rope latch; *spyzh*—a fence post (tr.).

SITUATION IN COLOR

1. The main inhabitant of Yalivets was, of course, the juniper bush. Frants planned the construction of the town in such a way as to avoid harming a single bush on any of the three sides of the slope. Since wood was in short supply, most of the buildings were made of gray slabs of stone that in some places are known as *gorgany*. The town's main colors, therefore, were green and gray—even fewer colors than are found in Hutsul ceramics. But, if the gray was the same everywhere, the green had many shades. Although that is not quite right—it would not be accurate to say green. Better—greens. There were so many greens that everything seemed unbelievably colorful. And that was before you even count the thousands of radically different dots of purple, red, pink, violet, blue, azure, yellow, orange, white, green again, brown, and almost black flowers. Anna learned her colors from these flowers (Frants often thought of

that time as something perfect. Naming colors became for him a clear embodiment of the idea of the creation of the world and of mutual understanding). If you live attentively, there is no need for floristry in such a town. And that's how it was.

It is also necessary to imagine the omnipresent strips of nearer, farther, and distant mountains that were visible from every point in Yalivets. Also, the sky, clouds, winds, suns, moons, snows, and rains.

2. Around this stone settlement, there grew so many junipers that the smell of their warmed, soaked, cracked, and crushed berries, branches, and roots could be tasted in the air.

3. It is hard to imagine how Sebastian found the time to talk so much with Frants that he could remember so many of the latter's individual phrases. For they had only a year and nine months together. But most of what Frants said survived precisely because of Sebastian. It was from him that the Unsimple noted down those best-known phrases, which were later reproduced on the various parts of an enormous dinner service made at the porcelain factory in Patsykiv. The second Anna once even joked that all these sayings were thought up by Sebastian himself, and that the words "Frants said" were Sebastian's particular parasite words. Just like fuck, probably, really, yeah, just.

4. In any case, Sebastian himself said that Frants had said that life depends on whatever it is that you walk along. But what you walk along depends on where you are going. Thus, changing it is quite simple. It is more difficult with other defining elements—what you drink and what you breathe.

In Yalivets, everyone breathed the etheric resin of the juniper and drank *yalivtsivka*, a spirit into which the juniper entered in three ways. Because the water in which the sweet berries fermented had itself for years, from the very beginning, flowed from the sky to the earth, washing over the juniper, touching it and remembering it, and then that water was also heated on fires of juniper twigs.

5. Yalivtsivka was brewed in every yard. Fresh shoots were boiled in pots with spirit extracted from the juniper berries. Steam gathered on the hearth, cooled, and dripped down as thick gin. It also happened that sometimes heavy gin clouds hung above the rooftops. And so, when frost was on the way, alcohol would drizzle from the sky. When it reached the already cooled earth, it would freeze, and the street would be covered in a thin layer of ice. If you licked the ice, you could get drunk. On days like that, you had to get around by sliding across the ice. Although your leg will not actually have time to slip if you move so fast that the sole of your foot barely touches the ice.

6. The first Anna appeared in Yalivets when the town was already becoming a fashionable resort. Not long before that she had seriously injured herself after falling from a cliff, despite being attached to a line, and, for a long time, she ate nothing. It had given her a terrible fright, after all. The day after the accident she had gone all the same into the mountains and tried to climb. But it was useless. For the first time, her body refused to be a continuation of the rock. Something there was stronger than she was. She came to Yalivets and drank gin; she had intended to train, but she drank gin. She dared not even approach the cliffs. And not long afterwards she met Frantsysk. He made animated films that brought no fewer tourists to Yalivets than the gin did.

7. Anna felt like lichen scraped off the rocky shore of a cold sea. She just had to hold on in order to hold out. There was no other way. She really did not want to be angry. "God, don't let me harm anyone!" she prayed constantly.

The first time they met, she and Frants had spent the night in a bar into which they had both drifted quite by chance and then found themselves unable to leave until morning. The barman looked nothing like a barman, so they waited a long time for someone to order from. In the bar, they gave each other gin massages, had three gin inhalations, set fire to first-distillation gin spirit on their hands and stomachs, drank spilt gin from the table and drank from each other's mouths. Anna still could not imagine Frants in any other place.

8. That night, they lay next to each other on folding chairs and understood that, through a coincidence of bone and flesh, they were brother and sister. Or husband and wife. Even if this never happens again, Frantsysk thought, it still feels good to touch one another. And she thought about various trifles and strange things that happen or can happen at any time.

As they slept, fitting bone to flesh, and bone to bone, and flesh to flesh, their skulls were always touching at uneven places. They turned over, squeezed closer together, twisted around and moved away from one another, but their skulls did not separate even for a second. Sometimes, their skulls scraped against each other, catching on especially pronounced protrusions or cavities, and they woke often, afraid of this incomparable closeness that relied solely on their heads. Never again would Frantsysk and Anna experience such intense enlightenment and lucidity.

Outside, it began to get light. The main street of the town ran past the closed bars, the dark courtyards overgrown with vines that never ripened, the low stone walls, the high gates, and made its way towards the foot of a five-thousand-five-hundred-and-sixty-one-foot-high mountain, gradually turning into a barely noticeable track, which at that time of day gleamed white.

9. Anna's pregnancy was a time of shared happiness. What could genuinely be described as cohabitation, as a family.

They began their evenings early. They walked in warm fall coats along the remotest streets among the as-yet-uninhabited villas. They pretended that this was not their town. He held her hand in his pocket. As they walked, they stepped in time, each with their leg pressed so firmly against the other's that they could feel one another's muscles contract and their hip joints rubbed together in a peculiar way. She liked it that things were so simple. That the one who loved her was the one she loved. She felt for the first time the joy of not having to clear out in the morning. She told him things from the time before he had appeared and loved to hear him tell her about how he knew her. In the mornings, they spent a long time on the balcony breakfasting on honey, sour milk, dried pears soaked in wine, dried bread that had been fried and dipped in milk and various different types of nuts.

10. On the table next to the bath, there was an old typewriter with an unmovable cast-iron base; whatever they did not dare to say to each other they typed on a long scroll of the finest paper that they fed into the Remington. "I feel bad with people you don't know about," wrote Anna, "do they feel good now, do they feel good with me, does he feel good here. It's awkward and difficult with people who won't say what they like and

what they don't." Frantsysk typed something completely different: "Without doing any particular evil deed, bad people can do us harm—we have to be wary of their existence." "Good people stop being good when they start to cling to that which they are unwilling to give away," Anna wrote for some reason. And Frants: "Sense and pleasure exist only in details, one has to know these details to be able to repeat them."

After Frants's death, Sebastian found that typewriter. The paper was still in it. Later, he would often imagine real dialogues between living people made up of similar sentences.

11. Frants tried to cure Anna of her fear. He would lead her to the top of the cliff from the side where you could come out onto the top through a dense patch of mountain pine, from the back. Then he would take her in his arms and hold her above the drop. "Fate is not the most important thing," Frants would say. "The main thing is to fear nothing." But something in his method was not right.

He had studied her body better than she had. He could take Anna's own hand and touch her body with it in such a way as she had never done before and would never have been able to do. He handled her in such a way that her blood vessels, arteries, and veins tingled. He would spend hours showing her own beauty to her. Through all this, Anna began to understand how beautiful she was. Beautiful not for somebody else, but for herself.

And she became even more afraid that all this could be destroyed by falling against the rocks.

"I love my life," she said to Frants. "That's good," he insisted, "because other than that there is nothing, to not love it—means to renounce everything."

12. All the same, she did try once more. When Frants blocked her ears. Because he suddenly began to suspect that Anna was afraid not of heights but of the sound of silence that accompanies height.

Secured in every possible way, with blocked-up ears, pregnant Anna climbed up the stone wall, feeling somewhat awkward, because she was not sure what to do with her belly.

Frantsysk decided to climb alongside her. He painted directly onto the rock all the contours where her belly had pressed against the cliff. They abseiled down so fast that they burned their hands on the lines. For some reason, such insignificant burns often make it impossible to get to sleep. The next morning, moving daguerreotypes showing the silhouetted movements of the fetus across the cliff were already finished. The film turned out beautifully. It did not matter that it was short.

13. Frantsysk paid no attention to time. All of his films lasted only a few minutes. He created animations that were not yet possible. He received pleasure from the creation of rich moments that might never have happened

otherwise. If not for. If he had not noticed something, if he had not thought up some device, if he had not combined things in a certain way, if he had not distinguished between certain things—and many other if he had nots.

"Life is so short," said Frants, "that time has no meaning. One way or another it happens as a whole."

Frants dreamed of something radical. And he came to the conclusion that the most radical thing possible is to wait.

14. After the birth of their daughter, Anna decided to go into training again. She tried blocking her ears, but something still bothered her. Her inner ear was deprived of the vibrations without which it is difficult to sense the limits of one's own body.

She remembered her father's garden and injected herself with morphine. The vibrations began immediately.

But sounds began to behave strangely. It was as though they had lost their dependence on distance. Sounds flew at great speed, tightly bundled together in clusters, without coming apart in the air. Sometimes, one of these bullets would collide with another, changing trajectory in a completely unexpected way. During some of these collisions, both clusters would give off aural splinters and dust. They flew independently. Mingling together, scattering apart, soaring up, falling down or driving into the ground. When she climbed up to about four times her own height, Anna stopped among the opaque clouds of that cacophony. When she climbed higher still, the crashing sound of tiny particles of rock falling from under her fingers to the bottom of the cliff became unbearable.

15. Anna gave up climbing. But she didn't give up morphine. She would sit for days on the veranda, listening in on the lives of the many insects that lived around the house. Not even hearing the crying of hungry Stefaniia.

Frants tried in vain to change things. The best he could do was to squeeze a little milk from Anna's breasts and feed it to his daughter. But the opium had also developed a taste for milk. It drank first, and Frants would hopelessly squeeze the dried-out breasts. Frantsysk went to a witch who was known for stealing milk from cows and asked her to take Anna's milk. The child then began to eat properly. But, together with the milk, she consumed the opium. Frants thought that the child slept for days at a time because she was content at eating so well. At last, things were more peaceful. But when Anna's milk ran out and even the witch could not get a drop more out of her, Stefaniia went through genuine morphine withdrawal symptoms. The Unsimple barely managed to save her by boiling some poppy seeds in milk.

Anna began to do the same thing. The child slept and had fantastic dreams (some of them—and she was barely six months old then—she would remember for the rest of her life. Although it may have been that she remembered the feeling that she had had in those dreams, and the rest came to her later), and Anna listened calmly to the worms burrowing through the earth, to the cries of spiders making love in their tense webs, to the splitting of a beetle's thorax, crushed in the beak of a wagtail.

16. In the middle of December, Frants took Anna on his knee and told her to leave Yalivets. Anna got up, kissed Frants and went to the bedroom to take the child. Then he proposed something different—he challenged his wife to a duel. Because it was necessary for the little child's future life that one of its parents be dead.

Anna agreed and chose her weapon. They would go immediately to the snow-covered, windswept cliff and climb to the top by two different unmarked routes, with no safety precautions. Whichever of them returned would be left with the child. Despite the fear this instilled in her, she was sure that it was the only way she could defeat Frantsysk (it did not even enter their minds that they might both not return, and they told nobody, leaving the child in its cradle).

They barely made it through the snow to the cliffs. They took off their sheepskins, drank a bottle of gin between them, kissed each other, and set off.

17. For the first time, Frantsysk had to become a real climber (a first, but then it's not exactly my first first

time, he thought). For this reason, his descent from the top took several hours; it turned out that the hardened snow actually helped him—on bare rock, he would never have made it. Though it pained him terribly, he was not able to bury Anna until June, when the snow in the ravine had melted.

THE SECOND OLD PHOTOGRAPH— ARDZHELIUDZHA, 1892

1. A naked female back ends with a wide leather *cheres*, and below it is just a strip of dark fabric.[9] On the sharply bent forward neck hangs a fine string of large coral beads. The head is not visible. The arms are held downward, but bent at the elbows. The torso is slightly twisted to the left, so only the four fingers with which the right hand grips the left forearm are visible. The back appears almost triangular—so broad are the shoulders and so narrow the waist. Between the top edge of the *cheres* and the white skin is a little empty space. The shoulder blades and the ends of the collarbone are clearly visible. Below the neck, the little mounds of four vertebrae jut out. Where they end, the lines of two tensed muscles running down the middle of the back begin. Nearer to the waist, the distance between them is smallest, and the depth of the hollow is greatest.

9   A *cheres* is a wide traditional Hutsul belt made of leather (tr.).

A keyboard of ribs shows through only on the left—and not on the back itself, but on the side. But where the ribcage ends, the concave of the waist begins; the line of the waist curves back out to its previous width at the top of the pelvis.

From the contrast of the white back and the black *cheres*, it is clear that the light from the sun is at its most powerful. Although a barely visible shadow has appeared only between the muscles running along the spine.

2. The back is photographed from close up. To its right, in the background of the picture, stands a small horse, some distance away from the camera. The little Hutsul horse is quite old—all the best horses had already been taken away when the state requisitioned them to send to Bosnia—but all the same, it is well looked after. In place of a saddle is a long, narrow *lizhnyk*.[10]

3. During their first summer together, Frants and Anna went to Kostrych to see the panorama of Chornohora. The day was sunny, and they could see the entire ridge—Petros, Hoverla, Breskul, Pozhyzhevska, Dantsysh, Homul, Turkul, Shpytsi, Rebra, Tomnatyk, Brebeneskul, Menchul, Smotrych, Staiky, and part of the Svydovets ridge—Blyznytsi and Tatulska, and further away—Bratkivska, Dovbushanka, Iavirnyk. Behind them were Rotyla, Bila Kobyla, and Lysyna Kosmatska.

10 A *lizhnyk* is a traditional Hutsul woollen rug (tr.).

On the way back, just after Ardzheliudzha, Anna took off her shirt and removed her *postoly* from her feet, leaving her in nothing but a pair of men's trousers.[11] They were walking up the Prut river. From time to time, they went down to the water to take a drink. The river was so shallow that Anna could place her hands square on the riverbed, bend down to the water, and submerge her whole face. The tips of her breasts came close to the bubbling surface but stayed dry. Only her heavy brass crucifix, with its primitive depiction of the crucifixion, rattled off the stones. At such moments, Frants would catch a ladybird and place it on Anna's back, and the creature would run around between the drops of sweat, tickling her skin, and Anna couldn't even move a hand to brush it off.

After bathing, they kissed until their lips became completely dry. Because everything that is wet has to dry up. Their skin smelled like cold river plants in warm rivers between warm stones under warm winds blowing from beyond snow-covered Hoverla. If they had been able to commit these physical sensations to memory, so as to be able to call them to mind at any moment, their feeling of happiness would have been constant.

At that time, they still talked a lot and with great enthusiasm. Frants thought about how everything that is worth looking at changes when you have someone to show it to.

---

11 *Postoly* are traditional Hutsul leather shoes (tr.).

The horse carried only a pear box containing a camera and a sycamore keg full of *yalivtsivka*, and not once did it go down to the water to take a drink.

4. In 1883, when Frants returned from the cliff alone, the first thing he did, instead of feeding the child, was to accidentally stumble upon the very same keg whilst looking for alcohol. There was about half a quart of yalivtsivka left in it; he immediately finished off what they had not managed to drink together. Then he pulled that photograph out from between the pages of his *Larousse*, slid it between two rectangles of glass, throwing away the drawing that they had previously held, and placed the framed picture on his desk for good. He ground a handful of dried bilberries in a mortar, soaked them in warm water with honey and began to feed Stefaniia. Next morning, he went to the priest and told him to enter his daughter in the church records under the name of Anna.

5. Sebastian decided it would be right to put this photograph in Frants's coffin (he could not know that there was already someone else in this world who would always regret its loss). For this reason, perhaps, the picture did not survive.

THE TEMPTATIONS OF SAINT ANTHONY

1. Little Anna was given a miniature figure of Saint Anthony by the Unsimple. Anthony standing up straight, in a monk's habit, in one hand he holds lilies on long stems, in the other—a child. Despite his size, Anthony looked like a real statue when Anna laid her head on the floor and placed the figure a little way away, or—still looking up from the floor—when she stood him on the very edge of a table. Especially striking was the expression of pure devotion in his facial features.

The Unsimple said Anthony had been cast from melted-down lead that had previously been a bullet. The figure lived in a metal cylinder of the type soldiers use to keep tags with their names and the addresses of their families. Anna wore the shell around her neck on a long wire chain. From the constant rubbing of the copper, her skin was always marked with green stains. Frantsysk didn't consider this harmful. When the weather was especially fine, Anna would take Anthony for walks. She would take him out of his capsule and give him an airing somewhere in the grass. When she put him back in, she would place alongside him a little flower—a violet, a dog daisy, a plum or a linden tree blossom—so that Anthony had something to breathe in.

2. Anna herself smelled beautiful. Frants liked most of all when she fell asleep on his table. He would keep working for a while, though already paying more attention to his curled-up, sleeping daughter, and would then crawl up onto the table, put a book under his head, put his arms around Anna and lie for a long time breathing in the air she breathed out. He stroked her head, and sometimes, in the morning, Anna would wake up with short, broad, shallow scratches on her face—the hardened skin on Frantsysk's fingers had scraped her body.

3. Frantsysk was convinced that there was no more worthwhile activity than watching his daughter. Every day, he saw thousands of perfect images but for some reason never bothered to use his camera. As a consequence, he dedicated so much energy to memorizing these images that he sometimes caught himself thinking that he could not possibly go on like this. Because very often, by the evening, he could remember nothing of what had happened during the day other than those imaginary photographs (although, when Anna was

a little older, he could describe to her for hours how she had looked on any given day in her childhood).

4. Anna was six years old when she told her father that she could remember once sleeping in a large box that had been placed on a long, eight-wheeled trolley under a tree from which hung a nest with an opening on its underside. The little hatch was open, and from inside the nest the blue eye of a bird peered at her. And then from all around flocks of little white owls swooped down and landed in concentric circles around the tree—on the ground, on the haystacks, on the dog-rose bushes, on the well and the hayrick. And also on the wires that stretched between the electricity poles.

5. Frantsysk decided that this vision must be the result of the morphine and called on the Unsimple. They had a talk with Anna and eventually the seeress said that the little girl had dreamed it all. She warned Frants that the little one would begin to tell him more and more often of all kinds of wonders, would begin to ask whether or not this or that thing had once happened to her. That about certain things she would be unsure until death, about what had really happened and what was a dream because, for her, there would be no real or unreal, but rather different types of reality. But dreams have nothing in common with seeing into the future. Rather, they tell us how things can be.

6. Frants decided that his daughter should know at least one thing in the world perfectly, something she could speak about without hesitation. They started walking round Menchul Kvasivskyi to the Keveliv, which flowed into the Chorna Tysa, and Anna learned all the stones on its banks—how each one of them looked, which lay by which.

In the meantime, all of the Unsimple had crossed over the mountains and settled in Yalivets; they stayed there on and off right up until 1951, when a special *chekist* unit, disguised as UPA soldiers, used flamethrowers to set fire to the mental asylum where those Unsimple who had been tracked down and caught had been interned in 1947.[12] They had to get closer to Anna.

7. A few weeks before the beginning of the year 1900, Frants finished a very important animated film.

"To live is to untie and tie knots—with your hands and with everything else," he was once taught by an Unsimple snake charmer who gave him a whole bundle of grass snake skins. Frants had to untangle the skins and weave his own pattern from them. Logic lives in the fingers, and its categories are defined purely by what the fingers can do.

---

12 *Chekists* are members of the Cheka, the Soviet secret police during World War II. The UPA, the Ukrainian Insurgent Army, was a Ukrainian nationalist guerrilla movement during WWII (tr.).

He turned the bundle over and over in his hands like a rosary for many days and nights. Eventually, he had untied all the knots, but, when it came to making his own pattern, his fingers found it terribly difficult not to follow the existing surface. However, Anna was able to tie such impressive knots that the snake charmer decided to take Frants to the bridge where the Unsimple had made their home.

8. At one time, there had been a plan to extend this viaduct between the two parts of the mountain ridge that lay on either side of Yalivets. They had planned to build the middle first, and then extend it to the peaks on either side. Frantsysk imagined how eventually such a path would turn the whole way between Sheshul and Petros into one easy walk. However, that project turned out to be Yalivets's only impossible idea. Three arches, connected to each other but not with the hills (and much higher than the railway bridges at Vorokhta or Deliatyn), hung above the town in one diagonal line, beginning and breaking off in thin air.[13] On top, there was a fragment of wide road. This is where the Unsimple settled.

Frants climbed for a long, long time up a hanging ladder, which swung violently because the snake charmer

---

13   Vorokhta and Deliatyn are two towns in the Carpathian mountains that boasted impressive Austro-Hungarian-era railway viaducts. Today, they are disused and partially ruined (tr.).

climbed ahead of him. On top, the bridge seemed too narrow, so that it would be enough just to stumble and you would plunge downwards: onto the little roofs, the short streets, the narrow canals, the foam-like trees. But all around lay such beauty, it was like something in someone else's life. Everything was white, no other colors existed, even in the far away sun.

The snow-covered Unsimple smoked pipes and looked out at Farkhaul in the Maramureş Alps beyond the Bila Tysa valley. The conversation was simple—when Anna becomes a woman, then let her be an Unsimple. But, for the time being, they would always be close by.

9. And so the film that Frants completed was similar to a chain of knots.

It looked like this. The whole screen was filled with a multitude of tiny, separate, seething signs. These were all the basic symbols that Frants had managed to find on the patterns of *pysanka* eggs from all corners of the Carpathians.[14] Due to variations in size, configuration, color and speed, this mist of signs resembled an incredible cloud of different insects. One could make out ladders, wedges, half-wedges, triple-wedges,

---

14 Ukraine has a rich and complex tradition of decorating Easter eggs, some of which are called *pysanka*s, with different techniques and patterns found in each region of Ukraine, and indeed different parts of the Carpathians (tr.).

forty-wedges, yellow wedges, triangles, seams, checks, infinity signs, half-infinity signs, curls, spaces, crosses, scratches, curves, sparkles, stars, warming suns, half-suns, moons, half-moons, sparks, shining moons, moon streets, rainbows, beans, roses, half-roses, acorns, flowers, black brows, corn ears, heather blossoms, pine trees, cucumbers, cloves, periwinkles, oats, orchids, barrels, plums, potatoes, branches, soapwort, horses, sheep, cows, dogs, goats, deer, cockerels, ducks, cuckoos, cranes, whitewings, trout, crow's feet, ram's horns, hare's ears, ox's eyes, butterflies, bees, snails, spiders, heads, spindles, rakes, brushes, combs, axes, shovels, boats, flasks, grates, chests, girths, straps, knapsacks, keys, beads, kegs, sheepskins, powder horns, umbrellas, pictures, hankies, laces, bowls, huts, shutters, pillars, troughs, churches, monasteries, bell towers, chapels, twisted sleeves, decorated sleeves, diagonal stripes, needles, symbols that were beaked, crossed, toothed, braided, laced, frayed, winged, eyed, spidery, flowery, flat and numbered, princesses, crooks, curves, dots, marks, flasks, secrets, cherries, raspberries, flowerpots, sprouts, damselflies, windmills, sledges, hooks, honey cakes.

Slowly the movement of signs gained a certain order—like a powerful wind gathering many lighter breezes together. The symbols whirled somewhat like a bath full of water draining out through a small opening. Out of this there appeared a chain of signs that were tied together here and there by knots. The chain curled itself into a spiral and spun like a centrifuge. From the chaos, loose symbols began to fly toward the chain, arranging themselves into another chain—made up of signs arranged exactly in the same order—that closely followed the turning of the first. Then, both spirals flowed together into the vacuum, merging with each other more and more tightly, and took on the shape of the world tree. Calm descended. The tree produced flowers, the petals withered, the ovaries grew into fruit, which swelled, split, and thousands of the very same signs slowly and evenly descended onto the ground, piling up into a mound and losing their form.

10. They waited until Easter 1900 with the premiere. It marked the opening of the Yuniperus cinema, built according to one of Anna's sketches, along with a public reading of a pastoral letter from the young Stanislaviv bishop Andrei Sheptytskyi to his beloved Hutsul brothers.[15]

11. From that time on, the Unsimple really were always nearby. It only seems that Chornohora is empty. In truth, there is really too little space in the Carpathians. For this reason, people who live far away from one another are

15   Andrei Sheptytskyi was the Metropolitan Archbishop of the Ukrainian Greek Catholic Church from 1901 until 1944 and an influential figure in Ukrainian religious and social life. Before assuming this position, he was, briefly, bishop of Stanislaviv (today Ivano-Frankivsk). See also note 4 on p. 183 (tr.).

constantly meeting. So it is easy to imagine how it is in a small town at the intersection of two ridges.

For a few Dovbush *zoloti*, the Unsimple bought a small plot on the Market Square and built a small building there.[16] They covered the hut with eccentrically painted tiles so that it came to look just like a stove. In each window, they wrote one word—notary. But, on the windowsills, there stood whole rows of different-sized and differently formed bottles, so that anyone seeing it would assume that "NOTARY" was just the name of another bar. Lukač somehow saw to it that, in just one week, the whole roof had become covered in moss, and, above the doors, he hung a green awning. Inside, it was bare—opposite a small table (with one drawer), on high legs, stood a comfortable armchair upholstered in canvas.

In the armchair sat the notary himself, smoking one fat cigarette after another, the cigarettes placed in a silver ring soldered onto a tin rod, which was attached to the ceiling. Each cigarette was no longer than half the length of an average woman's hand. The notary kept busy by rolling the next cigarette while smoking the previous one.

While he was still young, he had decided that he must somehow control his own death and not rely entirely on

---

[16] Oleksa Dovbush was a famous Ukrainian outlaw and folk hero who operated in the Carpathians in the eighteenth century. Legends about his treasure are common in the Carpathians. *Zoloti* are gold coins (tr.).

the unknown. Therefore, he wanted to determine if not the date, then at least the reason for his death. He settled on cancer of the lungs and began to allow himself to smoke heavily in order to be doomed to such a death.

12. But all it took was someone to call in, and the notary would take the cigarette out of the ring, sit the visitor in his armchair, open the drawer, take out two sweet red or yellow bell peppers—always fresh and juicy—and with one hand he would open a large folding knife which hung from a strap around his knee, clean out the peppers, which he held in the other hand, and would ask what kind of *horilka* to pour out—*palenka, rakia, slyvovytsia, bekherivka, tsuika, zubrivka, anisivka,* yalivtsivka, *borovichka*—would fill the two peppers, give one to the guest, stand by the table, take a sheet of paper and sharp pencil out of the drawer, raise his cup, say "God willing" looking straight in the eyes of the visitor, drink, take a bite of the pepper, immediately pour a second, relight the cigarette (he kept his matches in his trouser pocket right next to his belt, and the striking surface was attached to one of the legs of the table), holding the cigarette in the same hand as his cup, and in his left hand holding the pencil, he would inhale the smoke deeply and finally was ready to listen.[17]

---

17   *Horilka* is the generic Ukrainian name for distilled spirits. The spirits named here are: *palenka*—pálinka, a fruit-based spirit originating in Hungary and some other central

13. The notary was known as the French engineer.

The Unsimple found him in Rakhiv and offered him this job because he looked both modest and heroic at the same time. He was the sort of man you felt you wanted to surprise with some extraordinary tale from your life. And the Unsimple needed as many stories and tales of this sort as possible.

In Rakhiv, the French engineer had been enlisting people to go to Brazil, writing out authentic tickets for a ship that would leave from Genoa. Once he really had been a French engineer. He lived for twenty years in Indochina, developing drainage systems and learning about opium smoking, Thai boxing, butterflies, orchids and Zen. At the same time, he wrote articles on ethnology and geopolitics for major European newspapers. Several of his letters were translated by Osyp Shpytko. They were published in *Dilo*, with specific emphasis put on the author's origins in the Orlyk family.[18]

> European countries; *rakia*—fruit-based spirit originating in the Balkans; slyvovytsia—plum-based spirit; *becherivka*—Becherovka, a Czech herb liqueur; *tsuika*—țuică, Romanian and Moldovan plum spirit; zubrivka—bison grass vodka, most commonly found in Poland (żubrówka); anisivka—spirit made with aniseed; yalivtsivka—gin; *borovichka*—bilberry spirit (tr.).

18 Osyp Shpytko (1869-1942) was a Ukrainian writer who emigrated to Brazil and wrote in both Ukrainian and Portuguese. *Dilo* (The Cause) was an important Ukrainian-language newspaper. The Orlyk family was a famous Cos-

The Unsimple visited Kryvorivnia and advised Hrushevskyi to bring the French engineer to Lviv. Having passed through Manchuria, Turkistan, Persia, Georgia, Odesa, Chernivtsi, Stanislaviv, Halych, Rohatyn, and Vynnyky, he finally arrived and got work in the ethnographic commission of the Shevchenko Scientific Society. He received funds that had originally been meant for Shukhevych and set off for Hutsul country. But the experience of the several small wars he had lived through in the course of his life could not allow him to betray himself as a folklorist. The French engineer made a detour to Budapest and managed to obtain all the papers necessary to have the right to enlist people for immigration on the territory of Austro-Hungary.[19]

14. In Yalivets, the French engineer dressed the same way every day from 1900 to 1921. (Even after 1914, the

> sack dynasty to which Pylyp Orlyk (1672–1742) belonged, a Ukrainian hetman in exile at the court of Charles XII of Sweden and author of one of the earliest European constitutions (*The Constitution of Pylyp Orlyk*, 1710) (tr., ed.).

19 Mykhailo Hrushevskyi (1866–1934) was an important Ukrainian historian and politician and one of many prominent Ukrainians who spent time in the Carpathian village of Kryvorivnia. The Shevchenko Scientific Society is a Ukrainian scientific society that was founded in 1873 in Lviv. Hrushevskyi was its president from 1897 to 1913. Volodymyr Shukhevych (1849–1915) was a prominent ethnographer who researched the Hutsuls (tr.).

French engineer sat in his office listening and noting down everything that various people came to tell him. The storytellers received a decent fee, and the noted-down stories, dreams, insights, and insane ideas were analyzed by the Unsimple). A broad, white flannel suit, made without a single button, striped white-and-green shirts, always unbuttoned, cork sandals. Only in winter did he wear a lizhnyk wrapped around his head like a hood.

It was the French engineer who taught Sebastian that self-awareness is found in the soles of the feet, and that one's perception of oneself can be changed by standing differently or on something different.

15. The idea for a whole new type of film was given to Frantsysk by the French engineer.

In Yalivets, there was a small gallery. Its owner, Lóci from Beregszász, was good friends with talented artists—with Munkácsy, Ustyianovych, Kopystynskyi. He introduced Romanchuk to Fedkovych, and also made several photo sketches for Vodzitska, namely for her *Girl Making Pysankas* (much later, when the latter had returned from Paris—and from Zuloaga). He was close friends with Ivan Trush. Lóci told him a lot about how plants can regain control of landscapes that have been ruined and abandoned by people. He even took him sketching near Pip Ivan, to places where trees had been felled. Many years later, Trush would return to this theme in his wonderful series *The Life of Tree Stumps*. And, after all, it was Lóci who first showed anyone Dzembronia, which later became a favorite place for many artists of the Lviv school. And he would regularly send Hutsul rarities to the Dzieduszyckis for their museum.[20]

16. Lóci himself painted the same thing his whole life—little wooden cowsheds (a separate one for each cow) on the Shesa plain, the wooden walkways between these, and the great overgrowth of sorrel that gradually consumed its own environment.

Though he was a professional gallery owner, he never displayed his own work. On the other hand, he often fell in love with the work of others. He would take his paintings cum lovers home for a time and live in their presence, carrying them with him from the bedroom to the kitchen, from the kitchen to the study, from the study to the gallery, from the gallery to the bathroom.

And Lóci's life was defined to a large extent by the painting that was living with him at any given moment.

17. In the gallery, some unusual things were practiced. Every day, Lóci re-hung the pictures, completely

---

20 These were all Ukrainian artists working around the turn of the 20th century, except Munkácsy who was Hungarian, and Zuloaga who was Spanish. Count Włodzimierz Dzieduszycki was a Polish nobleman and naturalist who also had a strong interest in Ukrainian folk culture. In the 1870s, he turned his large private collection of natural and ethnographic objects into a public museum in Lviv (tr.).

changing their dialogues. Often, the buyers, having chosen a picture one day, would not recognize it the next morning. The roof of the gallery consisted of a glass reservoir filled with rainwater. Lóci changed the lighting of the room by covering different parts of the reservoir with spruce branches. But the most important thing was that the pictures could be borrowed, like books from a library. Lóci put together orders for the most expensive hotels himself, taking into consideration each individual occasion.

18. Lóci was the only one in Yalivets whose vines produced quality, ripe grapes. His vineyard grew along a path between the house and the gallery. Each time he walked along the path, Lóci would pick off at least one cluster of grapes. And he did so from the appearance of the ovary to the final ripening. Although by September there were only a few dozen clusters left, they were as ripe as the grapes of Tokaj, taking full benefit from the vines' strength, which the picked bunches no longer drew on.

Although Frantsysk was friends with the gallery owner, even he had no idea that Lóci was working for the Unsimple.

19. The French engineer once told Frants what he had heard from Lóci.

Lóci had told him how an old man from Teresva had come and asked him to paint a picture that would show what is happening off to the left beyond the frame of a painting depicting the battle of Khotyn that he had bought there a year earlier. The old man suspected that from out there a cannon would be able to strike directly at the rearguard of the Ulans, and this thought constantly bothered him.

This is precisely why animation is better than painting, said the French engineer.

20. Frantsysk came up with a more precise method. He produced an enlarged reproduction of a famous picture for the second part of his film. For the first and third parts, he painted scenes showing fifteen seconds before the moment captured in the original picture and fifteen seconds after it. As a test, he used a recent landscape by Trush, *The Dnipro near Kyiv*, although in fact Frants was thinking mainly of Rembrandt's *The Night Watch*. Then he animated several still lifes by the old Dutch masters (although he destroyed all of these except a Jan van de Velde—the one with a deck of cards, a pipe with a long stem, and some hazelnuts) and the wonderful *A Fight* by Adrian van Ostade (an inn, drunk villagers, women hold back two knife-wielding men with mad looks in their eyes, everything has been overturned, someone is running away, others have fallen to the ground).

After this, he started on paintings of Mamai.[21]

---

21   The Cossack Mamai is a Ukrainian folk character and a popular subject for folk art (tr.).

The living paintings were such a wild success that, for every premiere, dozens of viewers would travel to Yalivets from all over Central Europe; the films were written about in major journals, and Frants had no time to make more serious work.

21. Even before the Unsimple had discovered the unusual nature of Anna's dreams, one of Frantsysk's ambitions had been to make a film based on a dream landscape.

He noticed that the mechanics of dreams are based on nothing other than the connecting of well-known things according to the principles of an unknown logic in a way that could never really exist in one single landscape. This means that the key to this logic is the unification of landscapes. In this, the order of the unification is crucial. When such a landscape is created, it populates itself arbitrarily. And then all the characters no longer display their natural traits. And—most importantly—the characters will populate the space very densely. Irrational coherence is absolute.

22. And also, thought Frants, good dreams are like good prose, which is characterized by the use of similes from different systems of coordinates, the refined distinction of individual details against the flow of a broader panorama, a transparent endlessness of possibility, an unforgettable feeling of presence, the simultaneousness

of all tropisms, the unrestrainedness of the unexpected, and the modest rhetoric of restraint. And they are also like good grass, which does not bring with it anything of its own but rather removes limits and transforms the lattice of the proportions of time and distance from a crystallized state to a gas-like one.

23. However, trying to make a film like that would be even more difficult than making *The Night Watch*. So, in time, he stopped saving dreams for later, enjoying them instead to the full at night.

24. In July 1904, Anna recounted one of her dreams.
 I'm standing on the level roof of a long, two-story building. The building stands in water. The water reaches right up to the top of the first floor, to the top of its high arches. There are three heads floating and one heron standing in the water. One head swims under an arch. Another wants to swim out from there. Down the stairs from the window of the second story walks a naked, tubby man. A dry hand emerging from round the corner tries to stop him. I'm also naked. I'm standing on the very edge. My hands raised upwards. Placed together. I'm about to jump from that height into the water. Immediately behind me is a round table. And behind it—a barrel with a jug. Around the table sit a monk and a nun, drinking something. Above the table, the barrel, the monk, and the nun, a tent is stretched across a dry branch. Beside the

building, the hemisphere of a dome with a chapel at the top has been built. Fire pours from the top of the chapel and a woman looks out of its window. She is looking at me. Far beyond the dome are a wide river, a green forest and high, blue mountains, like ours. On the other side of the building, a round tower has been built. On its walls, little men have been painted. The little men dance, jump and tumble over. One is taking a book from the sky. Two carry an enormous raspberry on a stick on their shoulders. The top of the tower is crumbling and full of holes. Little trees grow, and a goat grazes among the ruins. The water in front of the building ends at a long island. The island is bare and of red clay. At the end of the island stands a windmill. Beyond the island is more water. Beyond the water—a city. Two towers descend right down to the water. Between them is a stone bridge. On the bridge is a huge crowd of people with spears raised above their heads. Some of them stand along the barrier and look across the water in my direction. In one tower, branches are burning. Some kind of creatures are swimming between the towers. A man with a sword and a shield is fighting with one of them. Further, beyond the towers, is an empty, sandy place. In the middle of it stands a two-wheeled cart. Further still is the city. Buildings with sharp roofs, a tall church, a wall. And, in the distance, there are high mounds, or perhaps they are small, green, bare hills. On the horizon itself is another windmill. To my right, but beyond the water and the island, some figures stand on the shore. With their backs to me. Some sit on horses or on strange creatures. One is in armor and a helmet, another has a hollow tree stump on his head. Between them grows a dried-up tree. Half the tree is covered with a red curtain. In a great crack in the trunk stands a naked woman. On the uppermost branch sits a woodpecker—a very big one. A man is leaning a ladder against the tree. Quite far away behind them on a stone sits a bearded man in a monk's cassock, with a stick in his hand, looking at a book. He looks like my Saint Anthony.

Through the shutters in the round tower, which I've already mentioned, I see that, behind the other tower, something important is happening. But I can't make anything out, which really frustrates me. But all the same it's really good to be in the middle of all this movement. For a second, I look over my shoulder and see a distant fire. It makes the skin on my back and on the back of my legs hot. Somehow, it's clear that I have to escape from it into the water. I'm already about to jump, but then I look down and see a length of sharp wire stretched out below. I don't doubt that I can jump beyond it. But I still stand there. My hands are already a little tired, because they're raised the whole time. Suddenly, a shadow falls on my back, and it gets colder. I look up. Directly above me, a sailing ship covered in armor is floating past in the air. I see its underside. It's a flying ship. It flies past. The shadow disappears. Once again, it gets hot. Hotter and hotter. I want to take the step. But I see a man with a camera.

He's been hiding the whole time in a dark corner between my building and the tower with the paintings of the little men and the shutters. I don't want him to take my photograph, and I shout at him. The man waves his hands in denial and points at the flying ship. Everything in me feels how interesting this all is. The man hides the camera in the wall. He walks around the tower and disappears behind it. I stand up on my toes. I sway a little, then jump. I see before me the wire. I raise my whole body. I try to fly over it. But my body won't shift. I am neither flying nor falling. I start to cough. At great speed, I fly straight towards the wire. I hit it with the fingers of my outstretched hands. And with that I woke up.

25. Anna's dream seemed so picturesque to Frantsysk that he immediately tried to draw it. Anna corrected the drawing as he went. When they got to the people on the shore next to the tree and the man with the book behind them, Frants had the impression he had already seen this image somewhere. Only the point of view was different. But it was enough for Anna to color in the drawing with coloring pencils for Frants to recognize Bosch. Without a doubt: *The Temptation of Saint Anthony*.

In *Larousse*, Bosch was represented by *The Wayfarer*, from the collection at El Escorial near Madrid. Anna could not have seen any other reproductions, Frants was sure, he had always been by her side. No one had ever told her about *The Temptation* in her entire life. Frants had definitely heard neither mention of it nor allusion to it since the very beginning of her education. That meant that the seeress's prediction had come true—Anna's dreams showed how things could be.

But Frants could not let it lie. He ran off to Lóci and asked him to order at the first convenient opportunity an album of Bosch's paintings. Frants was prepared to wait a long time, just as long as he would eventually be able to confirm that something was going on here.

Lóci promised to order the album the very next day. And said that he had Bosch in his own library, but only one reproduction—*The Temptation of Saint Anthony*.

Anna without hesitation pointed out her naked figure in the upper right-hand corner of the central part of the picture.

When, at the very same moment, they both recognized two of the four main figures walking across the bridge on the left-hand panel of the triptych as Unsimple, Frantsysk promised himself he would make that film.

26. The work was tougher than ever before. Frantsysk was troubled by doubt. He constantly wondered whether he would be able to convey the mood, the color, the atmosphere, whether he would be able to decode all the secret meanings, whether it was right to show anyone something like this, whether Bosch would look ridiculous and tasteless, whether it would be a sin to reproduce all this filth and sodomy, whether he would

offend the Unsimple, whether he might call down some calamity on Anna, whether he had done someone harm consciously or unconsciously, whether art made any sense, whether he would live to the end of the work, whether something bad might happen at the showing, whether he would die suffering, whether he would meet his parents after his death, whether his Anna was waiting for him there, whether his people would ever be happy, whether there was anything better in the world than our beloved Carpathian mountains, whether it was worth thinking so much, whether it was worth remembering so much, whether it was good to tell everyone all this, whether it was necessary to speak beautifully, whether plants think, whether tomorrow exists, whether the end of the world had not happened already long ago, whether he could hold out much longer without a woman, whether he was under the control of the devil.

27. The exact answer to the last question would have been the answer to many of the others. Despite the fact that Frants was a devout Greek Catholic; that, in the frequent discussions in the gin resort, he always methodically attacked the Manicheans, the Cathars, and the Albigenses; and that he feared nothing on earth, for he was convinced of the rectitude of God's plan—despite all this, the devil appeared to him three times during his work on this film.

28. The first time, he did not show himself but only very laconically showed one of his traits. He was like a magnet.

Frants dreamed that he was lying on the floor. Suddenly, without making a single movement, not even tensing his muscles, he slid along the floor to the wall. Then slid back in the other direction. Then again and again, with intervals, now quicker, now slower. As though he were metal filings on a sheet of paper, and under the paper a magnet was being moved. Once he was even pulled up the wall—lying in the same position—and then delicately lowered to the floor.

After this, the devil asked him to follow carefully what was about to happen. He dragged Frants into the corner. It turned out that his teacher was asleep there. Frants was shoved toward the teacher and immediately pulled back. The teacher, not touching Frants's body and without waking up, slid after him. See, said the devil.

Frants didn't hear the voice but somehow knew what the devil had said.

29. In the second and third dreams, the devil used different variations of the same method.

The second dream was the shortest. Frants was standing in the street in Yalivets (the place was real, he knew it well). He was waiting for his Anna who had already appeared at the end of the street. Suddenly Beda's armored car drove up to him. Beda looked out through the top hatch and said that he had brought someone with whom they would now go and drink gin. From the side doors, a little fellow emerged and came up to Frants. Anna was getting closer. The fellow stood with his back to Anna and the car. He took from his inside pocket a bottle, pulled out the cork, and offered the bottle to Frants. And now everything happened. In the few seconds it took Anna and Beda to reach them, Frants had time to see several thousand different faces pass over the place where the fellow's face should have been, several hundred waistcoats under his unbuttoned jacket, several dozen forms of bottle, and more than a dozen shades of drink. When the fellow and Frants were no longer alone, the kaleidoscope stopped. The fellow smiled, Anna and Beda smiled. Frants drank first. The taste reminded him of greengage plums. He passed the bottle to Beda, and he—back to the fellow (Beda had not actually introduced them to one another). When it came to Anna's turn, Frants, for some reason, blurted out that she did not drink. Nobody, apart from Anna, was surprised, and nobody insisted. And Frants discreetly but tightly squeezed her finger. He already knew who this was.

30. After the third dream Frants went to the high bridge and told the Unsimple about Bosch. "So, in the tower after all," said the peak wanderer. Frants asked whether he should show anyone the now completed film. That depends entirely on your wishes, answered

the Unsimple. Although think about it, maybe it's not right to show our faces where you dreamed up this nonsense. And, for now, go home and look after Anna, we must wander a little among the worlds, but soon she'll be a woman and will know where to find us, said the *baimaker*.[22]

31. At home, Frants burned the drawing that depicted Anna's dream.

"In order to be happy," he told Anna, "you have to live without secrets; and, with other people's secrets, you should know only those that you can reveal under torture."

He was very afraid that the Unsimple might sooner or later come for the film, so he told Anna never to mention its existence. But, if someone were to want to find something out using torture, then she should tell them everything they wanted straight away. Not try to

---

22 In the original Ukrainian, *baïl´nyk*—the author's neologism is based on the word *bai* that is usually used as an interjection in Ukrainian and other Slavic lullabies (the repetition of its simple trochaic meter *báiu-báiu*, often truncated as *báiu-bái*, creates a soothing rhythm that lullabies are known for). The noun *baika* means "a tale, parable," while the verb *baiaty* (*baiat´*) in old Slavic and archaic Ukrainian forms also means "to tell" (as in *baiku baiaty*— to tell a tale, fictional story, fable, or parable); the author does not use its old Slavic noun form *baiun* (one who tells tales, fables) but introduces *baïl´nyk* instead, now endowed with magic properties (see more on p. 389) (ed.).

fool them, just tell the truth. Therefore, you must know that I've destroyed everything.

Frants packed the film into his tobacco pouch and went outside the town to burn it, or to throw it off a cliff or into a torrent. On the way, he thought: no matter how they torture her, Anna will tell the truth—there is no film. It is paradoxical, but that will be the only truth the torturers will not believe, and the torture will not stop.

In that case, it is a shame to destroy the film. Maybe it will come in useful someday. Let someone find it who will watch it, analyze it, think hard about it, and understand what these Unsimple are about, with their wanderings around the world. For it always gradually comes to light, how everything and everyone in the world are connected with everything and everyone else—by paths, of which there are no more than four.

32. Frantsysk went into a beech forest in which every tree had a hollow under its roots. He wrapped a lapel that he had removed from a long overcoat around his eyes so that he could see only where he was standing and began to run blindly around the forest. Several times he collided with a tree, but it was alright, because his eyes were protected. He ran uphill and downhill, until inside his hood all the sounds of the world were replaced by the sound of wheezing from the depths of his lungs. It was only then that he stopped and, without opening his eyes, reached out, found a tree, found the

hollow between the roots, and stuffed the pouch with the film inside into the hole, deeper in than one and a half forearms. And then he slowly made his way out of the forest. In these parts, this is easy to do without looking. You have to go upwards, following the slope of the ground. At the top, Frants took the ice-covered lapel off his head and looked at the forest. All the trees were identical and unfamiliar, between them curled endless intertwined lines of footprints, his eyes hurt from the shameless light of the moon.

33. Of course, it was winter. Of course, snow was falling. You could spin round, catching the snowflakes in your dry mouth.

34. At home, Frantsysk could not smell his daughter and thought that he really was living after the end of the world, which had happened not long ago. In the house, he could hear only the flow of water deep in the pipes, the contraction of the metal in the doors of the cold stove, the ultrasound vibrations of the panes of glass in the windows, it smelled of sulfur and coal—the pressure was changing.

Frantsysk ventured to glance out through the open doors of the balcony. The blanket, spread out in the garden, looked like a painful stain. Shivering from the cold, on the blanket slept a little girl who had never yet fallen asleep without her father. In order for a draft to be created, a little time is necessary. So, it began to smell of Anna after almost a minute. Frantsysk felt that he did not want her to become a woman.

35. After that night, the Unsimple really did leave Yalivets, somehow managing to throw their rope ladder back up onto the viaduct. The French engineer remained, not even stopping his work for a day. Frantsysk stopped making animations. Now he, together with Anna and the Serb Lukač who marked all his movements around the world by planting forests, occupied themselves with improving the town. Frants drank a little (usually, he would draw an equator of full shot-glasses across a circular table in the bar and would not move until he had emptied the whole row), but he refused all forms of gin treatment.

He built himself an orangery where he cultivated tropical plants. He observed the changing resemblances of the children of the dog Lukač whom he had had to kill in the orangery. Sometimes, he would take an axe in each hand and run like that all the way to Menchil. From there, he would bring back fresh *brynza* cheese, slinging an axe with *berbenytsi* fastened to each end, like a yoke with two buckets, across his shoulders.[23] He gave

---

23 *Brynza* is a kind of salty, white sheep's cheese typical of the Carpathians. *Berbenytsi* are small wooden barrels used for carrying cheese or other products by the Hutsuls (tr.).

interviews reluctantly, but diligently. He would insist that he made such different films in order to be able to live in different ways.

36. In 1910, the members of the Vienna parliament Mykola Lahodynskyi and Vasyl Stefanyk visited Yalivets with the sole mission of persuading Frantsysk to return to his work. Frantsysk made no objections and promised nothing. He received the MPs not at home but in the CPT hotel, which stood for Cheremosh, Prut, Tysa.

Lahodynskyi later recalled how Frantsysk Petroskyi had said that a Ukrainian state would be possible only when the Carpathian vector became the basis of its geopolitics, Carpathian cosmogony the model for its ideology, and the Carpathians themselves a nature reserve (Frants did not especially believe in what he said, for he hated the Hutsul desire to cut down, in the course of their lives, as much forest as possible, and the Hutsuls' failure to understand that there was now more and more rubbish that could not just be thrown away into the water).

37. As for Stefanyk, he told Frantsysk's Vienna acquaintances more. "Every human being," so said Frants, "can, in their lifetime, make a book. I say a book, although we began talking about films. Every human, but only one book. Those who think they have written many books are mistaken—they are always repeating the same

thing. You cannot escape your own book, no matter what you change. You can imitate, but not create. Your single book is defined by your timbre, intonation, articulation. Fate is a way of speaking. Although there is an infinity of books in the world, the number of genuinely good ones is finite. It must be finite, and there must be an infinity. This is what plants teach us. If the number of good books was not finite, the whole world would stop—or take to drink. I've written my book. I don't know whether it is good or not, but I've written it. And, in that regard, it's like this: it's already meaningless whether I have finished it or have not finished it, whether I rewrote it or merely intended to do so. Your book is just the same whether it's one page or whether its volumes fill a whole bookshelf. The voice exists—that's enough. Plots are necessary for your own curiosity. Plots are not invented, nor do they disappear. They are and they are. They can only be forgotten. All that I've learned and memorized in my life are a few landscapes that signified the joy of thinking; a few smells that were emotions; a few movements that absorbed feelings; a few things, objects that were the embodiment of culture, history, sufferings; many plants that were access to beauty, wisdom, and to all that in comparison with which we simply do not exist in the world. And many, many intonations. Unique, similar intonations, the meaning of which I do not know. Perhaps they will help us recognize each other in the place where nothing but the voice remains."

38. Stefanyk was also pleased when, after Lahodynskyi had gone to rest, they began to hurl all sorts of different insults at each other—you blind bat, you freeloader, you four-eyes, you brat, you whimperer, you mumbler, you stutterer, cock-eyed, you bandit, you ne'er-do-well, you intriguer, you layabout, you rascal, you glass-peddler, you incomer, you playboy, you nouveau riche, you lowlander, you highlander, you Bukovynian, you Boiko, you Lemko, you Hutsul—and then fell asleep.[24]

39. Two years previously, Frantsysk had first taken Anna to the place from which he had returned alone fifteen years earlier. Anna never managed to visit the place again, not even once. Nevertheless, this was the beginning of the only tradition their family had.

In the fall of 1913, Anna still was not yet a woman. At around that time, the birds flew over Yalivets on their way to Africa. Frantsysk felt it: a little longer, and it would be time for him to cry. The most important things do not happen according to your will, he thought, and asked Anna to make a large pot of coffee and squeeze the juice from four grapefruits the size of small pumpkins.

Frantsysk realized that he could not, when he closed his eyes, exactly recall the outlines of all the surrounding mountains, just as previously he had begun to forget all

---

24 Boikos and Lemkos are ethnic subgroups of the Carpathian mountains (tr.).

the unforgettable women's breasts that he had known. For this reason, he had to climb up onto the cliff in order to look at what he had loved so much. And he wanted to make sure, before leaving on his walk, that the coffee and grapefruit juice would be waiting for him when he returned.

40. He returned home with Sebastian, having re-familiarized himself with all the peaks. Frants proposed that he try living a while in Yalivets. Anna made up another bed in the spare room. For some reason, she had had the spare key to the room since morning.

Frantsysk felt that Anna's scent had stopped being that of a child, and that the Unsimple might come very soon, because the blood of the guest, like an airborne disease, had begun to mix in the air with the blood of the women of his kin already.

Sebastian wanted to sleep so much that he accepted with gratitude Frants's invitation to live a while in Yalivets.

And Anna thought to herself that it would be hard for Sebastian, trying all the time to be friend to the father and husband to the daughter.

Naked vine branches tapped on the window above the bed. Sebastian noticed that the rhythm of their taps could serve as an anemometer.

EXCESSIVE DAYS

1. In the morning, Frantsysk was awakened by a completely unknown smell. At first, he thought that a miracle had happened and that, instead of the expected winter, which was due to bring some sort of sense, the time of June rains and abundant greenery had come. But, when Anna came into their room in the early morning, Frants adopted a new calendar of smells, in which the seasons had a different order.

Reality exists for those who have no Anna.

2. Sebastian, for the first and last time in his life, made love with a woman he had known for only a few hours.

Even in Africa it was not like that. Although he identified the women who would become his at first glance, he was, nevertheless, always convinced that they would not end up falling in love. Although they would care for each other for a long time, talk about childhood and retell books in such a way that the number of books each read would immediately double, give one another food, wash and warm each other's bodies, point out things they had seen from different sides of the road. Only later would it become clear that at the base of such coexistence was a certain unconquerable tendency. In as far as it indicates love not for oneself, but for another, this coexistence implies extending one's access to the territory of that other. And it is possible to reach a place where further extension is possible only by going inwards, only under the skin. Thus it was with Sebastian.

As for the women, having seen Sebastian for the first time, none of them had the irrepressible desire to make love to him. The unavoidability of this became clear gradually—it was enough to live for a while in direct contact with him. This is precisely how it was in Africa. In the end, Sebastian knew such things only about Africa.

It was only after spending the night in Yalivets that Sebastian became convinced that Europe exists.

3. In the night, it snowed and winter began, a winter which that year would last until the middle of April. Because of winter's ability to be more multifarious than all other seasons of the year, each of its days was completely different.

And it was never good in the same way twice.

4. Anna couldn't believe that such an unlikely similarity existed—curved lines repeated one another, curving inwards or outwards, exactly following concaves and convexes, came together in such a way that the two surfaces felt not themselves, not the other, but the appearance of a third, perfectly fine line, which curved around, through and backwards of its own accord.

And such unities do not happen by accident. A sort of perfect delicacy, delicate perfection, which so easily passes from one to the other and to several generations to come.

Love does not imply mutuality, said Anna, and Sebastian kept silent, because he was aware now that she did not need an answer. It seemed to him that something in the world had moved, that he had caused some disturbance in the world. And, although lovemaking has no future, does not allow the use of the future tense, only with Anna could he imagine himself in old age.

Anna opened the window. Now the vines could no longer be heard, because the swaying branches simply flew into the room. But the wind died down not because of the absence of an anemometer—rather, such a heavy snow began to fall that it gradually pushed the wind downwards to the ground and covered it in itself. And, in the same measured and unhurried way, the snow drifted into the room and settled on the bed. In this way, the room was ruled by six fluids—saliva, blood, water from the snow, sweat, Anna's moistness, and Sebastian's semen.

5. In the morning, the three of them breakfasted together. They had to sit in a row along the long, narrow table, one side of which was pushed right up against the window. Sebastian had almost stopped smelling of Africa. And, since the smell of Anna's moisture had not yet washed off his hands, Frantsysk tried to decide how they should breakfast from now on: he-Anna-Sebastian, he-Sebastian-Anna, or Anna-he-Sebastian.

Anna was given a letter from old Beda. This time, the wrapping was from the same tea as she had made for the men for breakfast. She wondered what she would write back to Beda, if she no longer had any questions.

6. That winter Frantsysk suddenly realized—he had no photograph of himself for the article in *Larousse*. He could have gone to Chameleon and had his photograph taken, but Frants correctly decided that—since there were several hundred possible variants of the article—even the best photograph would be purely accidental. He would have to have his photograph taken each time the article was written anew. (And he had even once had similar idea for a film—he photographed one person every day in the same pose and in the same place for two years, then he played this series of evolutionary changes back at different speeds. Against the background of evolution, details become very distinct).

Thus, Frants found a strange way not just of regaining the past but also of recovering something completely unexpected.

7. After breakfast (eventually Frants decided that it would be most correct for Sebastian always to be in the middle and accepted that Anna would always sit by her man, while he would have to be close to Sebastian so that they could talk easily about everything), Frantsysk took the spare key to Sebastian's room from Anna, for the room would no longer be locked and he would no longer go in there. He read the letter from Beda and said that he had told Anna this once, because he had told her everything he knew, and that she already knew what old Beda had written. Obviously, she had been too small when this exact memory had been told, and it had been forgotten. If she wanted, she could hear it once again when he—as he definitely would—told their whole story to Sebastian.

And then Frants pulled from the bed the winter sheepskin that had been laid there for the summer and went to the Hotel Union where, in a room on the second floor, Yalivets's only contract killer had lived for several years now.

8. Shtefan was very surprised when Frants entered his room—in Yalivets, Frants could kill anybody he wanted without needing to hire an assassin—he was too well respected. Shtefan had just returned from a successful job in Kosmach and had to do a little work on his rifle.

Before Frants arrived, Shtefan had already managed to attend a church service and even take communion afterwards. But he did not swallow the wafer. He brought it in his mouth to the hotel and put it in a hole that had been made earlier in the wall with a drill. He loaded a bullet into his rifle, walked to the opposite wall and fired at the hole. It is a good thing he aimed well. Frants heard this shot between the first and second floors, while traveling in the elevator, which was pulled upwards by two workers turning a winch right up in the attic. Shtefan laid aside his gun and started to collect the blood from the wall. Frants opened the door. Now Shtefan should have smeared the rifle with the blood, but he did not want to do this in front of Frantsysk.

9. Frantsysk quickly explained his request.

He wanted Shtefan to do what Shtefan did so well—to follow him unnoticed. To track him like an assassin. Find a good place to shoot him from and the right moment to shoot. But instead of a rifle, Shtefan was to have a photo camera. Frants would give Shtefan three months' time. After this, he would take one hundred of his photographs and pay the rest of the money. The main thing was that neither Frantsysk nor anyone else should ever notice him. On hearing how much Frantsysk was willing to pay, Shtefan enthusiastically agreed, not troubled in the slightest by the fact that he did not even know what a photo camera looked like.

Among other things, this irresponsibility of Shtefan's meant that a lot of people were still alive. Shtefan—as is the wont of Ukrainians—was constantly taking on more commitments than he was able to handle. And so, some people waited years for the fulfilment of contracts, while some jobs were simply forgotten. But now Shtefan understood that, with Frants, delays were out of the question. He had been told that Frants knew those eighteen words which make the rifle tremble, and the target come by itself, crying, to stand right outside your window so you can take aim at it.

Frants showed him how the photo camera worked and left. Shtefan quickly rubbed the blood from the wall all down the barrel of his gun. He knew it was a terrible sin, and that he would belong to Judas, but he always did this so that the rifle never missed. Especially after the blood begins to boil.

10. Every day, Frants took Sebastian for a walk around Yalivets. The frosts were severe, and the ice rinks did not even begin to melt, even on sunny days. Finally, Frants had someone to talk to—it turned out that Sebastian, as a real marksman, was able to see just as much. One might have thought that they would engage in endless, serious conversations, because the problem of Central Europe is a stylistic one: but no—just a few words, pointing out things they saw.

When they went into the bars, they drank gin diluted with boiling water and washed it down with fresh juice made from slightly frozen apples that had been left on the trees in the fall and only recently picked from under the snow.

Sometimes, they went to the place where the first Anna had died, and Frants drew in the snow schemes of more and more divergent versions of the family history. There are things that are more important than fate, he said. Maybe culture. And culture is kin, consciously existing within it. Frants asked that the children of Sebastian and Anna visit this place. And also the place where Frants had met Sebastian (he almost added here the beech forest with the undestroyed film, but stopped himself in time, because, after all, he knew little about the Unsimple), and other places would appear with time. For time is the expansion of kinship into geography.

11. There were days when Sebastian would take his African rifle with him. On especially steep slopes, it provided good support. On one of these days, they spoke of their dreams for the future. Unsurprisingly, Frants's dream was more complicated.

Sebastian dreamed of being old, living on a small rocky island in a warm sea, of walking around in nothing but canvas trousers all year round, but of walking little, mainly sitting on a stone bench beside an empty, white hut, drinking red wine and eating dry goat's cheese all day, and looking at the few tomato plants, and not at the sea, in which he would bathe every evening until the Matthiola began to give off its scent.

Frantsysk, on the other hand, dreamed of a woman with several pairs of breasts.

Suddenly, Sebastian bent down and butted Frants in the stomach with his head, Frants tumbled from the snowdrift they were standing on while Sebastian turned a forward roll on the ground and, lying on his back, fired from his snow-filled rifle. On a nearby hilltop something rang out. After lying still for a moment, they made their way to the place and found Shtefan, pierced by a bullet wound and holding a smashed photo camera.

Sebastian had taken the light flashing off the lens for the reflection of an optic sight. Shtefan had overlooked the most important point: "No one should ever notice you," Frants had said. And, for such an oversight, one has to be prepared to pay.

And the fact that Frantsysk ended up without a photograph for the encyclopedia, that is another story. Fortunately, reduction still interested him.

12. After this accident, Anna decided she wanted to learn to be a sniper.

13. First of all, you have to grow to love your own body, said Sebastian.

And the place where it will all take place.

For the body is the gateway to the brain.

If you want to think well and quickly, that gate should always be open.

So that thoughts can come in and out freely.

Thoughts are merely that which filters from place through the body and through the body flows out again.

The freedom of donor-acceptor relationships.

To lie in the water and not sense its smell.

To look closely at grass and not sense its taste.

To feel with one glance the taste of what you touch.

The gate opens only when you love it.

Open up, you always open up so beautifully.

You can scratch with your nails, but you can also hold on with them.

Prolong your gaze, maintain your gaze, hold your gaze.

Transfer to the rifle the desire of your body to be in a place that you cannot reach.

If you grow to love the place, it will become the continuation of your body.

It is not you who shoots but the relief of the landscape.

It is not the head that thinks, but the body.

It is not the bullet that hits, but the thought.

Every thought is a desire that was able to enter and leave through the gate.

What you can do by yourself, do with nobody.

Say what you think and think as you feel in the moment.

Cry from tenderness, for otherwise you will never be so strong.

Watch your breathing, for only it can dictate rhythm.

Always remember about trees, they disappear and appear most reliably.

When you are very tired, stop being unbreakable and fall asleep.

Reach inside with your lips to your center.

Shooting into a window is like looking into a window.

Try to understand how black people make jazz.

Openness. Honesty. Gratitude.

14. In order to learn these and countless other subtleties of the art of the sniper, it is necessary to uncompromisingly adhere to a strict regime—to constantly make love, and to do so only in the open air. Long, lightly, powerfully, fast, gently, stubbornly, clumsily, beautifully, wisely, carefully, very carefully, wisely and beautifully. On the earth, in leaves, on moss, in trees, under trees, on hills, in hollows, in the wind, in the snow, on the ice, along the road, across the bridge, above the bridge, in the dark and in the night, in the light and in the day, before, after, and during eating, in silence and crying out. Stand. Walk. Sit. Lie. As much as was possible during that longest of winters of 1914.

That whole, long winter which lasted until April 1914, Sebastian and Anna barely came into the house. Anna said what she thought and thought as she felt in the moment. She cried from tenderness, for never in her life had she been so strong. Sometimes, when Sebastian was inside her, she seemed to want him to be even closer, and sometimes he was extremely close through several layers of clothing. When she bent over, he was convinced that something made him bend too. As though another layer of tight membrane had been created around his own skin.

    Excessive days.

THE THIRD OLD PHOTOGRAPH— MAYBE FOR *LAROUSSE*

1. Were someone to ask him unexpectedly, Sebastian would be totally unable to describe this photograph exactly and in detail, although he had seen it many times and it did not show anything particularly complicated.

It is possible that the very laws of reduction, memorizing and forgetting that so fascinated Frantsysk were at work to the full in Sebastian's relationship with this photograph.

"Faces are the best plots," said Frantsysk.

Frantsysk said: "Plots do not end and do not disappear. They can, from time to time, be forgotten."

Sebastian recalled the plot of Frants's face differently throughout his life, but never as it was in that photograph.

2. It was taken at Frantsysk's funeral in May 1915.

Frantsysk lay on a bench covered with a lizhnyk next to a hole in the graveyard outside Yalivets. The photograph had been taken in such a way as to show only Frants, and not the funeral. Frants was dressed in an embroidered shirt, cheres, and red trousers, arms folded on his chest, holding a cross made of two pencils tied together with a wisp of upland grass (an idea of Lóci's). The ring with the river stones in it, which Frantsysk had made for himself, had worn for years without taking off, and had then taken off but not thrown away, yet refused to put it back on, stuck out from between the pencils. The opening for the head and neck in the shirt was covered with a silk cloth.

The head itself lay (or, more precisely, stood) apart, a little further along the bench. The black beard and long gray hair were combed in such a way that, apart from the eyes and nose, the face was almost hidden from view.

3. Sebastian was not at the funeral, and he saw none of this. The little girl—Anna's daughter and his daughter, Frants's granddaughter, whom the latter had not lived to find out about—had been brought to Yalivets the day before the funeral. Frants had had his head cut off two days before that. Sebastian had been there. Afterwards, he waited until all the blood had flowed out, washed Frantsysk, combed his hair and dressed him in the shirt and trousers. He laid the head in a basket and covered it with ferns. And, the next day, the courier brought the infant from dead Anna.

The whole day, while Frantsysk was being given a ceremonial burial in Yalivets, Sebastian did not leave Frantsysk's granddaughter who seemed to have a sore stomach and cried constantly.

Sebastian could never memorize the photograph, perhaps because he could not imagine how things had been at the funeral, though he knew only too well what had happened before it.

4. In the spring of 1914, Anna could shoot better than Sebastian. At that time, he was again spending more time with Frantsysk, because Anna would take her rifle and go for several days into the mountains. There, she tracked animals, watched them and learned the thing about being a sniper that Sebastian could not know—what a sniper looks like from the opposite end of the rifle. She killed no one other than the gadflies that tried to land on the udders of the mountain sheep.

"I want you so much," said Anna, "that I don't know if I could fall asleep at all if I didn't want to sleep next to you so much." And when she fell asleep, she needed Sebastian's hand to be under her head. "I want to be your daughter and you to be my father. A father exists so that he can be dreamed of later."

5. Spring began only in April. During the winter, an immeasurable amount of snow had gathered, and it all

started to melt at once, regardless of whether it was on the northern or southern slopes, or of how high it was above sea level.

Down in the lowlands, dirty and overflowing rivers caused floods in various cities, but no one knew there how the snow melted in the mountains.

The waters also ran through Yalivets. Every building was washed away a little that spring. All because of the thickness of the winter ice.

On every street in the town were bonfires on which they burned leaves and branches that had slid out from under the snow. The burning of spring smelled different to that of the fall—severed vine stems, already full of juices, found themselves in the fire.

6. All spring, Sebastian waited in fear for the onset of his allergy, just as in previous years. But no allergy came. This place accepted him without resistance.

While he was waiting, he noticed that the trees opened up in the morning, right at the end of the night.

The whole of Yalivets knew about Sebastian already. Often, when visiting a bar with Frants, he would have to tell various groups of people about Africa. The same story but getting longer and longer. He was even invited to become a survival instructor at one of the town's guesthouses, but he refused due to lack of time.

7. Because just then Sebastian had a dream.

He and Anna were in town walking along a street that did not in fact exist in Yalivets. The street consisted of two rows of buildings standing on a bare slope. Behind the buildings was nothing but alpine meadows and the tracks of animals. The street led sharply uphill. The ground floors of the buildings all housed different bars. There were also tables in the interior courtyards behind closed gates.

They went into each bar in turn, went up to the counters, which were different in each bar, and drank a glass each of white wine in one gulp, memorizing the taste of different vintages from different vineyards, and they were told something unimportant but very interesting by the dozens of acquaintances sitting in every bar. Eventually they stayed with two acquaintances, also a man and a woman, for longer. The women talked about something while the man invited Sebastian to go for a swim.

They left the bar and went along the street, further up the slope. The street ended suddenly in the snow-covered summit of a mountain. They walked across it to the opposite slope. There was a large open-air swimming pool there. Sebastian went into it first. He dived under and swam under the water, feeling that there must be a current in the pool, as he was being drawn a little to the side. He surfaced and, treading water, realized that now it dragged him even more strongly. The same happened with his friend. They drifted towards the side of the swimming pool, which ended not in a wall, but in a rope stretched across the surface of the water. The nearer they got to the edge, the stronger the current became, as though all the water wanted to pour away beyond the rope. When they had been dragged to that point, they barely managed to grab hold of the rope. Their legs were dragged forwards, and they lay on their backs, hanging on to the rope. Beyond the rope, little white turtles rushed past them on all sides, being carried forward by the water and disappearing from view. Sebastian held on like this for several minutes. His hands hurt as they never had done in his life, so he decided to let go and plunge after the turtles. But first he raised his head and looked beyond the rope. There, the water formed an almighty waterfall, which created a high, smooth, seemingly unmoving wall. At the very bottom of the falls Sebastian saw everything that could possibly be in the world. Suddenly, the current completely calmed and immediately began to drag him in the opposite direction, painfully casting him out onto the land at the place where they had entered the water. Sebastian's whole body recalled the short swim with a strange sense of sorrow.

They got dressed and quickly returned the same way they had come to the bar, noticing that balconies that had not been there before had appeared on the buildings. The bar was empty except for two old women playing chess at a table that rocked every time one of them moved a figure on the board. In the numerous bottles on the shelves behind the counter there was not a single drop of drink. They had already decided to leave when the old women left their game and approached them. They then realized that these old women were their wives (Sebastian barely recognized Anna) who had been waiting for their husbands, without leaving the bar, for forty years.

8. Sebastian was so struck by this that, the next night, he tried to go back again to continue the dream. But, instead, he merely dreamed that he was tea with milk, mixed in the proportions that give the best color.

9. Anna calmly listened to the story and said that that may be so, but mostly things are completely different, because real pleasure resides not in the vestibular system but somewhere deep in the lungs, something about breathing, filling, emptying, air pressure. A long time ago, Frants had told her the same thing.

10. In the evening Anna, took Sebastian's shirt off him and put it on her own naked body. She sat him on the Biedermeier chair, which she had selected from all the chairs in the house, found an opened pack of Gitanes in the cupboard and put it in his hands. She tore four small strips from the *vereta* rug, took a bottle of "Pelican" ink and sat down at the table.[25] Sebastian lit

25 A *vereta* is woven cotton or woolen Hutsul rug, or a tablecloth (tr.).

up a Gitane and Anna dipped her finger in the ink and sketched primitive and crude drawings on the strips of cloth—a sun (a circle with a few large rays on all sides), a fir tree (a vertical line in the middle from which, on both sides, short, symmetrical, downward-pointing lines come out), a person (a stick, split in two at the top and the bottom, between the upraised arms a little circle, between the spread-apart legs a stroke pointing towards the earth), a flower (a large circle, tightly surrounded by smaller semicircles).

From between the pages of *Larousse*, Anna took out a dried hemp flower and stuffed it into a narrow, glass tube, while quietly reading entries from the encyclopedia. Having finished, she pulled the belt out of Sebastian's trousers and tied his hands behind the back of the chair so tightly that his chest muscles became absolutely flat. She bound his eyes just as tightly with her neckerchief. She pulled a razor from her pocket, opening it immediately with one hand, and without hesitation lightly cut Sebastian three times: on the shoulder, between the ribs, and across his stomach. The cuts for a moment remained narrow lines, then their edges came apart, the wounds opened, and the blood started to run.

Anna took the stub of the Gitane from Sebastian's lips and used it to light the tube with the flower in it. She took a few slow draws, holding in the smoke for a long time after each. Finally, she took the tube in her mouth by the end where the hemp was smoldering, and, with one breath, released a little smoke onto each wound. Then she inhaled all that was left, brought her mouth close to Sebastian's, and released everything she had. From the surprise Sebastian began to cough and lick his lips—the Gitane left a different taste on his lips.

Only then did Anna seal up the wounds with the painted strips of the vereta. And she untied Sebastian, who decided not to ask any questions.

11. That night, Sebastian dreamed that he and Anna were walking along a street that led out of Yalivets. Only instead of junipers and mountain pines, there were two rows of enormous flowering linden trees, which they somehow knew were about to start speaking; they would then have to either say nothing in response, other than a greeting, or answer very accurately. The trees were to evaluate something according to some criteria known only to them. From the sides and from above, through every gap in the treetops, shone an unavoidable sun—like sea water leaking through the holes in a ship, rushing around inside it, gathering in every nook and drawing it down to the bottom.

He walked along that corridor so purposefully, as though something were pushing against the back of his head. Alongside him walked many strangers, but, if one were to take a photograph of the street with the whole crowd, it would nevertheless be clear that the photograph was of him.

Sebastian could see a little way up ahead—underneath the trees lay piles of swept-up leaves, and he saw that the first smoke was already rising from them.

He knew that he was going to walk this tunnel forever, gradually losing himself through friction or light, until he finally passed into eternity, having finally become light.

12. Anna was a grateful student and taught Sebastian to set and give thematic dreams, using the greatest force in the world—vibration. In order to achieve such pleasure, all one needs is a little imagination, in order to learn for oneself to sense the vibrations of things about which you are unable to think, which you should know.

13. All early summer, Anna and Sebastian entertained themselves by pretending that Anna was pregnant.

They began to make love gently. They slept long. And lay in bed for a long time not getting up, making love once again. They would take leisurely strolls out to the meadow to get milk. They would come back by the place where trees had been felled, picking the berries nearest them, and make love one last time at the place where the brambles ended. On the way, they recalled their first days together, always finding some details they had not previously noticed. They ate dinner together on the veranda, always just the two of them, and went out somewhere for supper, but always ordered the healthiest food, and, when laying the table, they composed exquisite still lifes. They went to shops and tried on dresses meant for pregnant women. They rearranged the things in their room and planned how they would accommodate the child. They bought children's books in the bookshop for several years ahead, and Sebastian read them to Anna before bedtime. Sebastian washed Anna in the bath, dried her and rubbed her with scented oils. Before going to bed, they wandered through the most beautiful parts of Yalivets, poured heated-up rainwater on the pumpkins that grew in a large pot full of holes on the balcony, and drank tea made from medicinal herbs. When they had already lain down, Sebastian would stroke Anna's stomach under the soft blanket to send her to sleep, so that he could go out onto the balcony for one last cigarette.

In the middle of the night, Anna would wake him, and for a long time they would not sleep.

14. On June 28, Anna decided she wanted to spend the whole day on her own. She had to finish a letter to the Unsimple and send it with old Beda, who had come to Yalivets for only a few days—the Unsimple needed the letter, having come up with some great plan. Sebastian did not leave Frants's side. They conversed, moving through Yalivets, one on foot and one swimming along the canals. Then the survival instructor took their

photograph and hung around with them right through until morning, first with Beda and later—God knows where already, drinking wine, gin, and predicting terrible dangers for the careless Sebastian.

15. At the end of September, Anna went to MezMezőterebes and signed up as a volunteer with the Ukrainian Sich Riflemen.

The day before, the Unsimple had finally arrived in the town. Anna met with them at the French engineer's place, lay down to sleep with Sebastian on the gallery, and, in the morning, was already gone. There was also no trace in Yalivets of the Unsimple. Frantsysk was sure that she had either gone with them, or they had taken her away with them. Sebastian wanted to go somewhere, ask around, at least do something that seemed useful (half a year later he would be thankful to dead Anna for sending him the infant at the very moment when Frants was no longer with him, and he had to do something so as not to lose his mind from loneliness).

Incidentally, running around haphazardly looking for a lost person, asking everyone you meet, is not actually completely senseless. For in our mountains, where the waters gather everything and where the waters themselves gather in three places, finding a missing person is very easy—as long as they are not lying under the snow or under a rock. And, even then, the not knowing will last no longer than a couple of years.

But Frantsysk laughed at Sebastian's impatience and told him to sit still as a rock and wait. Because waiting is sometimes the most radical thing one can do. And, sure enough, three weeks later, the Unsimple came again and began to demand that Frantsysk let them see Anna. For the first time, Sebastian felt relief.

16. In October, a wounded Bosnian captain arrived in Yalivets from the front. During the destruction of the Buchach citadel, both his legs had been crushed. They had been amputated, but the imaginary legs hurt so much that it was recommended that the captain come to Yalivets for treatment. Later, the hopes of the doctors would prove justified: the captain would stop howling and even write the first volume of a short memoir about the start of the war. Gin really is an effective analgesic.

In the meantime, still in October, when the captain had only just been brought on a stretcher to Yalivets, he told everyone about the operation he had undergone in Horonda. The surgeon spent all his spare time in the famous Horonda inn with the commanders of the Sich Riflemen. There, he had met the most beautiful woman he had ever seen—Anna Yalivtsivska from the Carpathians. She had been the favorite sniper of Second Lieutenant Pelenskyi from Didushko's company and had advised the surgeon to send the Bosnian to Yalivets (very soon afterwards, the company left Horonda for Nyzhni Verechky). This was not only the second moment of relief for Sebastian, but also the ultimate one for Frantsysk. Anna was free. She was not with the Unsimple. There are things that are more important than fate.

War, it turns out, is one of them, and thus so is death.

17. The third relief for Sebastian could have come when they brought the child, but he did not allow himself this luxury and lived with that heaviness until the end of his life, sharing perhaps only crumbs of it, passing them on from Anna to Anna.

18. How Frantsysk lived out the final months of his life, Sebastian did not know exactly, because he saw Frants only from afar. In the simplest sense of that word. And only from below.

At the beginning of that very warm winter, Frantsysk moved for good out onto the balcony, isolating himself there from all contact. Sebastian met him only once a week in a bar where he would go to collect a full can of gin. Their meetings were sometimes accompanied by glasses of yalivtsivka with guelder rose syrup. Frants was touchingly friendly, but about family matters he spoke not a word. Sebastian listened as Frants told him about the latest movements of the World War so vividly that it was as though it were Sebastian, and not Frants, who had been sitting isolated on the balcony (or as though Frants had a pair of binoculars that could see for hundreds of miles in every direction and even look behind every tree).

Sebastian did not understand how Frants could find out the military secrets of both military blocks because he could not know how Frants lived on the balcony—vines, ivy, and the tops of young cedars all obstructed his view.

19. Back in Africa, Sebastian had noticed one interesting thing—people are very willing to examine things when they have to lower their gaze but are terribly inattentive when it comes to looking up.

In summer, he and Anna had spent a great deal of time on the balcony onto which Frants had moved—they grew pumpkins, smoked, and spent all day drinking cold maté that had been poured into a silver jug the night before. They saw everything that happened on the street. They could even guess at the content of conversations from gesticulations and lip movements. On the other hand, nobody ever—Sebastian was sure of it, because he never missed a single glance aimed at him—saw what they were doing on the balcony, that they were on the balcony. Because one would have to raise one's eyes (this, obviously, is something to do with anatomy, thought Sebastian).

Now, looking at Frants's balcony, Sebastian cursed himself that he had never taught Anna the main rule of sniping in a city: balconies are the most important thing.

(Much later, General Tarnavskyi retold Sebastian someone else's account of the lost street battle in Lviv in November 1918, and Sebastian again thought about snipers and the balconies on which these snipers had probably lived before the war.)

20. The leaves on the vines finally fell off one night and Sebastian was able to make something out through the ivy and the cedars. He saw a thin line tied to the balcony, stretching straight upwards towards the clouds. And nothing else in particular. But during their next meeting he warned Frants that he had noticed the line, that it was visible.

Frants explained nothing, and Sebastian was left with no choice but to believe his own theory, which was, he thought, most logical. The line from the balcony leads to a high kite—the kite is fitted with a bird-catching net—the net catches birds—the birds are escaping from their nests at the front—beyond Chornohora lives an ornithologist—the ornithologist puts rings on the birds—the birds are ringed—they fly across Chornohora—they get caught in the net—Frants examines the rings—Frants knows the ornithologist—Frants understands his ring codes—on the rings, nesting places are indicated—the birds are escaping from their nests—that means the front has reached those places. Frants lets the birds go and raises the kite again.

21. In April 1915, the battle at Gorlice began (Frants had named the exact location for the offensive the day before).

In May, groups of strangers began to pass through Yalivets: the Mazepists were returning to Galicia, the Galicians had been released from Thalerhof and Gmind, the Moscophiles were trying to catch up with the Russians, deportees were escaping from Russia, Russian spies were infiltrating the Hungarians, the Hungarians were weeding out the spies and hanging Hutsuls, the Hutsuls were crawling to the Romanians for some cornmeal porridge, Romanian bandits were hunting Hutsul girls, deserters and marauders were trying to avoid one another.

Most of the vagrants avoided Yalivets, but those who appeared in the town generally wore arms. In Yalivets, there was only Sebastian's African rifle.

22. With Frantsysk, everything happened very quickly.

So quickly that it seemed to everyone that the head simply fell off in mid-sentence, the way a pipe can fall out of your mouth—if you pick it up quickly enough you can keep smoking. They almost wanted to do the same thing with the head before the body collapsed. So that the end of the unfinished word would not disappear in the momentary pause.

They had been finishing their gin and guelder rose syrup when some bandits from Maramureş walked into the bar. They paid for their gin with boots that had marks made by wolf bites. They sat down behind Sebastian, Frants looked at them from time to time, for he was on his guard. He placed his machete on the table, the one he used when he visited the Serb Lukač to hack his way through the dwarf mountain pines that incessantly grew taller around his forest hut.

The front was retreating, but the birds had not yet returned. Frants had nothing to say and was telling Sebastian about the Unsimple—how, when someone is born somewhere, they sit right underneath the windows and think up that person's story, like earth gods. And that, because they could not invent a new story every time, they had dreamed up this war. He was about to tell Sebastian finally what the baimaker had thought up for Anna (it was very significant that she had not been Anna then) and where he had hidden the film with something the Unsimple were looking for.

Suddenly one of the bandits came up to their table and said he would buy the machete. "You won't buy it," said Frants. "Then I'll take it." "You won't take it." "Why?" "Because I need it." "And if you won't need it?" "Then you'll come to me." "I'm already here," said the bandit, "and I want to take it." "If you can hold on to it," and he looked not at the Romanian's hand, but into his eyes. The bandit turned his eyes away, reached out his hand, looked back, took his hand away. "I can cut your head off," he said in Ukrainian. "If you can—do it. Otherwise, perhaps you'd better say *good*..." And that was how their chat ended, because the bandit grabbed the machete and, without taking a swing, using only the weight of the knife, sliced off Frantsysk's head. Sebastian heard the rip of the severing tendons. Frants's body sat. The head fell onto the floor and did not roll. Like a clay pipe from a mouth. They almost wanted to quickly put it back in place and hear "...*bai*." The second bandit put a bomb down in front of Sebastian and the two men left the bar with the machete. Sebastian did not know what to grab first—the bomb or the head. In the end, he took the bomb and threw it into the open stove. At least the explosion went up the chimney. Bats took flight in broad daylight. The body fell onto the floor, knocking the head under the table.

23. The next day, the courier brought the infant girl from Anna. Sebastian understood why Frants had died—he had reckoned that he was immeasurably stronger because there was no other woman in the world whom he would be able to love. Not suspecting that he had a granddaughter. At that moment, Anna's daughter had been only a day's travel away from Yalivets.

WARS OF THE IMAGINATION— BRIEFLY

1. Why always war? This is what little Anna, daughter of Sebastian, asked when she began to understand the more complicated stories. Sebastian was horror struck—he realized that he really had spoken to the little one about nothing but war, that he had told her everything there is to know about war, even though it was already 1921. He really had taught her nothing except what might come in useful in war; he had been bringing her up like a soldier.

Why is there always war? She turned her head towards him and managed to articulate the question in the time it took the horse to leap over a dog rose bush. The horse puts its forelegs down on the ground. Sebastian leans back sharply so the horse's momentum does not make him strike the child in the face with his chin. Anna turns her head away and once again looks ahead. They speed across the hills. She doesn't wait for an answer too long—she's becoming similar to Anna, her mother.

Along the road, Anna is supposed to remember everything she sees. Then describe it as exactly as possible. And, in addition, she should identify the positions she would choose for shooting, and the points which could serve as hiding places for the enemy. Just a children's game, a first schooling.

2. That evening, a tired Sebastian took some paper and sat down next to a candle to add up the material consequences of war (this is how Sebastian illustrated Anna's lessons—in the form of geometrical tasks and formulas).

The war had taken: Frantsysk, the machete, Anna.

The war had given: the mysterious sea buckthorn forests around Yalivets, Anna, a few Russian bullets, the funeral photograph of Frants and one drawing by Perfetskyi.[26]

What things had he done that can only be done in a war? He had gone on reconnaissance once, dug a trench once, blown up a bridge once.

There were really very few traces. The war had, in truth, passed them by. So, why always war?

3. Back in the fall of 1914, the Yalivtsians decided that this war was not for them. They were in Central Europe and could not afford to have any larger interests. But when the South is fighting with the North, and the East

---

26 Leonid Perfetskyi (1901–1977) was a Ukrainian painter who was best known for depicting war scenes (tr.).

with the West, then they do it mainly in Central Europe where the Carpathians and their rivers are. And the worst thing possible in such times is to play the role of the peaceful population of the Carpathians or a strategically important point on a 1:50,000 topographic map.

For this reason, Lukač decided Yalivets had to disappear. He planted sea buckthorn bushes all around it, and after a few weeks these had grown so high that the town could not even be seen from any of the surrounding mountains. (To achieve this, everyone had to take part in digging a real defense system that had several rows of trenches with passageways between them—it was as though the whole town was playing the old Boiko children's game of moles, but it was the only way, Lukač assured them, to get the sea buckthorn to grow fast, high and thick, hiding the secret paths with its needles). Only the viaduct, where the Unsimple had once lived, stood out. They gathered all the gunpowder horns they could find. They laid them on the bridge. They opened the windows in all the buildings, and Sebastian fired an incendiary bullet at the powder.

The bridge jumped and flew up into the air; the blocks tumbled together and disintegrated into sand, which fell all at once onto the town.

(Those few Russian ammunition rounds—sharp bullets with a Cyrillic letter on the shell—had been left with Sebastian by some Lemko deserters in return from a little ether.)

4. Everything in the world is connected by no more than four steps. So said Frantsysk.

Everyone in the world knows each other through no more than four people. Sebastian knew Anna, Sebastian knew Lóci. Lóci knew Anna, Lóci knew Sebastian. Lóci knew Perfetskyi. The artist Leonid Perfetskyi knew Anna. Perfetskyi drew Anna in the Sich Rifleman legion. Lóci met with Perfetskyi in January 1919 in the temporary capital of the ZUNR, Stanislaviv.[27] Perfetskyi showed Lóci the drawings, and Lóci recognized Anna. He told Perfetskyi about the woman in the picture, and Perfetskyi—as Frants had done once in his films—said what had happened just before the moment captured in the drawing.

5. Anna was a born spy. She was able to get through anywhere, see everything, memorize everything, and, what was most rare, she could describe everything in exact detail. She often disguised herself in different outfits in order to cross the front line. That is how it was at Bolekhiv. Once, she had gone behind the front when the Russians began a counterattack. The Austrian units gave way, leaving our riflemen open. Three Finnish regiments came at us from three sides. Hand-to-hand combat

---

27 ZUNR is the abbreviation for the West-Ukrainian People's Republic (Zakhidnoukraïns´ka Narodna Respublika) that existed in 1918–19 in western Ukraine (ed.).

began. Many of our soldiers fell on the field: Captain Bukshovanyi, Ensign Stepanivna, Ensign Sviderskyi, Second-Lieutenant Kravs, and Corporal Frei were all taken prisoner.[28] The rest held firm and fought off the Russians. And suddenly, in the forest on the other side, Anna appeared. She was dressed as an old man, ragged, and leaning on a long stick. She went straight through them. It wasn't carelessness. Something was guiding her, something no one could guess at. She was chased by three soldiers. Anna took her staff in both hands. It had been honed and was sharp as a bayonet. And she made a stand against the three of them. She used it like a real rifle without bullets—as though using bayonet and butt. She pierced the throat of one, smashed the head of the second above the ear, but from the third she took a bayonet in the chest. The soldier couldn't pull the bayonet out from between her ribs, and Anna seemed

---

28 The description is based on a real battle that happened near Bolekhiv, western Ukraine, in 1915, in which the famous Ukrainian Sich Riflemen unit fought on the side of the Austrians against the Russians. Ostap Bukshovanyi (1890–1937) was an important Ukrainian military figure of the period. He served with several Ukrainian armies and then in the Red Army. He was shot in Leningrad in 1937. Olena Stepanivna (nom de guerre of Olena Ivanivna Stepaniv, 1892–1963) was a historian, geographer, civil activist, and one of the first women in history to serve as an officer in a modern army. She served in the Ukrainian Galician Army during World War I. She was later arrested by the Soviets and spent time in the Gulag (tr.).

to help him, grasping the blade in her fingers. The Russian became frightened and let go of the rifle, which fell towards earth; Anna began to fall forwards, but the rifle held her up. The bayonet had now come right out through her back. In one hand, Anna still held her staff. She barely managed to lift it and strike out at the rifle that wouldn't let her lay down. The rifle butt slid forwards and Anna fell, with the bayonet in her chest twisting inside her. Some more soldiers ran up and stabbed her as she lay on the earth, just as they were taught.

6. Perfetskyi gave the drawing to Lóci. Lóci brought it to Sebastian, telling him: "Open the envelope only after I've gone."

In the drawing, Anna did not look dead.

Her head lay on a little mound, her face was bright, her lips were not tense, her legs were slightly bent upward at the knees, one hand lay relaxed by her side, the other was thrown back at the elbow toward her head. There were none of the things one normally notices on a corpse—no hardness, no withering, no inflammation, no swelling, not even any sharp, stiff angles. But for the clothes, it would have looked like a classic nude in an art academy.

7. He could not accept that this was his Anna. Sebastian generally did not believe in Anna's existence beyond what he himself had witnessed—and this had been true also during her lifetime.

But, looking at the picture, he felt the same as he had on Saint George's Day 1914.

On the market square, twelve gypsy trumpeters from Subotica played long into the evening. Gin poured from the fire hydrants. Drunken Lukač planted some sort of shoots in the ground that grew before their very eyes. They swam and danced in the canals. They swung on all the swings and trapezes. When everyone had already fallen asleep in the street, Lukač took the gypsies, Sebastian, and Anna back to his place. The gypsies could barely manage to drink any more. Sebastian tried to get his arms around Anna, but each time she would somehow end up cozying up to the gypsies. Then the trumpets fell silent, and the singing began. They sang as though under the gallows. Until they all sobered up, remembered everything they knew, and got drunk again—this time for good. Sebastian and Anna wanted to make love somewhere in a corner, but it was no good, because she kept returning to the table as each new song began.

At dawn, they made their way home and had nothing to say. Behind them, the nightingales still sang, and, before them, the larks were awakening. They thought they would lie until daylight with their eyes opened, but they fell asleep as soon as they lay down in one another's arms. The last thing that went through Sebastian's head was that, tomorrow, a new life would begin.

He woke up two hours later wanting water. He ran to Lukač's hut. The gypsies had already risen and were making kasha on the fire. They barely greeted him. Sebastian could not understand what he had felt so close to during the night. And the whole day he waited for the night to come again.

8. Looking at the drawing, Sebastian began to think about how a bayonet enters the body.

From that time on, he constantly felt something like this: He is being stabbed. He is stabbing. A saber slices skin. The wound heals. He walks through the field among the still living but already killed. He slowly dies from a bullet in the stomach. Mud under his boots. Marching in columns. Crossing through cold waters. Purulent wounds cleaned by dirty fingers. Ragged fighters. Rainwater in bogs and trenches. The wheels of the cart have to be dug out. Trees in the way are cut down. Explosions nearby. Must stay down. Trees split. Columns of deserters. Hangings in orchards. Crawling in the snow. Black figures returning across white hills. Burnt fields. Inflamed eyes. Muscles hurt from sleeping in the cold. Frostbitten hands. Pain, exhaustion, cold. The constant effort and strain without which even finding food becomes uninteresting. All this Anna also felt. For the first time in the world—two people feel exactly the same thing.

9. In 1921, Sebastian stopped talking about the war, although his imagination was there always. Thinking about something, he always thought about something different to what he was thinking about.

But he began to tell the child about animals.

He began to miss Frantsysk most of all.

10. That same year, the French engineer died. Just as he had expected—from smoking.

It was already quite cold, so all the windows were shut. The shutters on the chimneys were also kept closed. The French engineer finished his last cigarette in bed; he did not put out the stub in the ashtray, but rather got up and, without putting on his long johns, walked across the room and threw the butt into the stove. He then took a drink of water straight from the bucket. Only then did he lay down to sleep in peace. But the stove was full of waste paper—mainly old rough drafts and notes for completely banal stories (it was strange, but, after the war, there were many more of these, and he simply had to throw them away; and on top of that, people had begun to come much less often to the office of the French engineer: some stories were just unspeakable, while others begged to be told both one on one and to whole gatherings). The paper caught fire from the cigarette butt and burned itself out in the closed chimney. The French engineer died sweetly from the fumes.

THE UNSIMPLE

1. They said the Unsimple would come to the funeral. Why they hadn't appeared for so many years, when they had been truly needed, nobody knew. Clearly, it was not something they needed to do. It meant that the death of the French engineer interested them more than Yalivets did during the war. Or perhaps the real war, outside Yalivets, was more interesting for them. Here, after all, nothing happened that the French engineer could not keep an eye on. If they really were still tied to Yalivets, then they would come in order to do two things: first, to collect something the French engineer had left behind, and second, to leave somebody in his place. Frantsysk said they were interested in certain people. Sebastian vividly recalled how Frants had shielded Anna from them, how he had spoken of the haunting of their family by the Unsimple. The fear that someone might take his (and his Anna's) daughter from him came—at least for

a few seconds—every hour. Now, it had become all-consuming and pushed Sebastian to his limits. They had to escape somewhere.

Anna slept, and Sebastian grated potatoes and fried some potato pancakes, so as to have something substantial to take on the journey.

He grated the potatoes, fried them, and thought about something completely different.

2. the unsimple are earth gods. people, who, with the help of innate or acquired knowledge, are able to do good or harm to others. that point is important—innate or acquired. they know something. at the same time this can also be learned. acquired. in this way, it is possible to become unsimple by learning something.

and the innate. they were interested in Anna's dreams. was this innate or acquired. it came from the morphine—acquired. but it came only to Anna. the morphine uncovered something. which means—innate. Anna explained some things to me, I learned some things—acquired. Anna said that not everyone could master her teachings. they must have certain characteristics. characteristics are the principal plots. they are intonations. intonations make the voice. something innate and unchanging—it can at most be imitated. to imitate, one must know. imitation is knowledge, because knowledge is imitation. they were interested because Anna knew something they had not learned. which means their knowledge is not limitless. they have to acquire it. to tie it together with certain characteristics. the unsimple are different. it is impossible for one person alone to acquire all knowledge. but each one for whatever reason chooses certain branches of knowledge. depending on characteristics. they are of all kinds—cowlike, horselike, catlike, doglike, chickenlike, gooselike, fishlike, froglike, mouselike. like all creatures that take nourishment from other creatures. there is also the snake charmer, the werewolf, the stormbreaker, the clouddriver, the peak wanderer. there is also the seer and the seeress. but the most important is the baimaker, the spellcaster. the most powerful is the spell—incantation, speaking, *bai*. bai is not a word. bai is many ordered words. a bai is already a story. for different causes there are different bais. bais are plots. a bai is a narrative, telling a story, a plot. motivations must also be plots. and, in order to find a bai for them, they must be told. in this case, narrative influences the choice of narrative and then the chosen narrative is narrated. the bai is narrated, the bai that influences, acts on the previous narrative-motivation and matches the direction in which it is going with the narrative-bai towards the narrative-effect. which means that there are only narratives. narrative is all actions, and all actions are narratives. among the unsimple, the baimaker is number one. his innate knowledge-characteristics—how to narrate (hearing, articulation, voice, intonation, rhythm, pace)—are strung together with acquired ones—what to narrate. the unsimple must know what to narrate. they need people's narrations—Anna's, the French engineer's, Beda's, MP Stefanyk's, General Tarnavskyi's. what they know, they tell someone else. but to whom. to Frantsysk, Anna, Lóci. afterwards Frantsysk makes such and such films, Anna builds such and such buildings, which then bai something to someone else. and these someones have something they can re-bai to someone else. they have. the unsimple do what they want. wanting also must be known from somewhere. to know is to hear a narrative. wanting is narrative, it is bai. wanting is had. unsimple want to have. the best way to have is to be able to narrate, to make narrations. whosoever narrates has everything. narration, therefore, is not only the greatest act but also the greatest thing, the greatest number. the greatest characteristic and trait. the unsimple have the most, do the most, signify the most, because they narrate. the mystery turned out very simple. knowing criminals A, crime B is dreamed up for them. the unsimple rule the world. the unsimple come when someone is born, or something is born, and think up their life. they narrate a plot. the narrative becomes the motivation, life is the effect of the narrative. and the motivation for a new narrative, which can be heard and retold. there is no life without narrative. because narrative is life. plots do not end, said Frantsysk. plots hide and emerge. stories, like infections, cause fever, are carried, are passed on, hide, come out and cause fever. they merge, separate, mix together, grow together, break in different places, overturn, crumble, are reborn. to gather plots. to combine plots (analysis, synthesis, deduction, induction, mythologization, de-mythologization, analogy, hyperbole, addition, subtraction, multiplication, division, accent, timbre, articulation, transfer, cohesion, instillation, elimination, tonality, speed, rhythm, chronotope, personification, allegory, synonym, antonym, homonym, construction and deconstruction, comparative linguistics). to give away plots according to place and time. such is the method of the unsimple. and this method is a result. for it is as it is said, ordered, related, refused, retold, forbidden, indicated, suggested. what is it for. in order to say.

bai is invisible medicine. the essence of all form.
the form of essence itself.

that which can be taken into the next world. that which is necessary in the next world. for there is nothing but voices, eternity and delight. your own eternity with your own voice your own bai about your own delight.

no work, no treasure, no strength, no body, no emotions, not far, not near, not much, not little, not sometime, not now, not sometime. your own eternity with your own voice your delight—your bai.

3. Sebastian gave all the potato pancakes to Anna for breakfast, because they had nowhere to go, because there was nowhere to escape to. The main thing is to fear nothing.

Sebastian went to the deceased, prayed (dear God, don't allow me to harm Thee!) for the narrative of the soul of the French engineer and waited until the Unsimple arrived. They asked Sebastian not to get in the way and to wait two days, even though this was the first time this family had sought the Unsimple out, and not the other way round. Sebastian promised not to take up much time and stepped inside. He told the baimaker that he wanted to be a baimaker. He asked to work as a barman in the bar that belonged to the Unsimple.

At that time, in Yalivets, the What's There Is There bar had become the most fashionable postwar locale in this fashionable prewar Central European resort. After the war, its address changed a little, leading to some unavoidable, basic misunderstandings. Despite it all, Yalivets was still, in the end, situated in the Ukrainian Carpathians, and not just in the Czechoslovak Republic. But Stanislaviv, Lviv, and Ardzheliudzha were on the other side of that forbidden line through Chornohora. Now, people came mainly from Prague, Brno, Bratislava, Košice, Karlovy Vary, and Uzhhorod to drink gin in Yalivets. And also from Podebrady and Nusli, from Německý Jablonec, Liberec, and Jozefov. With these foreigners, it was easier to communicate in Ukrainian than in German.

The Unsimple agreed to his suggestion without hesitation, but they did have one condition. And, as it happened, Sebastian also had only one condition. Both conditions turned out to be the same—Anna should be in the bar, beside Sebastian.

TO SAY OR TO STOP

1. Something had to be changed in the bar. Sebastian described to Anna several interiors that he thought he had been dreaming of his whole life.

Anna agreed that it was easiest to remember beauty through things. Things endure, they go from story to story. But true, original beauty lies in flowers, in plants, and in that from which these plants grow and into which they grow: water, open air, light, a little warmth, and a little cool.

They did whatever the girl wanted.

2. After ending her six years of military training, Sebastian did whatever Anna wanted. He did not see this as spoiling her. He just did not know what little girls needed (with a boy, it would have been different—Sebastian could remember well how he had felt at different times in his own childhood—although perhaps it would

have been worse, because he could not know whether his son would feel things in the same way) and was of the opinion that small people know very well when they feel good and when they feel bad. The most accurate way of summing up childhood is as the correlation between laughter and tears. Some of the Yalivets women tried to assist in Anna's upbringing, but Sebastian would not allow them access to the child and ignored their advice. Although the renovation of the pub left them with very little free time, Sebastian managed to tell his daughter every day about all the things he had learned from the lives of animals.

3. The pub was transformed into a bar that was open in several places, more similar to a garden. As for the things in the bar (other than tables and benches), everything was made of transparent glass.

Mainly, the glass objects held cut flowers.

4. In the meantime, Anna spent more and more time with animals. She especially loved snails. Sebastian liked snails because they seemed well mannered. Their reserve and lack of emotion demanded a more attentive consideration of their snail needs, sympathies, wishes, and intentions. Completely different manners of behavior, self-expression and communication give a generous space for mutual understanding. Anna felt happy when she put a snail on herself in a place from which it didn't

immediately want to crawl away. It thanked Anna by slowly and gently sliding across selected areas of her skin.

It was possibly because of this preference that, all her life, Anna was best able to imitate snails. When they began to make love, she became a snail most often and most enthusiastically. Sebastian suspected that, in this way, she was trying to show him how he was to behave with her. She never dared to say this to her father in words. Sebastian was surprised—how was it possible to know so well the secrets of animals. "I just didn't have anything to read," his daughter laughed.

5. And really, this Anna did not even read *Larousse*, because: Sebastian did not know French (he had not fought in French Africa, and Central Europe gives the possibility to communicate with one's neighbors in one's native tongue), Anna had constantly been becoming a soldier in her early years, then they almost never left the bar, going home only to bathe in winter, and, in addition, Anna heard so many stories in the bar that the eternal and timeless *Larousse* would have seemed like a two-day-old newspaper to her; and, finally, they fell in love in such a way that no encyclopedia could ever contain entries of any use to them.

Next after snails were lynxes and wagtails. Among the insects—crickets.

6. At that time, Anna was between ten and twelve years old. Once they bathed in several streams during

one short, sunny September day, taking the Keveliv down to the Tysa. They decided not to return to the mountains until it got dark. They knew that there would be no more river bathing that year and walking in complete darkness was even easier—the soles of the feet found the way as if by themselves.

Sebastian looked at Anna as she jumped into the river and crawled out onto a rock. He had never seen such women before. And he did not know if he ever would again—Anna would soon grow up, he could already see in her a hint of his first Anna. He felt guilty for not memorizing that beauty. He could not remember last year's Anna, or three-year-old Anna. It was always today's that moved in his imagination.

I don't have to remember this, said Sebastian to himself. Remembering childhood is a child's business. I want only one thing—to see the day when there will be no need to remember her as she was sometime, but when every day she will be as she is every day. I want to live only with her. I am her father and an adult man; I know what I'm talking about with my little girl. I don't have to memorize this—after all, she'll also have to have something to tell when she becomes a woman.

(Anna lay in the whirlpools between the rocks.)

All the same, he tried to remember things. She was a slender twig on a branch, whitened and honed, bent and dried by the river water. Dried by the river.

He had to plunge his face into the Chorna Tysa.

7. During the night, as they crossed the Dzhordzhova Pass and could no longer make out one another's features in the dark, Anna took his hand, stopped him, and said that a poem had come into her head. It was, probably, very clumsy, but:

> how sad oh anno
> oh how sad oh
> for in anno domini one hundred hundred
> it's not just your height I want
> just like a clay bowl
> fears the growth
> of the supple pine
> which will carry her efforts
> in those places it seems
> the wind will release too much
> very fine sand
> from those rounded hills nearby
> for eyes filled with stinging tears
> when you touch your cheek
> to the palm
> which I press
> fine hairs rise on your skin
> I don't know the bai
> for this sand
> how sad oh
> little girl
> in a black beret

in big boots
with a blade of grass
in your wide mouth
She gave the poem to her father Sebastian.

8. Throughout all these years, they worked in the bar, which really did very quickly become the most fashionable one in Central Europe.

Sebastian invited, as Frantsysk had once invited Sebastian, columnists from several major newspapers to try living in Yalivets for while ("And anyway," he wrote on the postcards, "in the newspapers, there's never anything really important, there's only what causes most of today's problems—an excess of information, which is impossible to retell... it is understood that a certain convention exists that forbids philosophers from looking around and describing certain things..."), to drink gin together and talk as people should talk in Central Europe—to ascertain which places and people we have in common, exposing in this way the multiple parallel spider webs in which we all find ourselves.

Yalivets became a paradise for writers, journalists, essayists, columnists and reporters.

They came for the gin, they came for Sebastian. Some he listened to, some he told stories to. He tried to avoid stories that covered a distance more than four steps.

9. And he and little Anna worked night and day, mainly together, sometimes sleeping in turns. The child grew up in the bar, washing glasses, cleaning the tables and the floor. Cutting flowers for all the glass vases. Sometimes they spoke, but now somehow differently. Now, they were only concerned with what they thought about whatever they had just seen.

10. Anna liked to have her photo taken, and even those who had never taken photographs before liked to take photographs of her. Only Sebastian did not like this. For this reason, only three photographs, taken and given to them, apparently, by visitors, survived. In one of them, Anna is almost ten years old. This photograph is the most interesting.

Sebastian's figure is somewhat blurred. It is no wonder, because, at that moment, he is spinning around. In both hands, he holds knives. You can see that he has already started to throw one—he is just letting it out of his hand. Anna grips Sebastian round the waist with her legs, her back touching his knees and her hair touching the ground. In her raised hands are a bottle of gin and a glass. Her smile is distorted by the rush of blood to her face and the centrifugal (centripetal) force (in such situations it is very hard to close an open mouth).

This was a trick they had for their clientele. They would go out into the middle of the bar and, without music, dance a complex tango. At the end, Anna would leap up onto Sebastian, they would spin round, Sebastian would throw knives at a target (throwing knives at a target was the most popular form of entertainment in the bar), and Anna would grab from a table a bottle and a glass, pour out some gin, and place the glass on a table in such a way that it would slide right up to one of the customers. She never spilled a drop.

11. After Anna's death, Sebastian tried to collect at least some of her photographs. He recalled guests who might have photographed Anna, found their addresses, and sent them letters with this single request. But, for some reason, nothing came of this. No one wanted to give away their photographs, even those who could understand Sebastian's suffering.

THIRTY YEARS
OF THE FAMILY S.

1. In 1921, when Sebastian went of his own accord to the Unsimple, he chose a strange form of freedom—to tell the Unsimple persistently about the life of his family. To make surveillance by normal methods impossible. In this way, he turned himself and his family into a sort of research laboratory for the Unsimple.

"To live in such a way," said Frants, "so as not to have secrets."

This suited the Unsimple fine, and they stopped interfering in the family's life—they believed that Sebastian's experiments with his own life were more inventive and more selfless than anything they could come up with.

2. Sebastian sent his observations to the Unsimple on ordinary postcards.

Their code could be called unprose.

The messages did not take the form of normal sentences but contained abbreviated records made according to a certain system of definitions that he used to give names to things he experienced—actions, impressions, days, people, stories, emotions, ideas, whole microperiods. The Unsimple decoded the unprose and were able to imagine even more than what Sebastian knew (though sometimes what they imagined was entirely different).

He would leave the postcards under a stone beside the road out of Yalivets. Old Beda, passing through from time to time in his armored car, would collect them and then himself address them to the Unsimple—he always knew where they were wandering and the post would be waiting for them in the places where they were due to spend the night.

3. Thus passed almost thirty years. In all that time, the Unsimple only came to Yalivets a few times. Then they spoke at length with Sebastian and collected any unmailed postcards themselves.

Chronology did not interest them, and, for Sebastian, it had never even existed.

4. There was only one period when he wrote nothing—in 1934, when the third Anna—his daughter and granddaughter—was born, and Anna, his daughter and wife, died.

5. In 1938, when Carpatho-Ukraine was created, the Unsimple did as Sebastian suggested—they bought a big bus, turned it into a bar, and Sebastian and little Anna set off in it for the capital, Khust. During this time, he put together several dozen pages of descriptions of the mountain regions for the government of Avgustyn Voloshyn, and, during a one-hour meeting with the head of staff of the Carpathian Sich, Colonel Kolodzinskyi, he put forth a detailed plan for the defense of the country by two hundred snipers ideally placed in positions that Sebastian had personally selected.[29]

Sebastian continued traveling around in the bar, like a wandering circus, even after the occupation of Carpatho-Ukraine—right up until 1944 when, instead of the Hungarians, the Russians came. You won't wander for long with them around.

Sebastian barely made it in time to register himself in Deutsch-Mokra, near Königsfeld, moving into

---

29 Carpatho-Ukraine was created in 1938 as an autonomous region inside Czechoslovakia after the Munich Agreement. It declared independence in early 1939 but was annexed by Hungary within days of the declaration. After World War II, it became part of Soviet Ukraine. It corresponds to today's Transcarpathia region of Ukraine, which borders Slovakia, Hungary, and Romania. Avgustyn Voloshyn (1874–1945) was a politician and Greek-Catholic priest who became president of the short-lived republic, which was defended by a paramilitary organization called the Carpathian Sich (tr.).

the home of a Tyrolian who had been deported by the Hungarians. (He left the bus-bar by the side of the road in Krasnishora and heard that a whole squad of Soviet spies had drunk in it for several days before drowning themselves in the Teresva as soon as they started up the bus and started moving.)

6. Sebastian and Anna lived the most primitive of lives in Mokra. They ate cornmeal porridge three times a day, Anna would graft the apple trees (she had such a good touch), Sebastian would cure people of their fears. And, at night, he played a complicated radio game, imitating on the air the activities of several radio stations belonging to a non-existent partisan group called The Earth Spirits.

7. In 1949, Anna was poisoned by rye ergot and began to see the Middle Ages.

The Unsimple said she had to be with them as soon as she became a woman.

Precisely for this reason, Sebastian did not show Anna their family places when she turned fifteen.

It was only in late fall of 1951 that they left for Yalivets.

The Unsimple had been wiped out in the spring.

And Anna became a woman in June.

She and Sebastian spent the whole summer and fall in uninterrupted lovemaking.

UNPROSE

1. not talk to w. the same way

(w.. — women—Anna is still little, and he thinks up affectionate names for her—he notices that the little girl becomes moody when he uses the same words he used at one time for her mother—even if very effectively—in the narrations he used to narrate to his Anna, at least a few words have to be changed, before they can please his daughter, even if they are only simple stories from Brehm—and the most important thing is not to speak the same way about making love—it is not only individual words and phrases, but also emotions that are repeated in descriptions—Sebastian crafts a whole erotic lexicon, making love to three generations of his women)

2. tattoo on hand

(Sebastian entertains little Anna by drawing little cats, fish, fir trees, rabbits and birds on his hands—Anna watches for hours as the drawings change, moving in different ways on the hand—once, in the bar, a frog trainer performs—his frogs are tiny, like brambles, and of different colors—most of them, however, are white—the trainer has a tattoo—a huge multicolored iris between his shoulder blades, its long stem wrapped around his whole body—Anna wants a tattoo of her own—they take a long time to choose, looking through an encyclopedia of the plants of the Carpathians—Anna remembers the drawings from her childhood—but she asks if she can at least have a little frog, like the performer's—on her palm—quite a painful place, but Anna can endure a lot—tattooing Anna, Sebastian thinks about the line of fate—but there are things more important than that—a tattoo on the palm will not be seen by many people—now Anna greets people by raising her hand—they make love, Anna looks at her palm and doubles herself up like a frog—after this she expels the air from herself, which in this case has entered her together with Sebastian—several hours after Anna's death the frog loses its color and turns white)

3. fear—the greatest temptation
   (Sebastian to Anna—"You are, and the world is together with you, and only fear can tear away parts of you and make another world next to you without you—it's tempting to be afraid")

4. to squeeze out an orange into the mouth
   lemon dries white

   (one of the bar tricks they invented—cut an orange in half, pour some gin into a glass—the customer drinks the gin and immediately throws his head back, opening his mouth—the barman squeezes the orange juice not into the glass but straight into his mouth)

   (Anna is very tired—Sebastian squeezes some lemon juice onto her skin behind her elbows, above her collarbone, on her stomach, between the tendons on her wrists, on her throat—the juice soaks in and relaxes the skin—little streams flow out from the lemon lakelets and dry up, leaving thick, white trails—in the same way your fingers go white if you peel a lot of lemons)

5. w. b.; yours but entirely other

   (w. b. — without biography—in Yalivets, everybody knows everybody—and all biographies are known—on their free days, Sebastian and Anna travel to resorts in the Prut valley—where there are lots of strangers, where nobody knows them—to Tatariv, Dora, Deliatyn and Luhy, Mykulychyn, Yamna—they stay in randomly chosen guesthouses for a few hours—simply to make love—they tell invented stories about themselves in trains and hotels—behave differently every time—according to chosen roles—Sebastian sometimes feels as though he has just met this woman—the same as with the apartments—often, after working at night, they spend the whole day in

the empty apartments of friends—they try themselves
out among other people's things, in other people's habits, look at albums of other people's photographs—or
with languages—they go to shepherds' flocks on the
mountainsides—speak Hutsul—ask for milk, *zhentytsia*,
huslianka, *vurda*, and budz—they listen to how the Hutsuls try to understand them, to what they say amongst
themselves about them).[30]

6. seventeen stones ahead
   (a long time ago, when Sebastian was training his
daughter like a soldier—they had an exercise—to cross
a river without stopping for an instant, jumping from
stone to stone—having glanced at the route from the
bank for only three seconds; they tried it again, when
the second Anna was pregnant—she took a look and
estimated seventeen steps ahead)

7. understanding is the business of the one who wants
to understand
   (this is a fragment from a years-long discussion between Sebastian and the Unsimple—they believed that
the problem of understanding should be solved by the
one who wants to be understood—Sebastian thought

---

30 These are all Hutsul dialect words for dairy products: *zhentytsia* is whey, *huslianka* is fermented milk, *vurda* and *budz* are different types of sheep's cheese (tr.).

the opposite—because vital here is the a priori impossibility of identical understandings—and he supports his point of view in practice—he always narrates as he wants to, yet he answers fully any questions arising from this—he says that he prefers spare rhetoric to excessive rhetoric—more meanings than words, and not the opposite)

8. epos of family places
(Sebastian, after Frantsysk, considers the foundation of every private epos to be the enumeration of imaginary conceptions about places in which the family history has happened—a sort of family geography of plants—in the case of the last Anna, the main points of the epos must be Mokra, Yalivets, Chornohora, Stanislaviv, Prague, Africa, Lviv, Trieste, Borzhava, Sharish, Bolekhiv, Petros, Chorna Tysa)

9. child—killer
(spring 1944—the last spring of the bus-bar—columns of trucks on the mountain roads—some vehicles stand for weeks—helplessness of the commanders—the only idea—go West—soldiers live in the trunks of their vehicles; during the day, they await the possibility of mobilization; at night, they wander in the surrounding areas—a few Hungarian corporals drink the whole night in the bar—Sebastian recognizes among them the two Romanian bandits who, twenty years ago, cut

Frants's head off—he points them out surreptitiously to Anna, as a fragment of the family epos—there is no way of knowing whether the bandit-corporals can remember Sebastian, but no one says a single word to anyone—in the morning, the Magyars go to sleep in the trucks, and Sebastian and Anna drive on a little—Anna asks him to tell her in detail what happened to Grandpa Frants—during the day, the bar is shut—Sebastian puts the child to sleep and goes to sleep himself—he wakes up from the feeling that someone is moving his pistol in his belt—he checks, the pistol is in place, and Anna is sitting beside him looking at the clouds—they are so transparent that you can see what is inside them—fine bubbles of dampness, like caviar on seaweed, vibrate on the narrow strips of dense plumes of steam, everything the same color as gleaming flint—in a few days, someone will tell how two Hungarians, who were in fact Romanians, shot one another in broad daylight in the vehicle where the corporals slept—Sebastian notices that two bullets are missing from his pistol, Anna is washing glasses—in order to kill the killers, he thinks, she would have had to go back ten kilometers by herself)

10. diffusion, to absorb one another, to be absorbed by one another

(a theory of reverse absorption opens itself to Sebastian—he experiments with roots—applies the findings to people—proves that a man, when inside a woman, not only releases fluid that is absorbed by the woman but himself absorbs some of the woman's moisture—according to the laws of empty capillaries and connected vessels—Sebastian believes that, in this way, a transference of substances takes place on a world scale, and this seems extremely important to him—in any case, he wishes to absorb the maximal amount of this extract)

11. cognac with onion soup; juice from the grapevine; porter with wild honey; gin with red ants

(an Arab back in Africa told Sebastian—first of all, teach your sons to make food, they will be wise and joyful—Sebastian does not have any sons, but he has a daughter, Anna—he teaches her to make food: tells her she shouldn't be afraid to invent things, like the finest adventures, for herself—making food for someone always makes sense, like bringing up a child or looking after plants—tasks that return us to the spontaneity of animals and birds, when the questions of what to do and what for do not arise—curiosity that can be given—the opposition of different elements and essences that can be taught to live together—the beginning of all tastes is in plants—because there is no end to them, there is no end to the making of food—Anna started from the bar—she would boil porter together with honeycomb from wild bees—she would serve hot onion soup straight after cognac, and you'd take another drink of cognac for your scalded palate—into a glass of gin she would throw a few dozen red winged ants (believing that to kill for food is not a sin), whose acid gave the spirit a burning quality—in the hungry spring, she would cut grapes from the overgrown balconies and gather the juice of the vine, in order afterward to mix it with gin in a proportion of one to one-half—and the same with everything)

12. rainy guesthouse

(during one of their trips to the Prut valley, Sebastian and Anna stop at a small villa, built in the Zakopane style—while they make love, it starts to rain—when such rains start in the Carpathians they last for whole summer weeks—why do I want you so much today—asks Anna—when she asks Sebastian something, she always does it in a childish way—like a daughter, and not like a wife—Sebastian also forgets that Anna is not a child—he answers simply, genuinely, carefully, vividly, and wisely—so that she will understand for the rest of her life—for a human being the friction and pressure of human surfaces are extremely necessary—the quantity of this is set in advance, like the number of beats of a heart—and we haven't for so long—Anna presents various parts of her body—the body—is the gate of the soul—the gate is open—the soul is revived by touch—follow a change in the strength of the downpour beyond the open window—otherwise you may not come down from flight—they come out of the guesthouse—come out of the forest—unexpectedly, the rain stops—they walk along the mountainside—Anna wants more—they make love in the overly warm grass under the rarefied air, which barely restrains the sunlight—Anna feels so good that the surfaces are changing, in such a way that they will want to talk about this tomorrow—if there is a tomorrow, if there is talk, if there are surfaces—because she is absent several times even here and now—she takes Sebastian with her—he is so far inside her that they think he is no longer visible—birds land on the ground and watch from up close—they look without shame at the birds and see the openness of great Anna who barely fits in their field of vision—they can give themselves no more to the sun, but they want to go even deeper—they head for (now Anna stands, like a naked little girl with a wide mouth) where it might be wet—they run into the forest villa—maybe we should move somehow, but let us lie still, because my head is spinning—outside the window, it is raining—I can give a lot of wetness—they lie still and hold one another—Sebastian imagines how Anna will feed for the first time just such a little girl—Anna dreams of seeing for the first time just such a little boy—it is not you that feels good, not I, not we, but the world—you made me like this)

13. story of a view along a cheek
    novel of lips
    whole essay in a matchbox
    (the last Anna is a few years old—these are the worst days of 1938—everything Sebastian tells the

little one at bedtime either ends badly or loses sense, because he eliminates the children's places from the narratives—children must be read to out loud, Sebastian is convinced—children must look at the book, daddy with the book, letters, paper with letters—children must want to wait to understand of the book for themselves—because they say: because that's what is written—to perceive many older voices, in order to better distinguish your own—our *Larousses* already ran out a long time ago—Sebastian makes strange books—he cuts up postcards and binds the fragments, puts the little scraps of paper together in little numbered bundles in matchboxes, writes all over the walls, the table, the bed, the doors—he himself writes the written—writes in different voices—in the evening, he lies down beside Anna and reads aloud the story of the view along her cheek, the novel of her lips, the essay in the matchbox, the chronicle of the lack of a chronicler, the epos of railway stations, the fairy tales of bird food, the philosophical tract of ivy—Anna listens to the different voices and tries to hear her own—and, indeed, something moved)

14. to kiss often
    a kiss through a sweater
    (throughout the day, Sebastian dozens of times firmly presses his open lips against clothed Anna and breaths out long and hard all the air in his lungs—through the

sweater comes warmth—and somewhere in the middle of the breath the skin at the place of this kiss becomes hot—if this is done often, then using one's own warmth one can perceptibly keep the kissed one warm even in severe cold—the sensation is strengthened by the magical significance of giving from inside yourself into another's body something which is life itself)

15. that inaccessible structure—like a brain, like a nut, like a closed hand, like a seed

(one time, Sebastian feels that a certain psychosis is developing inside him—he does not have and does not want to have any other women in between the Annas—but, during one of these times, he understands that the sense of the erotic is not the object but the path—the interrelation of bodily landscapes—entry, passage, staying, returning—the wonder of any journey—the path that leads itself—all-encompassing uniformity—a place where one can meet the universe—his psychosis is based on nostalgia exaggerated by inaccessibility—even neutral situations he sees as being either inside or outside—sometimes, he feels that he performs his wanderings along this path at full height—moving along, squeezing through, staying in one place, coming to a stop, collapsing, sliding along, falling in—only because the wanderings are imaginary does he think he is not living right, godlessly wasting the gift of life)

16. to see the Middle Ages

(1949—in the mountains a great hunger—Anna is eating raw rye grains, infected with ergot—she sees the Middle Ages, in which things from the present take place—chopped-off heads, tortures, fighting among refugees, the arrival of strangers, ruined faces, wide belts, grammar lessons, bestiaries, musicians at feasts, lack of food, cut-down forests, polluted rivers, mixing of languages, dried fruit, ulcerous diseases, insane exhibitions, lost chronicles, manuscript apocrypha, stinking clothes, dirty dishes, broken arms, crushed legs, stretched tendons)

17. six

(the last Anna is six years old—Sebastian is bathing her—he notices that four spots, slightly darker than her skin, under her ribs and on her stomach, are in fact underdeveloped nipples—he recalls Frantsysk's greatest dream—would he have dared to even suppose—his great-granddaughter with three pairs of breasts)

18. (One bundle of cards old Beda, for some reason, did not take from under the stone. They were found only at the end of the 1950s, during the dismantling of the Austrian military roads in the sub-alpine Carpathians. Every single one was a photograph from the famous Chornohora series that had been made in the thirties. The Soviets did not yet have any of their own

printed views of the Carpathians, and these, taken with a fish-eye lens, were taken to the local museum in Vorokhta. The pencil inscriptions on the back were hard to understand).

feeling of discomfort—this is the trace of a previous taste on the salivary glands that forces you to seek a new one

every period brings new slang; like a new way of life; languages pass more slowly than periods. They accumulate, take up more and more territory, squeezing out the canonical language—they mean more to us. Soon, Anna and I will get to the point where we can converse purely in our own phrases

summer of white wine; get used to Austrian green wine

met with the Colonel and Yaryi[31]

all periods pass (I see that already in my second child and third wife)

it is good to know that you are, that always, somewhere, you are

faith in that which was in childhood

to think about how a leg gets caught between legs and gets scraped

---

31 Rikhard Frantsysk Marian Yaryi (1898–1969) was an Austrian and Ukrainian military and political figure of the early-mid 20th century. He was a prominent figure in the Organization of Ukrainian Nationalists (tr.).

    she fell asleep by the stove with atlases of plants on her lap

    when you pee on moss you flatten moths that sit there pretending to be unfurled leaves

    now I shall never envy anyone, because I have seen tears of kindness

    she could have done more than (why are some women allowed to do everything, maybe because they are able do everything)

    trench diggers eat with their hands

    animation on the sun, on the clouds, on the moon

    deformation by twisting

    such a fullness of being that one could dissolve inside

    (If it were possible to know what these un-decoded messages meant—what they mean (my Annas were not, will not be, but are, always are—so good to know, that always, somewhere, they just are.) If we knew more human fates, said Sebastian. Often in this lies the main therapy of bai.)

    Now a selection of the postcards of Chornohora is kept in the museum of the Carpathian national nature reserve in Yaremche.

HAVE A MOST
BEAUTIFUL BAI
(FOR EXAMPLE)

1. Sebastian told only of how things could be, and, therefore, things were as Sebastian told.

In all the years before he began to speak, Sebastian did nothing but look and think about how to tell stories.

2. Sebastian spoke about how he could tell people about their lives in such a way that they would want to live forever, without changing anything. And people really did want to live forever and changed nothing.

Sebastian told how, even under interrogation, he would not tell everything about his love, about his loves with the Annas. And true enough—under interrogation Sebastian did not say everything, because he overcame himself and did not speak at all as he would have wanted to, in a way that he had never once allowed himself to speak in his whole life.

3. Afterwards, he told how he had never heard anything so strange.

He was taken right off the street in Königsfeld

They were already living in Mokra. Sebastian was walking home, returning from a forester's hut near Tempa. There, one forester had been crushed by a falling spruce. It did not kill him immediately, but he had stopped living—he just lay there, neither dead nor alive. The forester was not from around here. He came from somewhere near Bereziv, and so there was nowhere to take him. To just put someone in the ground like that would have been a sin, so, in the night, they came for Sebastian on horseback, with neither saddle nor bridle. He examined the wounded man and saw that he had forgotten how to breathe. He sat next to him and told the necessary story. The man from Bereziv remembered everything, got up, and invited Sebastian to come and visit him in Bereziv. He had to thank Sebastian somehow, but he was foresting now, so he decided to give Sebastian all he had—a lump of budz.

4. Sebastian stayed in the hut a little longer, because he wanted to hear something about Bereziv—he had never been there, although he knew many Berezivians.

Sebastian said that it was most interesting for him to listen to someone speak about a place he did not know. He would ask that it be described thus—as though you are walking, looking around, and saying what you see.

Then—as though you are riding a bicycle or horse (a little higher, which dramatically changes what you see), and then—as though you had climbed up to the top of a tree. And would always get out a map of the place and ask his interlocutor to illustrate with words everything that was marked there.

Sebastian perceived even wars, prison camps, and all sorts of cataclysms primarily from this point of view—you meet so many people who come from so many different places, people who have grown up and spent time in different places. Great shifts mix people together, and comparative geography becomes the basis of speech and ways of thinking.

5. Sebastian was carrying the lump of cheese to Anna for supper and breakfast. In Königsfeld, by the door of the tailor, as always, a table had been carried out into the street, and several men were playing cards. The rest looked on. Sebastian had learned from Africa to see the road he walked every day in comparison with the one he had walked the day before. Yesterday (and the day before yesterday, and the day before the day before yesterday), three of today's spectators had not been present. When he saw how they were looking at him he understood that they were there for him.

6. Sebastian could still escape—he could turn off between the colorful little wooden buildings, run through the gardens to the bank and swim among the logs of the

Brusturianka to the Teresva; the Teresva would carry him down to the Tysa; after a few days along the Tysa, he could reach the Danube, and then turn either towards Vienna or towards the delta—and, on the delta, there are countless places to hide for a lifetime.

After all, he knew that it is rivers that bind continents together best, because all places on a continent are connected by no more than four rivers.

7. Back in Africa, Sebastian had on more than one occasion had to cover great distances by means of rivers, not coming out of the water for days. He just took everything that he did not want to get wet from his pockets, placed it inside an aluminum canteen engraved with his name and regiment number, and swam in his clothes down the current, pushing his rifle, floating on a few sticks he had tied together, ahead of him.

Surroundings seen from the level of the water surface—when your view slides along parallel to the shoreline—are no less interesting than those seen from a bird's-eye view. And the sculpture of the riverbed is sometimes even richer. To say nothing of the fact that all the most interesting things in the life of human beings happen on the banks of rivers.

The last time he had done this, he had swum into a strange network of canals with water that was almost hot and contained an unearthly abundance of plant life on their beds; the canals led to the ruins of a submerged fort.

For some reason, it was precisely this that he dreamed of most often during the course of his life. Such was his nostalgic Africa. And also: transparent bays and a lot of turtles swimming.

But, at that moment, he could not swim off anywhere—Anna was waiting for her daddy.

8. In Königsfeld, Sebastian could probably have fired a shot—if he drew first, he could have hit all three, one after the other, so that they would have fallen down together in a heap. That was how he had once shot a blind hitman and his child.

9. Those were times when a great many armed people could be seen wandering around Yalivets, having moved their mutual hunt up into the mountains. It often happened that shots were fired first and only later was the body turned over to see who it was. Sebastian had had to keep his pistol somewhere near at hand, always at the ready—under the counter, next to the grapefruits, the frosted glass jar of cinnamon, and the large glass of walnut vodka he kept there for himself.

10. When the blind man entered the bar with his toddler sitting on his shoulders, no one even suspected that they might be dangerous. Sebastian was brewing coffee with hashish for four Rastafarians, who were playing at words with Anna—Anna named the same

thing in Ukrainian, Hutsul, Polish, German, Slovak, Czech, Romanian, Hungarian, and they guessed what meant what.

11. Sebastian had begun to think up such linguistic games for Anna after he noticed how easily she understood not only the appearance and manner of animals, but also their languages. Her fantastic ear heard in the language of animals more subtleties than there were words in everyday human speech. There had been a time when Anna had almost entirely gone over to non-human language, and Sebastian had answered her in the same way. Eventually, he came to his senses—a little longer and they would no longer have been able to speak to each other. And he had invented so many games that now they spoke about linguistics—often very complicated speculations—as though about something quite ordinary.

Their play with words climaxed with a game in which, for every word, Anna would have to think up a beautiful sentence in different languages, and from those sentences form a meaningful paragraph. The subject of the paragraph was mainly formed by moods and mechanics, by the way of thinking of the languages used, or was more rarely based on articulation—so that it would be pleasant, or sad, or funny, or scary, or however else, to recite the paragraph.

12. The Rastafarians were hired killers. But nobody was afraid of them because everybody knew. They were the first hired killers in Yalivets after Shtefan. The Rastafarians had come from Budapest and, on the orders of Nanashka from Szeged, were tracking down and wiping out all the merchants in the mountains—Jews, Czechs, Ukrainians from the Maslosoiuz dairy cooperative—who were trying to arrange the purchase and export of cheese horses.[32]

After arriving in Yalivets, the Rastafarians called in to What's There Is There and settled down for a few months, partially Latin-Americanizing the Carpathian town—they introduced Yalivets to maté, loose, colorful men's shirts (worn outside the belt), sung sambas, big knitted berets, as well as the habits of sleeping in hammocks, putting houseplants on the front steps in summer, and eating supper on the balcony.

They figured they could avoid chasing around the mountains after the merchants and would instead sit in one place and wait for them to come of their own accord.

13. Sebastian liked how they lived for days at a time on the bank of the river—they lay, bathed, looked at the water and the clouds, smoked, slept, said nothing, ate a string of cheese horses each, drew something with a stone on a stone, stood on their hands. Or just drank

---

32 Horses made of stringy, salty cheese are a delicacy of the Carpathians. *Maslosoiuz* means "butter union" (tr.).

gin. Like true predators, they soaked up the sun and moved sparingly. Sometimes, they took Anna along.

The girl was not bored with them.

14. Sebastian, for some reason, had absolutely no reservations when Anna went with the Rastafarians. Although, normally, he tried to shield his daughter from any customers in the bar who paid her any attention. Especially later, when the second Anna became a teenager, and he knew personally several serious people who came to Yalivets to sit in the bar and watch her hands or lips.

15. One of them was an anonymous sculptor.

Fascinated by the art of medieval sculptural ensembles, primitive folk figures, and ancient African statuettes, he made copies of wooden sculptures and sold the forgeries to collectors, sincerely believing that he was fulfilling a sort of mission, that producing enough of these figures could change the world for the better. In the Hutsul villages, he was not liked, because he tried to buy up, for huge sums of money, all the figures in the churches and cemeteries. In refusing him, the community was afraid that, someday, he would return and either steal something or burn the whole lot from despair.

They were not far from the truth. In Prague, the sculptor had recently been taken to court and given a huge fine for deliberate acts of arson on several little shops selling paper flowers. In this way, he defended true beauty.

Sebastian understood him completely.

The sculptor had visited several times already, since the first time he saw Anna. He sat by the bar, drank wine with water and sketched Anna's every move. He wanted to publish his own guide to anatomy for artists, which would be different from all contemporary notions of the structure of the body.

He said that Anna was a perfect model for medieval Queens of Sheba, rural tombstone pietas (Mary, Mary Magdalene, and Mary, mother of Jacob the younger and Joseph, and Salome), and naked Black queens (though from Central Africa—slim, tall with elongated heads, and very supple) all at the same time. For her appearance, her suppleness, her firmness.

16. At the same time, Anna had a strange feeling of faithfulness and devotion and an uncommon ability to dictate her own personal distance, which only she had the power to regulate. It was easy to make friends with her, but to seduce her was impossible.

And so, Sebastian did not even hint that she should be careful with the sculptor or the Rastafarians.

17. Incidentally, it was only after Sebastian had gone a few times after the nightshift to the river with the

Rastafarians that he became fully aware of how profoundly and sweetly one can do nothing.

18. Another of the Rastafarians' distractions, which Sebastian was particularly fond of, very soon gripped the whole town.

As they crossed the Yalivets market square, the Rastafarians would gather whole pocketfuls of chestnuts, great piles of which formed under the trees. And, throughout the day, they did various pleasant and complicated things with them—they threw them onto the roofs (and the chestnuts rolled down the tiles, hurtling onto the pavement as though from a springboard), they threw them into the drainpipes, they juggled with them, they rolled them across the table, trying to pass a chestnut between bottles to one another, they threw them up as high as the birds, they threw them to one another, they held a few in each hand and dropped them into the canals, they put them in the bottom of glasses before pouring gin on them, they gave them to strangers and friends, they left them behind on the banks of the river, on city benches, swings, and on the billiard table.

19. During their first week in Yalivets, the Rastafarians actually lived on that table. It so happened that, in the whole town, not a single free room could be found for them. And sleeping somewhere huddled in some corner was not for them.

The Rastafarians paid Sebastian for an hour of billiards but did not bother to take cues or balls. Instead, they took off their boots and lay down to rest. One asked if this was okay, Sebastian decided that it was, because they met the two conditions for playing billiards in the bar—they had paid for it, and nobody was ruining anything. After the first hour, the Rastafarians paid for another two, then for a day, and, finally, for one week in advance.

20. It was right in the middle of the grass season when they arrived, and there was a sea of grass all around. The Rastafarians smoked one joint after another and gave joints out to all the guests. Some holidaymakers became Rastafarians, while the journalists listened for hours to stories about Jamaica. The bar was so smoky that even those who were not smoking, whether they liked it or not, had to breathe in the burning hemp and sooner or later got high.

21. When Sebastian washed his and Anna's work clothes, the water became not dirty but yellow from the cannabinol sediment washed out from between the threads.

22. Little Anna was also constantly stoned.
(Sebastian recalled this in 1947, when, with the Chuhaister detachment, he stopped to spend the night at a house near Huta. After supper, thirty partisans started

smoking the same cheap tobacco, and, in the middle of the night, it was discovered that a baby that had been sleeping in the house behind a curtain had died from the smoke.)

At first, she was a little afraid—she felt so good that it really seemed as though things would stay that way forever.

23. Later, Anna also smoked often, but only in the presence of her father—he did not want their hemp experiences to be too different.

Once, after smoking hashish, she felt how God stretched out his finger from between the clouds, and she raised her own towards the sky, and the two of them remained silent for a few minutes in infinity, touching the tips of each other's fingers.

However, after a while, habits changed, and the time of hashish passed.

Curiously, much later, when she had grown up and Sebastian would tell her what he felt while making love to her, Anna would always remember her hemp-filtered perceptions of the whole world.

24. When the blind man with the child entered the bar, she was not smoking, only playing word games with the Rastafarians and playing reggae on the Jew's harp.

The blind man was dressed in a typical European suit—only Sebastian subconsciously noticed several oddly colored patches in various places on his jacket. On his shoulders sat a young child in a stained sweater. The blind man had no eyes, it was impossible to say whether the child was a boy or a girl. They made for the bar, the little one somehow steering the man with its hands. Three times it had to bend down low over the blind man's head before they reached the counter. It had to bend down to avoid the backs of chairs that had been screwed on to the ceiling upside down—Sebastian had made things so that all the furniture in the bar was replicated on the ceiling, as though in a mirror.

25. Not long before, it had been different: the whole ceiling had been studded with many different knives—blades pointing downwards and producing strange reflections and shadows; the blade forest created a unique acoustic and added a pleasant feeling of uneasiness. Sebastian took the knives down after a few Boikos, who were stealing horses on the Transcarpathian slopes to take to Galicia, got drunk, began to argue, grabbed one of their colleagues by the arms and legs, gave him a swing, and flung him at the ceiling.

26. The blind man placed his hands on the counter and ordered strong tea with vanilla, pure alcohol, and a few red berries of whatever sort. The child looked round the bar. Sebastian was measuring out the alcohol when he suddenly had the feeling something was wrong. He noticed the man's hands and also that the child made

a strange gesture, and, for some reason, he thought of one of his games with Anna

27. They started playing it after they had thought up a new life strategy for themselves—to have more theatricality in their behavior (they began to allow themselves the sort of mimicry that went beyond even what one would expect of a harlequin).

He would stand by the counter; he'd put his hands behind his back and push his shoulderblades right together, so that from the front only his shoulders could be seen; Anna would stand behind him, so that she could not be seen at all, and put her hands out in front of Sebastian; it would look like a large man with a small child's arms, so well would they synchronize Anna's manipulations and gestures with Sebastian's facial expressions and intonations. The game was called "Two barmen—two hands." This very allusion—two people, but two hands—put Sebastian on his guard. The man's hands still lay on the counter.

28. Sebastian turned away and took a couple of steps towards the shelves to take some cherries from a dish. On the way, he even managed to take a sip of the tea (he always tried complicated drinks when they were ready, before giving the glass to the customer), and it tasted good. Suddenly, he was seized by that feeling that he always had when someone unexpectedly, quickly, and

quietly ran up behind him. He really did not like this and, at such moments, was at his most dangerous.

Sebastian dropped the tea, turned around, grabbed his pistol (the child's hand was under its sweater), and shot twice. He shot so quickly that the child did not fall from the man's shoulders, but rather they fell together, just as they had stood, overturning several baskets of large, green apples and various dried fruits that decorated the bar. Sebastian jumped across the counter and bent down to the child, pulling its hand out from under its sweater—only now did he realize that the stains on the sweater had been made using fine painter's dyes and fitted together into an interesting abstract composition). The little hand gripped the butt of a large pistol.

29. Form that time onward, everything the Rastafarians did was dedicated to Sebastian. They drank only to his health, played with Anna, taught her to lie for long periods of time on the riverbed, looking up through the water (someone even took a photograph of this; when Anna died and Sebastian was looking for her photographs, he was sorry that the Rastafarians had not photographed Anna—they would have sent him everything they had, for sure), and left a few draws in every joint.

30. As a sign of gratitude, Nanashka from Szeged sent Sebastian a whole menagerie made of cheese. A horse, a ram, a deer, a billy goat, an ox, an aurochs, and a unicorn,

all life size, were delivered by some rosy-cheeked, big-boned bruisers, glistening from sweat and a little on the plump side, who worked for Nanashka as thugs, intimidators, henchmen, and hitmen, and whose job it was to do daily samplings of all the cheeses and *brynzas* at the local markets.

Just for Anna, Nanashka also sent beads made of hardened cheese and a few of Frants's sketches, in which you could see how he had tried to master the symbolism of the cheese horses.

31. When skiers began to disappear and the visiting police commission took an interest in Sebastian (too often, the missing skiers were last seen in What's There Is There), the Rastafarians took it upon themselves to track down a band of robbers who had been throwing skiers into a ravine, taking their expensive skis, boots, watches, and cameras, and selling them to tourist trains at stations on the Polish side.

32. That day, the Rastafarians threw a party especially for Sebastian, Anna, and a few of their friends, hiring out the whole bar for the entire evening.

One of them performed barman's duties, another cooked a delicious supper, putting a different type of hashish into every dish (sugared hemp flowers and salted seeds were served for desert [this is how Sebastian learned to live off seeds, and not necessarily just hemp, he simply collected the seeds of various plants, carried them in the pockets of his Hutsul belt and nibbled on them on hungry days]). Two others led a hired Hutsul band, which was made to play reggae (one day, I'll take you to this music, thought Anna about her dad).

At the end of the party, the Rastafarians wanted to exchange earrings with Sebastian. When they realized Sebastian had no earrings, they asked if they could at least do so with Anna. For this, they had to pierce Anna's ears twice with an arrow from a crossbow (the Rastafarians did not allow the use of firearms in their work), and each of Anna's earrings was divided between two Rastafarians.

33. Somehow, everybody forgot that the arrow had been smeared with a substance that prevents the blood from clotting. Her earlobes bled and bled. Neither herbs nor bais helped. Anna even lost consciousness from blood loss (it was like this, she told them later, suddenly all colors began to flash and change, but only the colors of the objects, without spilling out of the shapes of the objects themselves, and the weakness was more pleasant than any strength), until the effects of the substance passed. Sebastian took an interest in the liquid, and the Rastafarians gave him a whole bottle of it.

34. Sebastian passed the liquid on to the Unsimple for analysis. They may well have used it for their own purposes.

An ethnographer from Warsaw was staying in Vorokhta, and, having almost solved the mystery of the Unsimple, he was planning to write an article about how these illiterate Hutsul pseudo-sorcerer-charlatans were manipulating Europe and the rest of the world using plots. And just at that moment, he died, in the finest hotel restaurant in Vorokhta where, at one time, the young Frants used to go for his morning coffee with egg liqueur after entire nights spent drawing (the liqueur was just alcoholic kogel mogel, and you could choose which eggs you wanted it to be made from: they lay in a large box—different sizes and colors, spotted, monotone, almost transparent eggs, gathered among the mountain pine bushes from all types of mountain bird). This morning, coffee sometimes extended all the way into an evening meal of mushroom soup, roasted corn on the cob with trout pâté, broad beans in blackthorn sauce, frozen fillet of slow worm with cranberry paste and galangal vodka—two or three quarts of it.

35. The ethnographer was dining in the company of the stationmaster, a Roman Catholic priest, the director of a sawmill, and a doctor from the sanatorium. Suddenly, he began to sweat. Very soon, instead of sweat, drops of blood appeared on his skin. Blood clouded his eyes. He tried to wipe it off with his hand, but merely smudged the neat, red spots. The blood seeped incessantly. Red stains appeared on his spotless white clothes

and quickly got bigger, spread toward each other and merged into one wet redness. Nobody knew how to help. On his body, there was not a single wound, but blood flowed from every pore.

36. When the party with the Rastafarians was almost over, Sebastian thought about the infinity of wondrous knickknacks, objects, music, methods, spices, wines, and films which—as you are made sharply aware—will never, in your lifetime, situated as it is somewhere between the extremes of cold and heat, become a part of everyday life.

37. The Rastafarians gave them a very beautiful example of an Indian hemp plant in a stone pot and spent a long time telling them how joyous it would be to live with Anna and start a little plantation from this plant on the deserted meadows and mountainsides, with their maximal exposure to the sun. Because every plant is planted first and foremost for the joy of planting plants.

The next morning, Sebastian reminded himself not to forget to ask the Rastafarians how to look after the hemp plant, but it turned out that they had already, at long last, gone from Yalivets.

38. The blind assassin proved useful again in 1938.
Sebastian did not know how to take two pistols into Carpatho-Ukraine. He thought for a long time, until he

remembered the blind man's child. He took four-year-old Anna (not the same one who had been in the bar then) onto his shoulders, hid the pistols on her and went towards the checkpoint. The only thing he was afraid of was that the little one—gripped by a childish desire to shoot at everything—might pull the gun from its hiding place.

39. Sebastian, for some reason, believed passionately in the triumph of Carpatho-Ukraine because the plot seemed such a good one.

It was of crucial importance for him that the Ukrainian cause should begin in Central Europe. Although it is well known how a representative of the field reconnaissance unit of the headquarters of the Carpathian Sich, a committed nationalist who was traveling at that time around Transcarpathia in the bus-bar, reported to Commander Klympush his belief that Sebastian was guided more by the idea of landscape than the idea of the nation.

And maybe this was true, for Sebastian's enthusiasm somewhat cooled when he learned of the government's policy plans for forestry and saw how the citizens used autonomy mainly to destroy the trees, waters, and stones.

After all, questions of forests and woodlands have always been critical in these lands.

40. Despite a certain disillusionment (all the same, his main quality was contemplativeness—to see everything and to know what you see—which leads not to

indifference but to the acceptance of everything that occurs), Sebastian hurried to complete the mapping out of all the sniper positions necessary to turn the mountains into one enormous fortress.

41. At one of these positions—an incredible metal construction, somewhat similar to the Eiffel Tower, with a hole-ridden wooden platform at the top, broken stairs and narrow hatches between the different levels—Sebastian found a bottle of plum brandy, which he drank on the spot. Only after finishing it did he see, from barely visible traces, that a Hungarian-Polish diversionist group, the sort of which there were many at that time all over Carpatho-Ukraine, must have stopped there before him. The brandy turned out to have been poisoned (Sebastian's vigilance was not yet sharp enough to anticipate quite such a trick).

It got worse and worse. That is, Sebastian felt good, he liked fevers, but the strength of his juices had disappeared, his lungs barely managed to gather and release air, which was of no help anyway. For some reason, his arms began to look as though they had been burned and would have hurt dreadfully if not for the fever. He had to replace all the water in his body quickly.

42. He made his way further up into the mountains—he did not want to come home and die in front of the child. And he did not want to go to hospital.

Some time ago, he had made up his mind—if something happened to him, he would not call doctors and he would not lie helplessly at home. Instead, he would—like an animal hiding its own death—make for the mountains. The mountains would either cure or quietly swallow him.

43. He had already been in a hospital once. A long time ago, in winter, when he had just begun to make love with the second Anna, back in Yalivets.

He had contracted a strange infection after eating part of an apricot left over by a guest, a cavalry officer from a foreign army—an unimaginably stupid accident.

He had then been arrested, so as not to spread the disease, and taken to a closed mountain hospital that was located inside salt caves. Cavernous, white, underground wards without doors led into one another via short corridors that were a little lower, but just as wide as the rooms. In every ward, directly on top of piles of salt, lay the patients, wrapped in some unfamiliar leaves. Treatment consisted of periodic rubbing with extra-thick oil. The moans of pain accumulated (there seemed to be more individual voices than there really were) and wandered through the underground chambers, the extent of which could only be guessed at.

This hospital was one of the innovations of the Czechoslovak ministry of health, aimed at eliminating Carpathian syphilis and other viruses. The patients were held in prison-like isolation, sometimes for as long as they managed to stay alive.

44. Sebastian could no longer imagine what winter on earth looked like, and the salt stalactite next to him had almost touched the stalagmite below it, when one day Anna appeared in the ward.

This could mean only one thing—she had also been arrested; yet it meant something different. Loyal Anna, unable to get through to her father (though normally such prohibitions did not hinder her—guards would themselves show her the way along forbidden paths), had come up with the idea of going to work in the hospital as a nurse. There was always a lack of people willing to work there, after all.

Every day, she came to rub him in oil ("You are my finest cream," said Sebastian. "It's you who are mine, and you know why"), and every night—to make love. ("I want to have the same microbes as you," Anna insisted. "And anyhow, it's actually a good thing, because we won't get sick a second time.") By God's grace, she did not even fall ill. Soon afterwards, Sebastian was let out, and they returned home together.

Winter had not yet passed.

Sebastian did not dare tell Anna that there was no such thing as immunity against that disease. But, it seems, it is frightening only for those who have been in Africa.

45. As a young man in Africa, Sebastian had almost died from the very same illness.

But then it had been even worse—because of the African climate, exotic fungi grew in his lacerations. Nobody knew whether they were the result of airborne spores or whether they were a product of the infected body, but the fungi hurt so badly that Sebastian preferred to cut them off together with patches of skin.

Then he had also been at a sniper's post. It was in a large African city made of clay. He had to make just one shot and was waiting for his chance in a hot attic where there was room enough only to lie down and cut off more and more rotten skin.

Sebastian kept his eye glued to the optical sight. He saw exactly the same thing as was portrayed on the most expensive postage stamp of that country—countless white cubes of buildings, a few spindle-like spires, gardens, and overgrown orchards on the city's hills, the red clay of the narrow street, coffee brewers on the doorstep of a blue restaurant. His view differed from the philatelic one only due to the presence of flies in his eyes and on both lenses of the sight.

Alongside him lay his beloved African girl. From time to time, Sebastian wiped down her sweating body with a wet cloth, and she applied aloe juice to his wounds six times a day.

From then on, Sebastian's only erotic fantasy was lovemaking soaked in aloe. But, in Yalivets, not a sprig of it was to be found.

46. The Annas were never ill.

Once, when they were already in Mokra, the last Anna had wind sickness, if wind sickness can really be called a sickness.

Anna climbed up onto a mountain at the wrong place and did not manage to duck to avoid a bad wind. The wind went into her head and blew out all the smells.

Sebastian knew only one cure for such an ailment. He led Anna along a narrow path between two mountains and waited for the draft there to blow the bad wind out of her head. This is just what happened, only the new draft stayed in Anna and softened her head: they could change the shape of her skull with their hands. "Make it like yours," Anna said. "I really love your beautiful head."

Sebastian decided that there was no longer any point in driving out wind with wind—you just end up endlessly changing winds (at best you could stop with the one you feel most comfortable with). But wind can also be frozen out.

On the feast of the Baptism of the Lord, they bathed together in the Mokrianka river, holding their heads for as long as possible under water. A Soviet policeman arrested Sebastian, and naked Anna ran home through the whole village. The policeman wanted to hold Sebastian for at least a few days for performing pagan rituals during religious holidays but, in the end, gave him a bottle of arnica in alcohol and sent him away to rub it on his daughter. "I have children, too," said the militiaman.

47. Poisoned by the diversionists' homebrew, Sebastian did not go to Anna but crawled higher into the mountains.

He knew of a spring where he could replenish all the water in his body. He stopped frequently to tighten the bandages on his burned hands, which kept slipping off as he crawled. Even more frequently, he would pass out for several minutes. At those moments, he had the worst hallucinations possible—that he was stuck in a narrow crevice and could not pull himself through to Anna, who was balancing on a ladder placed across a chasm.

When he reached the spring, it was already night. He took a drink, wet his hands, and dozed off. After a while he awoke and, once again, put his hands into the stream but could not feel the water. And yet someone gave a deathly cry. Sebastian realized he was not washing himself but the burned hands of a woman who had also crawled to the spring and slept alongside him in the dark. (Something similar, though not very, had happened to him already. He and Anna, when spending the night amongst other people, would resort to an inconspicuous method—under the duvet he would put his finger into Anna. Once they had been sleeping in such cramped conditions that, waking up in the middle of the night, Sebastian had pulled his finger out not from Anna but from a Hutsul woman who lay on his left. And Anna was sleeping soundly, lying with her back to him, to his right—Sebastian had not noticed when they had fallen asleep, Anna had turned away, and he had unwittingly placed his finger somewhere else.)

48. By March 1939, Sebastian's hands had still not healed completely, yet every second day he sent a telegram to Klympush's headquarters, urging them to send troops to the sniper stronghold he had prepared.

Nobody listened to him, and all was lost (almost the same as had happened in Lviv because of the balconies).

The Carpathian Sich faced open battle.

This was the unnoticed first act of the Second World War.

Only it was four thousand versus forty. Blood flowed in the Tysa.

(A fraction of the Sich fighters escaped to Romania, but, before long, the Romanians turned them all in to the Hungarians, and the Hungarians—to the Galician Poles.)

Sebastian understood that, this time, someone had thought up a plot that was better than his.

49. But Sebastian believed firmly in the strength of his own presence. He knew that there could be nothing bad wherever he might be because he felt good everywhere.

You have to love places genuinely so that they will love you.

For this reason, after the massacre at Krasne Pole, he took his rifle and settled down in a comfortable position near Trebusha. One exceptional marksman can change several plots, especially if that marksman is the last one.

50. He waited, crouched down in a small trench near Trebusha, and waited for the enemy troops (Frants had been right: the most radical thing is to wait).

This is the way things happen, thought Sebastian. I wanted to be the most outstanding. Frants also tried to be the most outstanding, and what came of it? He stopped making films (because he was always aiming to make the film of films) and he let them chop off his head. Frants really could have been outstanding. But, if you are outstanding in everything except for just one thing, then you are already not the most outstanding. And anyway, for every most outstanding there will always be an even more outstanding. That is what happened with Frantsysk, that is what happened with Nanashka from Szeged, that is what happened to Klympush. And that is what could happen to him.

51. When the almost one-hundred-year reign of Nanashka collapsed, the bar was often broken into by the new boss's thugs who stomped around the mountains bristling with rifles and powder horns imposing their own order.

These were times when Sebastian found himself surprised every night by some new madness, although he had always been sure the previous night that nothing could surprise him anymore.

Sometimes, the thugs would cause him problems, but what could he do, since he called himself the barkeeper?

Then, in his mind, he recalled all his boyhood heroisms.

52. He had no doubt that, in their boyhood, men do their finest deeds. It is just a shame that afterwards nobody knows about them, it is a shame that boyhood feats do not count.

Sebastian, for example, was the best at jumping off roofs onto the tops of trees—he would leap without looking straight into the leaves. He would tear a passage through the leaves and, when already in the middle of the thick foliage, would grab one branch and immediately swing himself onto another.

53. Although it is true that there were some childhood adventures that were similar to those involving the thugs.

After such incidents, he would repeat to himself hundreds of times his own, invented, successful version of events, until he made himself believe that it really could only have happened like that.

Such stories were created literally once and for all. Seemingly, they were a sort of bai.

54. Crouching in the trench near Trebusha, Sebastian imagined how fine things could be in his little Carpathia,

which he, making use of universal chaos, would defend by himself.

He dreamed up a beautiful land around Yalivets in which there would be no rubbish, everybody would know one another's languages, and the highest institution would be the bureau of scripts where everyone would be able to submit something genuinely interesting, and the government would act on the basis of these plots.

Everything is ruined by "would."

55. In March, it gets dark early.

Lost in thought, Sebastian barely noticed the detachment of riders dressed in strange uniform and armed with long rifles. They were headed for Trebusha.

He took off his gloves, laid out a row of bullets next to his hand, and pressed his eye to the sight. The riders were speaking to one another (judging by their lips—in Hungarian) and looking at a map (the gothic script made it seem like the First World War had never happened). On their uniforms, he could make out the badge of the forest guard.

Sebastian took his rifle between his legs, wrapped it in a rag, put the bullets into one pocket, his gloves into the other, and crawled along the trench on his knees until he reached a large pile of stones. Then, he ran through the forest to the road and ran for another four hours without stopping until he reached old Beda's armored car which was hidden away in a ravine.

56. The armored car was hanging over the edge of a steep drop, secured by a cable to a thick beech tree. The upper hatch was open and the warm air coming from inside quivered above the opening.

Inside the vehicle, it really was warm. Old Beda was making wine and telling little Anna about Francis of Assisi and Frantsysk of Petros. Anna had brightened her stay in the car by making large paintings on the white walls (Sebastian had once drawn something similar on her mother's hands) and unceasing misuse of the verb form "is."

Wasting no time, Sebastian and Beda drank some wine and drove all the way to Kvasy, where the bus-bar was.

Sebastian had admitted defeat in his imaginary war.

57. They could hear the bus-bar before they saw it. And then they saw, fairly high up in the sky, a secret sign—six bank swallows, four golden orioles and one kingfisher. All the birds were flying back and forth after one another without, however, flying outside the limits of a certain hemisphere, like the beams of many searchlights pointed at the cloudy sky above a darkened city. They were held down by strong lines that converged somewhere behind a tall hayrick, in which there was almost no hay left after the winter.

Six four one, said Sebastian.

Beda opened a thick notebook and read out—six four one, in the world everything is as it is, and everything happens as it happens: in it, no value exists—and if it did exist, it would have no value. If there is any value that does have value, it must lie outside the whole sphere of what happens and exists. For all that happens and exists is accidental.

This meant that everything was okay, and they could safely approach the bus, which stood in a hiding place behind the almost empty hayrick, in the very place where the lines attached to the birds converged. And they were attached to the handle of the front door of the bus.

58. The safety signal had been given by an ornithologist who had once ringed birds on Chornohora, Hryniava and on the edge of the Hutsul world—in the Tsibo mountains—and who had known Frantsysk.

Ornithology had slowly transformed into ornithophilia—he had learned to make love with all birds that laid at least slightly larger eggs. They made love on the highest peaks where all around spins empty sky, and the entire earth is reduced to a static base for your feet. The birds gave themselves to him silently, just throwing their heads back and opening their beaks wide, struggling to keep quiet, lest their mates should hear them. Their mates hated the ornithologist that loved birds—the ornithologist was always surrounded by an agitated flock of male birds, screeching in inhuman voices. The lovers of my lovers, the ornithologist called them ironically.

Later, ornithophilia faded, and philosophy took its place. To be more precise—one tract by Wittgenstein. The former ornithologist knew it by heart and would always think which proposition it was appropriate to quote in a given situation.

59. Therefore, when the ornithologist was asked to watch the bar while Sebastian fought against the occupying forces, the ornithologist warned him that, on his return, the necessary signals would be given via the birds and Wittgenstein. In order to make the signals decodable, he gave old Beda a notebook with a handwritten copy of the *Tractatus Logico-Philosophicus*. For example, the sentence, "Each item can be the case or not the case while everything else remains the same," would be given by one bird of one type, two of another, and one of yet another (one two one). What such a sentence was supposed to signify was up to Sebastian to decide. In any case, Sebastian's conclusion that six four one meant everything was okay turned out to be correct.

60. The ornithophile was probably the most loyal customer at Sebastian's bar. Though, over the five years of the war, the bus had seen thousands of the most diverse clients. Among them were a few hundred regulars.

The bar functioned very simply. Sebastian drove the bus until someone stopped him. The customer got on to the bar and they drove on. If the customer did not want to go anywhere, Sebastian drew into the side of the road and the bar operated for a while in one place.

Some clients could travel for weeks in the bar without any aim whatsoever.

Some went too far, and Sebastian would have to turn back.

Sometimes, the bar would stop for a long time in some village or other.

Occasionally, they would have to unexpectedly pack up and hurry off somewhere.

It was possible to request that the bar arrive at a certain time.

And so on, and so on.

61. Sebastian managed to drive the bus, serve the customers, and bring up Anna. Before each town, he would stop and walk into it by himself, according to his old sniper's habit, to scout out the terrain in advance. As well as this, he also had to listen to all sorts of stories in order to be able to tell somebody somewhere something from someone. This oral postal service tired Sebastian out to such an extent that he could no longer remember what had happened where, when, and with whom. He was traveling in an epos which had nothing to do with him.

62. The only conversations he took part in entirely consciously with his customers were a certain kind of

mutual confession, devoid of refined stylistics but extraordinarily rich in plot—who loves or does not love what, who likes or dislikes what, who likes or dislikes the taste of something.

Sebastian considered such conversations the basic catechism, the compulsory first level of every coexistence.

And so, on meeting any of his guests for a second time, he knew just what the guest was used to and what he could suggest he try.

63. The bar was most popular in distant villages, where few people lived and where very little happened.

In such villages, every inhabitant had at his or her disposal only a few stories of his own. They told each of them a countless number of times to everybody they knew, just the same as those people had told their own few stories. Thus, there were always a couple of plots in circulation that were hard to divide into the experienced and the heard.

The arrival of the bus with its strangers gave the opportunity to connect with something different. And to tell anew your own stories, which, wrenched from the enchanted circle of listeners, again gathered weight.

64. Interesting things happened sometimes when friends got together with their friends and spoke about friends and told stories about friends of friends that they had heard from friends.

More than once it happened that people would hear bizarre stories from strangers that turned out to be about themselves.

Or: the conversation at one table would often be about someone who, unbeknownst to the speakers, was sitting at the next.

65. At one time, this was constantly the case with Severyn. Everyone talked about how he had taken some foreign tourists into the mountains after eating some weird mushrooms, how the tourists had gone crazy, and Severyn had gone blind but had nevertheless led the tourists back to safety. This story was told in various forms many times.

Nobody knew that Severyn was living with Sebastian then and was sitting in the bus the whole time. It was a good thing he could not hear all these fables, since he had stopped up his ears and nose with cotton wool soaked in gin in order to finally saturate the tumor in his brain, which he refused to allow the younger Mlynarskyi to cut out.

The ornithologist also heard many legends of all sorts about himself. In the bar, they considered him a wandering philosopher; with time, he, in the process of retelling the *Tractatus* again and again, stopped mentioning Wittgenstein.

66. Even odder than the ornithophile was, perhaps, the Pope's daughter. Nobody could know if it was true

or not, but the fact that she used to say that about herself was certainly true. And, in any case, nobody had any intention of contradicting her—everyone was glad to see the impossible.

The Pope's daughter wrote drunken plays. At least that's what she called her method of writing.

She was fed up with having to accept the fact that the most interesting things happened to her when she was drunk—the most important stories, the wittiest jokes, the most aphoristic thoughts, the most original ideas, the most paradoxical solutions to the most painful problems. And the tragic thing was, she felt, that a moment later you could not remember a thing. So, the Pope's daughter started getting drunk with a pencil in her hand and wrote down every word she said and heard. The dynamics of her plays depended largely on what she had drunk. Sometimes, near the end, the actors said completely incomprehensible things. And not just that—the Pope's daughter tried out another experiment: the author provided precise instructions indicating exactly the quantity and type of drinks the actors should drink on stage during the course of the play. It is no surprise that this led to some interesting improvisations that took the action to unexpected lengths.

Sebastian's bus was, for several years, her creative laboratory, study, studio, and home.

67. In 1942, the Pope's daughter was planning to write a play about some Gypsy children who ran away from a camp and the Hungarian gendarmes who were trying to find them. The gendarmes come to the conclusion that children can best be tracked down by a child, who can imagine how the children think and behave, and they call on the help of a girl-detective. The little girl finds the Gypsy children, though with some difficulty—the play raised the problem of the otherness of different cultures and civilizations (in reality, the children had been taken in by old Beda, who ferried them around in his armored car until the end of the war).

Eight-year-old Anna was required in order to study the language of children. The Pope's daughter gave her deceptively sweet young wine to drink.

When Anna had slept it off and sobered up, she told her father about the grafting of apple trees, pears, peaches, and cherries in such a way that Sebastian became convinced she had been on the inside of trees and had swum in their sap around their tubules.

68. From that moment onwards, the Unsimple, from time to time, gave Sebastian cigarettes that could not be smoked.

On the inside of the cigarette paper, the Unsimple drew plans, which Anna had to use to find certain trees and graft certain cuttings onto them.

They drove to the appointed places in the bar.

69. In general, travelling by bus was very pleasant. It was good for drinking and great for talking, you could see a long way from the bus, and somehow all dangers passed it by—either it got there a little early or was fortunately late.

It was not a problem that they often did not have enough food, that, in winter, they got stuck in snowdrifts or that their hands burned from washing dishes in icy water, or that they had to pee straight into the snow outside the door, that, in summer, it got so hot that they had to keep wetting their clothes in a tub of rain water, and that, at night, when it got cooler, it seemed that outside it was constantly raining—because of the swarms of insects on the windows, or that they had to serve drinks for free to the police and officers.

70. In the fall of 1944, the bus had to be abandoned in Krasnishora. That very day, Sebastian and Anna hitched a ride to Königsfeld with some villagers who had been to Teresva to pick up bicycles left there by the Germans.

71. Being unarmed, Sebastian still could easily have beaten up those three in front of the cobbler's workshop in Königsfeld. He did not even need a stick (and he could easily have come by a stick, because the trees, saturated with water, had become soft—it was the time when water and greenery had triumphed everywhere). Sebastian knew from back in the army how to maim with his bare hands. And, in Africa, he had taken part in some fairly

theatrical contests—fighting with warriors armed with knives, awls, razors, or knuckledusters ("It's a good thing I have Africa," thought Sebastian. "It makes it possible to always explain to oneself the origins of one's personal characteristics").

72. He approached the three and could vividly see the throat cartilages of the first crushed by a short, straight blow from his straightened fingers, the blood vessels on the temple of the second shattered by an open-handed blow from the left, the knee dislocated by his right heel, and the jaw of the third smashed by his right elbow.

But he had no right to fight.

73. To fight meant to kill, to kill meant to run away and spend your whole life hiding. At home, Anna was waiting.

Sebastian approached them first, remembering that, first and foremost, he must always remember to protect his life, and had time to greet them before they made to grab him (even more invitingly presenting their throats, cheekbones, knees, jaws, and solar plexuses), tied him up, threw him into the trunk of a Studebaker, and drove off in the direction from which Sebastian had just come.

74. What could they beat out of him under interrogation?

In interrogations, they try to get secrets out of you, not guilt.

Guilt (husband of a Sich riflewoman, sergeant of a foreign army, participant in colonial wars, brother-in-law of a famous decadent, Greek-Catholic, Ukrainian, contact with nationalists, Zionists, anti-Semites, white and black racists, anarchists, Trotskyites, monarchists, foreign journalists, scouts, monks, officers, government ministers, members of parliament, diplomats, ornithophiles, drug addicts, relatives of highly placed Vatican officials, hired killers, the murder of three hired killers (one juvenile), sniper, illegal possession of arms, banned books, hashish, daughter as second wife, pedophilia, petty entrepreneurship, private property, illegal crossing of borders, witchcraft, local inhabitant, time spent in occupied territory, participation in events in Transcarpathia in 1938–39, spying, sabotage, violation of the passport regime, supporting the nationalist underground, living in a border zone, illegal psychotherapeutic practice, Freudianism, Morganism-Weissmanism, Nietzscheanism, Wittgensteinization, deviation from the principles of socialist realism in narrative, fault-finding, sympathies with the West, pacifism, half-Lemko, resisting representatives of authority, non-participation in elections to the Verkhovna Rada, avoidance of the all-Union census, unwillingness to work, common drunkenness, illegal income, harboring criminals, observes poorly, listens carefully, remembers a lot, talks too much) does not interest them, because it is not a secret.

Live without secrets, said Frantsysk.

He does not know any secrets.

What does he know?

He knows thousands of places and words.

What does he remember?

He remembers thousands of places and words.

What does he forget?

He forgets thousands of places and words.

What does he recall?

He recalls thousands of places and words.

What does he make up?

He makes up thousands of places and words.

What does he speak of?

He speaks of thousands of places and words.

What does he learn?

He learns thousands of places and words.

What does he love?

He loves thousands of places and words.

What does he choose?

He chooses thousands of places and words.

What does he not choose?

He does not choose thousands of places and words.

What can he do?

He can see, know, love, remember, forget, recall, make up, speak of, choose, not choose thousands of places and words.

What does he do?

Loves, sees, learns, knows, remembers, speaks of, forgets, recalls, chooses, makes up, does not choose thousands of places and words.

What does he want?

To see, to learn, to know, to love, to remember, to forget, to speak of, to recall, to do, to make up, to choose, to not choose thousands of places and words.

What might he do?

See, learn, love, know, make up, not choose, forget, recall, choose, remember, speak of, do, want thousands of places and words.

What, then, is the secret?

How and for what he sees, loves, remembers, speaks of, knows, wants, might do, can do, does, forgets, does not choose, recalls, makes up, chooses thousands of places and words.

How and for what there are thousands of places and words that are seen, learned, known, remembered, spoken of, forgotten, recalled, chosen, loved, wanted, done, made up, not chosen.

And that is already not his secret.

He can go with confidence to the interrogation. Although, if you do not know at least one secret, pain cannot be avoided; but there is no need to bear it—it will pass somehow by itself.

75. On the way, Sebastian pressed his neck arteries in order to sleep a little before the interrogation. To sleep is to prolong time by half a lifetime.

They barely managed to wake him for the interrogation.

76. First of all, they offered him a cigarette. He took three or four cigarettes from a full pack of Camels.

You always have to remember to take a cigarette for later; even when they have only appeared in the present moment by some miracle, cigarettes are the best proof that everything is coming to an end (Sebastian knew one staunch fascist who had handed himself in to an American camp because, every day, they gave out cigarettes).

77. Then they introduced themselves, called themselves folklorists, told Sebastian to prepare himself for a lengthy talk, and appealed to him to be honest.

Sebastian decided not to mention a word about how he had been hurrying to Anna. That might have made them want to hold him for as long as possible.

And, as for honesty, he knew one pretty good method. In bai, just as in lovemaking, everything depends on rhythm. If you fall into the false rhythm, what kind of honesty can there be? Well-written sentences will lead to nothing. He decided to try the following pattern—six short, one long, one very short going upward from low down, one very long turning in a spiral, and two short unfinished to the right.

Sebastian focused his mind in such a way that he was able to hear his own voice before he even started to speak. And he liked that voice.

And, in the end, it had never yet happened that he had been unable to get the better of someone in a conversation.

78. Sebastian, for some reason, recalled a story one of the Rastafarians had told him about how Nanashka had had a little private prison in Szeged in which chance passersby were imprisoned in order to tell Nanashka all sorts of stories.

79. When Sebastian was released after a couple of hours and was once again on his way to Mokra via Königsfeld, hurrying to Anna, he could not understand why everything had gone so easily and painlessly. Was it because he had told the folklorists straight away where to look for Dovbush's treasure ("When it comes to valuables, it's better to come clean before the torture starts," he had taught Anna), or had he been right that endeavoring to achieve understanding in different languages really is the peak of existence. Although it could have been even simpler: either these people really were folklorists, or the false rhythm had helped. Both were possible.

80.   He did not reach home until the next morning.

Anna slept late into the day, as she had fallen asleep just before he had arrived home. Sebastian did not even take her boots off, so as not to wake her up, sat beside her, and waited while she so beautifully slept.

The cheese had begun to stink, so he fried it with caraway seeds while she heated yesterday's soup on some soft, wet branches: you soak bread, onion, wood sorrel, and tree-dried cherries in plum brandy, then boil these in water with sour cream, add oil, salt and paprika, and serve in bowls; to each portion you add a spoonful of vodka and eat it while it is still very hot. (As well as the necessary ingredients, Anna also added all the fried cheese to the soup.)

Then Sebastian said he had never heard of anything so strange.

IF ACCORDING TO THE MAP (LEGEND)

The brilliant historical essay about the psychology of Christian martyrdom entitled "Irrational Coherence Is Absolute" and written by Anna Sebastiani in Paris in 1976 has the following lyrical epigraph: **"That the saints went through this you will know after a century has passed. Todiaska, 1951."**

In all likelihood, this phrase is autobiographical and relates to Anna's meeting with the future martyrs of the underground Ukrainian Greek-Catholic church on Todiaska mountain. Judging from the place and the time, it happened during Anna and Sebastian's journey from Mokra to Yalivets.

If this is really the case, then their journey most likely followed this route:

Deutsche Mokra—Ruska Mokra—Königsfeld—Svydova—Berliaska—Pidpula—Todiaska—Blyznytsia (the last five are mountains on the Svydovets ridge)—Kvasy—Menchil—Sheshul—Yalivets.

SEVEN

1. It was so cold you couldn't even take off your sheepskin.

2. Sitting on the stone floor of the empty room, they made love so simply that Anna felt as though she had disintegrated into many parts, each of which was making love to Sebastian.

3. And he felt that he had learnt to fly, although he understood that this was because he was in Yalivets.

4. The cold could not penetrate into the open gaps in their clothing, because it was met by a surging heat with the distinctive flavor of scent-hallucination.

5. The main thing is not to be in a hurry to leave when nothing is holding you and you have time to talk.

6. If so—you are so big, and yet really—so small.

7. There is so much and so little of you.

8. That is good for the world, and the world is also good.

9. Although inside you the world is better than outside you.

10. The thing I want most is to touch my pregnant stomach together with you.

11. If you ever have another man, he will die because his woman is too beautiful.

12. Do not talk to me in such intonations—that is how they talk when the way is closed, when you cannot get what you want.

13. I am beautiful when you tell me about it.

14. Anna dozed off, sitting on Sebastian, her head rested on his shoulder, and he had to continue sitting like this, although he dearly wanted to straighten himself out and lie down.

15. Just as with the previous Annas, with this one, it was always like the first time in the world.

16. Later, old Beda came for Anna. Nothing had happened to the Unsimple. Plots cannot end. They had decided to go somewhere far, far away and were waiting for her in the armored car. Anna became terribly sad. Sebastian said he would not give her to anyone. She drank a lot of gin and began to cry. Beda came back again. Sebastian drove him away and threw a grenade from the window. Anna got drunk and began to think aloud about their family. Sebastian understood for the first time that she saw everything differently to how he did. She cried and tried to kiss his hands. He would not let her, she stopped crying and calmly asked permission to kiss each hand once. Sebastian allowed her, and she did what she wanted. The second hand she kissed for a very long time. He had to take his hand away to throw another grenade. Anna said he was doing too much for her. And she went to the door. Sebastian could not understand this. Remember, we talked about this? She turned round but did not stop moving and went out through the door backward. Sebastian made a gesture that Anna, when she was already by the armored car, could not resist trying to repeat for herself, as though she had become Sebastian's biographer. What could her father be doing at that moment? Searching for interesting things is the most human of all traits, her father had said. Thus, Sebastian said what Frants had said.

17. Sebastian could neither sit, nor walk, nor stand, nor lie.

18. The depths of his lungs were empty.

19. Three thousand times he thought the word Anna.

20. Not until evening was he able to do anything. But then it was four things at once.

21. He pissed in the snow.

22. He examined a tree in which some birds looked like overripe fruits.

23. With the end of his tongue, he touched the roof of his mouth, which felt strange from the cold.

24. And he prayed for the souls of the dead for whom nobody else could pray—for Frants, Lukač, old Beda, the French engineer, Lóci, the Rastafarians, the blind killer, his child, the ornithologist, Shtefan, Nanashka, MP Sefanyk, MP Lahodynsky, the artist Trush, the artist Perfetskyi, the survival instructor, the Bosnian captain, Second-Lieutenant Pelenskyi, Captain Didushko, Captain Bukshovanyi, Colonel Kolodzynskyi, General Tarnavskyi, his African women, Severyn, the younger Mlynarskyi, the Pope's daughter, Brehm, Wittgenstein, the Gypsy trumpeters, Anna, Anna, and Anna.

25. On the apple trees, in the old city gardens, there were a great many apples. Nobody had gathered them,

and nobody would. He pulled an apple he had picked the day before from his pocket. He took a bite and found one of Anna's long hairs in his mouth.

26. I love her and not myself, and she is, always is somewhere, just as beautiful. It is good to have somebody at least somewhere. If only to have somebody to whom to tell the story of the day, through which it is worth living for this very reason.

27. In the next world, those who feel most at home are not soldiers and not doctors, not builders and not gardeners, but tellers of stories, baimakers.

28. From the highest of the trees that Sebastian had planted in 1914, the magpies took flight and flew into the shadow of Petros.

29. Sebastian counted—seven.

30. In the ornithologist's notebook: seven—whereof one cannot speak, thereof one must be silent.

31. Among all the proofs of God's existence, this can be considered the best.

IMAGE CREDITS

On the front cover, "Wedding Attire in Yabloniv, Pidhiria" and "The View of Chornohora." On the back cover, "A Landowner in Kolomyia"; on the front and back endsheets, "Ukrainian Sich Riflemen. Lieutenant Karatnytskyi with His Corporals" (paperback edition) and "Hutsul Children in Zhab'ie" (hardcover edition). All images courtesy of Valerii Kovtun, artkolo.org.

On the last page of the front endsheets and the first page of the back endsheets of the hardcover edition, "Zhab'ie: A General View" (Kosiv: Art. fot. M. Seńkowski, 1927), available in the public domain. Image source: Biblioteka Narodowa, https://polona.pl

PREVIOUS PUBLICATIONS

"Essai de Deconstruction (An Attempt at Deconstruction)" from *Anna's Other Days*, translated by Ali Kinsella, has previously appeared in *Love in Defiance of Pain: Ukrainian Stories*, edited by Ali Kinsella, Zenia Tompkins, and Ross Ufberg (Dallas, TX: Deep Vellum Press, 2022).

Excerpts from *FM Galicia*, translated by Mark Andryczyk, appeared previously in *The White Chalk of Days: The Contemporary Ukrainian Literature Series Anthology*, compiled and edited by Mark Andryczyk (Boston, MA: Academic Studies Press, 2017).

An earlier version of *The UnSimple* in Uilleam Blacker's translation previously appeared in *Ukrainian Literature: A Journal of Translations*, vol. 2, 2007, and vol. 3, 2011.

Harvard Library of Ukrainian Literature
Recently Published

Forest Song: A Fairy Play in Three Acts
Lesia Ukrainka (Larysa Kosach)

Translated by Virlana Tkacz and Wanda Phipps
Introduced by George G. Grabowicz

This play represents the crowning achievement of Lesia Ukrainka's (Larysa Kosach's) mature period and is a uniquely powerful poetic text. Here, the author presents a symbolist meditation on the interaction of mankind and nature set in a world of primal forces and pure feelings as seen through childhood memories and the re-creation of local Volhynian folklore.

2025	appr. 240 pp.	
ISBN 9780674291874 (cloth)		$29.95
9780674291881 (paperback)		$19.95
9780674291898 (epub)		
9780674291904 (PDF)		

Harvard Library of Ukrainian Literature, vol. 15

Read the book online

Love Life: A Novel
Oksana Lutsyshyna

Translated by Nina Murray
Introduced by Marko Pavlyshyn

The second novel of the award-winning Ukrainian writer and poet Oksana Lutsyshyna writes the story of Yora, an immigrant to the United States from Ukraine. A delicate soul that's finely attuned to the nuances of human relations, Yora becomes enmeshed in a relationship with Sebastian, a seductive acquaintance who seems to be suggesting that they share a deep bond. After a period of despair and complex grief that follows the end of the relationship, Yora is able to emerge stronger, in part thanks to the support from a friendly neighbor who has adapted well to life on the margins of society.

2024	276 pp.	
ISBN 9780674297159 (cloth)		$39.95
9780674297166 (paperback)		$19.95
9780674297173 (epub)		
9780674297180 (PDF)		

Harvard Library of Ukrainian Literature, vol. 12

Read the book online

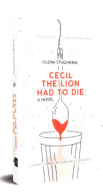

Cecil the Lion Had to Die: A Novel
Olena Stiazhkina

Translated by Dominique Hoffman

This novel follows the fate of four families as the world around them undergoes radical transformations when the Soviet Union unexpectedly implodes, independent Ukraine emerges, and neoimperial Russia begins its war by occupying Ukraine's Crimea and parts of the Donbas. A tour de force of stylistic registers and intertwining stories, ironic voices and sincere discoveries, this novel is a must-read for those who seek to deeper understand Ukrainians from the Donbas, and how history and local identity have shaped the current war with Russia.

2024	248 pp.	
ISBN 9780674291645 (cloth)		$39.95
9780674291669 (paperback)		$19.95
9780674291676 (epub)		
9780674291683 (PDF)		

Harvard Library of Ukrainian Literature, vol. 11

Read the book online

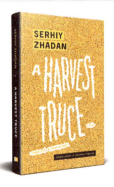

A Harvest Truce: A Play
Serhiy Zhadan

Translated by Nina Murray

Brothers Anton and Tolik reunite at their family home to bury their recently deceased mother. An otherwise natural ritual unfolds under extraordinary circumstances: their house is on the front line of a war ignited by Russian-backed separatists in eastern Ukraine.

Spring 2023	
ISBN 9780674291997 (hardcover)	$29.95
9780674292017 (paperback)	$19.95
9780674292024 (epub)	
9780674292031 (PDF)	

Harvard Library of Ukrainian Literature, vol. 9

Read the book online

Cassandra: A Dramatic Poem,

Lesia Ukrainka (Larysa Kosach)

Translated by Nina Murray, introduction by Marko Pavlyshyn

The classic myth of Cassandra turns into much more in Lesia Ukrainka's rendering: Cassandra's prophecies are uttered in highly poetic language—fitting to the genre of the dramatic poem that Ukrainka crafts for this work—and are not believed for that very reason, rather than because of Apollo's curse. Cassandra's being a poet and a woman are therefore the two focal points of the drama.

2024	263 pp, bilingual ed. (Ukrainian, English)
ISBN 9780674291775 (hardcover)	$29.95
9780674291782 (paperback)	$19.95
9780674291799 (epub)	
9780674291805 (PDF)	

Harvard Library of Ukrainian Literature, vol. 8

Read the book online

Ukraine, War, Love: A Donetsk Diary

Olena Stiazhkina

Translated by Anne O. Fisher

In this war-time diary, Olena Stiazhkina depicts day-to-day developments in and around her beloved hometown during Russia's 2014 invasion and occupation of the Ukrainian city of Donetsk.

Summer 2023	
ISBN 9780674291690 (hardcover)	$39.95
9780674291706 (paperback)	$19.95
9780674291713 (epub)	
9780674291768 (PDF)	

Harvard Library of Ukrainian Literature, vol. 7

Read the book online

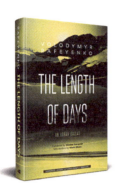

The Length of Days: An Urban Ballad

Volodymyr Rafeyenko

Translated by Sibelan Forrester
Afterword and interview with the author by Marci Shore

This novel is set mostly in the composite Donbas city of Z—an uncanny foretelling of what this letter has come to symbolize since February 24, 2022, when Russia launched a full-scale invasion of Ukraine. Several embedded narratives attributed to an alcoholic chemist-turned-massage therapist give insight into the funny, ironic, or tragic lives of people who remained in the occupied Donbas after Russia's initial aggression in 2014.

2023	349 pp.	
ISBN 780674291201 (cloth)		$39.95
9780674291218 (paper)		$19.95
9780674291225 (epub)		
9780674291232 (PDF)		

Harvard Library of Ukrainian Literature, vol. 6

Read the book online

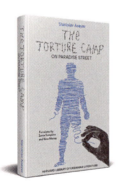

The Torture Camp on Paradise Street

Stanislav Aseyev

Translated by Zenia Tompkins and Nina Murray

Ukrainian journalist and writer Stanislav Aseyev details his experience as a prisoner from 2015 to 2017 in a modern-day concentration camp overseen by the Federal Security Bureau of the Russian Federation (FSB) in the Russian-controlled city of Donetsk. This memoir recounts an endless ordeal of psychological and physical abuse, including torture and rape, inflicted upon the author and his fellow inmates over the course of nearly three years of illegal incarceration spent largely in the prison called Izoliatsiia (Isolation).

2023	300 pp., 1 map, 18 ill.	
ISBN 9780674291072 (cloth)		$39.95
9780674291089 (paper)		$19.95
9780674291102 (epub)		
9780674291096 (PDF)		

Harvard Library of Ukrainian Literature, vol. 5

Read the book online

Babyn Yar: Ukrainian Poets Respond

Edited with introduction by Ostap Kin

Translated by John Hennessy and Ostap Kin

In 2021, the world commemorated the 80th anniversary of the massacres of Jews at Babyn Yar. The present collection brings together for the first time the responses to the tragic events of September 1941 by Ukrainian Jewish and non-Jewish poets of the Soviet and post-Soviet periods, presented here in the original and in English translation by Ostap Kin and John Hennessy.

2022	282 pp.	
ISBN 9780674275591 (hardcover)		$39.95
9780674271692 (paperback)		$16.00
9780674271722 (epub)		
9780674271739 (PDF)		

Harvard Library of Ukrainian Literature, vol. 4

Read the book online

The Voices of Babyn Yar

Marianna Kiyanovska

Translated by Oksana Maksymchuk and Max Rosochinsky
Introduced by Polina Barskova

With this collection of stirring poems, the award-winning Ukrainian poet honors the victims of the Holocaust by writing their stories of horror, death, and survival in their own imagined voices.

2022	192 pp.	
ISBN 9780674268760 (hardcover)		$39.95
9780674268869 (paperback)		$16.00
9780674268876 (epub)		
9780674268883 (PDF)		

Harvard Library of Ukrainian Literature, vol. 3

Read the book online

Mondegreen: Songs about Death and Love

Volodymyr Rafeyenko

Translated and introduced by Mark Andryczyk

Volodymyr Rafeyenko's novel Mondegreen: Songs about Death and Love explores the ways that memory and language construct our identity, and how we hold on to it no matter what. The novel tells the story of Haba Habinsky, a refugee from Ukraine's Donbas region, who has escaped to the capital city of Kyiv at the onset of the Ukrainian-Russian war.

2022	204 pp.	
ISBN 9780674275577 (hardcover)		$39.95
9780674271708 (paperback)		$19.95
9780674271746 (epub)		
9780674271760 (PDF)		

Harvard Library of Ukrainian Literature, vol. 2

Read the book online

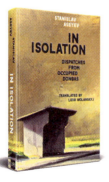

In Isolation: Dispatches from Occupied Donbas

Stanislav Aseyev

Translated by Lidia Wolanskyj

In this exceptional collection of dispatches from occupied Donbas, writer and journalist Stanislav Aseyev details the internal and external changes observed in the cities of Makiivka and Donetsk in eastern Ukraine.

2022	320 pp., 42 photos, 2 maps	
ISBN 9780674268784 (hardcover)		$39.95
9780674268791 (paperback)		$19.95
9780674268814 (epub)		
9780674268807 (PDF)		

Harvard Library of Ukrainian Literature, vol. 1

Read the book online

To discover more titles in the Harvard Library
of Ukrainian Literature, please visit
https://books.huri.harvard.edu